EARLY PRAISE FOR FAY'S MEN

Perle Besserman's light filled style matches Fay's sexual and spiritual passions and considerable intellect, by which she explores herself, more and less consciously. No navel gazer, she's heady. And a bit wry, so FAY'S MEN becomes a thorough study of her vulnerability BECAUSE of her strengths, the narrative taking us all over the world's surface: Asia, Europe, America, Hawaii, Africa, some time at sea, by imagery and metaphor. Fay seems "at sea" (or "in the air") as she determines her way with and through relationships, while her doubts are fed by her drive to explore, and live, versions of "enlightenment." A book to respect, not gallop through. Fay deserves our time, as she loves and suffers male sociopathies, however fascinating. Her men are not obvious. Can she be capable of love, and grief, knowing that she cannot save them, while they need her to obey and save their egos? A finely written, classic novel of human paradox.

~ Paul Nelson's most recent book of fiction is "*Refrigerator Church.*"

Fay's Men is a wonderful novel, abundant with adventures, humor, sensual detail and quirky surprises. Fay is a delight, a curious mixture of earthy, quixotic and spiritual. Travel with her and enjoy the ride.

~ Brigid Lowry - Bestselling author of *A Year of Loving Kindness to Myself, and Other Essays.*

Perle Besserman writes with an energy and detail that makes Fay's Men a delight to read. As Anne Lamott once said, a great character is like a great friend whose company you love and whose running commentary totally holds your attention. Fay Corman is just such a character. And her journey from Texas through New York and Japan to Hawaii is an absolute trip indeed.

~ Nina Killham is the author of three novels: *How to Cook a Tart, Mounting Desire, and Believe Me.*

FAY'S MEN

A NOVEL

PERLE S. BESSERMAN

Fay's Men
A Novel

Edited by Rudolfo Serna

Published in North America and Europe by Running Wild Press. Visit Running Wild Press at www.runningwildpress.com Educators, librarians, book clubs (as well as the eternally curious), go to www.runningwildpress.com.

Paperback ISBN: 978-1-955062-94-7
eBook ISBN: 978-1-955062-95-4

For Manfred, As Always

PART I

1
FERRY TO TANGIER

Dinner in Algeciras: paella and wine in an outdoor café on a dark, narrow, winding uphill lane opening onto a plaza, a lighted square. The air is salty. A woman's explosive laughter and children's shouts. Children everywhere, though it's well past ten. And babies in those high-wheeled straw prams you don't see in the States. We walk around town after dinner then sit on a bench in a Moorish tiled square lined with spindly palms. Everything feels fragile, delicate; a carnival scene charged with uncertain noises; a little girl in a pink tulle dress is strapped to a red and gold pony on a miniature carousel on a truck; she holds a cone of cotton candy, as pink and fluffy as her dress. We watch her go round on the carousel until her mother comes and takes her off. We drink sherry in another hillside café and don't talk—neither of us wants to mention the child.

The boat lurched and Fay stopped writing. As she closed the red leather diary, her glance landed on the clear blue inscription on the front page: "To Fay. I hope you will fill these pages as well as your trip with excitement and many happy events. Love, Erika." Her German sister-in-law. German and perfect. Perfectly German. The handwriting was round and looped, foreign and neat. Erika's house was neat, too. And her three children. The last time Fay had babysat for them she'd been beaten with the vacuum cleaner hose by Roland, the three-year-old. Wanting heroes, Erika had named her three boys Siegfried, Percival, and Roland. Fay propped her feet against the bar of her orange first-class deck chair and pushed her sunglasses back on her head. Erika had often scolded her for not producing a few heroes of her own. Fay took the scolding with a smile and said nothing; Erika's Teutonic orderliness intimidated her. She tucked the diary into her bag and pulled out a discolored pack of sugarless mints. She brushed a ball of lint from the top of the open package and popped a lozenge into her mouth, then, sighing, put the sunglasses back on. It was getting hot, all hints of a sea breeze abandoned.

"Seasick?" Ira mumbled from his half sleep in the neighboring deck chair, his eyes partly open and his hands folded over his stomach under the tent of a book. The first time she'd seen him sleep with his eyes partly open they'd been lying side by side on a blanket in Maine. Fay had brought her face close to his to see if he was breathing. Seeing Ira's blue eyeballs move against his skim-milk-white sclera had both fascinated and horrified her. She had contemplated kissing him awake but had barely grazed his nose when he awoke screaming, pleading with her not to bury him alive. Ira had later confided that their lunchtime discussion of Bergman's *Seventh Seal* had prompted his childhood phobia and recurring dream of entombment.

"Not seasick, honey. Just queasy."

"Take the Dramamine," Ira said.

"It makes me throw up."

"It's supposed to do just the opposite."

"Well, I'm sorry, it makes me throw up."

"You always did have paradoxical reactions to drugs. I suppose it's your strange genes," Ira said, using the same ironic tone he used with his female patients on the telephone.

Fay caught the eye of a handsome Japanese man with high cheekbones and a guitar case who was leaning against the boat railing with one foot up behind him conversing in heavily accented French with an animated Arab in a blue blazer. The handsome Japanese was tall for a Japanese person, but shorter than her, and probably ten years younger. He looked like a punk rocker, the kind of shaggy, footloose creature of the night she might have been attracted to before meeting Ira.

A troupe of musicians wearing soiled black tuxedos and white tennis shoes emerged from the stairwell leading down to the second-class deck. Propping fiddles under their chins and screwing their guitar strings taut, they launched into a romping version of "Fascination." Annoyed at the intrusion, the handsome Japanese and his Arab friend fled to the coffee bar. Fay reached over to tickle the back of Ira's hand. Directly opposite her, in the space between a smiling, yellow-toothed fiddler and an eccentric woman in a red bandana, red dress, and cork-soled red wedges who had begun dancing to the music on her own, a hirsute Spanish nursemaid was attempting to pour water from an earthen jug down the throat of a restive, beak-nosed little boy in a striped shirt. "*Chinga se*," the little boy screamed over the crooning fiddles, "*chinga se*," drowning out the vamping castanets. Then he kicked the hairy nursemaid in the shins. The eccentric woman in red made a face at the little boy then snapped her fingers and went right on dancing without missing a beat. A small crowd gathered to watch her; a man in a white linen suit with patent leather black hair executed a courtly bow and joined the dancing woman. Soon all the first-class passengers but Fay and Ira and the nursemaid and her foul-mouthed charge were gathered around the dancing couple, clapping their hands and swaying their hips in time to the music. A waiter carrying a bottle of Pellegrino on a tray leaned over a small table near the deck rail, examined his tip, sniffed with contempt, and wormed his way back to the coffee bar.

"We must look so American sitting here," Fay said.

"Mmm . . ." Ira was about to fall asleep again.

"Ira!"

"Fig Newton!"

"What?"

"Fig Newton . . . I'd kill for a Fig Newton," Ira said, now fully awake.

"Oh, Jesus . . . Don't start that stuff with me again, please. I thought I'd die at the hotel when you asked them to split up the lunch menu and the breakfast menu and make brunch. Europeans don't eat brunch. They eat continental breakfasts and a full course lunch, not bagels and lox . . . can you see asking that snotty waiter over there for a Fig Newton? Jesus Christ . . . and then when you made such a stink over the electric toothbrush . . ."

"Well, who knew they have only DC current over here?"

"You are a doctor; you should know about those things."

"That's right. I'm a doctor, not an electrical engineer. And what's wrong with being American?" Ira waved his hand at her, and Fay was instantly reminded of his Republican brother, Charles.

"You wouldn't understand," she said.

"What's a phoneme?" Ira asked.

"What are you reading there anyway?" She leaned over the armrest and looked into the book which he had now turned face-up. Tucked carefully into the spine of C.G. Jung's *Memories, Dreams, and Reflections* was a paperback edition of *Best Crossword Puzzles from the New York Times.* Ira snapped the book shut, but he was too late, Fay had seen inside.

"Philistine," she sneered.

The music stopped, and the musicians and dancers and their audience cleared the center deck, grouping into little knots at the rail or stuffing themselves into cramped, wire-backed chairs around sticky tables in the coffee bar—a hollow room consisting of eight tables with three wire-backed chairs each and a zinc bar, behind which a shelved mirror studded with aperitif bottles featured brown-edged ham sandwiches wrapped in cellophane. At one end of the bar a glistening espresso machine hissed and steamed like an autoclave, reminding Fay of the miscarriage she was here to forget.

Ira had been sleeping with his eyes partly open that night, too. For three years, he'd been flirting secretly with LSD and New Age "alternative therapies," not too successfully hiding it from his mainstream colleagues in the psychiatry department; the strain had left him permanently exhausted, had lined his face and hunched him over.

Fay had stumbled out of bed and was crawling around on the floor looking for her slippers in the dark when Ira woke up screaming that he didn't want to be buried alive.

"Get me a paper cup," she said.

"What for? Are you thirsty? What's going on with you? You're acting weird." Though Ira professed to get a kick out of Fay's "weirdness," he hated it when she got sick and needed him in the ordinary way of his patients. He hated it especially when she seemed to be losing control and coming apart. On the night he had asked her to move in with him, as they were exchanging life stories over cocktails in the Grill at Rockefeller Center and watching the skaters, he'd warned Fay not to need him. When she pressed him to explain what he meant, Ira had backtracked a little, saying maybe that wasn't the best way to put it. His mother, he said, was a very needy woman, who showed all the signs of clinical hysteria whenever his father would cut up her credit cards—which was often. Though she'd never had a job, Ira's mother had left him notes tacked to the refrigerator every day saying she'd gone "downtown"—presumably to look for one—when in fact she was compulsively shopping for hats. Ira had survived on peanut butter and jelly sandwiches he made himself. Telling Fay this, he paused a moment, then seeming to recall a related detail, added that in high school he'd been singled out and paraded around the classroom by a hook-nosed teacher for wearing his older brother's torn, castoff shirts. He said the teacher, Miss Murphy, had been anti-Semitic and made a point of informing the class that Ira's father was a millionaire —as if being Jewish and rich and too cheap to buy your kid a new shirt were related. Ira never told his parents about his humiliation at the hands of the hook-nosed Miss Murphy. Not that it would have mattered if he did. He and his father were hardly on speaking terms. And since his mother was too "needy" to intercede on his behalf, he said nothing about his problems at school and continued wearing his brother's torn castoff shirts. Ira rationalized his parents' indifference by convincing himself that he'd been adopted—until the day he met his mother's brother, an ex-boxer named Joe, to whom he bore an unmistakable family resemblance. Living with this constant reminder of the "seedier side of the family" hadn't sat well with his father, who'd lavished all his time, money, and attention on his first son, Charles—who was twelve years older than Ira and a superior athlete—sending him to elite boarding schools while Ira languished under the anti-Semitic Miss Murphy.

Fay removed the red plastic stirrer from her drink and chewed on it, nodding sympathetically, as Ira described his unhappy childhood. When he'd finished, she tossed the bitten stirrer into an ashtray, swallowed the last of her rum and Coke, and agreed to move in with him. A year later, they were married.

They had been married for two years the night she'd awakened to the miscarriage by the blood running down her leg. Feeling needy and hating herself for it, she lashed out at Ira.

"You're not going to faint at the sight of a little blood, are you?" Fay couldn't help sneering.

"Did you call Harris?" Ira swung his long bony feet over the side of the bed and searched for his glasses on the night table.

"Why bother, Harris? I know exactly what's happening. The book says to catch the stuff in a container so they can send it to the lab and see what went wrong."

"That's nice," Ira said. "I'm glad you know enough about medicine to be your own obstetrician."

"Honestly, Ira, you'd think that being a doctor yourself would make you a little less worshipful of the profession. To hear you complain about medical incompetence all these years . . ."

"Never mind," Ira found his glasses and his blood pressure cup and was reaching for her arm.

Fay pulled it away from him. "I'm going to the john."

"Pain?"

"Like period cramps."

"Oh, Fay . . ."

"Do you think it's finito?"

"Stop being flip, now's not the time."

"Will they put it in a bottle of formaldehyde?"

"Give me a break! Where's your bathrobe? We're going to the hospital, and you don't have time to get dressed."

Earlier that afternoon, in search of vitamin C for her cramps, Fay had ducked into Bemelmans Bar and ordered an outrageously expensive glass of orange juice. In the Carlyle Hotel powder room, she had stuffed her panties with toilet paper on noticing the tiny red spot that she'd pretended wouldn't lead to this. The sheer finality of Ira's words made her want to cry. Obediently, she let him throw a coat over her white terrycloth robe and followed him out the door.

The handsome Japanese man and his Arab friend emerged from the coffee bar.

"Order us some mineral water," Fay said.

"What for? We'll be docking soon. Bar's probably closing." Ira had put on his glasses and was now working openly at his crossword puzzle.

The bar *was* closing. People were returning to their chairs on deck. "Do you think that fellow over there is gay?"

"Who, the Arab?" Ira peered over his glasses.

"No, the other one."

"Who knows? Who cares?"

Fay now noticed that the Arab had a neat, pointed black goatee reminding her of Doctor Crumm, the gynecology resident who'd been bearded, too. Though she'd sat up in bed for two hours waiting for him, he hadn't apologized for coming late. Fay had considered asking the resident if beards were permitted in the operating room. Ira had grown a beard during his internship, but claiming it was "unhygienic," the chief of surgery had ordered him to shave it off.

"Was it absolutely necessary that they admit you at eleven o'clock? I mean . . . were you hemorrhaging?" the resident asked crankily.

"No." Fay hesitated, remembering how gruesome it could be, waking in the middle of a long dreamless sleep after two nights of uninterrupted emergencies on duty, or dashing for a pair of shoes in the middle of a shower, or worse, while making love. She and Ira's roommate, Douglas, were dancing the tango on the hospital's sunroof on a lazy summer afternoon when all the interns on emergency duty were called to a train wreck in the Bronx. Ira and Douglas had returned ashen faced.

"Six people dead and mangled, some of them beyond recognition," Douglas said.

The crank-up vinyl record player they'd bought on a lark in a junk shop on Second Avenue was forgotten, left to spin itself down until it had scratched away all the baize on the turntable. With this in mind, Fay gave Doctor Crumm an encouraging smile.

"Your doctor did this as a favor, didn't he? It's usually impossible to get a private bed so late unless it's really serious," he said.

"My husband is on the staff here."

Fay saw the resident frown as he bent over in search of her vein. "It did bleed. I think I lost the whole thing at home. There were no beds available till now." She remembered to avert her eyes from the needle so as not to pass out. "It's just that he wants to make sure."

Doctor Crumm took a coil of rubber tubing from his pocket, tied one end of it around her upper arm, and searched out her vein a third time. "Damn," he muttered.

"Why don't you call the nurse? They do it all the time, so

they're quicker." As soon as the words were out, she knew she'd erred.

Doctor Crumm glared at her over the tubing and said, "We've all got troubles. My wife's in her eighth month and she's still feeling as sick as a dog. I just came from there. We already have a little girl . . . two years old. It's rough." He pricked the vein in just the right place. After removing the tubing from her arm, adjusting the bottle of colorless fluid flanking the bed and taping the needle onto her hand, Doctor Crumm smiled at her wanly. When he reached the door, he looked at her and said, "I majored in English at Dartmouth."

"Who was your favorite writer?" Fay asked.

"Dickens."

"Mine, too . . . What's the IV for?"

"It's Pitocin. If you feel contractions don't get scared. If you can't sleep, your doctor can prescribe a sedative. Just ring the bell and ask the nurse."

"Will you tell my husband I'm okay and he can go home? He's looking in on a patient on the second floor. His name's Ira Corman."

Doctor Crumm leaned against the lintel and watched her from the doorway. Beyond him, Fay heard rubber shoes running on highly polished linoleum. Someone was worse off than she was. "Remember to tell the nurse if you begin to feel any strong contractions. They're going to take you up at seven in the morning. You should be out by tomorrow night."

"Send my best to your wife."

"Good luck, Mrs. Corman. Good night."

"Good night."

The television flickered soundlessly overhead. Fay hit the remote control "off" button. Propping herself against the pillows, she looked around the room and found it spacious, empty, brown, and green, like a room in an expensive understated British hotel. It didn't smell like a hospital room, and she was grateful for that. She looked out the window into the softly lit rooms of sleepless patients in the wing opposite hers, most of them drugged, unconscious of pain for a while. Here and there a television shadow flickered in reflection. Her cramps were gone. Checking the drip, she was surprised to find that the fluid level had dropped a quarter of the way. She traced it, watching it flow into her as she had traced the flow of life leaving her a few hours ago.

A nurse looked in and asked if she was comfortable. She was fine, thank you. Did she need a pill to sleep? No. She would be fine. The nurse checked the bottle. It's like being a baby yourself, Fay thought. People in soft shoes, drinking coffee and joking beyond your door—

"I'm going off duty now."

"See you later."

"Oh, no. You'll be home by the time I come back. Don't you worry now, honey. You'll try again and have another. They all do." The nurse, who spoke with a Jamaican lilt, smiled, flashing a prominent gold tooth; then she disappeared, leaving behind only the whisper of starch.

Fay was no stranger to hospitals. She had hung around during Ira's fourth year of medical school and, after that, his internship. She had even accompanied him once to a Saturday morning autopsy during his pathology rotation. In the basement, six floors below where she now lay, was the morgue with its rolling file cabinets and the dead inside, lined up in neat rows with their name tags looped around their big toes. In the adjoining lab, surrounded by six masked students, a tiny blond pathologist with a jaunty ponytail had performed the autopsy standing on a box. Ira had handed Fay a mask and asked the little pathologist if his girlfriend could join them. The pathologist, who was Polish and spoke with an affected British lisp, barely nodded before resuming her careful explanation of the symptoms of the liver she'd just unearthed and plopped onto an overhanging butcher's scale.

The corpse was male, huge and naked. The face (out of some atavistic fear or respect for the dead?) was swathed in bandages. The little white card dangling from the wire around the big toe read: Lopez, Roberto. He was jaundiced. The smooth hill above his sex was soft and golden. Above that, his stomach had been split wide open. The pathologist continued her litany of diseased findings, dropping organs on the scale then handing them to an assistant who put them back into the body cavity. Fay stood looking at the needle on the scale so as not to have to look into Lopez, Roberto's stomach. Without wanting to, she had begun to make up a life for him: he had four sons, he loved to dance, took his wife Margarita to a social club in Washington Heights on Saturday nights, favored loose blousy shirts and electric blue trousers, never wore a tie, but maybe a crucifix on a beaten gold chain. Under the bandages there was a tickly mustache that made his sons laugh when he kissed them. His arms, traced with strong blue veins, held Margarita close, as she pressed her breasts to his chest, dancing under the spinning blue and silver globe in the ceiling. In Mayaguez where he grew up, his favorite dish as a boy was fried plantains—Feeling faint, Fay had excused herself; ripping off the mask, she rushed into the washroom and scrubbed her hands raw with a nail brush she found on the counter.

She had reached overhead for a call button, then remembered that she wasn't allowed to drink or eat anything until after the operation. The scraping. Dilatation and Curettage. These days they sucked it out of you with a vacuum cleaner. She was terribly thirsty. She looked at the bottle hanging mouth down from the pole alongside the bed. The nightlight gave the liquid a pinkish glow. Still no contractions, not a quiver of pain since the nurse had helped her to undress and tucked her into the cool white bed. Ira had fiddled with the television set, shutting it off only after watching the last ten minutes of the Knicks game without talking to her. When the nurse left, he'd leaned over and whispered that he was going down to see a psychiatric patient who'd had a heart attack and had just been transferred to a private room from Intensive Care. Fay had peed in the scrubbed tile bathroom with the hand bar near the toilet that kept frail patients from falling. She thought she might like to go to the toilet again, but she was tied to the bottle and didn't want to risk twisting the tubing. She forced herself to stay awake by mentally checking off everything the Women's Collective pamphlet on pregnancy and miscarriage said was going to happen to her. First, find out the ingredients in every pill they popped into your mouth, the name of the anesthesia you'll be getting, the exact length of time in recovery, and how long afterward you'll have to refrain from sex. Most important, don't fret about the possibility of dying. True, freak accidents did happen during minor surgery, but the statistical probabilities of her dying were almost nil. Especially since she was in such good physical shape from all her years of dancing and yoga. It would not be her fate to be the one in ten million who choked on her own vomit because some sassy labor room nurse forgot to give her an enema before putting her under.

She pressed the call button. A tight-lipped nurse waddled into the room wearing a frilled net cap that reminded Fay of her high school home economics teacher. The nurse had the same watery blue eyes. The teacher's name was Miss Prince; she had flunked Fay for refusing to wear a hairnet while cooking.

"What is it?" the nurse said, looking at her sourly.

"I just wondered if it was important that I sleep."

"If you can't sleep, I'll give you a pill." The nurse had the same pointed reddish nostrils as Miss Prince, and she twitched them in the same way. "Do you or don't you want a sleeping pill?" she asked.

"I thought I'm not supposed to take anything before the surgery."

"Suit yourself."

"Thank you for coming," Fay said, turning toward the window to let the nurse know she could leave.

"It's my job," the nurse said, shrugging as she walked away from the bed.

Fay heard trees swaying outside in the dark. She knew there were green buds, the color of baby limes, sprouting on the branches. It was April. The nurse had left the door slightly open; a telephone buzzed softly. Fay rummaged through the drawer of the bedside table with her free hand and pulled out the jade Kuan-Yin pendant she had slipped into the pocket of her robe on leaving the house.

With the sky going from black to gray and all the rooms in the hospital wing opposite her couched in darkness, she had reached up to touch her face with her needle-free hand and found herself crying. The deeper she'd plunged into life, the less she'd gotten out of it. What was it she missed? Never could put her finger on that unnamable something—or nameable nothing, was it, the mysterious X that floated formlessly always just within reach, but was never grasped? She thought of Bette Davis putting out the dog and tucking herself into bed at the end of *Dark Victory*, smiling as George Brent went off to his medical conference and left her to die alone. Was Bette trying not to be needy, too? Fay looked at the bottle above her; the fluid was almost gone. She closed her eyes and drifted into a fitful sleep.

She awoke when the light came through the window, still feeling nothing. Her hand was numb; there had been no contractions. The IV bottle was empty. Rain splashed against the windowpane. The door opened and a red headed nurse entered, a real beauty, with freckles. The nurse pulled up the shades and let the gray morning light fill the room. Then she approached the bed and examined the bottle.

"Good, it's all finished," she said.

The nurse went to the open doorway and motioned to the two orderlies waiting in the corridor with a gurney, which they pushed into the room leveling it even with the bed.

"Do I go up now?"

"Yes, if you'll just help me by pulling yourself up a little. By the way, I'm Gracie," she lifted Fay, bottle tubing and all, and without any help from the orderlies, eased her onto the gurney herself. "Have you had any contractions?"

"I don't think so. No pain at all," said Fay, trying to keep her loose hospital gown from opening at the crotch.

"That's okay," said Gracie, holding Fay's gown closed and walking alongside the gurney as the orderlies wheeled her out of the room and into the corridor.

Fay laid back and looked up at the hospital corridor ceiling, then at the chrome ceiling of the elevator, then at the vaulted ceiling of the operating room. She saw Doctor Harris standing over her in a mask and green surgical gown. She noted that the windows were Gothic and felt the early morning cold through her cotton gown and the thin sheet Nurse Gracie had thrown over her just before entering the operating theater. She thought of saying something funny to Doctor Harris then changed her mind. An Asian nurse slipped Fay's legs into a pair of thigh-high booties. Promising to be back for her later, Nurse Gracie disappeared from view. "These are to keep you warm," the Asian nurse said. Fay knew damned well that the booties were there in case she went into shock and her body temperature dropped. Doctor Harris moved her onto the operating table and placed her legs into the stirrups himself.

"This will only take about half an hour," he said.

The anesthesiologist introduced herself as Judy, or Jillie, or Junie. The mask made it impossible to tell which. She was switching bottles, replacing the empty one with the Pitocin in it with something else, also colorless. I ought to contract so far that they're all flung out of the room, Fay thought. Judy, Jillie, Junie hovered over her. Maybe they were on closed circuit television, presenting a routine D and C to a class of fourth-year medical students.

"Think of the anesthesia as champagne," said the anesthesiologist.

"Dom Perignon?" Fay asked.

"My favorite is Piper Heidseck," said Judy, Jillie, Junie as she screwed on the new bottle, causing the floor to rush up like a fifteen-foot wave.

"Low class," Fay murmured. Doctor Harris laughed. The wave closed over her as she drowned.

There were two more miscarriages after that.

That was like a distant dream now, as the ship bobbed on waves, sending up a shower of spray over the rail. She could see land, purplish mountains. They'd be docking in Tangier soon, and Ira would get to see his Sufi sheik. And Fay would smile and nod her head a lot at the sheik's broken English questions, and the Sufi women, unaware that only three months ago she'd had a miscarriage and her womb scraped clean, would ask her when she was going to have babies. Ira would join the whirling, chanting circle of white-robed men and become unreachable in yet another of the myriad ways he had of becoming unreachable. She looked at her husband's hands, their long slender fingers. She scanned his face and neck, stopping at his ears (whose fleshy lobes reminded her of the Ceylonese Buddha they'd seen two weeks ago in the Musée Guimet), the un-aristocratic pug nose he had inherited from his mother's brother Joe, the slightly bulging stomach under its turquoise jersey sport shirt embroidered with the green alligator. Lulled by the light rocking of the waves, the steady creak of the boat's winches and the buzz of foreign conversation around her, Fay realized that she was still waiting for God to pull her out of her husband's rib and sculpt her into a perfect work of art. Pregnancy had fooled her into thinking she was on her way.

To avoid talking about the fissures the latest miscarriage had exposed in their relationship, Ira surprised her with a trip to Paris, Spain, and Morocco. Now, on the ferry, seeing the handsome Japanese man with the guitar reminds Fay of her recurring dream of giving birth to a little Japanese boy. She hasn't told Ira about her recurring dream. He'd insist she go into therapy, which is exactly what she does not want to do. She does not want to talk about her unsettling dream to a stranger. She wants to talk to Ira. But Ira is unreachable.

There was a loud thud and the clatter of lowering chains. The boat had docked. People were gathering their belongings and their children, smoothing their wrinkled clothing and preparing to disembark. The beak-nosed boy was still cursing his nursemaid.

"This is it," Ira said, getting up and taking her hand.

At the head of the stairs, Fay looked down at the pier. The handsome Japanese man with the guitar was having trouble with the customs agent about his passport. His friend was gesturing and talking excitedly in Arabic. A third man walked up flat-footedly and entered the discussion. The passengers behind them were being held up and not liking it one bit. "*Chinga se*!" screamed the beak-nosed boy. The steps leading to the pier were packed with people. Two massive German students tossed their backpacks over the deck onto the pier and hoisted themselves up on the rail, letting their legs dangle over the side of the boat. A steward waved them down but they ignored him. Anarchy threatened. Just then, a blue Mercedes touring car tore through the crowds on the pier, horn blasting, scattering onlookers and startling the passengers still on board into silence. Even the gulls perched on the masthead ceased shrieking. The car pulled to a stop. The Japanese man put on a pair of dark glasses, picked up his guitar, and, turning his back on the customs officer, gazed out to sea. A uniformed chauffeur stepped out of the car, walked up to the customs officer and showed him a paper. The customs officer nodded sulkily and stamped the handsome foreigner's passport. The Arab in the blue blazer, the flat-footed man, the chauffeur, and the Japanese man with the guitar all disappeared into the leather depths of the Mercedes and drove off. He must be a rockstar, thought Fay.

The passengers were bustling again. The demonic child screamed all the way down the stairs. A man called out in English for him to shut up. Fay stood in front of Ira waiting for her turn to disembark.

"How do you like it?" Ira asked.

"I don't know. We're not off the boat yet," she said without looking back at him. On the step-in front of her, the woman in red moved forward and Fay started her descent.

"By the way," Ira said, as if suddenly remembering something he'd forgotten to tell her before, something important, "did you know that if you write them close together without the apostrophe, man's laughter and manslaughter are the same word?"

2
BOYS AND GIRLS TOGETHER

Fay had been too intent on pursuing Donald Worth, a blue-eyed, NYU law student who drove a Beamer 320x, to notice Ira Corman reading Kafka every morning on the front steps of his cabin, obscured by the highly sought after "Desirable Donald." Ira's single claim to fame among the female counselors at Camp Waheeken was the ubiquitous black T-shirt devoid of slogans which he never removed even when swimming. If any one of those wise virgins had predicted it would be the Kafka and the slogan-less black T-shirt that would seduce her, Fay would have laughed in her face. Of course, she'd always been a sucker for antiheroes, but even so . . .

Maybe it also had something to do with the whooping cough ravaging the camp that summer, or with Steven, her most recent involvement back in New York (and the last person she wanted to see) threatening to show up and "whisk" her away in his red Mustang convertible. Whatever the reason, Fay ended up marrying Ira Corman.

On her wedding day, she overheard a tipsy Ira bragging to

his brother Charles about how he'd beat out the camp competition and landed her for himself. When Fay took her new husband aside and confronted him about it, he'd laughingly confessed to her his membership in a sizable cohort of Camp Waheeken admirers who'd been "totally mesmerized" by her "amazing ass." Responding to Fay's look of silent contempt, Ira quickly added that he'd only hung out with "those losers" because, "I was so in love with you that I needed an excuse just to hear your name mentioned once during my otherwise lonely and miserable workday."

Fay brusquely reminded Ira that she'd never seen him working, only sitting on the front steps of his cabin, reading—as he'd later confessed—a paperback collection of Playboy cartoons nested inside a hard backed copy of Kafka's *In The Penal Colony*.

Not to be outdone, Ira then informed her that he'd known all along not only that he'd "land" her, but how, because he'd had some bizarre ESP experiment going with his psychic best friend Sam Rubin, the long-distance perpetrator of Fay's seduction via telepathic suggestion. The Kafka ploy had been Sam's idea. He'd predicted that Fay would fall into a coughing fit on her way to the volleyball hut. Ira would put the book aside, and everything would change.

One minute she was upright, hacking away, and the next she was bent over in front of Ira, throwing up. Setting aside the Kafka, he rushed to her side. "It's all right, Fay, everything's going to be alright," he crooned. Holding her head with one hand, he massaged her back with the other. Gagging and spitting, she managed to get out, "Really, I . . . I'm sorry." Ira reassured her that there was nothing to be sorry about. He handed her an expensive monogrammed handkerchief which (forewarned by Psychic Sam) he'd borrowed from his father's dresser drawer and stuck into his backpack for just such an occasion.

"This is so embarrassing," Fay choked, still averting her face.

"You don't have to be embarrassed in front of me, I'll probably be seeing much worse a year from now," he said, leading her toward the steps of his cabin.

Fay wiped the tears from her eyes with the handkerchief, then dabbed as daintily as she could at a string of saliva still hanging from her chin.

"Why's that?"

"I'm going to medical school . . . Let me get you some water." Picking up the pseudo-Kafka, Ira disappeared into his cabin.

Fay refused the toothpaste-splattered glass of brackish water he offered her on returning but let him prop her against the pillow he'd swiped from the bunk nearest the door on his way out of the cabin.

"Isn't that mediocre?"

"Mediocre?"

"Medicine, I mean. For an intellectual like yourself."

"Me?"

"Well, every time I see you, you've got your face buried in Kafka."

"Oh," he ventured hastily, "that's because I'm prone to sunstroke."

"I think I feel okay now." Disappointed at the turn the conversation was taking, Fay got up and started walking toward the volleyball hut. "Thanks for the first aid," she called over her shoulder.

So had ended Phase One of Sam Rubin's psychically engineered seduction of Fay Watkins on Ira Corman's behalf.

Considering that throwing up in front of Ira had helped

establish a degree of intimacy between them, Fay had consulted him on a number of topics, and now was on the verge of asking how he felt about sex on a first date. They were sitting near a small bog deep in the woods behind his cabin when she changed her mind.

"You're going to get fired if you keep leaving your kids alone to kill each other. I can hear them all the way from here," Fay pointed toward Ira's cabin.

"My cousin owns this place," Ira said.

"Is Barry Porter your cousin? Are you kidding me?"

"Sure I'm kidding you," he said smiling.

Fay swatted at a mosquito and missed. "Why are we sitting so near a swamp?"

"Did you know that you and Donald Worth are the same morphological types, you're both Venuses?" Ira said.

"Where did that non-sequitur come from?"

Ira ignored her question. "It's got to do with facial structure, bones . . . things like that."

"Phrenology? You're a face reader?"

"It's not 'face reading;' it's a science taught in medical schools in France. I subscribe to the Journal de Morphologie. I figure it'll come in handy when I'm diagnosing patients."

"Do you read French?"

Ira wiped his hands on his shorts. "My friend Sam reads French. He knows Spanish and German, too. He started at Princeton when he was only sixteen."

"What's a Venus like?" Fay asked, not because she was interested, but because she felt sorry for Ira and wanted to get him off the hook, he was trying so hard.

"Very good-looking people . . . like, well, like the goddess Venus."

"Donald doesn't look like a goddess." Ira's stare was making her nervous. "What are Venuses like?"

"Well, they're very sexual."

"So what you're telling me is that I'm promiscuous."

"No! I didn't say that."

"What type are you?"

"Mars, basically . . ."

"Are Mars and Venus sexually compatible?"

Ira blushed. "Yeah, very . . ."

"I'll tell you what. Why don't I have sex with Donald Worth, and you have sex with Marcia Big Boobs? That'll keep us from spoiling our platonic Mars-Venus friendship. Everyone knows Marcia's crazy about you. Once you break her in, I might think about it. Otherwise, there'll always be this sex thing standing between us," Fay said.

Ira laughed out loud at her unintended double entendre, and she gave him a slight push. There was something touching about his gullibility. He smelled like trees in the rain. Donald Worth smelled like potatoes in a brown paper bag.

"Do you realize we've been sitting on wet moss all this time? I'll bet your shorts are all green in back."

Unaware at the time that it was a ploy to get her to turn around and give him a close-up view of her "amazing ass," Fay stood up and obliged him. "Let's get out of here."

They emerged from the thicket into the blinding late July sunlight. Someone in Ira's cabin was playing *Foxy Lady* on a flawed record album. Every time the song hit a chorus it blurred wildly, a soul-clawing caterwaul. "Will you cut that?" he yelled. The music stopped.

"See you around, Doctor Corman." Fay waved.

Ira mouthed something, but by then she was too far away to hear what he was saying.

. . .

On her first, and only, date with Donald Worth, she'd gotten a little high on two Screwdrivers and called him a misogynist after he'd mocked "lady lawyers."

"Don't tell me you're really against women going to law school!" she'd teased, softening her initial attack so he wouldn't think she was some kind of man-hater. The blue neon of the clock over the bar spun circles around him, weaving him into a tapestry of sparkling bottles, melting into the white sclera of his aquamarine eyes.

"Women lawyers inevitably stop practicing when they have babies," he muttered into his beer.

"The thought of having babies has never crossed my mind once," Fay said, adding that she'd decided not to marry before thirty . . . maybe never. That remark had gotten him mad enough to blurt out the real reason he'd asked her out, on a bet with the older guys that she'd go to bed with him, that it was about time a little tease like her got a lesson.

Sure, he was getting married in the fall and had no intention of bothering with her, but he couldn't resist the urge to put her in her place. And when she told him she intended to go to grad school after college, that she was probably smarter than he was, he threw back his head and laughed, squinting those aquamarine eyes of his and breaking her heart. There he was, hating her, and she was wearing her knockout purple blouse, the sheer one no man on earth could resist, and her mauve elephant-leg pantaloons and silver and turquoise drop earrings that almost touched her shoulder. A goddess. A Venus.

Fay had barely gulped down the last of her second Screwdriver when he practically dragged her out of the bar, piled her into the Beamer, and drove straight to Camp Waheeken without so much as a word or a glance in her direction. That was when she tried slapping him but missed, slamming her palm against the steering wheel instead and almost getting them into a wreck with the girls' softball field fence. "Get your hands off me, slut," he snarled, pulling up to her cabin with the tires screeching. Reaching across her, he threw open the passenger side door and dumped her out of the car like a bag of garbage.

Steven arrived the next day to "whisk" her away from camp in his red Mustang, as promised. It didn't seem to bother Steven that she greeted him sourly. He looked around, taking in the sky, the lake, and a troop of scrawny ten-year-olds en route to the soccer field.

"I like it here," he said. "I think I'll stay."

Fay told him not to be ridiculous. It was too late in the season to sign up for a job, but Steven wasn't to be put off by such trifling details.

"I can wait. I'm passionate, but patient," he said grinning.

To impress her point on him, Fay immediately took him by the hand to the owner's office. Barry Porter himself was there, decked out in regulation camp sweat suit, Waheeken Athletic Staff cap, ever-present whistle dangling from the braided lariat against his barrel chest. Barry twiddled the brim of his cap, rocked back and forth on his heels, greeted Steven with a handshake and, to Fay's utter horror, said, "There could be an opening soon. If certain people around here continue their lax ways, I'll need new help. Stick around."

Fay sent Barry a desperate look, "So late in the season?"

"You betcha," Barry said.

It started raining the minute they left camp and drove off in Steve's red Mustang. A thunderstorm was clearly in the offing; she could tell by the way the wind was blowing driveway gravel around and standing garden tools on end. Fay had reluctantly agreed to a pizza and the chance for Steven to explain why he was staying on at Waheeken even after she'd made it clear that she didn't want him to. As they pulled away from the front gate (with Anthony Kirsch, one of Ira's spies, kneeling behind a scrub pine, watching) Steven pressed a button and closed the black canvas top of the convertible. For some reason that really got her worked up, she started berating him for imagining that she'd ever be interested in someone who only last week had written to her that he'd decided to switch his major from Business to "Recreational Science"—which was nothing more than a fancy name for Phys-Ed.

By the time they were seated in a booth at Fabio's, facing an oily pizza drenched in tomato sauce, Steven, who had ordered them two beers and was sitting opposite her looking more unappetizingly jock-like every minute, was promising to leave Waheeken and give her time to think things over.

"I don't want to think things over. It's over! Just take me back. I can't bear this." Fay poked at the pizza with her fork, making heart patterns in the tomato sauce.

"Okay. I barged in on you, I'm sorry. Have a sip of beer."

"No, let's go back right now!"

Fay had just completed digging her third heart pattern into the pizza when it dawned on her that it wasn't Steven who was the problem; it wasn't even Donald Worth. It was that it was August in Maine and that she wanted to have sex with the least likely person she'd have imagined herself wanting to have sex with. She got up and started for the door. Steven asked where she was going. She threatened to walk the ten miles if he didn't drive her back to Waheeken immediately. Steven finished both their beers, left some bills on the table, and followed her out to the car, raindrops trailing down his cheeks like tears. They drove back to the camp in silence.

The rain stopped the minute they pulled up to the front gate. It was like the end of the Flood, a little miracle. All creation was dripping, the drops falling from the limbs of the brown oaks lining the driveway offering a steady ping to the macadam, and night was coming on fast, with a rainbow faintly showing. Crossing her arms in front of her chest for warmth and lowering her head, Fay got out of the car promising Steven to "Discuss it some more tomorrow." Then she ran toward the rec hall, where she expected Ira Corman would be practicing karate kicks with Ernie Rawlins, "the tattooed wonder."

But Ira was not in the rec hall, nor was he in the game room with Marcia Big Boobs who sat alone in front of the TV angrily knitting and watching a Nova replay of the first moon landing. Fay slipped out unnoticed and began wandering around in the dark. She was shivering and starting to feel a little faint. Her kids would be wondering where she was, needing help in pulling on their galoshes and navigating the swamp that the field in front of the mess hall was sure to be. A thick mist rose from the lake, making it hard to see in front of her. A frog emitted a belch from under the tiny wooden bridge leading to the bog. In opposition to her good sense, her limbs urged her on. It was dangerous, as she could slip in and drown, with nobody out there to hear her cries for help.

Ira was shooting baskets in the courts behind his cabin. The nightlights hadn't been turned on and she could hardly see the ball as she rushed forward and grabbed it out of his hands. It was cold and wet and smelled of moss. She shot it up and it hit the rim, then bobbled and missed the basket. Ira beckoned for the ball. Fay tossed it off the court and ran toward him, falling against his chest with a sob.

"Did he get violent? I'll bust his . . . who was it, Donald or that guy Steven, with the convertible?" he asked, nuzzling his chin into her damp hair.

Gobs of mist swirled up from the bog, lapped at their feet, and moved on to smudge the lights now flickering in the surrounding cabins and dish-clattering mess hall. They held each other close, both of them trembling. The basketball rolled off the cement into the tall grass lining the bog. They stood there not saying anything. At last, in an unfamiliar little cricket voice, Fay heard herself say, "I . . . I want to sleep with you, Ira. I didn't know it till today."

Ira brushed the wet hair from her forehead with one hand and massaged her back with the other, just as he had on the day, she threw up in front of him. It was his protection, she wanted; she knew that now. It was his doctor's bedside manner that was making her want to have sex with him right there on the basketball court before supper.

"I love you, Fay," he said hoarsely. "I've loved you from the first day. You kept saying we were only platonic friends, but I never felt platonic. I knew you'd come around to seeing it my way."

They kissed spuriously. Ira kept his mouth shut tight. He arched his body into an uncomfortable question mark as he pressed her close to his chest. Never mind his inexperience, Fay thought, guiding his hand downward toward the booty he'd coveted all summer. She looked up at the sky. Now black and clear, it revealed a Big Dipper resembling five perfectly aligned trays of ice cubes. She offered a silent prayer of thanksgiving to the Big Dipper, to Donald, Steven, and even to Barry Porter. Blessings on you all. Bless this Camp Waheeken, if you're out there, Great Goddess Venus.

At that moment, Benjy Dorfman—recognizable from the towering bootblack pompadour which he greased nightly with a Vaseline-and-Crisco combination intended for patenting—emerged from Ira's cabin, picked up the fallen basketball and dribbled it across the court. Halting in mid-dribble to avoid crashing into them, Benjy gazed heavenward. "You'll never see a galaxy like this in Brooklyn," he observed sagely.

"No way!" Ira said, concurring with the Crisco Kid—as

Benjy was called that summer and never again after. "Let's see the ball."

Benjy started toward him with a low dribble, Fay joined in, and soon enough the three of them were scoring baskets all over the place.

3
PILGRIMAGE

Like so many others of their generation during the "New Age" eighties, Fay and Ira were drawn to the spiritual teachings of the East. Discarding Existentialism for mysticism, they embarked on a mutual search for "enlightenment." Fay wasn't quite sure what enlightenment was but sensing that it had something to do with eliminating neediness, she enrolled in a yoga class. Ira, who'd developed a bad back playing basketball and hoping yoga might help, joined her. But Ira's back grew worse, and their yoga teacher suggested he take up Sufi dancing instead. To make up for Ira's painful stint with yoga, Fay accompanied him every Friday to a Brooklyn Mosque to whirl with a group of dervishes. Resentful at being segregated from the men and crammed into a small, hot room to dance with mostly veiled women, she was relieved when Ira's enthusiasm for dervish dancing proved short-lived, and the trip to Tangier, his last foray into Sufism.

. . .

With the muezzin's recorded call to evening prayers echoing in their ears, they scoured Tangier in a cab, searching for the Sufi meetinghouse.

Ira leaned forward and tapped the driver on the shoulder. "You speak English, right?"

"Sure, no problem. I tell you before. No address close to town. I take you further."

Beyond the window lay a flat stretch of beach road. Fay heard the thud of the surf as they sped away from the lights and cries of the *Kasbah.* The sand looked like the warm, powdery kind she enjoyed digging her toes into. She leaned against Ira's shoulder and fell asleep craving fried clams. She'd been dreaming of endless slamming doors when the cab pulled to an abrupt stop that jolted her awake. The driver, whose only visible features thus far were a sharp jaw and a dangling cigarette obscured by an oversized cap with a leather peak, got out, telling them to wait there.

Fay yawned. "Where's he going?"

"I don't know. He's lost."

The driver came back to the cab waving his arms for them to follow. She could now see that his face was pockmarked. Fay scrambled out of the cab and was slapped in the face by a cold ocean wind. Except for a scattering of crystalline stars overhead, the street, like the sky, was ink black.

"Here . . . maybe if you want . . ."

They followed the driver up a sandstone path to a squat row of whitewashed buildings with darkened windows in a lighted courtyard. In one of the buildings, in a door-less general store, an old woman wearing a black dress and kerchief and blue Keds high-tops sat splay-footed behind a marble counter. Turning his back on them, the driver spoke loudly to the woman in Arabic, making big sweeping gestures with his hands. The woman nodded her head and wrinkled her nose, frowning. Finally, the driver looked at Ira and said, "She say okay, you go upstairs. I wait here for you."

As the woman stood, Fay was startled to see three silent babies perched on a pillow-covered pedestal among the splintered crates of Coca Cola piled up behind her. Dangerously nearby, a coffee pot overflowed on a miniscule hotplate alongside a TIDE and BRILLO display. Emerging from behind the counter on Keds-silent feet, her bulky hips waddling only inches from Fay's face, the woman led them across the courtyard into an ill-lit hallway and up a short flight of stairs smelling of fresh tar. At the top of the stairs, she motioned them into a slope-roofed room, bare except for a candle in a dish on a water-stained wooden table and a narrow iron bed with clean white sheets, across which lay two stiff white hand towels.

"Think we've made a mistake? At this point, I don't care. I'm exhausted." Fay made for the bed.

Ira held out the paper with the Sufi meetinghouse address on it and asked the woman if she knew where it was.

"Ya, ya...dees number ten," the woman said.

A burgundy-colored curtain was strung up as a room divider a few feet from the bed. Expecting a washbasin behind it, Fay was about to draw the curtain aside and have a look, when someone coughed and it rustled.

"What's that?" Ira gestured at the curtain.

"Students, students, ya, ya . . ." The woman bobbed her head and gave him a reassuring smile. She had a bluish star that settled into a mole under her right eye.

A pair of black pointed shoes was sticking out in the space between the curtain and the floor. "That leaves out this place," Ira said, walking quickly toward the hall.

"I don't see what's wrong with it," Fay said breezily, slinging her bag over her shoulder. "No, thank you," she whispered loudly to the puzzled woman as she passed her in the doorway. She drew her finger, knifelike, across her throat and rolled her eyes, and the woman stepped back, frightened.

Captive to Ira's determination, they drove around in search of the Sufi meetinghouse for another three hours. Every so often, the driver would, wordlessly, pull to a stop, take the address from Ira, get out, and return shaking his head, his hands in his pockets. Finally admitting defeat, he closed down the meter and informed them that it was past midnight and he had to drive the cab back to the garage and go to his second job as a baker. Refusing their tip, he dropped them off at the pier where he'd picked them up. A pair of drunken Italian sailors lurched by with their arms around each other.

"You don't have a telephone number. You only know the guy as Yusef, no last name, and the address obviously doesn't exist. The next ferry to Algeciras doesn't come till seven, tomorrow morning, so we can't get back to the hotel. Let's just sleep here on the pier and wait for it."

Fay had to be careful not to sound as if she were rebuking Ira for being unrealistically stubborn about finding the Sufi meetinghouse or they would get into a big fight which she was too exhausted to pursue. As Ira paced in front of the pier, she consoled herself by removing her diary from her bag and scribbling: *"Fooling around with vitamin shots and visualizations for cancer patients doesn't make you Linus Pauling. Ira's problem is that he sees himself as innovative and daring when all he is, is a stubborn, introverted man of ordinary intelligence prone to hero worship."*

Sufism was the latest in the long line of "isms" defining Ira's spiritual quest. Fay had shared his experiments with meditation, LSD, the East in general. She'd even gone so far as to take Buddhist vows alongside him with a Tibetan lama in Colorado. The lama had given her a Buddhist rosary and the name "Ocean of Dharma." Ira had dropped Buddhism two months later. Fay had found its atheism appealing and investigated it further. Jessie Kane, her dance instructor, was a Zen Buddhist. Fay had stayed behind after Jessie's class to learn the basics of meditation. She was certainly no mocker of quests; it was just that Ira's, driven as they were by Sam Rubin, his purportedly "psychic" best friend and adviser, so often turned out to be occult rather than spiritual. Witnessing the course of that uneven friendship, Ira's loyalty to Sam continued to perplex her. At first, she'd found him charmingly boyish for trying to convince her that Sam was "psychically gifted from birth." She'd been amused by the bevy of invisible guardians Sam supposedly channeled to instruct Ira on everything from "important movies" to "malevolent influences" on his dating life. Ira referred to Sam's psychic power as "looking up." Fay had joked about it at first, saying she hoped Sam wouldn't look her up and put her in the category of malevolent influences. When Ira didn't smile, she dropped the subject.

Some months after she'd moved in with him and they'd just finished making love, Ira again insisted that it was Sam Rubin who had engineered the relationship telepathically. Fay laughed, saying Sam had to be some sort of pervert and that Ira was crazy to believe him. After that, Ira talked less about Sam's psychic powers and more about the Rubin family, and the outwardly observant Jewish mother who worked in the flower market on West 26th Street, bringing mammoth gladiola bouquets home to Brooklyn on Friday afternoons in preparation for the Sabbath, then took Sam and his sister and Ira out for non-kosher Chinese food on Saturday nights, as well as the moon-faced father who had driven a dog sled in Alaska before coming to New York to work as a bartender at a vaudeville cabaret called The Bowery Follies.

Ira's search for a surrogate family in the Rubins made Fay want to mother him. His vulnerability made her feel strong and protective. To bolster his self-confidence, she would have to show him that he didn't need Sam. She would do it gently. She would stop flying off the handle so as not to remind him of his mother. She would undo the harm Patsy Corman had inflicted by sending Ira to school in torn shirts and locking him out of the house until he'd removed his shoes first so as not to ruin her white carpets. When Ira turned fourteen, Patsy had lurched into a disastrous menopause and refused to let him into the house even with his shoes off. Ira never complained, and just spent more time with the Rubins. Then, whenever she could get her hands on him, Patsy took to slapping him about the ears and head, screaming, so the whole neighborhood could hear that, like his father, he had no idea of what she was going through, and accusing her estranged sisters Jenny and Hannah (whom Ira had only seen once from a distance at his grandmother's funeral) of stealing her inheritance. Feeling sorry for his mother, Ira had ducked her blows and fled from the kitchen as Patsy threatened to turn on the gas and put her head in the oven.

During a particularly violent bout one day, the doctor's wife next door notified the police, and Patsy was put away in a private sanitarium. After a month of shock treatments, she returned; the beatings stopped, and she no longer lifted her voice beyond a whisper. But the notes informing Ira she was "downtown" were tacked once again to the refrigerator door. Invariably, Patsy's shopping sprees would result in his father's cutting up her credit cards, and, lying in bed at night, Ira would hear his parents arguing through the strains of Charlie Parker's "Yardbird Suite" no matter how loud he turned up the music on his earphones.

Ignored by her husband (who slept in a separate room and, as Ira later discovered, had fathered a son during a thirty-year affair with his secretary), and with her older son away at college, Patsy had poured out all her misery on fourteen-year-old Ira.

Though he was already in his twenties when she met him, Ira claimed that Fay was the first woman he had slept with. He'd fallen in love often enough, but always with the impossible-to-reach big sisters of older neighborhood athletes; staring with mute yearning into their kitchen windows, hoping for a glimpse of them in their curlers as they shuffled from sink to stove in terrycloth slippers on hot summer nights with his heart wrenching at their fragility. Ira told her he'd grown up not so much desiring, as feeling sorry for women, pained by their secret torments, their monthly bleedings, their soft bare arms and frail fists, their high-pitched cries for independence, life insurance, furniture, separate bank accounts . . . all the things Patsy had been refused. Ira squinted, looking like a fourteen-year-old boy when he told her these things, and Fay took him for an ally, a man who was not dangerous, not like her father, always wanting something from her that she couldn't deliver.

Though every woman in her consciousness-raising group had warned her against it, Fay jumped headfirst into the rescue mission that was to become her marriage. Her upbringing had prepared her well. As the only child of a bitterly frustrated Catholic mother who had survived several miscarriages and a botched hysterectomy by the time Fay was a year old, and a military father whose greatest ambition was that his daughter become America's first female four-star general, Fay was accustomed to playing the hero.

On the Texas army base where she'd grown up, everyone, even her teachers had called her "Buddy." She'd played football with the boys from the time she was nine. No girls' soccer for her. Hiding her burgeoning woman's body in baggy pants and daddy's oversized camouflage shirt, wearing combat boots and no makeup, her thick black hair pulled into a tight knot and pinned up under her helmet, she conspired with her father to maintain her image as his "Number One Son." To her mother's horror, Fay's efforts paid off only too well. By the time she turned fifteen, she was a full-fledged member of her father's male inner sanctum of beer halls, billiard parlors, and weekend poker games. Though initiated into sex that same year by one of her football "buddies," Fay had never associated sex with love until she met Ira.

In her letter announcing her engagement to her parents, she described her fiancé as a "fair-skinned introspective person who complements my hyperactivity." Because she wasn't aware of it herself at the time, she did not say that she loved Ira for being everything her father was not: gentle, shy, and deferential toward women. Or that his mother had branded him with an indelible fear of needy women who threatened to bury him alive in his sleep. Or that Ira had only survived his mother's assault by turning to Sam and his army of invisible guardians. Or that it might be too late for her to undo the damage. Oddly enough, Ira wasn't the first of her lovers with a fixation on threesomes. She seemed to have a penchant for attracting men eager to share her with their best friends—like Paul, her first serious college boyfriend, a Columbia doctoral candidate in philosophy who wore a wool shirt that scratched her face when they made love on the sofa after curfew in the basement lounge of her all-women's dorm at Barnard. Being allergic to wool, Fay would inevitably break out in hives the next morning. Dates with Paul were predictable. They would spend their evenings drinking vodka and tonic at the West End Bar and arguing about Heidegger's Nazism with a group of doctoral candidates from the philosophy department. Those unresolved debates would be followed by short bouts of determined lovemaking on the sofa in the basement lounge of her dorm while Paul's best friend,

Noel, waited for him on Broadway in his black Porsche with the engine running.

One night, instead of immediately going upstairs to her room, Fay had sneaked out behind Paul and followed him into the street. Their lovemaking had taken longer than usual, and she was curious to see if his friend had grown tired of waiting for him and driven off. But Noel was still parked there. As Paul got into the car, she heard him call out angrily, "You'd better get yourself another traveling partner, I'm sick and tired of this routine." Then he stepped down hard on the gas pedal and the two of them sped down Broadway.

Fay was genuinely surprised when Paul and his friend turned up again the following Saturday night. Wary, but eager to see what would happen next, she suggested the three of them go out together. Maybe buy a bottle of red wine and drive up to the Cloisters. Both men were game.

When Paul jumped into the passenger seat of the Porsche next to Noel and didn't show any sign of moving, Fay crammed herself into the baggage space behind them. The drive uptown was uncomfortable, the Cloisters had long closed, and she was soon sorry for having suggested it. But Noel seemed determined to make a success of the evening, driving until he found a safe place on the heights to park so as to get an unobstructed view of New York lit up at night. They passed the wine bottle back and forth and got pleasantly tipsy before making the trip back to Fay's dorm and the inevitable scratchy lovemaking session on the basement sofa with Paul.

On the last Saturday night before her final exams, Noel invited Fay to his Riverside Drive apartment for a drink alone. Paul, he said, was busy preparing for his dissertation defense and had asked him to fill in for him. As they entered the building, Noel handed the keys to the Porsche to the doorman along with a five-dollar bill. When Noel's back was turned, the doorman winked at her. When they'd entered the apartment and removed their jackets, Fay noticed that she was inappropriately casual in her baggy cargo pants and T-shirt next to Noel, in his expensive black shirt, gray silk ascot, and tight gray slacks that exaggerated his narrow little buns. She watched as, swaying his hips ever so slightly, he walked to the bar to pour her a glass of sherry. As she sipped her drink, Noel kissed her on the nape of the neck. It was a gratuitous, birdlike little kiss that felt more dutiful than romantic. Then walking away from her without saying a word, he stopped in front of an ornate mirror bordered by gargantuan-sized seashells to straighten his ascot before disappearing into the bedroom. Shutting the door behind him with a definitive slam, he left her standing there, astonished and alone.

Fay had never laid eyes on Paul or Noel again after that night. Only months later, when she saw them walking hand-in-hand on Broadway as she was coming out of Butler Library, did it dawn on her that they were gay and using her as a foil, like Elizabeth Taylor in *Suddenly Last Summer*. She'd conveniently forgotten about that humiliating ménage a trois—until the night Ira brought Sam to the apartment to meet her for the first time.

She had worn a skin-tight mandarin silk dress with a Mao collar.

"Ah, Madam Panderer, so glad to meet you," Sam piped in a fake Chinese accent, his eyes eating the flesh off her hips and breasts.

Sam had sour breath and carrot-red hair.

"Nice to meet you, too" Fay said coldly, detesting him on sight.

Ira picked up on their mutual animosity immediately. But he was too hell-bent on creating the happy family he'd never had to consider that his wife and his best friend might not like each other. Seeking to defuse the tension between them, he seized on the one topic involving Sam that still seemed to amuse her.

"Why don't you give Fay a morphological reading," Ira urged.

Sam pretended to demur.

Unable to resist baiting him, Fay said archly, "That's right, you're a face reader as well as a psychic. From what Ira told me, I was under the impression that you dwelled strictly among the gods and didn't bother with mere mortals like me."

Taking an adenoidal deep breath and releasing it, Sam took a step toward her. Fay stepped back. The stink of him was not to be borne. Even the expensive cologne he'd doused himself with couldn't hide the sulfurous vapor of his breath. She had all to do to keep from gagging, as wrapping his clammy, nail-bitten fingers around her chin and tilting it upward, Sam leaned in and scanned her face.

"You were right on, Ira. She's definitely a Venus type. The heart-shaped face, that black hair . . . and of course those beautiful green eyes are a dead giveaway. Highly sexed, Venus types . . . very nice for you, Ira. Very nice indeed." Sam let out a lascivious whistle.

"I told you she was gorgeous," Ira said.

"Can we stop now? I'm feeling very uncomfortable."

"On the contrary, we're paying you the highest compliment. Venus, Aphrodite, in Greek, is the goddess of love, after all, my dear Fay." Rolling his eyes and tweaking a non-existent mustache, Sam played the Victorian villain. He was certainly dressed like one: a starched high-collared shirt, three-piece black suit, gold watch fob, and shiny black high-top boots. A regular Jack the Ripper.

Fay shuddered. To deflect Sam's villainous gaze, she asked

quickly, "And what about Ira? He told me he was a Mars, and that Mars and Venus are perfectly matched."

"Oh, no. That's where he was wrong," said Sam with a sneer. "Ira's a Saturn. You can tell that right away, from the hexagonal shape of his face."

"And what are Saturns like?"

"Secretive . . . an iron fist in a velvet glove."

"And what type are you, Sam?"

"Mercury. A perfect triangle. Named for the god of psychics, the mediator between the dead and the living."

"And the god of thieves, too, if I remember correctly," Fay added.

"And the divine messenger, ruler of medicine, don't forget the helmet, the winged sandals, and the caduceus," Ira quickly interjected.

"Oh, yes. The florist's delivery boy," Fay said, removing Sam's hand from her chin.

"Its obvious Fay doesn't put much stock in all this." Sam turned to Ira, giving her the opportunity to slip away into the kitchen with the excuse that she was going to open a bottle of wine before they sat down to dinner.

Taking her bag with her into the public toilet at the entrance to the pier, Fay changed into jeans and a sweatshirt. When she came out again, she saw her shadow engulf Ira's and wondered whether he hadn't come to resent her strength.

"Do you need help?" He extended his hand as they prepared to jump over a waist-high fence.

"No. I can make it easily. Just catch my bag." She made a graceful leap. "I could go for a joint."

Ira looked at her sulkily. Yes, he'd probably grown resentful of the independence he'd sown back in the early days of their relationship, probably wished she wouldn't push through restaurant doors ahead of him and jump over fences without his help. He was probably sorry that he'd married a woman who had not only failed to give him a child, but also now seemed out of control, heading for a life that didn't include him. Yet, being Ira, he remained mute, watching haplessly as their marriage crumbled.

The pier was perched on wooden stilts at the end of which stood a small, unoccupied watchman's station. Since the decent hotels were too far away, and even if they did find some rundown sailor's hostel closer to the harbor, they wouldn't have time to get to the early morning ferry. So they decided to spend the night on the pier. Using Fay's bag as a pillow, they sat down and, leaning up against the windowless wall at the rear of the watchman's station, fell asleep to the sound of water lapping against the pier's wooden stilts. They hadn't been there for more than fifteen minutes when a man in uniform shocked them awake with a flashlight. Aiming it directly into their eyes, he asked in broken English what they thought they were doing sleeping on government property. Blinded by the flashlight, Fay had the strange sensation of being suspended inside a kaleidoscope, whirling and fragmenting into a million purple and silver bits of stars and half-moons. Then the center of the kaleidoscope cracked open, and she saw herself climbing up the side of a cliff wearing the black robes and straw sandals of a Japanese Zen monk; she was holding on to an outcropping of rock, not daring to look down, and was about to fall when, above her, a man whose face she couldn't see extended his arm and pulled her up.

"You scram," yelled the watchman, pulling Fay roughly to her feet. "You no good hippies. You get out of Tangier!" Ira, she noticed, was already standing and made no effort to intercede on her behalf. Fay briefly thought she might still be asleep and dreaming they were still searching for the Sufi center. Only this time they were not riding in a cab but standing on a street in front of a pier surrounded by vomiting sailors and pimps and dope pushers peddling their wares beneath the artificial glow of colored lights in the narrow alleyways of Tangier harbor.

"Come on, let's get out of here," Ira at last took her hand and led her away from the pier.

They walked for a few blocks before sitting down at one of the empty tables in front of a café whose open window revealed a man roasting a great hunk of meat on a spit above a glistening bib of fat.

"What next?" Ira asked.

"We sit here all night, I guess."

"I have a headache."

The proprietor of the café stuck his head out of the window and, seeing they had no intention of ordering anything, went back to basting the meat.

"He's not going to bother us. Let's just sleep here."

"I can't."

"I can." Yawning, Fay stretched out her arms on the table in front of her and lay her head down. "I can sleep anywhere, even standing up if I have to."

"Well, I can't."

Fay sat up and stroked Ira's forehead with her fingertips. "This'll cure your headache. You love this, don't you?"

Ira had just closed his eyes when an Arab boy of about twelve approached their table, pulled up a chair and sat down next to her. He wore a black wool lint-covered jacket, khaki trousers, and no socks with his expensive-looking kidskin shoes. The boy was so stoned that his head lolled like a puppet's before falling against Fay's shoulder; drool trickled down his chin and he stank abominably.

Ira opened his eyes and pushed Fay's hand away. "I know

you don't believe in demons," he said, "but after tonight I think you'll change your mind." He got up and without looking at her, charged away from the table. The boy's head slithered from her shoulder with a thump.

"He's only a kid. I hope he didn't hurt his head."

"I hope he busted it, the junkie bastard!" Ira exploded.

Seeing her husband so uncharacteristically angry, Fay followed him in silence. A few blocks away from the café, under a tree in a vacant square, Ira spotted a bench and sat down, motioning for her to join him.

"We'll take turns sleeping and watching your bag. We don't want our passports stolen. You sleep first. I'll watch. We'll do it in fifteen-minute shifts, okay?"

"Okay."

Fay had barely fallen asleep before entering a dream, in which the handsome Japanese rocker glimpsed on the ferry to Tangier was asking Ira if he'd mind making a bargain with him and his friend. The same Arab man with the pointed black goatee who reminded her of Doctor Crumm standing beside him grinning lewdly. Ira said he wasn't interested in bargains. The Arab stepped forward and offered "one thousand dollars for a half hour with the lady." Ira told him to "Beat it!" and the Arab disappeared from view. The Japanese rocker then sat down on a bench under a palm tree across from them and stared at Fay, sphinxlike, for what felt like hours. At last, with daylight filtering into the purple, mauve, and black-fringed sky behind him, he stood up, bowed to her with his palms touching, and left.

Fay woke and checked her watch. It was five. Ira was sleeping soundly next to her with his eyes partly open. A man in a striped *jalabiya* was sweeping the street with a twig broom, scattering the night's detritus as the sun inched slowly into the sky.

4
MEXICO CITY

Fay was eighteen and bent on using what her mother referred to as her "God-given gifts" for the good of humanity when she linked up with a Mexican medical school dropout named Sergio Ruiz and became a revolutionary. She met Sergio in a San Antonio bar famous for its puffy tacos. He was twenty-eight, brown-skinned and a head shorter. He was shy, wore big round glasses and told her he'd been raised in the hills outside of Cuernavaca in a villa with a swimming pool and twenty barefoot peasants in help, adding that, when he was sixteen, his father had turned him out of the house for trying to unionize the twenty peasants who worked the family estate.

Sergio was drinking beer and half-heartedly watching a baseball game on the TV over the bar when Fay walked up to his booth and asked him if he'd mind if she sat down.

"Sure," he nodded, making it hard to tell whether he minded or was inviting her to sit.

Fay slipped into the booth opposite him. Then she ordered tequila without ice and told him she was a lapsed Catholic in need of redemption. She said it partly because she was sure

Sergio didn't understand a word she'd said, and partly because she'd already had two tequilas and was drunk.

"You can solve your problem by coming down to Mexico and working for the revolution," Sergio said in only slightly accented English.

"This isn't real. I'm dreaming this conversation."

"I'm Sergio Ruiz." He reached across the table and shook her hand.

"Fay Watkins. Did you ever want to be someone you aren't?"

Sergio looked her in the eye, "A woodcarver once, when I was a kid."

"What are you now?"

"A seeker after social justice." Fay noticed that the bottle he drank from was slightly chipped at the mouth.

"You're going to cut your lip on that bottle."

Sergio pointed to the door. "Let's get out of here and go for a walk." A month later, Fay was living in Mexico City studying crowd control and training as a demonstration monitor. Her roommate, also American, was a medical student named Margo who had divorced her husband and left her two daughters with her mother in North Dakota in order to attend, as she put it, "the only medical school in the hemisphere that would have me." Margo was on a U.S. military scholarship. She'd served five years as an air force nurse before becoming radicalized and still bore the traces of her military training: her side of the room was always neatly arranged, her desk spotless, her medical books lined up on the bookshelves ready for duty, and her personal belongings tucked out of sight in khaki rayon bags. Not like Fay, who lived out of her open suitcase.

Sergio had dropped out of the University Medical School in the Pedregal district to organize full time, leaving Margo in charge of student demonstrations like the upcoming protest against the jailing without trial of an important labor union activist. Under Sergio's instructions to cover their link to the student radicals and establish their identity as a pair of American *muchachas* out for a good time, Margo and Fay spent many hours flirting and drinking tequila with the regulars at an artists' café in the Zona Rosa called The Laughing Horse.

It was there Fay met Humberto, her thirty-seven-year-old lover, a penniless film director to whom she contributed most of the money her father had given her when she told him she needed some time before college to think about what she wanted to do with her life. Though she'd already won her dance scholarship to Barnard on early admissions, her guidance counselor, certain that she was experiencing a "temporary identity crisis," had convinced her parents to let her spend a semester perfecting her Spanish in Mexico City. The guidance counselor, who was forty, recently divorced, and whose name was Brown, wore loafers with tassels and had a crush on her.

On the night Humberto finished cutting his "life's work," a film called *The Laughing Horse*, he celebrated by piling Fay and Margo and his leading man, Felix, into his red Volkswagen Beetle and driving in circles around the Paseo de Reforma honking the horn. Felix, who by then was stinking drunk, started pawing at Margo's breasts. Margo hissed into his face that he, like all men, was a *hijo de puta*, and Felix jumped out of the moving car into the middle of traffic threatening to kill himself if she didn't take back the insult against his mother. Humberto stopped the car and snatched Felix out of the way of an oncoming door-less and windowless bus jammed with farm workers. Fay suspected they were replaying an almost identically harebrained "traffic scene" from Humberto's film to impress the two *gringas*.

When he wasn't out on the road exhorting peasants to drop their hoes and join the cause, Sergio slept on a couch in the living room of Margo and Fay's flat. Two days before the march, Margo was out taking an anatomy exam and Sergio, in a new crisp blue denim shirt Fay hadn't seen before was eating breakfast when he suddenly looked up from his poached egg and announced that he and Margo were getting married so he could get a green card and legally cross the border. It was raining lightly. Fay had just closed the door and returned from the hall after having paid the bread man. She put two fresh rolls on a plate and placed it on the table in front of Sergio. Watching him as he mopped up the runny egg yolk from his plate with a chunk of his roll, she was struck by the certainty that he was about to be lost to her—not because he was marrying Margo (even before Fay had opened her suitcase, Margo had announced that she was a lesbian and was having an affair with a woman radiologist at the hospital, so the marriage was clearly a political convenience)—but because she needed more time alone with him to absorb what he had found and she was still searching for. It was as if Sergio had suddenly appeared to help her solve her "temporary identity crisis" and was now just as suddenly abandoning her.

"When's the wedding?"

"Tomorrow at noon, at the American Embassy."

"Will you throw me out of the flat?"

Sergio laughed. "I'd like my coffee now."

"Well, I can't live here with you and Margo as a married couple."

She turned to the stove and heated the coffee, then poured warmed milk halfway into a mug and waited.

Sergio buttered a roll and passed it to her. "You know, I used to sneak the best food from my mother's pantry and bring it to the peasants who worked on our estate. By the time I was twelve I was an avowed enemy of the capitalist government in the United States and an urban guerilla in my own country."

The coffee pot hissed. Removing it from the stove, Fay poured coffee into Sergio's mug, added sugar, and placed it on the table in front of him. Then, fixing a mug for herself, she sat down. As she took the first sip, it suddenly occurred to her that there was nothing to worry about; everything was working out exactly as it should. Although she wanted to say something to that effect to Sergio, she couldn't put it into words. Instead, the fact of perfect cosmic order in a chaotic world seemed to announce itself in the appearance of the sun, which was just then driving a red ray through the rain and smog of the city, pouring into the window behind him, and dancing off his plate as he fed the remains of his roll to Margo's cat licking at the leg of his chair. That, too—Sergio bending over with the bread, the cat's tongue working away at the chair—somehow promised the possibility of perfection in things just as they were. A moment of illumination that passed too quickly.

After they'd cleared the table and washed the breakfast dishes, Sergio unrolled a large Mexico City street map and pointed out where the demonstrators from the medical faculty under Fay and Margo's command would feed into the line of marchers en route to the Zocalo. He placed his finger directly on the spot where the rally ending the demonstration would take place, in front of the platform where he was scheduled to give the keynote speech. Several Mexican film and television stars and a popular leftist folk singer had agreed to appear with him as well. Stationed at opposite ends of the Zocalo, wearing white armbands and carrying megaphones, Margo and Fay would keep their contingents in line. It was all to be done legally and peacefully. Sergio had registered with the city government, obtaining both an official permit and an unofficial promise from the municipal police captain himself that there would be no harassment of the demonstrators. In exchange,

Sergio had promised the captain a peaceful protest march and left him a thousand-dollar bribe.

The weather on the day of the demonstration was perfect, the sky blue and cloudless, the air free of the usual stink of diesel fuel—no cars, no scooters, not even a city bus in sight. The crowd of onlookers lined up three rows deep behind the sawhorses on both sides of the Paseo de Reforma were in a holiday mood. Even the policemen on horseback were smiling as they let themselves be photographed. Slogan-painted banners hanging from the windows of office and apartment buildings billowed lightly in the wind: red, yellow, royal purple and dragon green. Women at the windows threw colored confetti into the air.

Standing next to Humberto in his tweed jacket with the familiar beige suede elbow patches and ever-present pipe sticking out of the front pocket, Fay thought: If I'd seen this short, bandy-legged, barrel-chested Mexican with the Indio cheekbones and mica chip eyes walking the streets in San Antonio, I'd have taken him for just another illegal alien with a grim mestizo face. I'd have passed him by, never knowing he was a Communist who'd held a grip for Godard, or that he spoke flawless French and liked sitting on the bed naked, playing the guitar and singing Oaxacan folk songs after making love.

A single helicopter suddenly appeared in the empty sky and made a loop over the crowd, and a young man in a brown corduroy suit standing behind the sawhorse pointed at it shouting, "CIA!" He was immediately joined by a group of teenage girls who, laughing as they pretended to shoot the helicopter out of the sky, chanted in English, "CIA! GO AWAY! CIA! GO AWAY!" The helicopter pilot responded by narrowing his loop and buzzing the chanters. Three men in civilian clothes peered out of the helicopter's open doorway. Two of them waved enthusiastically to the teenage girls.

A small ruckus exploded out of a side street, and a monitor hurried over to inform Fay that the police were turning their horses on a rowdy cluster of white-coated medical school students. She hurried after the monitor to confirm the report, which, though it turned out to be only a rumor, didn't dispel the worrisome air of restlessness now underlying all the gaiety. On returning to her assigned post, Fay was about to convey her concerns to Humberto when the "start" signal came in the form of a white handkerchief held aloft on a stick waving to her from the sidelines. A chanting group of demonstrators carrying labor union banners had already begun streaming from the side streets. Linking arms with Humberto, Fay led her medical student contingent forward, their hoarse chants merging with the unionists in a moment of ethereal harmony before lapsing into a guttural roar.

A woman marching directly in front of Fay was wheeling a toddler in a collapsible stroller draped with a Che Guevara banner. As the demonstrators were stopped at a crosswalk awaiting the policeman's signal to move forward, a man suddenly bolted from the sidelines and pitched a tomato at the banner. Fay saw it coming, and breaking rank, rushed in front of the stroller catching the tomato full in the chest. Unhurt, and loudly cheered by her linemates, she returned to Humberto's side wearing the splattered mixture of seeds and tomato juice on her chest as a badge of honor. Spotting a group of counter demonstrators in front of the Hilton, she raised the megaphone to her lips and shouted in English: "Cowards! Free Vallejo!" The pony-tailed mother of the toddler in the Che Guevara stroller thrust a fist in the air and chanted along with her. Soon everyone in Fay's line was chanting in English, "Cowards! Free Vallejo!" Even the mustached policeman rocking on his horse alongside her seemed to be keeping time to the rhythm of the chant.

The demonstrators were marching faster now, almost approaching a run, as onlookers started breaking free from behind the sawhorses to join them. Humberto had picked up the pace and she had to hurry to keep up with him. When the marching band up ahead broke into a defiant version of *Guantanamero*, the protestors switched from chanting to singing—until the music was suddenly interrupted by a cacophony of screeching flutes and blasting horns. Drums boomed like cannon fire, which was soon followed by the clearly detectable sound of human screams. Fay's contingent was the first to panic. Breaking through their well-organized lines, the white-coated medical students began scattering in all directions. Taking up the megaphone, Fay shouted for them to return to their ranks, but the marchers were too intent on fleeing to obey her. Humberto was still gripping her free hand so hard it hurt. Fay tossed aside the megaphone and heard it crunch under her feet as she ran alongside him. The place at her right was empty. Her line mate, a scruffy teenage boy in sandals had fled. The pony-tailed mother had been pushed out of view by the surging mob, and the child still in the stroller was left behind. Fay reached for the stroller, but before she could grab hold of the handlebar, a gray-haired man emerged from behind her and lifting the child, stroller and all, ran with it toward the disintegrating lines in the rear. Fay looked around for a monitor, for anyone wearing a white armband who might help her regain control of the scattering marchers, but the monitors, too, were dispersing in a desperate attempt to avoid the crush of whinnying, prancing horses now tangled in the same maze of bunting, imprisoning the fleeing mob. Offering no resistance, Fay let Humberto pull her forward into the mass of panicked demonstrators blindly tearing through the bunting and running toward the Zocalo.

A Black girl holding a trumpet high over her head ran alongside them, her hair brushing against Fay's cheek. Spotting the white armband, the girl pulled at Fay's sleeve, screaming for her to do something. "They're shooting! They've opened fire at the Zocalo! They're killing us!"

How could that be? If it were true, why was the marching band still crazily blasting and drumming and screeching away up ahead? Trapped, unable to move forward without being trampled, Fay could now clearly make out the steady burst of gunfire coming from the Zocalo. A horse reared inches from Humberto's face. He ducked, almost lost his balance, but then righted himself, never letting go of Fay's hand. A woman in a white doctor's coat who had been hit and was bleeding was thrust against her by a no longer familiar policeman on horseback. Fay tried shielding the woman from another round of blows, but the policeman was too quick for her. Guiding his horse between them, he swung a truncheon cursing, first at one, then at the other. Fay narrowly escaped being struck as Humberto, forcing open a path through the throng of bodies and horses, dragged her toward the sidewalk. Ignoring her protests, he pulled her along and started running in the opposite direction of the Zocalo, not stopping until they'd reached a deserted narrow street behind the Reforma. There, in front of an apartment building, his breath coming in gasps, he grabbed her by the shoulders and propped her against the stone façade of the entrance, then, resting both hands on the walls on either side of her, he covered her body with his. They remained there breathing steadily in unison for about fifteen minutes until Fay assured him that she was ready to return to her apartment.

When she arrived, Sergio was sitting at the kitchen table in a bloodstained shirt. He was still wearing his shattered glasses.

The bloodstains, he told her, were Margo's, not his. Except for his broken glasses, he'd gotten away unharmed. Margo had suffered cuts and bruises on her arms and legs, two requiring stitches, but other than that, she'd been lucky to escape anything more serious. She was ready to leave the hospital, but it wasn't safe to pick her up yet; the emergency room was crawling with police. He would be leaving for Cuba in a couple of hours, but Fay wasn't to follow him. She was about to protest, but Sergio cut her off. No, it was best that she return to San Antonio as soon as she could book a flight out. He might write to her, but she wasn't to worry if she didn't hear from him for a while. His messages were sure to be intercepted.

Removing his shattered glasses and placing them in his bloodstained shirt pocket, Sergio got up from his chair, pushed it aside, and walked past her toward the door.

"Good luck, muchacha," he said. Then flashing the victory sign at her from the doorway, he slipped out of Fay's life as deftly as he'd entered it.

5
GOD-GIVEN GIFTS

Fay's fifteen minutes of fame had come and gone during Ira's internship on a Saturday, with the sun slicing one sharp ray through the lettering on the Polish butcher's window across the street from their Yorkville tenement. She was still slowly inching her way toward a B.A. at Barnard—where she'd earned a reputation for being "eccentric" because during a snowstorm she'd tracked to school on skis. But beyond that, she was basically viewed as a loner, known only sketchily to her few New York acquaintances as an anti-war army brat from Texas whose father was a career army doctor. Her fiercely devout Catholic mother—working as a receptionist at the San Antonio Marriott, on whose stationery she typed her letters disapproving of Fay's politics, her living in New York, and "shacking up with that Jew"—was not a subject for discussion at all.

Mrs. Engelhardt, the janitor's wife, was leaning out the ground floor window of her apartment on the day Fay was "discovered." Fay greeted her before stepping inside and climbing the corroded staircase leading to her own apartment on the top floor. She was so excited that she had to stop on the second landing to catch her breath before climbing again past the corner apartment of a Cuban exile couple who were arguing in elegant Castilian Spanish, up to the third floor, where the sun knifed through the broken skylight. Finally, she reached her door, heart still pounding with the thrill of what had happened on the Lexington Avenue bus stopping for a red light in front of the parking lot that had once been the School for the Deaf. A woman with brown braids arranged on top of her head like a crown, wearing a pale-yellow silk suit, had approached her and asked if she'd done any modeling.

"No, why?" Fay said.

"I just thought you might. You have the height, the facial structure, the body . . ."

They were just passing Bloomingdale's. Fay's stop was eight blocks away. "I'm a dance education major at Barnard," she said, her hands wet and the nape of her neck prickling with anticipation.

"Have you ever done TV?"

"No, I haven't."

"You'd be perfect for commercials. You strike me as the travel ad or soft drink type."

"I've never modeled . . . I . . . I'm a dancer," Fay said.

"You'd probably photograph smashingly with those green eyes and those high cheekbones," the woman said.

"I inherited the high cheekbones from my grandmother."

The woman didn't seem to hear her. "Here's my card," she said. "I get off next. The name's Leorna Mann, I'm with Sherman, Hopewell and Brand—you've heard of us, I'm sure."

Fay had not.

"The number is there on the card. Call me."

The bus pulled up to the next stop. The driver opened the doors and the woman with the braids folded into the Lexington

Avenue crowd. Fay missed her stop and walked the twenty blocks home from Spanish Harlem in a daze. Digging into her saddlebag-sized purse for her keys, she came upon a small hand mirror and appraised her looks through Leorna Mann's eyes: abundant black hair caught up in a dancer's knot, green eyes, high-bridged nose, and high cheekbones—the misused and tainted "God-given gifts," her mother cherished so.

Leorna Mann's office at Sherman, Hopewell and Brand was carpeted in real Bessarabian. An expert thrift shopper, Fay noticed it the minute she walked through the door. Leorna Mann wore a black dress and black high-heeled pumps, looking more imposing than she had on the bus, her hair still braided. When Fay saw her get up from behind her desk and come forward with her hand outstretched, she was reminded of Ira's brother's wife, Erika. The two women shared the same taut skin, lean arms and year-round tan that came from playing hard tennis in the Hamptons on a regular basis. Mann was a German name, too. Fay tried not to be intimidated. She remembered pretending for Ira's sake that she was really enjoying herself immensely listening to his brother Charles tell her every time she came to the Amagansett house that Sonja Henie, the ice-skating star, had owned the place next door. "She was a Nazi sympathizer, you know," he'd say, pouring drinks as Erika shook her head and pouted. "It's a matter of local fact." Then Charles, a balding cardiologist who had once called Fay a Communist in a heated political exchange, wouldn't say another word to her for the rest of the weekend. Fay pictured Leorna Mann dragging exhausted Nazi frogmen from the water and leading them up the wooden steps to the weathered house with the glass wall facing the dunes. The spies were blond, with sand-colored mustaches, and they drank brandy from snifters painted with kingfishers.

"I really am glad you came," Leorna Mann said. "I was afraid you might think I was putting you on. But then I wouldn't have given you my card, would I?"

Fay noticed the outlines of a full slip under Leorna Mann's smart black dress. A woman who wore a full slip had to come from out of town; she was probably an import from the Midwest who had carefully cultivated a Boston Brahmin accent. Fay, also an import, wore neither bra nor slip under her tie-dyed skirt and white peasant blouse. Nor was she wearing stockings with her sandals. Nor had she fully shed her Texas twang.

Leorna Mann took her to meet "the staff," four crew cut preppies with pencils behind their ears. The preppies mumbled "Hello" in unison and looked down at their yellow memo pads. Fay tiptoed behind Leorna Mann into a room marked "Quiet," where a director and camera crew were preparing to shoot a cream cheese sandwich. Sprouting earphones, the professorial-looking director waved his hand, the cameras whirred, and an actor in a loud red blazer purred into an offstage microphone about the thousand and one ways you could use Kraft in the kitchen. His announcement was followed by the clarion call of a baroque trumpet. Leorna Mann led her out of the studio into a corridor, stopping in front of a chrome cylinder that turned out to be an elevator, which scooped them both inside. At the fiftieth floor, the elevator opened and disgorged them into a glass-enclosed room dominated by a fig tree. A thirtyish man with a red face and patrician features, his vest flaunting a shameless display of a Phi Beta Kappa key, standing behind a desk.

"Miss Hopkins?"

"Watkins."

"Yes, Watkins . . . nice to meet you." He did not offer her his hand. "You don't mind if I call you Fay, do you, dear?"

Leorna Mann said, "This is Dave Wilkie, Mr. Sherman's assistant. He'll tell you everything you need to know. I'll be in my office. When you're ready, just ring yourself back down to twenty and the receptionist will show you where to go. We'll have lunch, hmm?" Leaving behind the scent of sandalwood, she stepped into the elevator and was swept out of sight.

Dave Wilkie emerged from behind his desk then and asked Fay to turn around so he could have a look at her ass. Without uttering so much as one of the barbs that had earned her some notoriety at Barnard for being "liberated," she walked calmly toward the elevator, pushed the button and entered it. When she reached the lobby, she fled from the building onto Madison Avenue and vomited against a fire hydrant.

Arriving at the yoga center on West Seventy-Second Street, where she taught four classes a week, she fell sobbing into the arms of Olga, a Parthenon-thighed fellow instructor who calmed her with deep breathing exercises. When she had sufficiently recovered, she went to the locker room to prepare for her master class. As she was changing in her cubicle, trying to banish the image of Dave Wilkie's pornographic leer with her exhalations, she heard a woman whose voice she recognized as belonging to a student of hers named Phyllis say, "Sure she's pregnant."

"Eets a veecious rumor," said another of her students, a Frenchwoman they called "Pixie."

Phyllis, who was double-jointed and could sit in full lotus posture, but whom Fay didn't like because she was coarse and giggled during the meditation period, spoke again. "And it's not even Richard's, either. They're divorced . . . they have been for ages. Why do you think she's wearing all those loose smocks these days, huh? Why do you think she's losing her waist . . . too many belly breathing exercises?"

"When I was pregnant, my waist was the first part of me to go," called a third woman from one of the toilet stalls.

Fay stood in the changing cubicle silently staring at her unpainted toenails as her students badmouthed the nice New Age couple from California who owned the yoga center.

"I heard something about them being divorced for a long time, too. They keep the partnership going for the business."

"Yeah. She's got a lover ten years younger, the fella with the motorcycle that shows up every Thursday," Phyllis said.

"Do you zink zat's why Fay is taking over so many of her classes?"

"They say when you're pregnant you're not supposed to do the inverted postures."

Fay waited for her students to leave the locker room before coming out of the cubicle. She washed her face with cold water and brushed her hair, tying it back into a severe bun. A long black strand curled around the spigot. She stared at it for a minute or two. Then, putting on her serene yoga teacher smile, she entered Studio A and greeted the women, who were seated in a circle on the floor waiting for her.

She made two bad mistakes in class that day, but her students pretended not to notice, not even when she almost lost her balance while demonstrating the Locust. She'd been thinking of interrupting the class to tell them how Dave Wilkie had asked to look at her ass; of chastising them for spreading ugly rumors about the owners of the yoga school, maybe saying something about yoga being not only a set of physical exercises but a spiritual practice. She was still thinking about delivering a little lecture on "cultivating compassion" after the relaxation period that closed the hour. But then Phyllis, the coarse redhead, executed a perfect Full Lotus while standing on her head and Fay decided to dismiss the class without saying anything at all. She was there to teach Yoga, not preach to them. If she antagonized her students—especially the redhead, who wore a four-carat, marquise-shaped diamond ring to class and enjoyed platinum card status for having brought six new members to the yoga center from Great Neck—they might complain about her to the management, and she didn't want to lose her job, because she needed the extra cash for vitamins and monthly visits to the chiropractor. Luckily, she'd kept her mouth shut. She had a penchant for saying just what was on her mind at the wrong times. Still, part of her wished she'd told Dave Wilkie off, or at least complained about him to Leorna Mann; a professional woman like that was surely a bit of a feminist, would have lent her a sympathetic ear. No, better not to have mentioned it to Leorna Mann. Funny, it was easier to talk to Olga, who was a lesbian, than to Leorna or the yoga students, who were straight and aligned themselves with men like Dave Wilkie. Women like Doreen, her mother, who was always ready to condemn one of her own kind for taking offense at being propositioned because she wasn't wearing a bra, saying she was asking for it by sticking her tits in her boss's face. What did she expect from men, pigs, they were. God help me, Fay thought, I'm on the verge of becoming a moral tyrant—judge, jury, and executioner all rolled into one—just like her.

She clapped her hands. "Okay, ladies," she said, "that's it for today."

6
HOUSEKEEPING

Like Sergio Ruiz, Patsy Corman also entered Fay's life unannounced, but under entirely different circumstances. By the time she and Ira's mother met, Fay was no longer eighteen and a naïve revolutionary seeking grace in other people's political causes. Living in New York with Ira for two years had cured her of that. But not without transforming what had begun as a search for redemption in political activism into an as yet undefined spiritual quest.

Since Fay and Patsy had never been introduced, had never even spoken to each other on the telephone, neither of them was prepared for their meeting on that gray November morning. It was Ira's birthday, and to honor the occasion his mother had taken it into her head that her son's apartment needed cleaning. Having parked her Lincoln alongside a fire hydrant encircled by a wall of trash, carrying a mop and a bucket filled with rags and assorted cleansers she mounted the stairs behind the janitor. Judging from the veiled black velvet hat, mink coat, and green alligator pumps she was wearing, Patsy clearly had no intention of cleaning the apartment herself. Certain that neither Fay nor Ira would be home in the middle of the day, she'd given the janitor fifty dollars to clean it, and was following him upstairs to make sure that he did.

Ira was still working the morning shift at the hospital but was due home by noon. To celebrate his birthday, Fay had canceled her classes at the yoga center and was in the middle of preparing his favorite meal. She was peppering and buttering a steak in the kitchen, wearing only a pair of bikini panties and one of Ira's white hospital jackets when the janitor's key turned the lock. Thinking it was Ira coming home early she grabbed a spatula, hoisted herself onto the kitchen counter, hastily undid her front buttons and exposed her breasts. Crossing her legs and holding the spatula aloft like Miss Liberty, she burst into a breathy Marilyn Monroe rendition of "Happy Birthday." The janitor took one look at her and sped back downstairs. Then Ira's mother herself appeared in the doorway. Before Fay could button up and invite her in, Patsy bolted down the stairs in her green alligator pumps, leaving behind her mop and bucket filled with rags and cleansers. Fay picked them up and took them inside. Ira arrived a few minutes later, distracted and rubber-legged with exhaustion.

"Your mother was here," Fay pointed at Patsy's cleaning utensils.

"You're kidding! Where'd she go?"

"I bared my breasts and scared her away."

"Don't take it personally; my mother is a very sick woman."

Ira laughed as he walked past her into the bathroom and left the door open behind him as he peed. Fay hated it when he did that.

"I know, but she just left me standing there feeling like the great Whore of Babylon."

Ira flushed the toilet. "I'll call and tell her to apologize. What's for lunch?"

Ira's new habit of hunching his shoulders, combined with the first signs of his thinning hairline had conjured in Fay the first of her daily surges of guilt. To the point where, for Ira's sake, she'd stopped carping about Sam, even going as far as allowing his detestable friend a generous slot in what she'd come to view as the foreign film version of her life.

Only a week before, Ira had informed her that, "statistically-speaking," she could expect to outlive him by eight years, and be healthier, too. Guilty about the prospect of her robust American widowhood, Fay had assured Ira that she was definitely not looking forward to spending eight years in a retirement home without him. Yet at the same time, she secretly cherished her greater endurance, her power to outlast him. Was it, she wondered, simply a matter of hormones? Ira was always making fun of her "strange genes." Did he do that to pump himself up, knowing all along that she was stronger and would live longer? Thinking she ought to stop feeding him red meat, she watched him chew his steak.

"Do you love me?" Fay hoped Ira would stop chewing long enough to say he did with all his heart.

"What's wrong?" He got up from the table, tossed the leftovers on his plate into the trash and placed it in the sink without running water over it. Fay looked at the gristle, the globes of fat forming on the plate, and bursting into tears, ran into the bathroom and locked the door.

"I love you, Fay. I want to marry you for god's sake," Ira moaned, pressing his body against the bathroom door.

"Next week?"

"Yes, next week."

Fay wondered if there wasn't something to Sam Rubin's psychic powers after all; if, just to spite her, he hadn't worked it out so she'd be captive to Ira's welfare against her will, bonded to him by a kind of telepathic Crazy Glue that could turn even the corroded staircase in the hall outside their apartment into a stairway to heaven at the barest hint of his footsteps. Maybe it was Sam's mind control that compelled her to sit in the apartment alone for hours pretending Ira was there with her when he wasn't, talking to the astral Ira as if he were sitting at the table across from her, chewing on his steak as he had been a few minutes ago. Ira didn't even have to be there in the flesh, his presence was so real, so necessary. At times she felt herself becoming Ira—slowly making his way home from the hospital, his thinning hairline bathed in the shaft of light knifing through the broken skylight out in the hall, turning the key in the lock, pale and rubber-legged with exhaustion, not wanting to hear about Patsy—not wanting to talk at all. Fay wondered whether Sam hadn't indeed managed it so Ira would possess her, body and soul.

Two months before taking his medical board exams, without informing her, Ira stored a box of Sam's belongings in their apartment. When she opened the already crammed front hall closet and found Sam's old coffee pot, rusty toaster, stained sleeping bag, and shoe-stuffed backpack and demanded they be thrown out, Ira refused.

"Sam's going to California on business, and I'm returning a favor."

"What favor?"

"He gave me a reading on the questions I can expect on the medical board exams."

"Tell me you're kidding. Tell me you don't really think Sam knows the questions the examiners themselves haven't seen yet."

"I sure do."

"I don't believe what I'm hearing!"

"If you screw your face up like that, you'll get wrinkles."

Fay headed for the door. "I'm taking a walk. I need some air."

Ira did not try to stop her.

After two hours of aimless wandering, she walked into a diner and ordered a cup of coffee. Leaving the cup on the counter, she went to the pay phone on the wall near the women's toilet and called Ira to apologize "for being such a harpy." Ira told her he missed her warm body in bed and advised her to come home right away. Which she did.

On their honeymoon, Ira stayed out too long in the sun and got a nasty sunburn. Feeling it was her fault for insisting on Puerto Rico when Ira preferred Canada, Fay sat up all night in their mildewed hotel room, wrapping him in wet compresses and killing insects. Falling asleep once during her vigil, she was awakened by what sounded like someone typing in the next room. Not wanting to disturb Ira, she decided against calling the front desk and, slipping on a tank top and a pair of shorts, went downstairs to complain in person. Swearing that no one was occupying the room next door, the clerk leaned over and made as if to pat her hand. Leaping out of reach, Fay raced back upstairs and found that Ira had rolled off the narrow bed and was lying on the floor asleep with his eyes partly open, his sunburnt body a mass of insect bites. The typing had stopped. Waking Ira and quickly packing their bag, Fay tossed his windbreaker over his shoulders and fled with him into the predawn darkness.

Getting married was a mistake. Fay knew it on the first morning of their life together as newlyweds in their Yorkville tenement apartment when she was awakened by a siren to find herself alone in bed. Ira, wrapped in his ash and semen-stained terry cloth bathrobe (which she hated and periodically, but unsuccessfully, tried to get him to throw away), was sitting at the table, reading Jung under the fixed death's head gaze of his study skeleton. Accompanied by a recorded warning echoing through a loudspeaker, fire engines blared up and down York Avenue all that morning.

"DON'T ALLOW RUBBISH TO ACCUMULATE IN YOUR HOME . . . HOME . . . HOME. RUBBISH BREEDS FIRE . . . FIRE . . . FIRE. PROTECT YOUR HOME, YOUR FAMILY, YOUR LIFE . . . LIFE . . . LIFE . . ."

Fay placed a sprig of fresh parsley alongside Ira's omelet, but he never noticed it. When he finally looked up at her from his book, his eyes were glazed.

"Why don't you say something?" she said.

"Because there's nothing to say."

"Please, Ira, talk to me."

"I'm too tired to talk. I was half asleep on my feet during rounds yesterday, and the day before that I almost fell asleep in the middle of taking a patient's history."

"I'm sorry to be such a burden to you."

Leaving his omelet uneaten, Ira got up from the table and threw himself down on the sofa.

"You're not a burden," he said, falling asleep before she could answer him.

Five years of intensive Jungian analysis hadn't put a dent in Ira's fear of being buried alive in his sleep, but that didn't seem to faze him. Jung was still his idol. Fay hadn't been in therapy at all but had no fear of dying. What did continue to dog her, however, was the enigma that came in the form of her attachment to Ira. She could never figure out how two people could be so attracted to each other and so estranged at the same time. What she did know was that by presenting himself as a victim, Ira had robbed her of her defenses and caused her to grow cunning, witchlike, and dangerous, even to herself.

What next? Now that, imperceptibly, they'd emerged from their cocoon of prolonged adolescence into what Ira liked to call their "productive phase;" just as—also imperceptibly—they would enter old age and die. Why shouldn't Ira feel productive with a medical degree and a certificate from the Jung Institute on his wall, entitling him to an office full of patients on completing his psychiatric residency next year? While she was still plodding along as a dancer and making peanuts as a yoga instructor, Fay didn't feel very "productive" in the way that Ira defined it, and she resented him deeply for fooling her into believing she wasn't "needy" and could stand on her own two feet. Then, again, what could she expect of a man who remained as oblivious as a stone or a block of wood to the fact that they'd shared the most intimate moments possible between two human beings, that he'd filled her with his sperm, that he'd peed in front of her, that she'd wrapped him in wet sheets and saved him from a scarring sunburn, cut his hair, babysat for the demonic children of his Republican asshole of a brother . . . *merciful God,* she thought, doesn't it matter to this man that I trusted him enough to offer my veins to him when, unlike his fellow medical students who were practicing on oranges, he was learning to draw blood?

Being born male had endowed Ira with the power to set the ground rules of their relationship, and to alter them according to his shifting whims. And he was a doctor, which had earned him the right to be taken seriously by the world. Her only tools were her good intentions and "God-given" good looks. Babbling of equality for women, she had fooled herself into believing she had changed the rules of the oldest game in the world. Then, realizing that the game had been fixed from the beginning, and fearing failure, she'd rejected the old ploys—but not the desire to please—and found herself dancing in limbo. Armed with nothing but her desperate sincerity, Fay wondered if, as her mother's latest letter warned, she wasn't already on her way to hell.

7
UNBRIDLED

How sweet were those six, seven, and eight-hour love marathons on the rickety bed near the window with its brown, stained shade drawn almost to the floor, the heat banging extravagantly through the naked pipes; joint butts, a mountain of apple cores and gum wrappers overflowing an ashtray perched on top of Ira's coffee-logged copy of *Gray's Anatomy*. Now that they were married, it was hard to believe they were the same couple who'd bundled up in ski jackets after all that glorious lovemaking to brave a blizzard, tracking through unploughed streets to the East River promenade just to throw snowballs over the rail at passing tugs, Ira screaming, "You're crazy, Fay Watkins! I love you!"

Developers had long since demolished the seafood house on Third Avenue where, after these winter forays, Ira and Fay had stuffed themselves with clam chowder and steamed lobster tails dripping with butter. And a fifty-story, all-glass condominium now stood where the little art movie theater used to be. Sitting in the last row watching re-runs of Jacques Tati films and fondling each other until they got so aroused, they'd have to hurry back to their overheated flat, where, arms and legs aching with love weariness, they'd fall into the rickety Salvation Army bed, still smelling of early morning sex, and start making love all over again.

Lately, Ira had taken to chiding Fay for "romanticizing" their poverty. Fay said she wasn't romanticizing their poverty; it was the unbridled animal pleasure, the tenuous lie of innocence that she missed so much.

Their passion had already begun to ebb by the time Ira's internship ended, but the relationship had yet to enter its currently full-blown contentious phase, when Ira passed the medical board exams with a mediocre score that belied Sam's psychic coaching. Determined to keep the peace, Fay said nothing about Sam and threw a party instead.

Thinking none of her Zen or dance or yoga friends would mix well with the medical crowd, she crammed the railroad flat from end to end with Ira's hospital acquaintances. The first to arrive was a Filipino doctor she recognized only vaguely, who greeted her waving a bottle of Johnny Walker Red in one hand and a stack of paper pill cups— "courtesy of the supply room staff"—in the other. Fay took the bottle and cups to the kitchen then hung a sign on the wall designating a windowless cubicle she'd painted cerulean blue and pasted over with silver stars as "Pot Luck." People started streaming in. Two surgery residents, claiming they were no longer smoking pot because of the latest rumor from the pharmacology department that it left significant brain damage, had removed the bottle of Johnny Walker Red from the kitchen and were pouring generous shots into the pill cups. Ira took her aside and asked why she'd invited the surgeons. Fay said she found surgeons more sociable than other doctors. Giving her a dubious look, Ira walked toward the food tables.

Passing through the cerulean blue room on her way to the

kitchen, Fay clambered over a mountain of coats and a nude couple. At least someone was having fun.

As she was removing a tray of half-charred cheese puffs from the oven, a stoned intern approached her waving a joint. "Partake, dear hostess?"

"Not now, Pete. I'm trying to salvage my canapés."

"Do I detect a note of hostility?"

"No, fury!" Fay grabbed the joint from his hand, taking three deep puffs before returning it. Over his shoulder, she could see Ira engaged in deep conversation with Gail Breyer, the psychiatry department "hottie," with her melon-shaped breasts, thick black Dutch boy bangs, and pouty red lips. After sorting out the least burnt cheese puffs Fay retrieved the joint and, dismissing Pete, smoked it down to a glimmering ash. Whereupon Pete fell down on his knees pretending to be a begging dog. As Fay circled him trying to get out of the kitchen, a nurse entered with the information that her date had drunk four boilermakers and was puking his guts out in the toilet and that she needed to call for a taxi. Fay motioned her lazily toward the telephone on the wall. "It may not work. We haven't had a chance to pay the bill." Fay wasn't sure if she'd spoken or thought that. The nurse made her phone call, pleading with the dispatcher in Haitian Creole. Pete had stopped being a begging dog and was sitting at the kitchen table describing in detail how he and three Pittsburgh prostitutes had holed up for a week in a motel room enacting the entire pocket version of the Marquis de Sade's *Justine*. Fay was studying Pete's big red hunter's hands and hairy knuckles when Sam-the-so-called-psychic appeared in the doorway with an African princess wrapped in a tie-dyed dashiki. Fay looked again. She was hallucinating. It wasn't Sam, but the Filipino doctor, talking to the Haitian nurse on her way out of the kitchen.

"Where've you been all this time? Don't you want to socialize?" Ira charged past her toward the refrigerator and began digging for cubes in an ice tray with a fork.

"I am having psychic experiences—like your friend Sam," Fay said, grinning beatifically.

"You'd better lay off the pot."

"Here we go, ladies and gents!" Pete pulled himself up from the table, slapping Ira on the back before weaving toward the "Pot Luck."

"Was that lug trying to put the make on you?"

"Vicariously . . ."

"You shouldn't be leading him on."

"Didn't your mother warn you that I was oversexed?"

"Isn't it time you learned to exercise a little self-control? Oh, never mind." Ira flung his arm forward, then immediately withdrew it. Forgetting that he had just filled the ice tray with water, he lost his balance, sloshing himself and the cheese puffs. "Damn it!" he muttered as he left the kitchen.

Fay remained at the table in a pot haze coping with a new round of hallucinations: a barefoot Japanese night watchman in leggings and a short blue kimono with a huge bunch of keys dangling from his rope belt, banging on a drum and crying, "The Hour of the Rat," a party of noisy revelers, also wearing kimonos, sitting on the floor of a windowless cubicle and passing around a long pipe, a jug of rice wine heating on a nearby hearth . . . She looked up from the table to see two policemen, one stepping forward to tell her that the neighbors were complaining about the noise. She opened her mouth to say something to them, but Pete stepped in front of her and handed each of the policemen a cigar. Taking the cigars and grinning, the policemen disappeared. Fay got up and herded out her guests.

The next day, while Ira was asleep in the bedroom and she was sitting spread-legged in a chair in the kitchen, searching the windows of the tenements across the street for signs of a life in better order than her own, Fay saw a man in painter's coveralls spreading a tarpaulin on the floor of an empty apartment. He was young and wore his black shiny hair long over his ears. As he moved closer to the window, she saw that he had a black mustache and a cigarette dangling from the left corner of his mouth. The bare arms sticking out of his coveralls were long and white and hairless, almost womanly. Suddenly he looked up and saw her watching him. Then, circling around, prancing a little, he continued laying the tarpaulin. Fay wanted to stop looking at him but couldn't. She went to the telephone on the wall, pretended to dial, and mouthed a conversation. The painter dropped the tarpaulin and came up to the window. Now she saw that he was indeed young, and quite handsome, with thick, glossy black hair, a high Olympian nose and a smooth face—except for the ink brush of black over his lips, which were wide and pendulous. The painter stared back at her through hooded, cobra eyes. Arching his head, he took a step back into the room and bent forward from the waist as if to pick up his brush from the floor. Then, thrusting the cigarette away, he stood facing her again, holding something up for her to look at. He appeared to be taming a snake, making passes over it, cajoling it between his fingers, rocking on his heels, swaying forward and even perhaps—though she couldn't hear him—crooning. Fay shivered. The painter's glutted penis stood erect, aimed right at her, coaxing her to join him. Shocked, but unable to stop looking, Fay turned her profile to him; from the corner of her eye, she could see him massaging his penis, taking his time, caressing it lovingly. Soon he was brushing it briskly, then faster, until he was mauling, bruising, slapping it, with his eyes closed, his head thrust toward the ceiling, his tongue snaking out of his mouth. For what felt like an eternity, he stood luring her to his pleasure. Fay pressed the telephone receiver against her stomach until it hurt. With his lips parted in a triumphant sneer, the painter shot a great white stream in an arc across the room. Then, matter-of-factly wiping his hands on the front of his coveralls, he buttoned his fly and gave her a courtly bow.

Fay placed the receiver back in its cradle, went to the refrigerator and took a long drink of cranberry juice right out of the bottle. She wondered whether she'd just been unfaithful to Ira. She thought about her inertia, about using her five missing dance education credits as an excuse not to get her Masters degree. All the people she knew were productive, scrambling around making important telephone calls and flying to conferences, "accomplishing things." Why wasn't Fay doing the same, her mother had admonished in her recent letter. What had happened to all that energy since she'd gotten married? Had it been transformed into lust by her latest inordinate craving for kinky sex? Or had she always gotten her kicks from watching and being watched?

At Camp Waheeken, where they'd first met, Ira had watched her every morning as she intentionally made her way past him. Given her predilection for shy, boyish-looking men in glasses, knowing he'd be sitting, hunched up, on the steps of his bunk staring at her, not daring to say good morning. Fay had deliberately worn her seductive lime green halter top and white shorts on the day she took sick and he came to her aid. When she got to know him well enough to joke about his wearing a long-sleeved shirt and jeans when it was so hot, Ira had endeared himself to her by taking off his glasses, squinting up at her and reminding her that he had a tendency to fry in the sun. And later, hearing him describe himself as "basically pugnacious" when he was so obviously not.

Maybe it wasn't Ira's shyness but his voyeurism that had turned her on even then?

Fay's own letter responding to her mother's latest litany of complaints against her was still lying on the kitchen table waiting to be signed off. In it, she'd written that she'd stopped going to Mass. That she was no longer a believer. That she was still "window shopping" (using her mother's phrase) for a clue about what to do with her "God-given gifts." Window shopping, indeed! She briefly thought of describing to her mother how a pervert of a house painter across the way had only a minute ago flashed her in the window and how, unable to tear herself away, she'd stood there watching. No way she'd write that, of course. But she did add the following postscript:

"Hey, Doreen, I think you ought to know that your daughter just committed adultery in her heart. And guess what, she wasn't struck dead and sent straight to hell!"

8
THE GOLDEN KIMONO

It was a windless New Year's Day, and the cross streets along Second Avenue were heaped with stiff gray slush that had at first thawed with the false promise of rain and then just as suddenly hardened with unexpected frost that turned to ice. Reminding him that the disc jockey on the radio had only a minute ago warned of "dangerous driving conditions," Fay suggested that Ira buckle his seat belt. But Ira refused, saying he'd rather be thrown out of the car and die, than pinned down and boxed inside. Didn't she remember he had a phobia about being buried alive?

Fay stared out the snow-stained window on the passenger side, safe and snug with her seat belt fastened thinking Ira and his phobia could both go to hell. If he wanted to be a schmuck and drive without a seat belt, let him.

The Amagansett house was closed for the winter, and they'd spent a sour New Year's Eve in Charles and Erika's Fifth Avenue apartment with people they hardly knew. No matter how hard Fay tried to avoid it, their opposing politics always came up when she and her brother-in-law were in the same room at the same time. And New Year's Eve was no different. Except this time, Charles, surrounded by his Republican friends, had the advantage.

"You could say everyone here, except for you guys, is slightly to the right of center. Any problem with that?" Mike, one of Charles's gray-suited cronies, leered at her, giggling like a serial killer.

Fortunately, Mike's mouse of a wife, also in gray, had defused the threat of an argument by passing around a plastic-covered sheaf of baby photos, so that when midnight struck, instead of kissing and toasting in the New Year with champagne, they were all looking at mouse babies and gurgling the way grownups feel they have to when confronted by other people's ugly offspring.

Charles's wife, Erika, managed to under heat and over butter the casserole, and Fay had suffered from the runs all night, waking up grouchy, which, in addition to pissing off Ira, got them off to a late start for their New Year's Day brunch date with Ira's patient, Nick Pernal, and his wife, Loretta, in Rye.

Ira woke up grouchy, too, asking her in a querulous tone whether she'd walked the dog they were watching for a friend who'd left town for the holidays, and responding when she told him she had, that, if Nick Pernal weren't such a high fee-paying patient, he would gladly have given up the socializing and the icy drive for a comfortable day in long johns and a pair of woolen sweat socks watching football on the tube.

"The Dog was obnoxious," Fay said, "The Dog" being the dog's name.

Fay did not advise Ira to forget his obligation to Nick Pernal and stay home, because he was touchy enough about being embroiled in a messy case involving a Hungarian patient who was breaking up with his wife on account of hashish, and she wanted to take his mind off: 1) the questionable medical ethics involved in taking on both the Hungarian and his wife as patients, and 2) the fact that he was on the verge of being investigated by the psychiatry department ethics committee for a possible breach in doing so. It was all too complicated. Better to go out even if she didn't feel like it than sit around the house watching him brood all day.

"Ira doesn't like for me to pester him about his practice," she'd told her mother during one of their infrequent phone conversations. When her mother hadn't left it at that but had tried forcing information from her, Fay snapped, "I'm just a hick dancer from Texas, what do I know about Ira's practice? Besides, I'm barely hanging in as far as this marriage is concerned, so please bug off!" After which her mother had mumbled something anti-Semitic about Jewish doctors and hung up.

They were on the East River Drive when Fay, still ruminating on last night's disaster, remembered Sheila, the woman in the shocking pink satin pants suit and triple animal cracker-shaped chain belts sitting next to her. Hardly touching her food, Sheila had spent dinner silently studying Fay's face. Only when the tiramisu dessert arrived did she break her silence to comment on Fay's "perfect skin" and ask if she used mud packs and got regular facials. Fay said, no, she didn't use anything on her face but Dr. Bronner's castile soap, and Sheila had turned away to study the face of the redheaded woman to her left who'd been haranguing the publisher of New Age books sitting next to her.

"You'll have to leave New York soon or you'll die of emphysema," the redhead was saying.

"We're always a step ahead, the human race," the publisher, who hadn't been listening, addressed the table at large. "Soon there'll be transplants for everything. No bodily death. We'll adapt ourselves to the changing environment, as always. It's cyclical."

Fay was about to ask the publisher for specifics when she was hit by the first of the many stomach cramps awaiting her that night.

They left the Willis Avenue Bridge behind and traveled north on the Major Deegan Expressway, with Ira cursing the old man in the '78 Pontiac in front of him for taking up two lanes at once. By the time he pulled their red Nissan into the Pernal's frozen driveway, skidding wildly and almost tearing into the holly bushes lining the side of the house, the day had brightened somewhat. Or was it that, in Rye, streets covered with powdery snow instead of gray slush made the day seem brighter than it did in the slag-heaped city? That every mansion on the street that signaled privilege, also might have helped. Thanks to Loretta Pernal, Fay knew, for example, that the huge Tudor with the two turrets on the southwest corner had been imported stone by stone from an English manor house in Suffolk (England, not Queens), and that the eighty-nine-year-old recluse who had once owned the now defunct Montgomery Ward department stores roamed alone through the thirty-two rooms, which included a harem built in "the Turkish style" to accommodate the sexual eccentricities of the Jazz Age nouveau riche.

Nick and Loretta Pernal and their brood of four, a Venezuelan live-in maid named Manuela, and their Afghan hound, Ludmilla, had recently returned to the States from Japan. Using only a meager portion of Nick's vast trust fund, they'd bought a small version of the Tudor house on the south-west corner during a depressed market for "only" seven hundred and sixty thousand dollars, though by now it was worth at least two million. Theirs, with its yellow cross timbers, falling chimney, and un-renovated art nouveau kitchen was, by the usual neighborhood standards, the most "modest" house on the block. Loretta, a diehard city dweller who hated the suburbs, had confided to Fay that she'd let Nick have his way in exchange for a bargain: two years in a city abroad for five years in a suburb with good schools in the States, so the kids could at least learn to speak English without an accent, since, as far as Loretta was concerned, they were American after all. Assuming a mock Spanish accent, Loretta had mimicked her husband's umbrage. "'Norte Americano, you mean. Colombians like me are Americano too, eh?'"

All in all, it was a tense household, and Fay never felt comfortable there.

She was about to pull on the door knocker, but Ira pushed ahead of her and rang the bell. A woman called out that the door was open and they entered. Inside, all was warmth and steaming coffee. Seated at the table on the sun porch off the living room was a couple Fay didn't know. The four Pernal children had been dispersed for the holidays among aunts, uncles, and grandparents from both sides of the border eager to see them after their two-year absence. Manuela was visiting a sister in Suffolk County (Queens, not England), and the house radiated suburban peace. Ludmilla lay in front of the fireplace with her elegant muzzle tucked between her, disturbingly, for such a big dog, dainty paws. Through the leaded windows a weak sun cast indecisive rays across a table heaped with pita bread, smoked fish, hummus, falafel, and a variety of Middle Eastern salads.

The couple on the sun porch was so soft-spoken that Fay had a hard time catching their names when the husband got up and introduced himself as Jorge and his wife as Dolores. Moving in closer, she heard them tell Ira that they were

Brazilian architects, longtime friends of Nick's, and that they were planning the Pernals's Carnival trip to Rio. Apologizing for their host's absence, Jorge laughingly added that Nick was still upstairs nursing a New Year's Eve hangover.

"Milk is on the table," Dolores said, holding out two steaming mugs of coffee.

Fay thanked her, saying she'd take hers black, then, as an afterthought, asked if Brazil was anything like Mexico, which she hadn't visited since she was eighteen. Still mindful of Erika's casserole-induced bout of the runs, she put down the coffee and asked if there was tea.

"Over there, on the sideboard," Dolores pointed to a jade-glazed Japanese teapot on a stone heater.

Just then, Loretta came in from the kitchen carrying a tray of hot scones. She wore a black cashmere sweater and slacks, a thick medieval cross on a silver chain, and the whitest of tabi on her feet. "What's this about Mexico?"

Aware that Jorge was staring at her, Fay poured tea into one of the matching jade teacups surrounding the pot.

"Fay was just asking if Mexico is anything like Brazil, and I was about to tell her that the one big difference is that she can leave the penicillin home if she goes to Rio." Then turning his attention away from Fay, he addressed the others. "But, since we're planning a trip into the Amazonian jungle, and there's a good chance we'll get to see the initiation ceremonies of the few remaining tribes there, we might need to take penicillin along. What do you think, Dolores?"

"Are you talking about cannibals?" Ira intercepted, chomping on a fish sandwich, his eye on the massive television set in the adjoining den.

Ludmilla barked, announcing Nick's entrance in a yellow turtleneck sweater and yellow linen slacks. Unlike Loretta, he was barefoot.

"You'll catch cold," Loretta said.

Nick smiled, placing his hands over his eyes. When he took them away, Fay saw that his face was puffy and gray.

Loretta goaded Nick about his hangover, but before Fay could tell if the Pernals were on the verge of a fight, Dolores had turned the conversation back to Brazil. Nick suggested they all move into the living room, but he and the other two men continued talking at the food table. Fay lingered briefly over the teapot. Then, accompanied by Ludmilla, she followed Loretta and Dolores into the living room. The men soon joined them, and Nick put on a CD, and the sexy, muted tones of a samba seemed to calm everyone down. Loretta briefly disappeared, then came back into the room holding a floor-length golden kimono under her chin.

"I designed it on paper and the dressmaker carried out my instructions to the T. It's made of the finest Japanese silk," she said.

"But this is absolutely magnificent," Dolores approached her and pinched an edge of the kimono's sleeve.

Loretta put on the kimono and modeled it for them, her hands fluttering across the silk. Then taking it off with an impatient gesture, she carried it back upstairs. Not wanting to appear envious, Fay hadn't asked if she could try it on, but now, seeing Loretta return without the kimono, she wished she had. Pretending to be interested in the numerous photographs of the Pernal children on the mantel above the fireplace, Fay remarked on the resemblance between Loretta and a teenaged sylph in a string bikini.

Loretta said, "It's nerve-shattering to be cooped up in one place for very long. Even with Manuela, it's a madhouse of kids and skates, and Nick's high-strung, high-maintenance dog, subject to false pregnancies, and his daughter on weekends, who, by the way, is the double of his first wife." She glared at

Fay for having picked the wrong child to admire then added, "Anything to keep Nick happy . . . just so he won't fall back into the old well of nostalgic Latin despair, which, thanks to Ira, hasn't happened since we got back from Japan. Knock wood," she tapped the mantel lightly, her big turquoise eyes welling with tears.

Taken aback by Loretta's outburst, Fay changed the subject. "Have you met your neighbor in the turret house yet?"

"Not really. We see the maid come in at nine when the bus comes to pick up the kids. He's terribly old I understand, and almost totally deaf. Would you care for a Mexican beer?"

"I think I'd like one," Dolores said, coming between them before Fay could answer.

The sun was shining in earnest now. Nick opened the window to a gust of pine-smelling air. The high flames in the fireplace faltered slightly.

"It's too cold in here," Loretta said.

Nick shut the window. Jorge was sitting next to Ira on the sofa, listening to him pontificate on the subject of drug-induced altered states of consciousness. Taking a book off the shelf, Nick joined them. Words like "peyote," "spirit guide," and "shaman," drifted across the room. Loretta laughingly asked Dolores if Jorge had "gone native." Dolores merely shrugged and rolled her eyes. Nick changed the CD, replacing the samba with Ravi Shankar. Ludmilla suddenly jumped up and threw herself against the window with an eerily human-sounding sob.

"It's the black dog," Nick said. "Let her out, Loretta, will you?"

As Loretta absently opened the door and Ludmilla galloped past her, Fay caught a quick glimpse of the long black coat and pointed muzzle of the intruder outside. Loretta closed the door and walked back into the living room. Saying he was not in the mood for Indian music, Jorge asked Nick to put on something by Mozart, then, turning back to Ira, said, "It seems that this tribe in the Amazon has developed a very sophisticated form of dream analysis."

"How do they do it?" Ira asked.

Struck by the lunacy of the conversation, and afraid she might say something to that effect and embarrass Ira, Fay quickly turned to ask Loretta the first thing that came to mind. "Is it easy to hire maids in Japan?"

Giving her a quizzical look, Loretta said, "We had Manuela with us, so I didn't have to find one. But then, we've always been lucky that way."

The unstoppable Jorge was still going at it. "Apparently, the elders of the tribe sit with the children each morning, encouraging them to relate their dreams . . ."

"Nick, do you mind if I turn on the TV to get the score?" interrupted Ira, clearly annoyed with Jorge for intruding on what was, after all, his professional turf.

"Not at all," Nick said.

Fay focused her eyes on the stiff pleat in Loretta's slacks as she followed her into the kitchen. Startled by a sudden loud noise outside, they stopped at the same time and almost crashed into each other. A man was screaming. Fay heard him but could not take her eyes off the infuriatingly perfect pleat in Loretta's slacks or she might burst out laughing because Jorge was still blabbering about shamans to Ira, who, no longer even pretending to be interested, had gotten up from the sofa and was now watching television in the den.

Loretta opened the kitchen door and hurried outside.

"Nick! Nick!" she screamed.

Without stopping for their coats, the three men rushed out the open kitchen door. Fay walked back to the front hall and found Dolores putting on Loretta's mink coat. It was too long for her, so long that she had to lift it as she stepped out the front door and daintily made her way down the ice-covered driveway.

For the second time that day, Fay wondered why Nick hadn't strewn the driveway with salt or sand. Someone could get hurt. Then she remembered that Nick had a hangover. She went upstairs. The door to the master bedroom was open, and she walked in. Opening the closet and immediately locating the kimono, she took it out, gently removed it from the hanger, and put it on. As she was tying the silk cord on the inside of the kimono, she looked out the window and saw: Loretta, frozen in black against the snow, standing in the middle of the road; Ira, brown and drab in corduroy slacks and oatmeal-colored sweater, standing next to her with his hands in his pockets; Dolores, swathed in mink, watching from the driveway; Jorge, halfway hidden behind two men in boots, lumber jackets, and plaid shirts, standing spread-legged behind a green pickup heaped with shrubs, "Hayden's Nursery" painted on the door; Nick brilliantly illuminated in yellow, and still barefoot, staring down at Ludmilla lying in the road.

As Fay stood inhaling the kimono's fragrant temple incense, she heard Dolores shriek, "Loretta! What is it?"

Loretta didn't answer her. She was staring down at Nick, who'd fallen to his knees with his arms held out in front of him to form a cradle.

Fay looked at herself in the full-length mirror on the wall opposite Loretta and Nick's bed. Slipping off her shoes, she walked toward it with the doll-faced expression and mincing gait of a Japanese geisha. But the mirror was right alongside the window, and no matter how intently she focused on her reflection, she could still see and hear what was going on outside.

"I'm sorry, I'm sorry, I'm so sorry," one of the booted men was saying over and over again. He had a blond ponytail sticking out of the back of his navy ski cap. "But there wuz the two of 'em, tearing like mad around the corner . . . the big black one, and then this one. The black one got away in time and ran off. But this one—this one crashed right into the truck . . . at an angle, almost like on purpose . . ."

No one said anything after that.

Nick got up, holding Ludmilla's limp, shaggy body in his arms, her too-dainty front paws aimed en pointe at the road. He took one slow, barefoot Kabuki step toward the house, then another. Fay slid her fists into the vast hanging sleeves of the kimono. Loretta, Ira, the two nurserymen, Jorge, and Dolores looked like snow statues. Fay pictured them all coming to life at her signal and the whole Kabuki play running backwards to the beginning. In her version, the icy front path would be covered in cherry blossoms. Inside, huddled around Ludmilla, snoring in front of the fireplace, they would talk about things that really mattered to them, make noble New Year's resolutions they could not keep, but would forgive each other for it. Loretta would give Fay the golden kimono. Ira would take her to Japan, and she would be kind to him.

Fay slipped out of the kimono and hung it back in the closet. She heard sparrows chirping. Looking through the window, she saw the old man standing on the front steps of the mansion across the road tossing breadcrumbs into the snow.

9

STRANGE MEDICINE

It's one of those perfectly luminous May days in New York, and Professor Bob Burns, chair of the psychiatry department is being honored at a reception in the NYU faculty lounge overlooking Washington Square. Holding a glass of champagne in one hand and a copy of the department newsletter in the other, Fay stands on the terrace in her best party outfit, a black silk pants suit, looking down into the playground at a toddler in overalls staging a tantrum. She is searching for a flat surface on which to set down her glass when Eleanor Burns walks up to her and introduces the balding young man alongside her as the psychiatry department's newest member. Thanks to the heavy metal music thundering from a passing boom box in the park below, Fay misses the new doctor's name and is relieved not to have to ask when Bob Burns himself appears to cut off any further conversation with an elaborate display of affection toward his wife. It's no secret that the couple's recent public kissing and cuddling are intended to stave off rumors that they were on the verge of divorcing before the plum offer from Washington came (Bob's been appointed head of the National Institute of Mental Health, and the social-climbing Eleanor has chosen to cast a blind eye on her husband's affairs. Hence, the divorce talk has ended—at least for now).

Bob is known for being a snazzy dresser. Today he's wearing a midnight blue custom-made suit worth a small fortune and a maroon and white striped Hermes tie. He is sixty-two but looks to be in his early fifties; he's short and lean with a pointed face that reminds Fay of a prairie dog. Bob once told her that he stays in shape by swimming laps for an hour every morning in the New York Athletic Club pool. Fay has never liked Bob much, but ever since he's been targeting Ira's parapsychology research as a possible cause for revoking his attending privileges at the hospital, her mild dislike has turned to active resentment. Still, even putting aside her antipathy toward Bob, Fay herself would have to admit if pressed that she, too, has qualms about Ira's departure from the psychiatric mainstream. Normally she wouldn't have thought twice about her husband's latest short-lived fad if he hadn't cryptically asked her to meet him in his office late one night and made her promise not to tell anyone about it. Ira hadn't yet entered fully into his "consciousness altering" phase, hadn't grown his prophet's beard, or taken to wearing smocks and beads, or been branded as having "gone off." That was to come after the drug experiments—when the NIMH had stopped funding LSD research and "going off" was no longer fashionable. How like Ira to be out of step with fashion. To be out of step, period.

Carrying a pizza and two beers in a shopping bag, she'd arrived at his office at about eleven o'clock on a cold February night to find him seated yogi-like on the floor in front of his desk, staring at the Turkish prayer rug on the wall opposite with a strangely skewed grin on his face. He did not turn to greet her as she entered.

"I've taken two micrograms of LSD," he said sweetly, like a child admitting he'd just eaten all the cookies in the cookie jar. "Stay here with me and see that I don't hurt myself. Take notes. Don't talk, please."

Sitting there in his baggy green turtleneck sweater, his long legs loosely crossed in front of him, Ira had reminded her of "Will," the rag doll her mother had sewn for her when she was six and in bed with viral pneumonia. Believing her mother's claim that the doll had been sprinkled with holy water and was therefore infused with healing powers, she'd stubbornly refused to part with it long after it had fallen to shreds and was unrecognizable. Disturbed by the memory, Fay briefly wonders if that mind-altering drug experiment was the first indication of Ira's "falling apart"—and her own stubborn refusal to acknowledge it. Should she have warned him then? Salvaged his career (and their marriage) before it had fallen to shreds? Had she been wrong to reflexively cave into his demands so as not to hurt his feelings?

The pizza had gone cold and rubbery by the time Fay remembered she was hungry. She ate two slices and drank both beers. Ira didn't speak, move a finger, or twitch an eyelid for five hours. Outwardly, nothing happened. Yet, on observing him emerge from his drug dream, Fay knew instinctively that something dangerous had been set loose in him, and that their life together would never again be the same. It didn't take long for him to bear her out. Heedless of his own demand for secrecy, Ira had bypassed the professional academic journals and announced his consciousness-expanding drug experiment to the press only two weeks later. Provoked by a Newsweek story referring to his department as a "hotbed of mind-altering drug research," Bob Burns (a fellow Jungian, and once Ira's staunchest supporter) had launched his campaign to ruin him.

Guilty for her role in Ira's professional slide, Fay had been overly protective of him since then. Always on the alert, she trained herself to gauge the right moment for snatching him out of harm's way—like now, at this party, for example. But Bob is standing in front of her talking, and he's still Ira's boss, so she plasters a fake smile on her face and pretends to listen.

Over Bob's shoulder, she spots Ira in the lounge talking to a man with an FBI crew cut wearing an outrageously checkered polyester suit and sandals with no socks. Suddenly Ira looks up, waves at her, and steers his companion toward the terrace. Desperate to head them off, Fay quickly excuses herself and faking an urgent need for the toilet, rushes past Bob into the lounge. Someone taps her wrist with a "Hi," as she enters. It's Natalie Jaffin, one of the few people here Fay actually likes, a child psychiatrist who is dying of a rare blood disease. Planting a quick kiss on Natalie's cheek, Fay promises to call her tomorrow then pushes through the crowd, coming full stop against Ira's barrel-chested companion, her high heels only just avoiding crushing his bare toes. Her usual social anxiety is operating overtime today, and she's a bit too apologetic, but the man laughingly assures her that he's okay.

"Honey, this is Tom Clerkson. He's on leave from the Stanford Research Institute; we work in the same area . . ." Ira puts his arm around her, electrifying, always amazing how such small, husbandly gestures can be so privately erotic in public.

A sweating student waiter in a white jacket appears with a tray on which Fay can finally set down her now empty champagne glass before returning Clerkson's determined handshake.

"Nice to meet you."

"Likewise . . . What's that you've got there?" He points at the newsletter she's still clutching in her now print-blackened left hand, gently removes it, and places it alongside the champagne glass on the waiter's tray. A nice gesture, but even as she thanks him, Fay remains wary. Clerkson strikes her as one of those loony academic pariahs Ira is on the verge of becoming. He's certainly dressed the part.

"Tom's also into parapsychology." Ira confirms her suspicion in a loud voice, unaware that Francis Waltham, Burns's spy (and soon-to-be successor) is eavesdropping on their conversation.

Fay tries, but fails, to alert Ira to Waltham's presence with a nod in his direction.

"He's been studying clairvoyant subjects like Sam Rubin at SRI. You know . . . they publish that parapsychology research journal . . . the one I showed you that printed my query last fall."

"So, you came all the way from California for Dr. Burns's sendoff," Fay positions herself in front of Ira so as to block him from Waltham's view.

"Actually, no, I confess I'm only here because of Ira." Clerkson looks down at the bare toes sticking out of his sandals as if noticing them for the first time. He's so badly dressed and out of place that Fay feels sorry for him. Still, he makes her nervous. He could be egging Ira on to something that will get him thrown out of the psychiatry department for good.

"Isn't it great that Tom's agreed to dinner and a "looking up" demonstration from Sam at our place tomorrow night?" Ira gives her his shamefaced "I've been a bad boy" look.

Barely hiding her anger, Fay asks jokingly, "Are you planning to steal Ira's favorite psychic so you can study him in California?"

"Share, not steal, Mrs. Corman. From what Ira tells me, Sam Rubin sounds like the real deal," Clerkson says breathily, "and I've been working in this field for over thirty years, starting back there at Duke, along with Rhine and the Psychical Research Society . . ." He pauses then adds in a conspiratorial whisper, "Your husband's making quite a reputation for himself."

No longer counting on the party noises to drown out their conversation, Fay notes for the first time that Clerkson has a southern drawl, undoubtedly picked up at Duke. Seeing that Waltham has edged in closer, she offers a caustic, "Glad you think so."

Clerkson responds with a bemused smile.

"Here, let me give you our address and telephone number. I'm on a three-month sabbatical; we're living out in my brother's house in Amagansett while he and his family are sailing in Florida. It's on Long Island. Do you know the area at all?" Ira scribbles the information on the back of his business card and hands it to Clerkson.

"Hey, I did my psych residency out at Islip. I know the area for sure."

The room darkens as the sun passes behind a cloud. Fay glances at her watch. It's four o'clock, definitely time to go. She gently tugs at Ira's arm, urging in a low voice that they leave now . . . the long drive . . . the expressway clogged to Kingdom Come . . .

"Looking forward—"

The two men exchange a collegial hug.

"Tomorrow night, you said. Dinner, was it?"

Ira's eyes plead for Fay's assent.

"It'll be a simple, cold supper, a salad and smoked salmon sort of thing." Fay hopes the scant promise of food will put Clerkson off. Judging from the way he's been scouring the canapé trays, he's a big eater. "Do you mind? The train takes awfully long, two hours or more from Penn Station to Amagansett, and you probably won't get in till late."

Clerkson bows slightly: "Not at all. I'll eat anything you put in front of me."

"And Sam? If he's going to demonstrate his amazing psychic powers, won't he require special food?" Fay's first hint of outright sarcasm, and she only regrets it a little. She's run out of sympathy for Clerkson and now resents him for teaming up against her with Ira and Sam.

"I'll bring a couple of bottles of wine . . . any favorites?"

"Don't bother, we've got a cellar full of wine. Anyway, I don't think Sam will be drinking much.

"Oh, no, he'll be busy drawing from a different realm of 'spirits,'" Clerkson says, chuckling.

Fay tugs harder at Ira's arm and deftly moves him toward the door. "See you then," she says.

Waving a beefy paw at them, Clerkson is already considering a tray of miniature frankfurters wrapped in dough blankets.

"It's past four. Let's be fast, okay, honey? No side hellos, let's just amble swiftly past Waltham, and out the door . . . There!" Fay takes a deep breath. They're safely out in the hall near the elevators and no one has noticed them leave. Ira's out of danger—for now, anyway. Burns will be tucked away in Washington; Ira will be on sabbatical, far from the psychiatry department and the prying eyes of his enemies. She'd like to confront him about inviting Clerkson and Sam to dinner without asking her first, but now's not the time to start an argument. Not here on the street. She'll make up some excuse not to ask them to stay overnight, maybe suggest a motel. She can worry about that tomorrow.

"Want me to drive home?" she asks as they cut through Washington Square Park toward the garage.

"Yes, you drive," Ira wipes his forehead with a balled-up handkerchief. "I've had three glasses of wine to your one."

A bare-chested black man wearing a tightly bound red

bandana on his head suddenly leaps out of the bushes in front of Fay and tries selling her a handful of "loose joints."

"No, thanks," she maneuvers past the loose joints man. Past an ear-phoned jogger on skates looping along to the music of the spheres across the pitted moonscape the city has become, past a man in a camouflage jacket playing a gutted upright piano under a dying plane tree at the entrance to the park. Why, she wonders, has she grown so morbidly attuned to such details? Or is it because she drank champagne on an empty stomach that the homeless man playing that gutted piano under that dying plane tree has set off a runaway train of unrelated thoughts about Sam's latest catastrophic predictions about the fate of the planet. Only a few days ago she'd scoffed at Ira for believing him, and they'd argued. But now, as she leaves the park, Fay wonders if Sam's dire predictions might not be so far-fetched after all.

It turned abnormally cold the night Tom Clerkson arrived with Sam Rubin in tow, each carrying a bottle of expensive West Australian Shiraz, Tom offering a flurry of apologies for being two hours late: the train had stalled between Southampton and Easthampton. Sam, all in black—windbreaker, shirt, jeans, and sneakers—attempted to kiss Fay's hand but she snatched it away from him. His familiar clammy touch and rank breath had evoked the usual surge of disgust. But tonight, seeing him standing in the doorway, she detected a streak of criminality in his ugliness she'd never noticed before—the sloped forehead, scraggly red beard and hair, the thick-lipped smirk of a comic book villain capable of doing harm for no reason except that he enjoyed playing his little game of pretending to be attracted to her, using her as bait to further ensnare Ira. One part showman and nine parts con artist, Sam could always be counted on to cause her grief.

As soon as they'd finished their promised cold supper, Ira hustled his guests into the study. Refusing their invitation to join them, Fay left saying she was going to watch a DVD in the den. An hour ago, she'd blown up at Ira for inundating her with unwanted guests, and he'd apologized, promising this would be the last time. Unconvinced, she'd remained short tempered and grumpy throughout the evening.

She'd just turned off the TV and was dozing when Ira burst into the den and startled her awake.

"It's incredible; you've got to see this for yourself! Grabbing her by the hand, he pulled her up from the sofa and hurried her toward the study.

Fay instinctively shrank back. But Ira would not let go of her hand and continued nudging her forward.

Clerkson was sitting hunched in an armchair at the far end of the study with his head in his hands when they entered. Sam, a glass of wine within easy reach, slouched in a director's chair opposite. His eyes were half shut, but Fay felt him gazing right through to the core of her. Suddenly Clerkson sprang out of his chair and started babbling excitedly, his forehead glistening with perspiration.

"In all my years as a parapsychology researcher, I've never come across anyone like Sam here. I deliberately said not one word about myself on the entire trip, gave him not one clue, and in a minute or two he's managed to reveal everything about my past—personal details nobody could possibly know but me—that I was an only child, including every one of my numerous childhood illnesses, the objects in my room when I was ten, my mother's hospitalization for depression after she and my father divorced . . ."

Interrupting Clerkson's outburst, Sam turned to Fay and

said, "Why don't you take a pencil and paper and write a name on it, any name you choose, then seal it in an envelope."

"Yes, go on, Fay, you're a neutral party, you have nothing to lose," Clerkson urged. "We know that in ESP experiments, the positive attitude of the investigators influences the course of hits positively. If a skeptical or neutral party is brought in, there are usually a larger number of misses."

". . . Which suggests that we can influence each other psychically without the need for communication devices like telephones or computers," Ira added, and would have said more if Sam hadn't silenced him by telling him to sit down.

Hoping to put an end to the evening, Fay picked up a pencil and notepad from Ira's desk and, with her back turned to Sam, quickly wrote her maternal grandfather's name on the front page. She removed an envelope from the drawer, tore off the page on which she'd written, folded it and slipped it into the envelope before removing the protective tape and tightly pressing it closed.

"Now burn it, the whole thing, in the ashtray," handing her a pack of matches, Sam sat back and caressed his wine glass with his short, square, nail-bitten fingers.

Clerkson returned to his armchair and Ira hovered behind him, both watching her as if transfixed.

When the flames in the ashtray had died, leaving a pile of black ash, Sam got up and quickly intercepted Fay by the wrist. Recoiling from his touch for the second time that evening, she demanded brusquely, "What was the name?"

Sam let go of her and said matter-of-factly, "Nicholas Ashton. Your maternal grandfather." Then wiping his mouth with the back of his hand, he turned to Ira. "Your wife is a perfect transmitter. Perfect."

"Bravo!" Clerkson sprang from his chair.

"Would you be willing to try one more, Fay? You're very

good, you know," Sam softened his tone and was actually coaxing her, rewarding her for her obedience. "Take a deck of cards, don't let me see it. Pick one, put it in a sealed envelope, and place it anywhere in the room after I leave."

This time Clerkson didn't have to persuade her. Fay went and fetched the cards and the envelope on her own.

"Come and get me when you're ready." Sam walked out of the study, closing the door behind him.

Clerkson wordlessly tried signaling her to hide the envelope containing her chosen card behind the bookcase, but she ignored him and stuffed it under a sofa cushion instead. Then she called Sam back into the room. Ira nodded approvingly as Sam, again piercing Fay with his eyes, returned to the director's chair and sat down.

"Over there," he pointed confidently at the rosewood hutch in the corner of the room, where, to Fay's astonishment, the envelope was tucked behind the glass.

"But that's not . . ."

"Take it. Open it."

Fay quickly pulled the envelope out from behind the glass, tore it open, and saw her card: the jack of clubs. Immediately returning to the sofa, she lifted the cushion, and found nothing there.

"A great magic trick, Sam."

"It isn't a magic trick. It's a gift I was born with. It can't be learned, like a trick. You ought to know, because you were born with it too."

Fay chuckled. "Maybe, but I can't take it seriously. I have other priorities. And now I'm going to bed."

For all the drama and flash of Sam's telepathic display, nothing could dispel the distinct, if unspoken, aura of gloom remaining: Ira was pale and shrunken, Clerkson noisily dyspeptic, and Fay had a throbbing headache. Only Sam was now alert and cheerful, as if infused, vampire-like, with the energy he'd sapped from his audience.

Clerkson looked at his watch as the clock over the fireplace chimed half past midnight. "I'm afraid we've overstayed. When is the next train back to New York?"

"Of course, you're not going back tonight." Ira stretched out his arm to bar him from leaving. "There are more than enough rooms here," he laughed nervously.

"Alright, but only till tomorrow. Then I'm returning to good old laid-back California. You Easterners have always been too intense for me."

Fay yawned loudly. "Oh, pardon me . . . Ira's right, Dr. Clerkson—"

"Hey, why so formal suddenly? Tom . . . please call me Tom."

"All right, Tom. So you're staying?"

"Looks like it, ma'am." Lightly resting his hand on her shoulder, he guided Fay toward the front hall staircase, with Ira and Sam following behind. Leaning his great bulk in closer as they approached the stairs, Clerkson squelched a burp before whispering into her ear, "Of course you're aware that, behind all the bluster, Sam's really very fragile and requires lots of tender loving care."

"He's Ira's responsibility, not mine," Fay snapped. "I don't go in for the paranormal. The ordinary world is enough for me to cope with." Then, shaking his hand, she said, "Good night, Tom," and walked away, leaving Ira to settle his guests in their respective rooms.

She was sitting up in bed reading a heavily blue-penciled copy of Ira's latest article when he opened the door and tiptoed in a few minutes later.

"You were away a long time."

"Ssh . . . you're talking too loud . . ."

"Don't worry; our esteemed company can't hear me. They're at the other end of the house."

Ira climbed into bed and placed his long legs between hers. "Mmm, you're warm—typical of a choleric type," he teased.

Putting the article aside, Fay kissed him on the cheek. "Tell me, doctor, why do I love you even when I'm angry at your shenanigans?"

"Because I've hypnotized you, my dear. Didn't you know that the psychiatry department secretaries all think I'm Rasputin, and that I have magical seductive powers over beautiful young Czarinas like you?"

Fay kissed him again, less enthusiastically this time. "I wish you'd stop wasting good money on expensive editors when, like all your work, this article's sure to be savaged by your critics," she pointed down at the manuscript on the bed beside her.

"Why, what's wrong with it?"

"You know what . . ."

"You'd have been so happy if I would just sit in my office dispensing pills to rich depressives, wouldn't you?" Ira looked away from her. "Who knows? Maybe you're right. Tonight, for a moment, watching you and Sam, I had the sudden urge to delete all my files, trash all the data and forget about publishing my findings."

"As long as you brought it up, let me remind you that just being in the same room with Sam makes my flesh crawl," she shivered.

"Please, Fay, don't start on that."

Registering her displeasure, Fay unlaced her legs from his; her abrupt movement caused the pages of Ira's article to scatter and slide off the bed. She was about to bend over and pick them up when Ira pulled her back. "Leave them," he said.

"No, I want to pick them up now."

"God, you're stubborn."

Having collected the pages and restored them to order, Fay sat back on her pillow. "If you really want to know, it's not just Sam I hate, but what he's doing to destroy you . . . I hate the way he's ruining your career, everything we both worked so hard to build."

Ira gently stroked her hair. "I can't, darling—you know I've never been as grounded as you are . . . that's what you always say, isn't it?"

"It's true, I am more grounded than you, but you've got to admit that I'm also more intuitive—even Sam said so." Fay turned away from him and buried her face in her pillow.

"Poor Fay . . ." Ira whispered, grazing his lips against her hair.

No response. She'd fallen asleep with his incriminating article still in her hand. Taking it from her, Ira placed it on his night table. Then turning off the lamp, he shifted his body away from her to face the window.

PART II

10
RETREATS

Jessie Kane was already known in dance circles as a thirty-year-old wunderkind who'd started her own company with a National Endowment Arts grant when Fay entered her Classical Japanese Dance class at Barnard for the first time. Jessie's interest in Zen had been sparked by her training under Eric Hawkins and two years of studying Noh and Kabuki in Japan. Reputed for her austere style and her Japanese formality (she'd become a master at tea ceremony and flower arranging during her stint in Japan), Jessie had surprised everyone by welcoming Fay into her inner circle almost immediately.

Fay admired Jessie for her arty Japanese kimonos, painted silver toes and frizzy henna-dyed hair, worn in what she laughingly called her "punk monk" cut. She was flattered by Jessie's whimsical postcards, which she found almost every day in her mailbox before class: a mysterious calligraphic line against a bare white ground; a black-and-white photo of a Buddhist shrine somewhere in Japan; a koan asking her about her original face before she was born. Though the cards were never signed, the enigmatic smile Jessie gave her when she entered the mirrored practice room and took her place at the barre, convinced her that Jessie was communicating something even more important than dance. Wordlessly, through those strange, unintelligible Japanese characters, she sensed that Jessie was guiding her toward the spiritual path she'd been searching for. Fay was both awed and puzzled by Jessie's method. She wondered whether she would ever be worthy of the wisdom contained in her postcards.

At the end of Fay's last semester at Barnard, Jessie invited her to join the dancers' Zen group that meditated in her loft on Wednesday nights. From the moment she removed her shoes at the door, walked in, and sat down cross-legged on the black cushion, Fay knew she'd found her way. She loved Zen for its starkness, she loved the stories Jessie told her over tea about her antic Zen master, Ryuho Roshi, who, after visiting Jerusalem and dancing with the Hasidim, was determined to found a zendo there. How he had come back to his monastery in Japan and chosen Eikei Tanaka out of all his successors to open it in a blue Arab house on the Mount of Olives donated by a wealthy Japanese supporter. How, while visiting Jessie in New York one summer, Eikei (a no less eccentric Zen master than Ryuho Roshi) had gotten up at two in the morning and washed his laundry in the bathtub and hung it to dry on the roof. Fay loved the idea of a Zen master who did his own laundry at two in the morning. She couldn't get the image of him standing on Jessie's roof in his nightshirt hanging socks on a television antenna out of her mind, and she was determined to meet him. The opportunity came sooner than she thought.

When George Corman died of a heart attack on a golf course in Short Hills, leaving his wife Patsy with five million dollars—twenty-five thousand of which she immediately gave to her hairdresser as a birthday gift—his sons Charles and Ira hired a lawyer to prove their mother incompetent. As a result, each of them was awarded a two-million-dollar trust fund, and Charles, the elder, was appointed executor of his mother's estate. Following his accountant's advice, Ira immediately bought a first-floor office in a luxury condominium on the Upper East Side and to placate Fay, a loft in Soho, not far from Jessie Kane's combined dance studio/zendo. The paint on the walls of their loft had barely dried, however, when he announced that he was taking a six-month sabbatical from his psychiatric practice and flying to California to join Tom Clerkson and his breakaway team of SRI researchers to work with Sam—now a celebrated "channeler" whose spirit guide, "Samuel," was gathering as many as fifteen hundred devotees a sitting at a thousand dollars a head.

Ira's final defection from the mainstream medical community had been a long time coming, but not unexpected. At first, Fay did not try to hide her disapproval of his plan to drop everything and "go a-channeling," as she put it. But Ira was determined to go, and she knew that nothing she could say or do would get him to change his mind. That he never once invited her along only added to the insult of being left behind. Not that she would have wanted to be anywhere near her despised adversary. Still, that didn't stop her from secretly hoping Ira would ask her at the last minute to join him.

Only a year ago, Ira's rejection would have left her numb and barely able to function. But her life had taken a different turn since then, and she was too immersed in her dance career and, increasingly, her Zen practice, to lament their impending long-distance marriage. At least for now, the benefits of this new stage in her relationship with Ira appeared to outweigh the drawbacks. To begin with, the telephone did not offer him the luxury of spending long minutes staring at her in silence while she loudly lamented their growing estrangement. Ira had certainly been more forthcoming in his nightly phone calls during his previous exploratory trips to California than he was when they were sitting across the table from each other at dinner in New York. Not once, when he was away, did he tell her to "look into it" (meaning go into therapy) whenever she'd complained. There was definitely something different about the way he spoke to her on the phone. Away from her, Ira, it seemed, had grown more affectionate. Maybe his flourishing partnership with Sam's "past-life therapy" success in California had helped. Whatever it was, Fay was genuinely happy for him. If living apart from her could bring about such positive changes, why should she begrudge him? Besides, she told herself, long-distance marriages were becoming more common among professional couples—and even more so among her "dharma friends." It wasn't unusual for practicing Zen couples to separate while one partner took a year of intensive monastery training. One woman she knew had even taken her fifteen-month-old daughter with her to Japan while her husband remained in New York. Ira was taking off to "follow his bliss," why shouldn't she? Though patience wasn't one of her virtues, Fay knew that her turn would come. And soon. All she had to do was wait.

Ira left for California on a cold, raw day in January. Fay had just seen him off at the airport and was unlocking the door of the loft when the telephone rang. It was Jessie, calling to say she was laid up with a severely sprained ankle and needed a favor. A big one. Would Fay be willing to take over for her and manage the dance company's upcoming Israel tour. Fay immediately protested that she wasn't up for such a big responsibility. Reminding her that she'd already been with the company for five years and was the only one she could fully trust to take over for her, Jessie persisted. Fay countered by expressing misgivings about her lack of managerial experience. They went back and forth like that, until Jessie changed everything by saying how disappointed Eikei Roshi would be if Fay didn't go to Israel in her place.

An hour later, she was in the elevator on her way up to the studio, still not sure she was the right person for the job. But when she entered the loft and saw Jessie actually lying there, her frizzy hair un-hennaed and streaked with gray, dazed by painkillers and hardly able to talk, but making an effort to prop herself on one arm to say how relieved she was not to have to cancel the tour and how this was a great opportunity for Fay to fill in, because someday she'd have to take over the company anyway—Fay swallowed her misgivings and promised to do her best.

As she was leaving, Jessie reached over to the night table and handed her a piece of paper on which she'd scrawled the address of Eikei Roshi's Zen center in Jerusalem. Then she directed her to the closet and told her to take out the Macy's box she'd find there, saying it was a gift for the roshi.

On a freezing, sunny February day, exactly a month after Ira's departure for California, Fay stood in front of a sandstone Arab house on the crest of the Mount of Olives with the box containing Jessie's gift in one hand and a greasy brown paper bag stuffed with falafel and pita sandwiches in the other. She knocked and was surprised when Eikei Roshi himself appeared in the doorway. Given his status, she'd expected him to have an attendant monk. Jessie had described the roshi as "very traditional, very Japanese," adding that he'd been born into a samurai temple family consisting of several generations of Zen monks. The black-robed man who faced her in the doorway did not match her expectations: he was tiny, about fifty-five, and his too-big-for-his-body-head was as bald and shiny as a melon. His face, however, was golden and fierce.

Leading Fay to a room behind the zendo, the roshi asked her to sit down on a floor cushion at the Japanese-style table while he went to the kitchen to fetch tea. She noted that his robes were made of thin cotton and that he was barefoot despite the cold.

"No central heating," he apologized, returning with the steaming tea. "Only in lower belly, best central heating system." He patted himself on the navel, crossed his legs, and sat down without having to use his hands for balance.

Shivering, Fay opened the greasy bag and offered the roshi a falafel sandwich. He took it and smiled. "Fourteen years is enough falafel for traditional Japanese monk. I now get word I go home to Japan and eat raw fish again."

Fay placed the box on the table. "For you."

Setting his falafel sandwich aside, the roshi clasped his palms together in thanks and immediately began opening the package. "Ah . . . beautiful," he murmured, removing the sweater, and holding it up to the light. "Beautiful wine color, so young looking, my sister will say I become young boy again. Very beautiful. Thank you, Fay-san." He made a little bow then continued to admire the sweater, occasionally smiling at her with the open face of a child, all the fierceness gone.

"It's from Jessie," Fay said, reddening.

"I send Jessie thank you card," he paused to refold the sweater and neatly placed it back in the box. "Thank you for bringing it."

Fay wished she could follow him to Japan.

"Roshi, I want to see my face before I was born. That's why I've come here to you."

Pouring her a second cup of fragrant green tea, the little man shook his head and purred. "No need to study with anyone. You sitting on your own diamond mountain and you run around the world looking for it. 'Where is my precious diamond mountain?' you cry. All the time right there with you. Only you dream you lost it. But it is right there," the roshi picked up his sandwich and started eating.

Fay sipped the tea and felt her face grow warm. What was he talking about? A magic mountain? No, a diamond mountain. It didn't matter. All she wanted was to remain seated on the floor across from him for as long as she could, silently watching him eat his falafel sandwich.

The roshi did not say he would be her teacher. He didn't even say he'd see her again. At the end of the interview, as he led her out the door, he told her he was probably going to remain in Japan as vice abbot of his monastery. Then, handing her a small bronze Buddha, the names and phone numbers of two of his American students in Jerusalem, and a Japanese sutra book with the English translation on facing pages, he encouraged her to keep meditating with Jessie's group in New York.

As Fay walked downhill to the bus stop, she looked over her shoulder and saw the roshi standing in the doorway, waving. *So this is the way it happens*, she thought.

The next three weeks passed in a blur of red desert skies, grilled fish dinners along the Sea of Galilee, and tented oases flanked by date palms. The company received enthusiastic reviews from three knowledgeable Israeli dance critics familiar with Jessie's Japanese wabi choreographic style, and the tour proved Fay capable not only of moving dancers around the stage, but of settling their petty disputes and staving off major upheavals as well. Much to her surprise, she was also good at handling company finances. Before the trip she'd warned Jessie that she had absolutely "no head for money." Jessie had given a little laugh and put her arm around her saying she had every confidence in her not to run off with the take. Fay now realized that she'd been so cowed by Ira's using her "strange genes" as an excuse to keep her out of his financial affairs, that she was shocked when, perusing accounts at the end of the tour, she found that she'd not only managed to cover company expenses but had four hundred dollars left over. Fay attributed her success to her meeting with the roshi. "When the student is ready," Jessie had told her, "The teacher appears." At the time, Fay thought she was referring to their own meeting, at Barnard, but now she knew it was Eikei Roshi Jessie had been talking about.

On her last day in Jerusalem, Fay returned to the zendo on the Mount of Olives, hoping for another interview with the roshi. This time the door was locked and, though she banged on it for a long time, no one answered. A grizzled donkey stood tethered to the fence of a neighboring house. It watched her with interest then brayed as if to tell her there was no use her knocking like that, the roshi wasn't there. When the donkey lifted its lip and sneered at her, Fay turned away from the zendo and walked back to the bus stop.

In a handsome yellow villa surrounded by purple bougainvillea bushes, she found Diane, the dress designer from Hawaii whose name was first on the list the roshi had given her. The friendly, curly-haired woman served her iced tea. Then, apologizing for their brief meeting, Diane handed her a business card, saying she was just passing through Jerusalem on her yearly visit to her mother and was leaving that night, but that if Fay ever found herself in Honolulu, she was welcome to sit zazen with her group.

In a rundown Arab house near the Damascus Gate, she located Eric, a martial arts teacher, the second American on the

Roshi's list. A short bullock of a man with cropped hair, Eric informed her that he was originally from Brooklyn and offered to teach her karate at half price if she became a dues-paying member of the Jerusalem zendo. Turning down the karate lessons, Fay wrote a two-hundred-dollar check to the Mount of Olives Zen Center covering a year's worth of dues and mentioning her second unsuccessful visit to the zendo, asked him if the roshi had already left for Japan.

"You must have gone there on a Wednesday, his day off. He's sleeping inside, but he locks the zendo and won't answer no matter how hard you knock. He's a very private person," Eric said, his low voice trailing off into a whisper.

"Oh . . . my plane leaves tomorrow, at two in the morning, and I wanted to say good-bye."

"It's obviously not your karma this time." Giving her a wistful smile, the karate teacher tucked the check in his pocket. "Hey, I just made some fresh soymilk. Why don't you sit down here on the porch and have some?"

Fay didn't usually like soymilk, but she was thirsty, and Eric's was cold, and delicious. When they'd finished drinking and washed the glasses, Eric demonstrated some basic karate moves in exchange for which she showed him a few yoga postures. It wasn't until the sun started casting pillar-sized shadows across the ochre walls of the Old City that Fay returned to her hotel and packed her bags.

Five months after that first meeting with the roshi in Jerusalem, she received a blue airmail letter marked with a Japanese postage stamp:

Shofuji
May 8, 1984

Fay-san:

I will be London beginning of June till middle of July. (10 Primrose Court. Chalk Farm). We take sesshin (Zen meditation retreat) in June, second Saturday and Sunday. Only weekend sesshin. Then, one-week sesshin from July 4 to July 10. If you want to take sesshin please come anytime. During sesshin everybody stay in zendo. Please bring your own sleeping bag or blanket. As you know, English people are not so clean and zendo atmosphere is not like Jerusalem zendo—dark and poky little room. Please let me know when you come. I go back Japan end of July. You can stay London zendo cheap after sesshin is over.

Please take good care of yourself.
Eikei Takano

When she called Ira in San Francisco, the message on the answering machine in his sublet said he was on an extended retreat in Tahoe and couldn't be contacted. Fay told the answering machine she was making arrangements to join Eikei Roshi for sesshin in London and wouldn't be home when Ira returned but that she would call him when she came out of sesshin.

The earliest she could get out of New York was July 3, and her flight was delayed and didn't land at Heathrow until midnight. It was one o'clock in the morning before she arrived at the zendo, a narrow row house on a shabby cul-de-sac with a pub on the corner. The lights were out, and everyone appeared to be sleeping. She gave one quick jab at the bell, and a slender, silent figure she took to be male opened the door, took her suitcase, and led her through a narrow hallway up three flights of stairs into a spacious room with only a futon and several floor cushions for furniture. Leaving her suitcase on the floor alongside her, her escort walked out of the dimly lit room. Fay wondered if she was meant to unpack and lie down. Adjusting her eyes to the gloom, she looked around. There, in front of an artificial fireplace casting the only light in the room, sat Eikei Roshi. She jumped and let out a little cry. His baldpate shining in the glow of artificial firelight behind him, the roshi had been transformed from the puckish elf she'd met in Jerusalem into a slit-eyed samurai with a gash for a mouth and a square iron jaw.

"You sit down here," he growled, pointing at a black meditation cushion in front of him.

Fay's skirt was too narrow for her to cross her legs without revealing her underpants, so she opted for sitting on her knees in a cramped, painful ball, her mind numbed by jet lag.

"We face each other again," roared the roshi.

Why is he talking so loud? Does he want to wake up the whole house?

Fay gulped. "Yes. It's been five months since we last met in Jerusalem."

"No, I do not mean Jerusalem. It took you a century to come. Finally, your karma has brought you here."

Except for her father, Fay hadn't admired and feared anyone so deeply since she was nine. Only this time it wasn't Ben Watkins sitting on the edge of her sickbed with his chest full of medals, holding a long needle and exhorting her to be a brave little soldier and take her penicillin shot without crying; this time it was the embodiment of the Buddha sitting in front of her with the cure for all suffering. Tears filled her eyes and she bowed her head.

"Sesshin is very hard, very painful," the roshi continued in the same loud voice, his palms resting open in his lap. "But you can do it. Forget everything except for your breathing. Counting your breaths. Breathe . . . one, breathe . . . two, breathe . . . three. Eating . . . breathe one, sleeping . . . breathe two, walking . . . breathe three . . . You become breathing until there is no Fay-san, only breathing in the whole universe. Nothing more. You sit in lotus posture with back and neck straight. Zen is not ecstasy, not intellectual answer to problem, only counting breaths and bravery. Wake-up bell is at four, so you must go to sleep now." The roshi dismissed her with a wave of his hand.

Fay rose to her feet; her knees shot with needles, she picked up her suitcase and wobbled to the door. The slender figure had reappeared on the landing and was motioning her to follow him down the hall. Stopping in front of a door marked WOMEN, the figure, which she could now make out was in fact male, nodded at her before continuing down the stairs. Fay opened the door and walked into the room. The streetlight shining into the curtain-less window illuminated an indoor clothesline strung with bras, socks, and panties and a floor covered with women in sleeping bags. An artificial fireplace like the one in the roshi's room was built into the far wall. In the corner nearest the door, alongside an empty rush mat, she put down her suitcase. Too tired to undress, she dropped onto the mat and promptly fell asleep in her clothes.

11
SAMURAI TRAINING

The roshi had warned her that sesshin would be hard—but Fay was not prepared for the shock of being cast among thirty silent strangers every minute of the day for seven days: sleeping fitfully, jumping up with her heart tripping for fear of missing the four a.m. wake-up bell; eating the same Spartan meal—tofu, brown rice, and a few paltry greens—from tiny wooden bowls with chopsticks at odd hours; then sitting in a constipated stupor on the toilet of a single postage-sized WC with a crowd of strangers queued up in front of the door grimly waiting their turn.

No matter how early she arrived for zazen, the roshi would already be seated on his black meditation cushions in front of the altar, as stone-faced as the statue of the Buddha behind him, the long wooden stick used to awaken sleeping or fidgeting meditators ominously laid out in front of him and the timing bell and clappers alongside.

Worst of all was sitting cross-legged for hours on her cushion in excruciating pain under the ferocious gaze of the tight-lipped roshi as he toured the zendo wielding the long wooden stick, shouting, "March on bravely!" The mere whisper of his black monk's robes grazing the hardwood floor was enough to strike terror into her heart. Afraid she might scream if he were to stop behind her and whack her hard between the shoulders, she'd lose count of her breath and have to start over again each time he mercifully passed her by. Sweat dripped from her armpits, staining her cushion. Tears and snot streamed down her cheeks, but she didn't dare raise a hand to wipe them. At one point, the pain in her knees was so bad that her legs started twitching. Fearing to disturb the people on the neighboring cushions—a skinny young man with a platinum-blond ponytail to her left who she later discovered was a Scottish Laird, and a plump, cheerful-looking grandmother to her right—she pressed her fists into her thighs, distributing the pain until the twitching stopped. Though sitting periods lasted for only twenty-five minutes, it felt like hours before the roshi's bell signaled release into a numb-limbed, silent stiff walk around the zendo led by the shadowy slender figure who'd escorted her the first night. The man was apparently some sort of major domo, for he frequently stole away after lunch to consult with the roshi in his room before tiptoeing down the stairs to mysteriously whisper into the kitchen wall phone.

As Fay sat counting her breaths on the third morning, she was suddenly gripped by a stabbing stomach spasm so sharp that she fell face forward on her cushion. At that moment someone lightly touched her shoulder. Turning around, she saw that it was the major domo kneeling alongside her. Leaning close, he whispered into her ear, "Interview." Fay looked at him uncomprehendingly. "Interview with the roshi," he whispered into her ear again, his breath smelling of garlic and cloves. It was the first human contact she'd had in three days.

Eikei Roshi sat in his third-floor eyrie, as distant and hard as the diamond mountain she'd been attempting to scale on her cushion.

"I'm having terrible stomach pains," she said. "I'm afraid I might scream."

"So scream," he said, laughing.

"Roshi, my guts are going to come flying out of my mouth if I have to go on sitting like that."

Without so much as blinking, the roshi picked up the little hand bell near his cushion and rang it.

"Next!" he called, motioning for her to leave.

Holding on to the walls of the narrow corridor, she made her way downstairs, muttering under her breath as she had when goaded to the breaking point by her father, "*I'll march on bravely just to spite you, you son of a bitch.*"

During the eleven-thirty work period on the morning of the fourth day, as Fay was performing her assigned chore of dusting the altar and lining up incense sticks for the afternoon meditation, Eikei Roshi himself suddenly appeared alongside her and silently motioned her upstairs. When they reached the third floor, without changing his stone-faced expression, he led her to a door across the hall from his room and opening it ushered her into a small spare kitchen with a low table surrounded by cushions on a tatami-covered floor. Closing the door behind him, the roshi slipped out of his robes and hung them on a wall hook. Seeing him stripped of his all-powerful, black-robed persona, Fay could hardly keep from laughing. He looked so puny standing there in his white cotton T-shirt and pantaloons that she had to resist the urge to run her finger over his shiny baldpate. She was at least two heads taller and could probably send him sprawling with one quick jab.

"Now, what is wrong with your stomach? You vegetarian?"

"Yes, except for eggs and cheese, and occasionally fish."

"Never mind that. Let me see your belly."

Fay stuck out her stomach.

"Too big around diaphragm, too much yoga exercise, maybe, and not enough deep-belly breathing. Look at me."

Fay looked down at the roshi's potbelly.

"Ha! Rinzai Zen belly! First time you ever see such a strong belly. Punch!"

She resisted. Antic was one thing, but being asked to punch your teacher in the stomach?

"Punch!"

She rained a few tentative blows on his protruding belly.

"Ha! Nothing! You must eat meat. You have constipation? Or sometimes diarrhea, no? Never beautiful golden pagoda, only loose intellectual worm shit. Never make gas? Ah . . . if you make gas like this"—the roshi delivered an enormous fart—"you get instantly enlightened!"

Fay winced, recalling her father's daily challenges, their early morning push-ups while her mother was out at Mass. Her father laughing, still pumping red-faced beside her toward the floor as she heaved and gasped for breath, wishing he would just die right there. When she'd fall exhausted to the carpet before hitting thirty, he'd get up and give her a rousing slap on the back, yelling, "Don't go chicken on me! I said thirty consecutive push-ups!"

I'll march on bravely just to spite you, you son of a bitch.

The roshi suddenly spun her around and tapped her on the spine. "Here, this is stomach point. Here . . . can you feel how tight it is?" Fay felt a shaft of pain coursing through her stomach and pulled away from him.

"Poor Fay-san, your head is in your stomach! Hahaha!" The roshi abruptly let her go and turned his attention to a saucepan on the stove. Picking up a wooden spoon lying on the counter, he heaped the saucepan's contents into a bowl and set it on the table. "Here, you sit down and eat Japanese white rice and chicken and you feel better. English people's macrobiotic diet very terrible food. You eat chicken and you get well. You will see. I know. I know you from before you were born."

The roshi handed her a pair of chopsticks, fixed a smaller portion of chicken and rice for himself, then, bringing a glass pot filled with green tea and two porcelain cups to the table, he sat down opposite her, brought the bowl close to his face and started eating with great noisy slurps.

Picking up her bowl and bringing it close to her face, Fay took a few tentative mouthfuls. Soon she was slurping loudly like the well-dressed businessmen at her favorite Japanese restaurant on Broadway. The slurping had always put her off, but now it seemed a perfectly natural way to eat. Noisily smacking her lips along with the roshi, Fay realized that this was the first meat she'd tasted in years. And it was delicious.

12
GREENHOUSE PERSON

London. July 14, 1984

Now that sesshin is over and I'm the only resident in the zendo, Eikei takes me along on his early morning shopping trips through Chinatown in search of Asian vegetables, silky tofu, and imported Japanese miso. Afternoons, we either go to the movies, or to Marks and Spencer's for the slippers and Swatches he intends to bring back to his favorite monks at the monastery. He's teaching me to cook traditional Japanese breakfasts: seaweed and crushed soybean stew poured over rice, says it'll cure my stomach problems once and for all. I don't know . . . it's mushy and hard to eat first thing in the morning. But I trust him, and I'm starting to get used to it (The terrible stomach pains haven't come back since the day he fed me that chicken and rice dish). We spend hours sitting at the low table in the upstairs kitchen, talking and drinking tea. He shocked the hell out of me one morning by removing a pack of Kents from the pocket of his pantaloons and offering me one—which I refused—initiating a ridiculous debate about cigarettes and cancer that went nowhere. If he weren't my Zen teacher, I'd have left him then and there, rather than sit around inhaling his second-hand smoke.

What else but "karma" (a word the roshi uses a lot, which makes me uneasy, given its associations to Sam Rubin and the channeling crowd in California) would have drawn me to him in the first place? Or left me speechless when he goes off on one of his Japanese chauvinist rants about Westerners as slovenly, undisciplined, lacking in traditional manners, and obsessed with our health. When I once got up the courage to ask him why he teaches us, he said it's because today's Japanese monks are even worse! Somehow, his low opinion of his Zen students doesn't seem to include me, or maybe I've convinced myself I'm the exception to the rule. Otherwise, why would he bother with me? Could it have something to do with what he calls "bravery-mind?"

Of course, Ira would say it's an Oedipal thing, that I'm replaying my love-hate relationship with my father. And he'd probably be right. Just yesterday Eikei told me he'd served in the Japanese Navy. I can't say I was surprised to hear it, since he never stops boasting about his samurai lineage, the centuries of warrior blood running through his veins. He treats me like a new boot camp recruit—same as Ben. Screams bloody murder when I leave the light on behind me, or let the water run. Yelling, "I show you Zen way of cleaning!" snatching the vacuum cleaner out of my hands for being too slow or for leaving dust balls in the corners. OK, so it's the old 'Number One Son' game I'm playing again, proving I can be better than a real son—or, in this case, monk. The rewards are uncannily the same: they always involve food, a sacred communion. Like the roshi, Ben was a wonderful cook. Come to think of it, his breakfasts were pretty exotic, too: ham and onion and jalapeno pepper omelets, black bread and hot cocoa smothered in thick, fresh cream. We'd wash the dishes together afterward in the same meditative silence.

On Wednesdays, when Doreen went straight to work from Mass and he didn't have to be at the hospital until nine-thirty, Ben let me help him cook oatmeal. He taught me how to stir the lumps away. I loved clasping my fingers around his on the warm wooden spoon handle. Warm and safe, his smooth doctor's hands promised me a life of continued protection. I relished being his 'Number One Son,' told myself that I was special, that playing football was so much better than being a "Daddy's Girl," like my golden-curled rival Harriet, captain of the cheerleading team.

Feeling "special" is probably what keeps me here sitting in the kitchen drinking green tea with my chauvinist samurai Zen teacher after we've meditated and chanted, freshened the water cup in front of the Buddha, and vacuumed and dusted everything in sight in the spare, dark, 'poky' little zendo. While the breakfast rice is cooking, we listen to the hourly BBC news bulletins on the radio, which Eikei needs me to translate for him, because he doesn't understand the newscasters' British accents. At least we don't argue about politics, like my father and I did when we listened to the news in the morning . . .

Oh, and the roshi smokes two packs of Kents a day and eats pork chops—habits I'd never associated with Buddhist monks before, and he talks a lot about "farting" and "shitting." For example, he loves repeating his favorite story about a monk named Chu-san (now abbot of one of the most illustrious temples in Kyoto) who, at the moment of letting down his drawers in a rice field during a bout of dysentery, startled a frog, and was immediately enlightened. He gives me the same puckish grin every time he tells that story. After hearing it for the sixth time, I couldn't resist telling him he was "anal obsessive"—which cracked him up. Yet there's something so childlike and innocent about his farting and shitting talk that, instead of having its desired effect (which I assume is to shock me into enlightenment), it no longer fazes me at all.

The two of us travel around London in identical navy-blue monks' work suits. I bought mine from a tall (that is, tall for a Japanese) novice named Gempo who spent six months in an English immersion school in Hampstead. He stopped by last week to visit Eikei before returning to the monastery in Japan. Seeing myself in my monk's suit in the mirror last week, I thought I might as well go all the way and cut my hair. Doreen would have a shit fit if she saw my new Jessie Kane "punk-monk" cut. Would probably think I'd turned dyke and run wailing to her priest.

Maybe Ben was right when he said the stork made a mistake and dropped the wrong bundle down our chimney. Or could it be that I'm paying my mother back for telling me when I was ten and still starving for her affection, how she'd cried, "Oh, it's not a boy!" and refused to look at me when the nurse placed me on her belly minutes after I was born. I remember weeding alongside her in the tomato patch of her tiny vegetable garden, when she turned to me and asked, "What was all the pain for?" Coming out of the blue like that, her question made no sense to me. I was too young, still groping to understand what I had done to hurt her, but I knew my mother well enough by then to know how much she resented me for being born a girl. When I got older, and more spiteful, I used to think of her hysterectomy as punishment for rejecting me—

Fay had just finished sewing a seam on the roshi's ceremonial undershirt and was jotting notes in her diary when he walked into the kitchen. She pocketed the diary. He took the shirt from her, turned it around twice and unleashed a guffaw that shook the walls. "You sew seam backwards! Exactly like my teacher Ryuho Roshi, typical intellectual greenhouse person!"

Greenhouse-person was the roshi's code word for incompetent. Fay shrugged. "I never did learn to sew."

"You exactly like Ryuho Roshi," he shouted. "He terrible at sewing, planting . . . terrible at everything with his hands. Only talk, talk, talk. One day when a very young monk, Ryuho was on garden duty. He supposed to plant tree in front of monastery gate. So he dig up a little soil with a spoon and stick tree into the ground. By next day, tree was dead . . . roots outside, leaves all gone. The abbot very angry, and he shout at Ryuho in front of all the monks. Ryuho ashamed, so he disappear. He like you, very sensitive . . . too sincere. He run away to Manchuria for six months, and nobody find him. Abbot and Ryuho's mother sent people, but nobody find. One day, Ryuho come back by himself, standing outside monastery gate with long hair, dressed like beggar, dirty, like London hippie."

"He came back to the monastery?"

"Yes . . . because like you, Ryuho Roshi very pure person, very honest and sincere enlightenment seeker, very artistic. You dancer, Ryuho poet. Both of you spoiled by talent, not able to work with your hands. Not like me, a wild human being with no fixed ideas. I don't like people who thinking, thinking, thinking all the time. I like people who talk direct, concrete, no beautiful words, no dream talk, like these English greenhouse people. I like wild, crabgrass people like Tano Roshi, the abbot of my monastery since Ryuho Roshi retire. Tano is my best friend. We train together from the time we young monks. Tano just like me—no mother, no father. But he even worse off. I have grandmother to raise me. But Tano put in basket when born near a hot spring and brought up by farmer family. Always working hard. Beaten from the time he five years old.

When he put into temple at sixteen, he already tough guy, survivor."

Eikei lit a cigarette and took a long drag. "Later, during war, Tano lived in underground tunnel he dig with his own hands, right on American army base. He steal food every night from PX and stay alive for three years like that. All his teeth fall out from no calcium. At end of war, he put up white handkerchief stolen from American PX and was liberated. After war, he live by drawing dirty pictures and selling to American GIs. Tano very great artist. He never marry or have lady, but know how to make real pictures of lady vaginas, details of hair and everything. I just like Tano, never have lady. But I can tell size of human being vagina from looking at ear . . . and penis, too!" he shouted.

Fay blushed. The roshi's smutty talk made her uncomfortable. Stories about monks being enlightened in the middle of shitting was one thing, graphic descriptions of genitals were another. Lately, this kind of talk had grown more frequent. She and Eikei would be riding the escalator in the Underground after a trip to the Regents Park Zoo, and, in a loud voice, he might suddenly comment on the width of the giraffe's vagina or on the length of the penis of the tiger in the neighboring cage. Taking it as part of his campaign to change her from a "greenhouse person" into a "crabgrass person," however she might try to appear unfazed, even forcing a wild, high-pitched laugh now and then, the blushing always gave her away.

He especially seemed to enjoy regaling her with raunchy stories about the Tokyo geisha who serviced the monasteries and, with yakuza backing, chased away the local freelance hookers who tried to intrude on their business. She wondered if he was exaggerating just to see how she would respond when he described the mixed public bathhouses he'd frequented, where female attendants specialized in "penis massage."

One afternoon, as they sat in Hyde Park eating Kentucky Fried Chicken from a striped jumbo tub, Eikei said, "I know high-class geisha in Tokyo who specialize in massaging three, four penises same time."

"How do you know about that?" Fay asked, her phrasing stiff and childishly slow. "You said you 'never know lady'." They were sitting close enough for her to smell the liquor on the roshi's breath. She had thought he might be drinking but had never actually caught him at it.

"I know everything!" he boasted, giving her his, *don't-be-so-slow-witted look*. "I never meet anyone like you before—except maybe Ryuho Roshi. Completely pure, too pure . . . must learn swimming in dirty water. A real fish must swim everywhere. A pure fish die right away."

He grunted, wiped his hands on a napkin, and said, "Your skin too tender, Fay-san. When storm comes, hard times, you scratch and bleed too easy. Your father give you good training, but you still not tough enough."

Craving initiation into his swaggering monk's world of bar hostesses and crabgrass abbots, Fay pleaded for him to teach her.

"We see," said the roshi.

Later that night, after the evening meditation was over and the three zendo regulars who never missed a sitting had drunk their tea and gone, Eikei, a cigarette dangling from his lip, swaggered around the tiny kitchen straightening the bamboo blinds and watering the philodendron on the windowsill. Fay sat at the low table watching him. Suddenly he turned from the window and, giving her his puckish grin, picked up where he'd left off that afternoon in Hyde Park: "You have to be born survivor, like Tano and me, by karma. I come from old samurai Zen family, Japanese temple family . . . born lucky. Karma, that is karma. You have not so good karma . . . born in Texas . . . greenhouse girl . . . Catholic, guilty about sex . . . afraid of sin. God Jesus Christ weak and hanging from cross, saying 'Be pure, like me.' I don't like weak Christian god. Better Jewish god, like in Israel, big fighter. My best Zen student is Israeli paratrooper, army man, like samurai warrior. One lucky piece of your karma, you born to army family. Not Japanese . . . not man, that unlucky . . . but still, your father train you good."

Turning on the water, the roshi doused his cigarette with a hiss and tossed it into the trash pail behind the curtain under the sink. "They made me Zen monk at six. My grandmother shave my head and force me to memorize sutras, beating me on bald head with a bamboo rod until bleeding. Then mother and father both die, forcing me to survive alone. I learn snake's way, cheating way to move around in this cheating world. Not like you, only straight way, fixed, sincere, too pure." He sniffed, then straining the day-old leaves his survivor's instinct compelled him to save every night after supper, poured himself another cup of tea. "I sell black market cigarettes to American GIs, and ice cream in the park."

"And then what?"

"Become Zen monk!" he roared, grinning, on the verge of a great, belly-shattering laugh.

Fay's lips quivered in anticipation of laughing along with him. But the roshi turned serious suddenly, leaving her with a stupid leer on her face.

"I had temple teacher," he continued, "my father's friend. The old man say I must get enlightenment by five years in monastery or I must come home to work in village temple. I did not want to return to that small poor village and be slave for old man who beat me. So I decide to throw out everything, become hard stone-head, and on April 22, 1955, I become enlightenment person!"

Fay felt her legs buckling at the gravity of the confidence the roshi had just shared with her.

He lit another cigarette. After a reflective pause, he shook his head and said, "But I live in the West for too long with people like you. Getting spoiled, so Western in my thinking now that when I go Japan my older sister say I have 'foreigner mentality.'" The laughter broke loose then, raucous and wild. Again, just as quickly turning serious, almost grave, he said, "But you are basically enlightened too. Right now. You must know this. Without theory, without books, you must see that Buddha is here now. Zen is everyday life. You drink tea; that is Buddha. You walk, that is Buddha walking. You cry, Buddha cries. There is no need for Buddha, for Jesus Christ, for God. Everything is God, without beginning or end, with every breath you are breathing. Everything is Buddha . . . even cockroach. My policy is to tell you these things only three times. If you too stubborn to learn, I not bother with you. There is not enough time. Death cannot be cheated. Pain cannot be avoided. You must start by being humble, accepting pain with bravery mind."

How she wished she could prove her bravery mind to him that very minute. What could she do? Release a great cloud of enlightenment gas? Leap out the window and fly over London? She could do neither. All she could do was sit in front of the roshi like a clod, waiting for him to make her worthy of enlightenment by transforming her from a puny Texas greenhouse girl into a wild crabgrass monk.

"Do you remember landing at London airport?" he asked, gentler now, almost conversational. "It is like that. Flying above the weather, it is always sunny, clear. Then when airplane begins to land, clouds appear—many, many clouds full of rain. But you know that sun is always shining above those clouds, like your essential nature, always shining, always clear."

"Why can't I see it?" Fay let out a wrenching cry.

"Because Fay-san, like you tell me, you always 'window shopping' for truth. Because you always thinking, thinking, thinking." The roshi leaned over and rotated his finger in the air near her temple. "You want to see Buddha nature like it is movie inside your brain. You make pictures; then when outside world is different from your pictures, you become disappointed. Like you tell me your husband Ira-san disappoint you."

"Because I want him to be the perfect partner, and he isn't . . . neither am I," Fay whispered.

"Typical Western mentality. Why do you need partner? This I do not understand. A man once came to me in Jerusalem zendo and say he was going to India to surrender to his guru. What is all this talk about surrendering to a guru, or a partner, or even to a Zen teacher? You yourself already perfect as you are! Don't need anybody—" he stopped, disgusted. Then pointing his finger at her, he said, "Ah, but you not yet clear. When you clear, you will see this."

"Will you help me, Eikei?"

"You must help yourself, train and discipline yourself. As Dogen Zen master say, we all enlightened, but we must train our own bodies and minds until not even one trace of dust remains. We must become like white sheet of paper, with no ideas. Remember, Fay-san, I will not come and pat your back or tell you I am so sorry it hurts. If you need psychologist, you go get treatment. I am no psychologist. That remind me . . . Your husband call and leave message two days ago, when we out, but I forget to tell you. He say he missed your phone call when sesshin finished. Say no need you call him back, he not wanting to disturb."

Fay blinked and said nothing.

"Maybe you think I stone-hearted forgetting Ira-san call you. But, like I tell you before, Zen monk have no time for relationship problems."

London. July 22, 1984

The honeymoon is over. I can't do anything right. Eikei fluctuates between ignoring me and shouting in my face that I'm wasting his time. I tell myself Zen masters are supposed to be like this: antic and unpredictable. I console myself with his intermittent displays of puckishness, when his black monk's robes give way to ordinary street wear (polo shirts and baseball caps are his favorite "civilian clothes"), and his growls turn into belly laughs. "I am formless," he says one day, after I've accused him of being inconsistent. "Stop looking for your fixed picture of me. I never same person because I change with every situation, new every second, not like you with stuck cassette tape inside your head."

Lately, when we go shopping, he slips away from me and disappears into the crowd. I have to run to keep up with him, never manage to finish a sentence within earshot. Not that it matters; he's so bored by what I have to say that he yawns in my face. For two days in a row he didn't ask me in for breakfast, so I went out to the pub on the corner and had a stale scone and a disgusting cup of white coffee. I sat in the booth wondering what I'd done to make him so angry with me. I came up with plenty of reasons, not the least of which was that he'd suffered a lot at the hands of the American military, and my father is, after all, an American army officer. Maybe just looking at me reminds Eikei of the GI who bought ice cream from him and called him "Shorty" or "Nip." He told me his mother's family lived in Hiroshima but didn't say if they were there when the bomb was dropped. Said he was sleeping in his hammock below deck on a navy ship fifteen miles away from the city when it was erased from the map. Claims he's such a sound sleeper that he "snored right through the blast of a thousand suns," which exploded close enough to his ship to tilt it upright in the water.

Yesterday, at the Chinese noodle shop in front of the old gas house where we eat lunch almost every day, he got testy when I offered to pay the bill. He always insists on paying for me, and, since he depends on pocket money from his monastery supporters and I have plenty of my own, I thought it would be a good idea if I paid for a change. I was totally unprepared for his response. He got purple in the face and started pulling the check out of my hands. "What you think, I cripple? Cannot pay own bill?" he yelled. The Chinese woman behind the cash register motioned me over and gave me a handful of cellophane-wrapped fortune cookies free of charge. She felt so sorry for me. Her gesture must have shamed him. At least he stopped yelling. Then he got up and paid the bill without saying "You have nice day, missus," as he always did, and rushed out of the restaurant. I ran all the way after him, saying how sorry I was. Finally, when I caught up with him he said, "You make me nervous. I getting headache from your neurotic, your over caring . . ." His English lapsing, the roshi quickly walked away from me. I caught up with him again. "Please don't be mad," I said. He lit a cigarette. "Okay, okay. Everything okay." Frowning, he threw the newly lit cigarette on the pavement and stamped it out. What if he gets cancer? I thought. What'll I do without him?

"I promise I'll stop over caring," I said, amazed that all those years of living with Ira hadn't expunged my neediness.

I was fast walking behind the roshi, my shadow towering over his, when a pumpkin-faced old woman with a carbuncle on her nose stepped into my path and put down her shopping bag. "You should be ashamed of yourself, girlie!" she cried, causing three women standing in front of a fruit stall to turn around and stare at me. Desperate not to lose sight of Eikei, I stepped around the shopping bag and caught up with him.

We'd reached Piccadilly Square when, seeing I'd calmed down a bit, he turned to me and said, "I never worry. If I can't get what I want, I can't get it. That's all. Otherwise getting big headache."

Adopting the most normal tone of voice I could manage under the circumstances, I said, "So does that mean you never have plans? None what-so-ever?" Despite my efforts, the question came out as the whiney, nine-year-old plea for daddy's indulgence I've always hated.

"In the situation."

"Immediate?"

"Yes, in the immediate situation. So, if I cooking monk in monastery I never plan menu. I go to market and look at what they sell that day. Fresh vegetables, bean curd, eggs. I cook what I find."

"No advance-planning menu?" I persisted.

"No. If advance planning, I lose chance to find something new, unexpected—like avocados, maybe."

I knew I had to tread lightly, keep him on the topic of the monastery, since talking about the old days there usually gets him into a better mood.

"If I go to market with list and cannot find what I want, I become disappointed, like you, no? Better to expect nothing. Zen person expects nothing. Accepts everything."

Our truce established, we traveled back to the zendo on the Underground without saying a word to each other. Eikei tilted his head and read the advertisements posted above the windows. For a maddeningly long time, he sat there feigning interest in a business school that promised potential students a higher salary and a more rewarding job. We reached our stop and silently climbed the stairs to the street. At the front door of the zendo he turned to me wearily. "Please, Fay-san, today no tea. I tired.

Must lie down and take nap, then bath before sitting. Very sorry, no tea."

Feeling as if he'd slapped me, I raced upstairs past him into my room, slamming the door behind me.

The next day, the roshi was his old friendly self again. We spent the afternoon eating strawberry ice cream sundaes and reading newspapers in a Shaftesbury Avenue teashop, across from the movie theater where we'd bought tickets for the six o'clock showing of The Seven Samurai. It was opening day, and the line curled around for blocks. Eikei said it was the fifth time he'd seen the film, and when we finally got in, he slept through most of it. When the lights went on, he sat up and, as if continuing a nonexistent conversation we'd been having, said, "Best student is best fighting partner, like you and me, Fay-san." Not wanting to provoke him into changing his mind, I hid my pleasure at being complimented and said nothing. This time as we rode the Underground back to the zendo, he was very talkative and never once looked at the advertisements. He was sitting in the seat opposite me. Leaning over, he said, "Roshi like samurai general. Monks like samurai sergeants."

"Do you think I can ever become a samurai sergeant?"

"You? Greenhouse person? Maybe you have nervous breakdown if I hit you hard like I hit Chu-san. One winter I hit so hard between his shoulders during sesshin, he get weak lungs and have to spend one year in hospital for T.B. Stick in monastery is very long, not short like here. I beat Chu-san to make him work hard chopping wood. I make him tough. Then I take him to movies and buy him nice pork cutlet for supper."

'Well,' I thought, but didn't say, 'at least you've taken me to the movies. I can do without the beating and the T.B.'

"Maybe one day . . . maybe you become samurai sergeant, too," he mused, scratching his chin.

My heart was pounding so hard against my ribcage that I

was afraid he might hear it. I was on the verge of asking if he'd let me train with him at the monastery but knowing how quickly his compliments could turn into insults, kept my mouth shut.

We'd reached Chalk Farm station and were walking toward the staircase leading to the street.

As if he'd read my mind, Eikei said, "But it is very hard to do samurai Zen training in married life. Monastery life impossible for married lady like you, Fay-san."

"Ira and I are living apart, roshi."

"Not good. Married lady must take care of husband."

"That's not the kind of marriage Ira and I have. Besides, the last thing he wants right now is a wife who takes care of him. He needs to be off on his own. And so do I."

"You get divorce?"

"No. We just need some time away from each other."

We were on the street, and I was preparing for the usual race back to the zendo, when, to my utter amazement, he stopped, looked me straight in the face and said, "Okay, Fay-san. You come to Japan, train in monastery. But first you call and ask husband. If he not approve, you go home."

Ira was back in New York, and uncharacteristically chatty, when Fay finally reached him in his office. He told her that he'd joined a fitness club and started jogging, and, oh, yes, he'd begun writing a book on past-life therapy. Without stopping to let her get a word in, Ira buoyantly informed her that "Samuel" had correctly predicted a forthcoming six-figure offer from the New Age division of a prominent New York publishing house —which was why he was in the city, and on his way to a meeting with his editor when she called. Knowing he was in a hurry, Fay cut the conversation short, telling him only that she'd decided to join Eikei Roshi for a summer training period at Shofuji monastery in Japan. Sounding genuinely delighted, Ira offered to pay for both their air tickets. "Just use your credit card, for the tickets, for all your expenses. It's the least I can do. You don't know how happy it makes me to see that you've found your true spiritual path," he said. Seeing Ira's offer as yet another way of buying her out of his life, yet not wanting to appear ungrateful, Fay thanked him. Giving him Shofuji's location and telephone number, she was about to ask if he'd be back to meet her in New York around Labor Day when she returned from Japan, but after quickly telling her he loved her, Ira hung up.

PART III

13
SHOFUJI

Narita Airport was as clean and spare as a zendo. And, except for the brisk little policemen in white gloves shouting "*Mushi mushi*!" into walkie-talkies while directing pedestrian traffic, almost as quiet. The Arrivals Lounge was crowded with diminutive "company-men," all wearing exactly the same blue suits, all carrying identical gift boxes of XO Napoleon brandy. One white-haired gentleman had an authoritative air about him, but that was the only thing that distinguished him from the rest. Fay knew that the Japanese prized conformity and condemned individuality, but she was truly startled at seeing how alike they were.

The roshi was annoyed with his Tokyo hosts, the Hanakawas, for being late. When father and son finally appeared, he scowled and pointed at his watch. The two men responded with a peremptory bow and as far as Fay could make out, some excuse about the traffic. But she could tell that the roshi wasn't mollified. The son, Omu, who spoke a bit of English, introduced himself, and then his father. He wore a blue blazer, gray slacks, and Gucci loafers. Fay guessed him to be about thirty. He was slightly taller than his taciturn father, who had greeted her with a grudging nod without shaking her outstretched hand. Watching the roshi quibble with his hosts made her uncomfortable. Seeing that, despite his robes, no one at the airport had taken particular notice of him unnerved her. The customs officer had treated him rudely, scattering his underwear in search of hidden gifts from London, and the curbside porters in front of the Arrivals Building ignored him and went right on smoking and spitting when he shouted at them for help with the luggage. What unnerved her even more was that under the fluorescent airport lights the roshi's skin was no longer golden, but the color of Dijon mustard.

On their way to the car, Omu explained to her in halting English that the House of Hanakawa had supported Shofuji Monastery for six generations, and that his grandfather had favored old Ryuho Roshi while his parents were partial to Eikei. Omu shyly admitted that his family had never entertained a Westerner before, but he assured her that, as a student of their beloved roshi, she was most welcome. Fay had trouble adjusting to his punctuating every sentence with a bow and found herself dropping her head to her chest whenever he did. From the moment the Hanakawas came into view, Eikei ignored her entirely. Having shoved her into the back seat of their black Rover sedan along with the luggage, he launched a boisterous Japanese conversation with his chain-smoking companions.

They got stuck in a stomach-jolting stop-start traffic jam on a clogged two-lane highway. Omu, who had graciously crammed himself into the back seat alongside the mountain of luggage to give her more room, was smoking as well. It didn't seem to occur to him to ask if she minded. Fay looked out the window at the bleak industrial landscape dotted by skeletal bridges leading to enormous heaps of landfill and rickety shanties bordering the graffiti-sprayed freight cars on the tracks alongside the highway. Everything was so ugly. Except for the sky . . . which was luminous, stunningly mauve with pollutants and punctuated by a resplendent setting sun. Feeling carsick, she pressed the electric button and rolling down the window, stuck out her head. When she was five, on her first Sunday outing in her father's new green Buick, she'd vomited all over the back seat and been made to clean it up herself. *I will not vomit on the back seat of this car. I will not embarrass Eikei on my first day in Japan.* She took four deep breaths of fume-laden air and valiantly fought off her nausea. Groggily, she watched the immense orange ball of sun play hide and seek with the smokestacks lining the fields beyond the railroad tracks until the traffic started moving again.

She was still wet, hardly out of the Lilliputian shower in her dollhouse-sized hotel room when the telephone rang. Omu, who had not been exaggerating when he said her room would be small, was waiting for her in the lobby, right on time. Despite the shower, Fay was exhausted and longed to sleep. She dreaded meeting the rest of the Hanakawas and talking Pidgin English with Omu. She chastised herself for never having asked Jessie to teach her at least the rudiments of conversational Japanese. Straightening up, she did a few deep knee bends, slipped into her clogs, and throwing a red and black shawl over her shoulders, went downstairs.

Of course, Omu was smoking. Everybody in the lobby was smoking.

"You like raw fish?"

"Yes. Yes." He was walking too fast for her to keep up with him.

"You eat everything?"

Fay noted his stylish haircut. "Yes."

"Okay. Good."

Together they speed-walked through the wide, clean streets of an elegant residential neighborhood. Then Omu made an abrupt turn and entered an underpass that turned out to lead, not to a subway station, as she thought it would, but to a subterranean mall lined with shops and restaurants. Ushering her into an open sushi bar, he removed his shoes and set them on a platform into a row of perfectly aligned footgear of all shapes and sizes. Fay did likewise.

"Higashiyama!" Omu announced. "Oldest Japanese restaurant in Tokyo!"

Fay followed him into a tatami-covered room and was immediately confronted by the Hanakawas, who, like their shoes, were also lined up and silent. Mama and Papa sat on cushions at the head of a low table, Tomoe, Omu's pretty wife, was seated to their right, and the roshi was seated with his back to a scroll painting in a tiny alcove, the traditional place for honored guests. He had changed into a soft, flowing beige robe and matching tri-cornered brocade hat that looked positively elegant. A cushion had been left empty for Fay between the young Hanakawas. She lowered her eyes as she walked past the roshi to her seat. Perching uncomfortably on her knees, she looked across the table and found Mama Hanakawa giving her the once-over. Evidently satisfied with what she saw, Mama Hanakawa smiled and handed Fay her business card, which was printed in Japanese on one side and said "Managing Director" in English on the other, along with the company name and address. Mama Hanakawa had a round playful face, and a gold tooth that flashed when she smiled. But her jolly appearance was deceptive. She snapped orders at the kimono-clad waitress, made rude faces at her taciturn husband, and bullied the roshi. Before long, using Omu as her translator and gesturing with her plump, square-tipped fingers, Mama Hanakawa turned her full attention to Fay.

"She say you go Nikko, Nara, Kyoto, Kamakura. She say why you want bother going to monastery? Monastery boring place. Monks not good monks. Much more interesting sights in Japan," Omu repeated his mother's advice, smiling at Fay as he did so.

Tomoe, Omu's pretty wife, sat mutely at his side.

"Thank you. I'll try to see them all," Fay said, waiting for Omu's translation.

Leaping from her cushion with a great snort, Mama Hanakawa responded angrily, "She ask why you waste time with corrupt monk like Eieki?" Omu's face turned red as he translated his mother's outburst. Then he added a comment of his own: "I thought roshi bring someone fat."

Thinking she had misunderstood, Fay looked at Omu's lips and asked him to repeat what he'd said.

"Fat." Omu motioned with his hands in front of his chest, simulating big breasts.

The kimono-clad waitress poured sake all around. Omu drank and grew more voluble. No longer interested in Fay, Mama Hanakawa berated the waitress for a breach of service. At the head of the table, Eikei Roshi and Papa Hanakawa were drinking sake fast and punctuating their boisterous conversation with loud laughter. The sushi arrived, superbly displayed on an edible doily of pink radish flowerets and octopus-stuffed seashells. An exquisite miso-dipped tofu and shredded turnip salad dish came next, followed by foamy white custard on a glazed white plate. The roshi interrupted his boisterous conversation with Papa Hanakawa to call to Fay from across the table, "Wall, you don't have to eat it."

"What?"

"Wall!"

"He mean whale," Omu intervened.

Eikei nodded and resumed talking to Papa Hanakawa.

"I can't eat that," Fay said in a loud voice, shocking even Mama Hanakawa into speechlessness. "I'm against killing whales."

Omu, whose business specialty was food processing, said politely, "Yes, but you Americans kill cows, so many cows for hamburger. Japan fishmen must kill whales, must use every product."

Fay turned to Omu's pretty wife. "Very beautiful food."

"Yes, traditional Japanese," she answered in perfect, British-accented English.

"You speak English!" Fay said.

Tomoe put her hand to her mouth and giggled. "You do Zen," she said pettishly, then sat back on her cushion, mute and lovely as before.

Omu said, "Zen, well, I do not sit . . . Zen is not for young people in Japan. It is like church in America. Most people my generation don't care religion, don't go temple except for funeral."

Resuming the hangdog expression he'd worn when translating for his mother, Omu settled down to the serious business of eating whale.

Trays heaped with food kept coming out of the kitchen: eel in black lacquered boxes, fried tofu, clear soup, pickles, rice, an oily sliver of salmon on a ruffled lettuce leaf.

"March on bravely!" the roshi shouted. Papa Hanakawa laughed so hard he almost choked.

At the end of the meal, filled to bursting with sake and every dish but whale, Fay put on her shoes and staggered back to the hotel accompanied by Omu and his pretty wife. The roshi and the elder Hanakawas had gotten into the family sedan and driven off into the night without so much as a farewell.

"Do you know Tano Roshi, the abbot of Shofuji

monastery?" Tomoe asked testily. With her in-laws gone, she'd grown bold.

"No, but I'm looking forward—"Fay answered.

"He is a very funny man."

Fay wanted to ask Tomoe what she meant by "funny." Strange? Eccentric? But Omu wouldn't let her get the words out. "All roshis different. My mother calls Eikei a 'corrupt monk.' Tano Roshi is . . . ah, funny. And the old Ryuho Roshi is crazy." He put his finger to his temple, and his wife slapped it away, laughing. But not before remembering to cover her mouth with the other hand.

Perched on a mountaintop surrounded by modern suburban sprawl, Shofuji looked more like a theme park than a venerable Zen monastery. Subdivisions leading to and away from it were being gashed out of every neighboring hill and hummock. The citizens of the surrounding towns were frantically building carports the size of airport hangars, annexing them to their matchbox houses, and the air was abuzz with the incessant jackhammering, sawing, and droning of an ambitious highway construction project designed to span the one-hundred-plus-mile-distance between Tokyo, Mishima Prefecture, Mount Fuji, and the Sea of Japan.

The detours leading around the construction sites invading the once quiet countryside took half an hour to navigate. Eikei slept as the taxi driver pointed out to her what was left of the scenery in unintelligible English. Fay kept telling herself she'd done the right thing by coming to Shofuji . . . to Japan, in general. But when they finally pulled up to the front gate and stopped in front of the Main Hall, she was tempted to order the taxi driver to take her back to the airport. Eikei, now awake and sitting next to her in glum silence, smoking up a storm, and probably still angry at her for letting Ira pay for his plane ticket, was sorry he'd invited her to Japan and would be glad to be rid of her. Suddenly, he jumped out and started pulling the luggage out of the trunk. The driver remained seated behind the wheel, not making a move to help him. Now was the time to say she'd changed her mind and wanted to go back to New York. Or she could stay. Too late. Eikei was already beckoning to a tall, black-robed monk who'd come out of the Main Hall and was approaching the taxi.

Fay paid and over-tipped the driver; then, inhaling and counting, "One" as she exhaled, got out of the taxi. Leaving the bags in charge of the monk, Eikei walked up the porch steps of the Main Hall, and without so much as giving her a backward glance, disappeared inside. The monk slammed down the trunk of the taxi, and the driver sped off in a shower of gravel.

"The zendo is closed, so you won't be sitting in meditation today. I'm to show you to your *daishi*—women's quarters." Fay did a double take: the tall, black-robed "monk" was an Englishwoman with a shaved head and a crazed look in her eyes. No introductions. No welcome. The woman picked up the bags and swinging them over her back like a teamster, led Fay down a cinder path away from the Main Hall.

"The monk in charge of the zendo hates meditation, so he just locks it up," the woman said sourly as they passed a bamboo grove surrounding a lotus pond.

The picture-book prettiness of the scenery could not dispel the overall despondency of the place, or of the Englishwoman's contempt, or of Fay's mood as she followed behind her. Beyond the bamboo grove there was a huge wooden building fronted by a raised platform. "The kitchen," snapped the Englishwoman. Fay looked into the open doorway. A roaring fire in an open grate cast a sinister glow across the smoke-stained walls of a cavernous room. Two simmering vats hanging over a cast iron hearth resembled a pair of medieval witch's cauldrons. No one tended the fire. The kitchen was eerily empty.

They reached a small cottage in a bowl-shaped clearing bordered by cedar and pine trees, and the Englishwoman led Fay inside. The cottage was hotter than a boiler room.

"You'd better get used to it . . . Japan in July. People are known to drop on the streets like flies. There's no air-conditioning in the monastery. And no heating in winter. You either boil or freeze to death—nothing in between. Part of Zen training entails overcoming your vulnerability to the elements."

"I'm Fay Corman," Fay put out her hand.

"Priscilla Devon," mumbled the Englishwoman, turning away to lead her into a tiny wooden toilet. "Here's the water closet and bath. It's a complicated affair that takes the better part of an hour to heat—that is, if you can't do without warm water. And you're not to waste water or leave the gas on and asphyxiate yourself during the night."

Fay wished Priscilla would leave so she could pee and make herself a cup of tea in the kitchenette she'd spied on entering the cottage.

"Morning service is at 4:30 in the Main Hall. I'll fetch you, but you are responsible for waking up on time yourself. I do hope you've brought an alarm clock. The last American woman who came thought she'd be awakened by the monks' bell. But we're too far from the monks' quarters to hear it, so we women must make do on our own."

Fay was now desperate for Priscilla to leave; she had to pee so badly. To her relief, Priscilla started to walk toward the screen door. Then she suddenly stopped and glared down at the sandals Fay had left on the porch. "You aren't supposed to wear your own sandals. There's a pair of regulation straw sandals in the wardrobe. You'll wear those at all times."

Fay nodded.

"And I strongly advise you to remove your lipstick, no perfumed soap or cologne, either. You're not to stimulate the monks." Pushing aside the screen door, Priscilla abruptly walked out, and Fay made a dash for the toilet.

At her high school in San Antonio, where she'd been admonished by Miss Prince for not wearing a hairnet in cooking class, Fay had developed the knack of turning for comfort to "Buddy," her alter-ego. As Priscilla's footsteps crunched down the gravel path separating the women's cottages, it was "Buddy" who mimicked her low, British-accented growl: "You're not to stimulate the monks . . . no perfumed soap . . . and no cologne, either." Then it was Fay again, responding in her own voice: "Fuck you, Miss Priscilla Devon."

Shofuji Monastery
Mishima Prefecture, Japan
July 28, 1984

The monks love Tano Roshi for his leniency, his fondness for washing machines, vacuum cleaners, and cars. Anything that will make their lives easier. There are at least three cars here, even a snappy red Toyota pickup truck. Still, monastery life remains a hybrid blend of the latest in modern conveniences and medieval squalor. A case in point: the twenty modern self-flush Toto toilets for guests, back-to-back with the twenty matching lime pits servicing those of us who live here. As Shofuji's newest recruit, I'm in charge of cleaning them all. Not that I mind. The toilets are far away from Priscilla, who spends the work periods proving herself as strong and tough as the monks by pruning branches in the orange grove and lugging cordwood to the kitchen from what's left of the forest that borders the monastery.

Though I do my best to stay out of her way, she always manages to catch up with me on the path to the refectory when we're going to breakfast. Tano Roshi has permitted me to take off after I've finished cleaning my toilets, and Priscilla insists that he's only cut me slack because I'm a "guest" and not an actual "novice-in-training." She sneers as she says the word "guest." Then she starts her Jane Eyre torture routine. Did I know that old Ryuho Roshi is locked up in a hut above the Main Hall and that he's dangerously psychotic? That he sometimes escapes on full-moon nights and appears stark naked outside my cottage windows and howls like a dog? "Surely," she promises, giving me her perversely gleeful smile, "you'll be treated to one of his visits soon, especially as his beloved mother died in your cottage and is believed to haunt it still."

I'm tempted to ask Priscilla why she's chosen to remain at Shofuji if she hates it so much, but I don't want to give her the satisfaction of a reply. Instead, I pick up my rags and water bucket and head for the toilets where I'll be alone and at peace.

"Don't forget, you're to clean out the pits by hand," she calls after me, flushed with sadistic pleasure. "No sponge-on-a-stick here!"

"Up yours," I mutter, giving her the finger as I walk off in the opposite direction.

With Eikei nowhere to be seen and only Priscilla for company, I wake up at precisely four every morning, roll out of my futon, wash my face, brush my teeth, get into my monks' suit and straw sandals, and step out into the darkness. Staring down at Priscilla's raw bare feet on the path in front of me, I pad along in the glow of her "torch"—British for "flashlight"—though "torch" most aptly suits her Inquisitorial persona.

We arrive at the Main Hall even before the monks are awake. Once there, I sit on a bench near the open toilet nibbling on a green tea biscuit I've hidden in my pocket while waiting for the hacking, spitting, peeing monks to prepare for the meditation period that precedes the early morning sutra chanting service. (By the way, Priscilla was lying when she said I wouldn't get to meditate; the zendo monk may hate sitting zazen, but it's his duty to open the zendo every morning and lead the meditation and chanting. And hate it or not, as long as he's here, he's got to carry out his duties or he'll be beaten for insubordination.)

Priscilla swishes by in her black robes like Torquemada. She points to the women's platform behind a screen separating us from the monks (It's no better here for women than it was with the Sufis in Brooklyn). The lantern-faced zendo monk pushes aside the screens to the porch and the lonely sound of the morning bell announces the first period of zazen. Ting! Ting! Ting! We sit for thirty minutes, after which the sullen zendo monk signals us to our feet and hurries us out onto the wooden walkway leading to the Main Hall. Awkward in my straw sandals, I make flapping noises as I run along last in line. Priscilla turns to scowl at me, and I am very pleased.

Most of the monks here at Shofuji are from temple families; they're men in their early twenties who consider themselves unlucky for being eldest sons forced to become priests so they can inherit the family business. They are, for the most part, lazy and disgruntled. Some of them already have their fiancés handpicked for them by their parents. These are the ones who rush through services and sleep during zazen in order to make the time pass by quickly. They can't wait until the day they leave here so they can sleep late while their wives cook, clean, make babies, and keep their parishioners at bay. Needless to say, they have no interest in "enlightenment." In the old days, they had to remain at the monastery for two years. Now the training period of Zen temple priests has been cut down to six months!

The second most common variety of monk is the one born into a lower-class family that hopes to climb up in the world by producing a priest. The zendo monk is one of these: a barely literate farmer, but tough and shrewd with a taste for hard physical work and equally hard drinking (what Eikei would call a "crabgrass person"). The third kind of monk is rare: we have only one, as far as I can tell. They're often in their late thirties, men with university educations and promising careers whose search for the answers to life and death questions caused them to turn their backs on the world and become monks, some even leaving their wives and children behind. Most come from well-to-do families. Hiro-san, the head monk, is one of these. He is small, delicate, and wears round, wire-rimmed glasses. He appeared at my side one morning as I was standing at the post-breakfast bonfire watching the garbage burn.

"I was a political leftist before I became a monk," he said in lightly accented English. Just like that, with no introductions, not even telling me his name or asking mine.

"So was I," I said.

"I am Hiro-san." He reached into the sleeve of his robe and handed me an orange. "I was educated by Catholic Brothers all my life, in English . . . I even think in English . . . Western religion, philosophy, later, Marxist politics. I wanted to change the world. I thought Japan was backward."

A Catholic Marxist! Here, in the unlikeliest of places, was the Japanese mirror image of Sergio Ruiz!

"Then what?"

"I attended a lecture by Ryuho Roshi at my university. I came to challenge the roshi, to heckle him. I called out while he was talking, asked him how Zen proposed to change the world, make it more bearable for the suffering masses. The audience was stunned at my rudeness. One of the monitors was about to throw me out of the lecture hall. But Ryuho held up his hand signaling that I was to be allowed to stay. He looked at me quietly for a few seconds. Then he said very gently, 'Who is it

that wants to change the world? Find me this man first and then talk to me of change.' That confrontation resulted in my becoming his monk."

"Yes, that sounds like Ryuho Roshi. I never met him myself, but my dance teacher, who was one of his first students in the States, said she knew he was her Zen teacher after meeting him for the first time at a tea ceremony. She said all it took was seeing him whip green tea in a bowl." I threw the orange peel into the fire, watching it curl and blacken. "And now, do you still consider him to be your teacher?"

"No. Tano Roshi is my teacher since Ryuho Roshi became sick."

I was about to ask Hiro-san about the mysterious "sickness" that kept Ryuho Roshi locked up in his mountaintop hermitage, but I was interrupted by the agitated zendo monk who wedged himself between us and started tossing garbage into the fire, spreading sparks everywhere. "You go working! Clean shitting place!" he jabbered at me in broken English. Hiro-san tried calming him down, but the zendo monk turned on him and the two of them got into an elaborate Japanese argument, so I left.

Except for a glimpse of him on the morning of a patron's banquet, on her way back to her cottage after cleaning the toilets, Fay hadn't seen Eikei Roshi since the day she first arrived at Shofuji. As she was standing on the porch, about to push aside the screen door, she looked down and saw that he'd left her a box of strawberries, a packet of Emmentaler cheese, and a tin of green tea biscuits. Recalling how he'd hurried past her along the cinder path in his beige stocking cap and wooden clogs with a cigarette dangling from his lips, changing direction so as to avoid meeting her, she wondered why he was leaving gifts at her door and giving her the silent treatment at the same time? She thought of asking Hiro-san about the roshi's strange behavior, but decided it wasn't appropriate. She was a novice (Priscilla would have said "guest") in a Zen monastery and had no right to special treatment. Eikei had left her food to let her know he hadn't forgotten her. She would have to content herself with that.

A week later, shortly after the morning sutra chanting service, the zendo monk knocked on the door of her cottage to announce that the abbot was leaving for Europe and wished to interview her informally in the kitchen.

On the raised platform that served as the monks' dining area, Tano Roshi stood among his three attendants directing the packing of his dozen trunks and cartons with a soft, fleshy index finger. A small, conical-shaped volcano with glutinous skin, slashes for eyes, and two thick lines for a mouth, he bellowed instructions at the scurrying monks in a deep bass voice, his imperious finger-pointing belied by his jovial delivery. It was the first time Fay had seen him up close. In the mornings, when she was sitting too far back in the woman's section to get a good look, Tano Roshi would enter the Main Hall poised on the balls of his feet with the portly grace of a performing walrus. With one deft fling, he would cast his red silk bowing mat to the floor, bow three times before the Buddha on the altar, roll up his bowing mat, and scurry out of the Main Hall before the monks had finished chanting the last line of the Great Vows. His outfits were lavish, produced with an eye toward elevating his height and social status.

Tano wore his colorful reputation like a badge. Monks and monastery supporters alike boasted about his wartime career as a sketcher of dirty pictures. Everyone but Priscilla seemed impressed by the abbot's artistic talent and humble origins. Driven by British class snobbery, Priscilla never ceased to dwell on Tano Roshi's "bad taste." This only increased Fay's interest in him. She took to watching him more closely during morning services, turning her attention away from the sutra book and following his every move. She soon found herself eagerly looking forward to his ceremonial displays of sartorial splendor: the sunflower-gold robes and saffron surplices, the purple brocade vests worn inside out with the label showing. She marveled at Tano's dancer's sense of timing, his graceful hand gestures, the confidence with which he had forged such a unique and magnificent persona. She thrilled to see him prance into the Main Hall and depending on his mood, boom or whisper the sutras while fingering his amber rosary beads with his eyes closed, his features disappearing into their soft mask of flesh as if they were being stretched taut under a nylon stocking.

Now here she was, standing face to face with the remarkable Tano Roshi himself, holding her "interview gift," the bottle of Jamaican rum she'd bought for him in London, in her outstretched hand. For three weeks she'd kept it hidden in her suitcase, waiting for the occasion to present it, never imagining that her first interview with the abbot of Shofuji would not only take place in the kitchen, but that it would also be her last—for he was to die of a myocardial infarct almost two years to the day of their first meeting, in Italy, while enjoying a ride in a Venetian gondola.

"Firewater," Tano said, laughing. "Stomach on fire, you drink that." He pointed his soft plump finger at his navel.

"Caribbean firewater," Fay said.

"Make crazy," Tano replied, giving her a cunning grin.

They both laughed, and the interview was over. The abbot clapped his hands once, and, loading themselves up like mules, his three attendants carried all twelve bags and cartons outside and deposited them in the bed of his red pickup truck. Fay stood watching as Tano Roshi and his driver got into the front seat and shortly after careened down the circular driveway. She was still standing there when Priscilla crept up behind her and said, "He's a wonderful Zen teacher, but he hates women because his mother abandoned him at birth. He calls us *akema*, evil spirits."

"Then why do you study with him?"

"Because he is the only enlightened monastery abbot in Japan who will let me study with him." Priscilla turned sharply and walked away, her straw sandals crunching against the driveway gravel.

It was the first time Fay had heard anyone at Shofuji use the word "enlightened," and it worked on her like a subtle poison. Plagued by doubts, she wondered whether Eikei was really enlightened, or if he had faked it, hiding the lie under his quirky Zen master façade. For days afterward, instead of counting her breaths on her meditation cushion, she tormented herself with questions. Could unlikable, vicious, immoral, and crazy people be enlightened? She pictured Tano Roshi, that brilliant shifting bundle of amorphous flesh, sketching hairy vulvas and frying pork chops in his private kitchen, the fragrant smoke purling from the chimney making her mouth water as she cleaned the lime pits. Tano didn't look or act like an enlightened person. But then, what did an enlightened person look like? Ryuho Roshi? But he was locked up in his hermitage, rumored to have hair down to his ankles and nails like tiger claws. She compared Eikei and Tano, the two most commonly agreed upon "enlightened" people at Shofuji. Tano was soft and easygoing; Eikei was hard and testy. Both were "crabgrass" monks who'd been scoured raw by years of Zen training; neither, as far as she could tell, was "needy." They were the opposite of "needy," in fact. What happened to you once the bottom dropped out of your ego? Did you never again need a friend or a "partner"? Was enlightenment like Jamaican firewater that made you "crazy"? Could that have been what Omu and his wife meant when they'd laughed about Ryuho Roshi? Poor Priscilla had certainly been driven crazy by Tano Roshi's strange ideas about women. Imagine working with a Zen teacher who called you an evil spirit! Fay was glad Tano had gone off to Europe leaving Eikei in charge. Eikei was a drill sergeant, but at least he didn't think of her as an evil spirit. A greenhouse person, yes. But all Westerners, including men, were in that category.

Fay longed to hear more from Priscilla. She desperately missed speaking intimately in English to a Westerner, to an experienced woman Zen practitioner, like Jessie. But Priscilla never gave her an opening. She was too intent on killing her ego to make friends with Fay, too busy chewing the poisoned capsule of her womanhood down to a fine powder of time-released rage.

Fay spent her free time rolled up in her futon falling in and out of sleep. She dreamed she and Ira were lying in a sun-drenched meadow in the English countryside, that he was handing her a bouquet of buttercups. She dreamed they were dancing at a wedding, that she was wearing a black velvet dress and star-shaped diamond earrings, and that Ira leaned over and nibbled at the diamonds in her earlobes. The dreams left her lethargic, with no appetite, and she frequently skipped meals.

She wondered if Shofuji wasn't driving her a little crazy.

14
FUNERAL SEASON

Shofuji Monastery
August 3, 1984

We have a constant stream of guests, so I've been scouring the toilets from top to bottom every day. Instead of tiring me out, all this physical work has made me manic. I've been on a cleaning binge. Yesterday, when I got back from cleaning the toilets, I still had so much energy left that I dusted every inch of the cottage, polished the floors, washed the windows, did the laundry, and hung it out to dry. I'm trying to be very "Zen" about it all. Just going along with each moment, taking it as it comes. I don't want to think about what will happen when I crash.

Priscilla came by to say she was taking the weekend off, staying with friends in Kyoto. What friends? Who would have Priscilla as a friend? Of course, I didn't ask her. We stood in the doorway of the cottage staring each other down for a while. When Priscilla saw that I wasn't going to invite her in, she cleared her throat and said, "I don't suppose you could do me a favor?"

I gave her a suspicious look. "What is it?"

"I've left enough cat and dog food . . . well, you see, um, there's a small army of stray animals who've collected themselves around me, um, particularly a dog—my number one problem—Ryuho Roshi's abandoned pet."

Amazed that Priscilla could actually care for anything besides her own precious enlightenment, I relented and invited her in. Refusing the invitation, but still standing in my doorway, she said, "I'm surprised you never spotted him. He's quite bedraggled, really. Looks like a ghost running through the bamboo grove."

"No, I never have," I said.

Priscilla looked down at her chapped red feet and said, "Well, I've been feeding him since Ryuho Roshi abandoned him, and several wild cats who can take better care of themselves than poor Sherau . . . that's his name. It means 'white'."

"What about the monks? Why don't they look after him?"

Her pity obviously reserved only for animals that didn't talk, Priscilla said disdainfully, "Haven't you learnt about them yet? They torture animals. I've seen them kick Sherau in the ribs and set fire to the cats' tails . . . They're brutes. Besides, Tano Roshi has imbued them with his own superstitious hatred of animals—particularly cats, who, he says, embody evil female spirits."

Not wanting to hear more, I promised Priscilla I would care for the animals and wished her a pleasant trip.

Beset by rainstorms, the bamboo grove came alive and moaned. The pine trees shivered and tossed their branches over the roof of Fay's cottage, and the wind shook the fragile windowpanes so hard that they cracked. One morning after breakfast, she found a note from Eikei on the kitchen bulletin board instructing her to "clean toilets twice today. Big funeral ceremony. Make sparkle for monastery patrons."

Later that morning, as she was hurrying from her cottage to an early lunch, she heard the telephone ring in Hiro-san's office behind the kitchen. There was some garbled shouting, and then Hiro-san himself ran out into her path. "It's for you. A man's voice from America!" He cried into the rain, his arms flailing like millwheels.

Ira, it must be Ira. Fay ran toward the office.

She picked up the telephone just as the monks started chanting the meal sutra. She knew they would not wait, that if she wanted to eat, she would have to talk fast. She wished they would slow down the chanting, but they seemed to be hurrying it along even faster than usual. With the indulgent Tano gone, Eikei's strict rules against lingering over meals wouldn't spare them the time.

"You sound good," Ira shouted in answer to her hello. "A little detached."

Knowing he wanted to hear the code words that would absolve him of responsibility for her neediness, Fay laughed. "It's my samurai Zen training."

Ira laughed, a shivery sound that rattled and echoed across the storm-tossed telephone lines.

"What about you? How's the book going?"

"Great. I'm in L.A. working on interviews with Sam. Tom and the team are back in San Francisco compiling the case data."

"Really? How long are you going to stay in California this time?"

"As long as they need me. I'm booked for a month of past-life therapy workshops, and they're already oversubscribed, so I can't say. They're being held at the Beverly Hills Hotel. But

Sam and I are always on the move and you're staying in one place, so it's best if I call you. You can always leave a message with Tom Clerkson in San Francisco if there's an emergency. I'll try to call you every week anyway. I can't tell you exactly what day, but I'll keep you informed of my whereabouts."

The call was on its way to being over. She would have to speak fast. "Sure . . .

Let's both keep each other informed of our whereabouts," she said wanly.

There was a pause; then, in an unfamiliar, gravelly voice, Ira said, "I love you, Fay. Never forget that. I love you."

She waited for him to beg her to take the next plane to L.A., to come back into his bed, because it was too awful without her, but he didn't. "I love you too," she said. Then the roof shook and the line went dead.

Fay placed the receiver back in its cradle and stood staring down at Hiro-san's open accounts ledger with its unintelligible Japanese squiggles. Then she looked up at the calligraphy on the wall, and below it, at the stained teapot on its hotplate and realized she was about to cry. Wiping the gathering tears from her eyes with her sleeve, she tiptoed back to her place on the tatami mat at the long narrow bench that served as a dining table and sat down among the monks. In a few minutes her knees would be numb, her ankles prickling. She would have to eat twice as fast as everyone else to catch up. Fumbling with her bowls and chopsticks, she struggled not to think of Ira. She remembered Eikei telling her once that he didn't love anyone, not even his mother or his sister. There was no room in samurai Zen training, he said, for messy female notions about love— Samurai didn't fall in love. To them, love meant sacrifice, loyalty, and honor. She repeated the words in her head, keying them to the pace of her chewing. But it was no use, she'd been infected by Ira's passionate declaration of love, had even begun to imagine that, like her, the monks, too, were brooding, tired of the rain, tired of endlessly cleaning the monastery, sick of rice and pickles, curious about the telephone call from far away, and hungry for a bit of messy female love themselves.

Hiro-san sat at the head of the table munching on a salted plum. The telephone call coming in the middle of lunch seemed to have unsettled him. He flitted, making an awkward charade of ignoring her, chanting shrilly and snapping his fingers to show he was angry with the cook for passing the food around too slowly.

Eikei arrived as they were reciting the last meal sutra, his face red and pinched. He joined the chanting in a high, cracked voice that grated against Fay's spine and made her want to stick her fingers in her ears to shut it out. She could feel the food turn in her stomach, a bolus of pickles, radish, salted plums, seaweed soup, turnips, rice, and cold chard. Two days ago, they'd been served fresh tomatoes, and she'd lunged at them greedily. She thought about the packet of cheese Eikei had left at her door the day before, and her mouth watered. Sherau had been standing next to her on the porch, sniffing at the cheese as she stooped to pick it up. But when she had tried coaxing the dog inside, he'd turned away, running off and disappearing into the bamboo grove. Sherau had continued to pay her occasional visits, but she could never get him to come inside. She wondered where the dog had spent the night during all that rain.

Eikei announced a free hour after lunch while he and the senior monks prepared for the funeral ceremony. As Fay was standing in front of the kitchen door putting on her sandals, he came up behind her and tapped her on the shoulder. "Okay you sit in Main Hall with ladies," he said tersely. "Good opportunity to see typical Zen-style funeral."

At two o'clock the mourners started trickling into the Main

Hall. As Hiro-san directed Fay to her seat, he informed her that the deceased had been a local schoolteacher with many friends and relatives from abroad. She wanted to ask him if all funerals were as elaborate as this one, with its massive flower displays and fruit baskets, swirling clouds of pungent incense, and most unusually, the never displayed Zen master's traditional red lacquer High Seat standing at the center of the hall in front of the golden-faced Buddha on the altar. But before she could open her mouth to speak, Hiro-san had already gone.

Fay's seat among the women was close enough to the oversized photo of the deceased on the altar for her to study the elderly kind face of a man with a sad smile and pouches under his eyes. Eikei had told her not to wear her blue monk's suit but a black "lady dress," and judging from the elegantly dressed, made-up women in black designer suits and veiled hats, wearing pearl necklaces the size of pennies, she saw why. In her capacity as "novice monk," Fay, of course, wasn't wearing any jewelry or makeup, and her black skirt and blouse were salvaged from the wrinkled "civilian clothes" in her suitcase, which left her feeling like a bag lady who'd stumbled into a Chanel fashion show. Because the women were all dressed alike and showed no outward signs of grief, she couldn't tell which one of them was the widow—until the woman sitting in front of her, closest to the altar, quietly wiped away an occasional tear with a lace-edged handkerchief. Gathered opposite were the men, all wearing the same black three-piece suits, white shirts, and gray silk ties, all perspiring and wiping their faces with the same expensive oversize handkerchiefs. Judging from the affluence of the guests, Fay knew the monks would dine in style that night.

A sudden rustle in the doorway announced Eikei Roshi and his entourage. Fay caught her breath at the sight of him in his magnificent gold brocade clerical robes and royal blue surplice. Carrying the traditional Zen master's red lacquer fly whisk under his arm, his immaculate white tabi barely touching the floor, Eikei approached the High Seat with the stiff, deliberate movements of a Kabuki dancer accompanied by a chorus of sutra-chanting monks and the eerie clamor of cymbals, drums, and bells. Taking the High Seat, the roshi assumed his by-now familiar stony "sesshin face," wearing it like a theatrical mask throughout the formalities following his spectacular entrance.

First, a man in a black cutaway carrying a folder slipped out of the men's section and stepped up to a microphone on a small dais that had been specifically constructed for the occasion to one side of the altar. The man in the cutaway removed a sheaf of telegrams from the folder and started reading condolences in a shrill, singsong voice. When the last telegram had been read and the condolence reader had returned to the men's section, Eikei slowly rose from the High Seat, and turning around to face the altar, took three slow ceremonial steps before removing a lit incense stick from its holder, tracing a circle of smoke around the photograph of the deceased. After replacing the incense stick in its holder and sweeping away the smoke with his fly whisk, the roshi returned to the High Seat. Fay marveled at the choreographic perfection of each dramatic gesture, however small and insignificant it might appear to the mourners who were discreetly hiding their yawns behind their handkerchiefs.

Again, the man in the cutaway approached the microphone, this time calling on members of the funeral party to speak. Several friends and relatives got up and made speeches, most of them brief. But then a heavyset man with beautifully manicured fingernails came up and talked at length to the photograph, engaging the dead man in a one-sided conversation laced with laughter, and even a few tears. An unexpected display of emotion for a Japanese man, Fay thought, stifling a yawn.

She looked at her watch. It was four o'clock and the ceremony showed no sign of ending. She folded and unfolded her legs under her long black skirt. The mourners stopped coming to the microphone. The monks chanted. Eikei recited a poem in the high-pitched, nasal voice of a priest in a Kabuki play. Fay was on the verge of falling asleep when the roshi suddenly let out a ferocious yell: "KAAAAATZ!"—It was the traditional Rinzai Zen enlightenment shout Eikei was forever talking about but would never demonstrate for her no matter how much she pleaded to hear it. And now he was crying it out in front of an audience that had no idea what the yelling was about and didn't care. In fact, the man in the black cutaway hadn't even waited for the roshi's "KAAAAATZ" to end before returning to the microphone to resume reading condolence messages.

Eikei had had enough. He turned and abruptly left the Main Hall with the monks trailing after him.

The rain never stopped all that day. The ground was glutinous with mud, and the gutter pipes gushed noisy streams of water from the kitchen eaves. At five thirty, when the funeral guests had finally left, Fay took a meager supper along with the three novice monks who hadn't participated in the funeral ceremonies. Together they sat wordlessly, slurping their soup. The main dish was cold, unseasoned chopped chard. She reached for a salted pickle and mixed it in with the chard. She needed greens badly. In the mirror above the sink in her cottage bathroom, she had been watching daily as her skin grew dry and patchy from lack of oil.

She was washing the supper dishes when Hiro-san came out of his office behind the kitchen. "You look miserable," he said. Then putting his finger to his lips, he whispered, "Meet me outside when you're done. I have something for you. It's a standing fan from Tano Roshi's secret storehouse. Keep it in your room. Don't tell anyone. It will be paradise."

The fan was huge and clumsy, but the cottage was so humid and airless that she didn't have to think twice about accepting Hiro-san's offer. As she was dragging her prize through the mud, Kosen-san, a burly monk with a reputation for violence, jumped out of the bathhouse and blocked her path. He had a towel wrapped around his head and was bare-chested, wearing only black cotton pantaloons. In his hand he held a white shopping bag. Thinking he intended to grab the fan away from her, Fay took a step back. But to her surprise, instead of trying to take the fan, Kosen-san handed her the shopping bag. "For you," he said.

"Me?" She had never talked to Kosen-san. She'd stayed out of his way because Priscilla had told her he was an alcoholic with a black belt in karate who would knock down whoever happened to be standing next to him when he got drunk.

"Fruits," Kosen-san pointed at the shopping bag. "Fruits."

Fay looked into the bag and saw three bananas, three perfect Sunkist oranges, and a small green pineapple. "Thank you. Thank you very much," she took the bag from him. Now, with both hands full, she could only bob her head up and down to show her gratitude. Out of words in any shared language, the two of them stood looking at each other awkwardly. At last Fay took a step forward, the burly monk stepped aside, and each went their separate ways. Halfway to the cottage, when she thought he was out of earshot, she called out to the trees in the bamboo grove: "Thank you, Kosen-san, for the funeral fruits you filched from the altar! Thank you, Hiro-san, for the fan! Thank you both!" Answered by the sound of her own voice echoing through the valley, she hurried along, dragging the fan behind her with one hand and carrying the fruit-filled shopping bag in the other.

She was met at the cottage door by Sherau, the wettest dog in creation, an overjoyed mass of dirt and glistening fur. The dog eyed her unblinkingly, before running across the porch to eat from the bowl of soggy kibble she'd put out for him early that morning. When he'd licked the bowl clean, he hopped onto the ledge of the porch seeking shelter under the eaves. It was all the frightened dog would do to escape from the rain. He seemed to be limping. But no matter how much Fay pleaded with him, Sherau would not come into the cottage. Too exhausted to coax him further, she went inside and closed the door. Another funeral service was scheduled for the next day. Eikei had left her a second note on the kitchen board, letting her know in his inimitable English that he expected her to attend. Hiro-san had warned her that midsummer was 'funeral season.' But one funeral had been enough; she'd come to the monastery to practice Zen, not to attend church ceremonies or entertain wealthy patrons. Her enthusiasm for monastery life was waning fast; now she was exhausted, and all she wanted to do was sleep.

Looking out the window, she saw Sherau prick up his ears. Someone in the valley below was playing a melancholy tune on a flute. The dog began to howl. Keeping perfect time, waiting always for the last notes of the flute to die away, Sherau lifted his muzzle to the sky and howled along with the music. Fay didn't dare move for fear of startling him. The dog and the music stopped at exactly the same moment. It was as though old Ryuho Roshi was communicating with her through his dog. Again, she tried coaxing Sherau inside. At first he ignored her, then, edging a little closer to the screen door, he eyed her with a look of mistrust.

"I don't blame you," Fay said. "The way you've been

treated around here, why should you trust me?" Knowing that pain was the price of too much human contact, both dog and master had become hermits. Ryuho Roshi was hiding in his mountaintop hut; his dog had taken refuge on the porch of her cottage. They would both be okay. Neither of them needed her. Anyway, she was only a temporary "guest" at the monastery. Once she'd gone, both dog and master would again be at the mercy of their karma and the waywardness of the monks with whom they shared the mountain.

The rain fell interminably. Fay switched on the fan and aimed it at the futon. Then she stripped down to her panties, slipped into a T-shirt, and lay down. Peeling one of Kosen-san's oranges and eating it slowly, she reflected on the strange dream that had become her life. In the course of a single day, Ira had told her he loved her; Eikei had delivered his thundering KAAAATZ! and Ryuho Roshi's dog had serenaded her. What was next?

When she woke up, it was dark and her alarm clock read, one. Too early to roll out of the futon and prepare for morning service. A cow down in the valley had interrupted her sleep with its mournful lowing. Fay buried herself deeper into the futon. When she next awoke, sunlight was pouring through the window, the alarm clock read, eight-thirty, and Eikei was calling her from the doorway.

"Fay-san! What happen? You miss morning service. You sick?"

"No, I'm just tired."

"Ah . . . you thinking, thinking, thinking. Nothing come out," he said amiably.

"You wouldn't understand," she mumbled into the pillow.

"What you say?"

"I'm tired."

"Tomorrow, you come with Hiro-san and me to French restaurant. You feel better. Okay?"

Food again. She was sick of being ignored, then lured like a child by the promise of food. The game had grown stale, and she no longer wanted to play.

"You meet these people I introduce through friends. One is a medical doctor, like your husband. The other man owns French restaurant, like in Paris."

She longed to tell him to shut up and go away, to quit stuffing her with food and start treating her like an adult, like Hiro-san, or like any of the other monks, even Kyu-san, the cook, who was only nineteen. She longed to stop the Zen game of being treated like shit and then stroked. She couldn't take it anymore.

Eikei pushed aside the screen door and came inside. It was the first time he had ever entered the cottage. Men were not permitted in the women's quarter, not even roshis. Here she was in bed, to the bargain, in her T-shirt and panties, with her cropped hair sticking up in clumps and her eyes red from having cried herself back to sleep.

"You look terrible," Eikei said, sitting down cross-legged on the tatami mat opposite her. She noticed that, despite the heat, he was wearing his antic weskit and ridiculous woolen stocking hat.

"You don't look so good yourself."

Pointing his finger at her, Eikei laughed. "Ira-san call you and make you lonely for home, no?"

"Yes."

The roshi moved close enough for her to reach out and touch the index finger he was pointing at her. She felt the warmth of his body then remembered that she had forgotten to hide the forbidden fan when he'd appeared at the door. Standing there, noisily blasting air at them, it was the perfect emblem of her greenhouse frailty. "Hiro-san gave it to me," she said apologetically, pointing at the fan in the hope of deflecting his gaze away from her. In all the time they'd spent together, Fay and Eikei Roshi had never so much as shaken hands, and now they were sitting only inches across from each other in her cottage, close enough for him to look at her in her T-shirt and panties with the same appraising gaze he'd reserved for the giraffe at the London Zoo—maybe even measuring the size of her vagina, too.

"I know. I tell him to," Eikei said softly.

"You did?"

He nodded.

The cow moaned in the valley. "She kept me up all night," Fay said, grateful for the opportunity to change the subject.

"You sleep today. Tomorrow we go to French restaurant. Big supporter treat us in style." Eikei sprang up from the tatami without using his hands and walked to the door. Stopping in front of it, he lit a cigarette. Then without looking back or saying good-bye, he stepped out onto the porch.

Fay got up and watched the roshi walk down the path leading away from the monastery toward town. She did not return to her futon until his beige weskit and stocking hat were no longer visible among the trees.

15
THAT EXTRA JAW MUSCLE

Shofuji Monastery
August 12, 1984

Mr. Yamato, the owner of the French restaurant, came to pick us up in his custom-designed Toyota Camry. Priscilla was not invited, so I was the only woman in the car, and, of course, the conversation was entirely in Japanese. Eikei sat up front with Mr. Yamato, wearing the same princely outfit he wore the night we dined with the Hanakawas in Tokyo. Let me see, that was at Higashiyama's, on the night of our arrival . . . How many eons ago? Hiro-san sat between me and Mr. Yamato's nephew in the back seat pretending I didn't exist. Without the roshi ordering him to, he didn't dare translate so much as a word for my benefit. So I spent most of the forty-five-minute drive to Hakone making up my own version of the men's conversation, imagining sexist jokes at my expense, stock market quotations, monastery gossip, and every anti-American cliché I could conjure up to divert myself. After a while, I got so bored, that I asked the nephew in French how he liked the Tour D'Argent, because Eikei had mentioned as we were getting into the car that he'd trained with his uncle as a chef in Paris for two years. The nephew didn't even look at me, no response whatsoever. The uncle, however, had apparently understood my question, and interrupted his conversation with Eikei to inform me—through Hiro-san, whom he addressed in Japanese from the rear-view mirror—that, apart from the names of food and wines, neither of them had learned much French. For some reason, this struck me as hilariously funny, and I burst out laughing. Too long and too loud, as it turned out, because Eikei swiveled around and glared at me. Women, I remembered too late, do not speak in Japan unless they are spoken to; decent women do not laugh out loud with their mouths open—and I had done both. Fortunately, we pulled up to the restaurant then.

We walked down a steep flight of carpeted stairs and through a vestibule smelling of overcooked egg and were ushered into the restaurant proper and seated at a table elaborately set with gold-rimmed dinner plates and sculpted crystal goblets. We were the only diners, as Mr. Yamato had closed the restaurant to the public for the evening. A second monastery patron joined us a few minutes later and was introduced as "the doctor." Something about him—maybe it was his handsome silver shock of hair, or his distinguished tweeds and Sulka tie, or his refined manners—prompted me to say a few words to him in English, and the doctor gave me a polite English reply. He also shook my hand Western style instead of bowing, which made me almost giddy with gratitude. Unfortunately, the doctor's English was limited to polite greetings, and he soon displayed a penchant for launching long Japanese monologues. Though he did make an effort to include me by making eye contact and waiting for Hiro-san to translate his monologues for me into English. That is, until Eikei got annoyed at the interruptions and ordered Hiro-san to stop.

The meal opened with a traditional Japanese tea ceremony, with Hiro-san doing the officiating. That took almost an hour. By the time we finished I had a splitting hunger headache. The waiter passed around a basket of hot towels and then a tray of Japanese hors d'oeuvres accompanied by several bottles of red and white wine. First there was sherry, then cold sake, then an awful resinous Japanese Blanc de Blanc, then an excellent French Chablis, then a passable German Moselle . . . and on and on it went. I made so many trips to the toilet that Eikei suggested in a loud voice, in English, that I change seats with Hiro-san "before you have accident!" Feeling my face go red, I looked around the table to see if anyone had taken note of my humiliation, but the men were all too busy talking and drinking.

"You like?" Mr. Yamato pleaded with me after every sip of wine (As the only Westerner at the table, I had been appointed chief wine taster).

"Ah . . . very . . . ah, crisp," I said, trying not to wrinkle my nose as the resinous Blanc de Blanc burned its way into my gut. After six and a half glasses of assorted wines, it was impossible to distinguish a glass of port from a Margarita. Besides, I was having enough trouble keeping my trips to the toilet to a minimum so as not to ruffle Eikei's feathers.

Seated to my right, Hiro-san, his nose red from drinking, wasn't eating a thing. Not that there was anything much to eat: not one slice of bread, not so much as a pat of butter had been placed on the table. We weren't even served water; the crystal goblets having been appropriated for the endless flow of wine. At last, the waiter appeared with a tiny fish paté, which I tried eating slowly with all the appreciation I could muster, since Mr. Yamato's eyes were trained directly on my mouth. The sauce swimming around the paté, a sugary Japanese plum wine concoction, made it virtually inedible. Still trying to be polite, I looked up at Mr. Yamato after every bite and enthusiastically nodded my approval. A creamed green tea soup followed next, then a tepid rolled fish filet in another version of the inedible Japanese plum wine sauce, each course accompanied by a new bottle of wine. I felt like a guest at a Roman orgy getting ready to retire to the vomitorium before resuming the next round of eating and drinking.

Through the wine cloud that floated over the table, I heard the names "Dogen" and "Hakuin," and realized that the doctor was haranguing Eikei with "Zen talk"—one of his least favorite dinner topics. "When eating, just eat. When sitting zazen, just sit zazen. No need philosophical talking." He'd admonish me whenever I tried engaging him in serious conversation over breakfast in the London zendo kitchen, or at the Chalk Farm Chinese restaurant over lunch. Eikei had the same sour look on his face now, but since "the doctor" was a big Shofuji supporter, he couldn't tell him to shut up the way he would have if I were haranguing him with "Zen talk" while eating. Though I noticed that the roshi wasn't eating much, and he only sniffed at the wine as it came his way. I had already drunk three glasses of the latest by now unrecognizable wine, and our Francophile host was standing over me with yet another refill. I pretended to take a sip, then pushed away the glass as he left to fetch the next bottle.

An abbreviated slab of tissue-thin beef soaked in watery mayonnaise and green onion relish was served next, propped between a slice of whole wheat toast on one side and a thick heel of rye bread on the other. I was surreptitiously reaching under my blouse and opening the top button of my long black funeral-skirt-for-all dress-up occasions when the waiter placed a salad in front of me consisting of four strips of shredded cabbage and two carrot slivers soaked in the same watery mayonnaise as before, only this time accompanied by chicken bits.

When, as all good things must, the meal finally ended, I

allowed myself a final visit to the toilet. On my way, I could not help remembering the monks back at Shofuji eating their rice and pickles while the roshi, his head monk, and his American "guest" were sitting in an ersatz French restaurant being stuffed like geese and getting drunk. Poor Hiro-san looked ready to fall off his chair, yet he went right on bowing and smiling. Is there no limit to Japanese courtesy? I wondered. Or is it all those years of samurai Zen training that keeps him upright? It was getting awfully hard to tell where one began and the other ended.

Eikei suddenly stood up in the middle of one of "the doctor's" monologues. "We go, Hiro-san," he announced snappishly, in English.

Undeterred, "the doctor" continued arguing his case for Dogen, founder of the rival Soto Zen sect, as the greatest author of classical Zen literature—thereby deliberately insulting Eikei's strict Rinzai lineage. To no end, for Eikei had already left the table and was headed for the exit.

"How you like?" Demanding a final verdict, Mr. Yamato stood in the vestibule smiling at me.

"Magnifique," I said, trying to keep from falling over. To Hiro-san, I said, "tell him I especially liked the second Japanese wine, the Chateau Brilliant 1977, the one he said Queen Elizabeth liked so much on her visit to Japan. It was as good as the French."

Beaming with pride, Mr. Yamato presented me with gifts from behind the cloakroom counter. I felt like an ingrate as I accepted the medallion embossed with the restaurant's fleur-de-lis logo and a dozen long-stemmed, fuchsia-tinted white roses. "Arigato! Arigato! It was wonderful, just wonderful!" I called over my shoulder as I drunkenly tottered up the stairs and out the front door.

When I stepped outside I saw Eikei heading toward a kiosk across the street in search of cigarettes, cutting a weird monkish figure in his robes as he pushed his way through a group of leather-jacketed bikers lounging against their parked Harleys. From the expression on his face when he returned, I saw that he was ready to explode, and that his fury was directed at me.

"People should not talk philosophy when they eat!" he screamed into my face. "Eating time is no time to spoil taste of food with philosophical talking! Make sick! I don't like intellectuals!" Hunching his shoulders, he rushed over to Mr. Yamato's waiting car, got into the back seat, and slammed the door shut before I could get in. I opened the door and since he wouldn't budge, had to climb in over him. I was nauseated and dreaded the long drive and the prospect of vomiting all over the roshi's elegant robes. So I tucked myself into a ball as far away from him as I could. Hiro-san was already sitting up front. Mr. Yamato had remained behind to close the restaurant, and his wife, making her first appearance of the evening, was our designated driver. Mrs. Yamato had big pink curlers in her hair, talked with a cigarette dangling from one side of her mouth, and drove like a maniac. Evidently enjoying her droll patter, Eikei threw back his head, slapped his knee, and roared with laughter at everything she said. The more he laughed, the more furious I got; I had to resist the temptation to lean over, open the door, and push him out of the speeding car.

Leaving my gifts behind on the seat, I was the first to jump out of the car when Mrs. Yamato pulled up to the Main Hall with brakes screeching. As soon as Eikei got out, I stalked up to him and, emboldened by drink, told him in no uncertain terms that he had no business insulting me in public. Eikei was in the middle of trying to light a cigarette with a damp match that refused to be lit, and I'd clearly caught him by surprise. Mrs. Yamato stuck her head out of the driver's window and waited to see what would happen next.

"Fay-san, why you angry? You tell me. I walk you back to cottage." The roshi took hold of my arm.

"No! Let go of me!" I pulled away from him and ran down the cinder path toward the cottage. I heard him exchange some words with Mrs. Yamato; then she started the car and drove off.

I stopped running only when I'd reached the lotus pond and was too far away for Eikei to catch up with me. Something compelled me to stop exactly at that spot and look up. There were so many stars overhead that they appeared to be crowding each other out of the midnight sky. They reminded me of the passengers in the Tokyo subway, crammed into the trains by the white-gloved "pushers" stationed at every door. I couldn't believe how alike they were, those masses of silent and impassive stars, and those Japanese subway riders, equally silent and impassive in the middle of all that pushing. No one complained. No fights broke out. No one seemed to resent being crammed into the trains, and the pushers themselves weren't particularly hostile or aggressive. On the contrary, they were very courteous as they shoved people through the doors into the trains. Exactly the opposite of the New York subway, where the smallest thing could set off a fight at any moment, and where, at the time I left, homicidal maniacs were pushing riders onto the subway tracks on an average of once a week. How, I wondered, did the Japanese manage to be so brutal and so civilized at the same time? And where did I belong in all this?

It wasn't exactly a moment of great spiritual awakening, but standing at the lotus pond looking up at the stars did spark an insight into my troubled relationship with Eikei Roshi: I'm the subway rider and he's the "pusher." According to Japanese custom, he has to be courteous to some extent, but it's his job to push me into the train. Knowing from experience that I won't break because I'm desperate to get on that train, that I'm determined to reach my destination no matter what. On the other hand, I'm not a Japanese subway rider but an American greenhouse person walking around in monk's clothing pretending to be Japanese. And, being American, I'm always questioning authority, always bucking up against the system, and, from the roshi's Japanese vantage point, always inappropriate. Worse yet, I'm a woman. He's told me more than once that I'm his "bad karma" from a past life, come back to haunt him. He says it jokingly, but if he really believes that, why shouldn't he resent me?

Eikei certainly isn't shy about letting me know when I'm getting out of line. I'm sure he deliberately staged the little scene in front of the restaurant to test me by "pushing" me back into my place on the enlightenment train. True, he was furious with "the doctor" for spoiling his meal and ruining his evening with "Zen talk," but his outburst was clearly aimed at me. Who better embodies everything he dislikes about Westerners? A case in point:

We took the last weekend in July off and traveled together to Kyoto. As we were sitting in a noodle shop eating udon soup, Eikei suddenly looked up from his bowl and said, "No matter how long you live Japan, you never learn to eat noodles like real Japanese person."

Having just finished slurping noodles with what I believed was the requisite amount of noise, I asked, 'Why not?'

Eikei pointed to his jaw and said, "Because Japanese person have extra jaw muscle right here."

I laughed so hard I sprayed a mouthful of soup and noodle bits in his direction. "Sorry," I covered my mouth with my napkin until I could catch my breath and stop laughing. "You don't really believe that, do you, roshi?"

"I serious. Japanese scientist write this in newspaper. I read long time ago."

I hadn't noticed until then that, behind him, perched like a

Buddha on an altar, the gargantuan Sony television had been turned on, and that every table was filled with diners slurping noodles with that extra jaw muscle while watching a Buddhist priest deliver a sermon.

"Like everything else in Japan, eating noodles is tradition," Eikei said. He would repeat that word in every shrine, temple, and tacky souvenir shop we visited in Kyoto. But when pressed, even he had to admit that the core of Japanese tradition has long been lost. It's especially obvious in the empty formality that passes for Zen in the great temples whose abbots, like American televangelists, tour the country in their Mercedes limousines dispensing spiritual advice to the masses. I turned on the television set in my hotel room later that night in the hope of seeing one of them. Instead, I got a videotaped tea ceremony repeated every hour on the hour on the same cable station offering "Pornographic Dreams" in English. In a sense, that's what Eikei would call a true Zen experience. After all, if, like Bodhidharma, the founder of Zen in China, you know that there's "Nothing holy," and it doesn't matter whether you deliver a sermon, perform the tea ceremony, or draw and sell dirty pictures . . .

I thought of old Ryuho Roshi sitting in his own excrement in his little mountainside hut. Was it too much purity that had broken him? Hiro-san once told me that, early in his Zen training, Ryuho had undergone surgical removal of his gonads to reduce the sexual urges inhibiting his meditation. The once revered Shofuji abbot was said to have been in love with a high-class geisha versed in the art of tea. It was even rumored that before he'd entered the monastery, when he was still a university student, the geisha had secretly given birth to his child, a girl who'd grown up and become a famous tea master in her own right.

Could sexual deprivation be the reason so many of the monks are alcoholics? Often, after the lights-out bell has been rung at night, I can hear them laughing as they pass around a smuggled bottle of sake in the bamboo grove behind my cottage. Once, someone even brought a radio and I heard them dancing to disco music. Listening to their muffled laughter, I remembered how Mama Hanakawa had referred to the Shofuji monks as "corrupt," hinting at what I now guessed were their homosexual proclivities. I can't say that it shocked me. Tano Roshi hates women. Eikei, who claims to know so much about penises and vaginas once boasted to me that he was fifty-five and still a virgin. I've read enough Japanese history to know that "the art of male love" was at the core of samurai training, and that this, too, is still a big part of Zen "tradition."

Interestingly, none of the Japanese Buddhas and Bodhisattvas I saw in the Kyoto museums and Zen temples looked like fierce samurai. They all had loving smiles and gentle feminine faces, like their original Indian counterparts. One statue, a Kannon, the Bodhisattva of Compassion, even had breasts! And Miroku, the Buddha of the Future, had the same sad, doe-eyed gaze as a medieval Christ at the Cloisters.

Maybe Eikei was right. Maybe I am too Catholic and too "pure"—not cut out to be a "samurai sergeant" after all. His dilemma is that he invited me to the monastery in the first place, and his Japanese sense of "virtue" compels him to honor me as a guest. Unlike Priscilla, I have a rich American husband who is paying my way, which means I have to be treated with respect, like a monastery patron. I am both his worst nightmare of a "greenhouse person" and his ideal student in that, thanks to my father's military training, I can take anything he can dish out in the way of humiliation, blows, indifference. Someone as steeped in Zen as he is knows enough to recognize the real article when she appears on his doorstep. No wonder he doesn't know what to do with me.

. . .

Fay lies curled up in her futon dreaming she's in London walking through Chinatown, past the tofu factory where she and Eikei buy fresh curds every day. The owner of the factory, a round, smiling Chinese woman with black-penciled lines for eyebrows is offering her a "free sample." Behind her, three laughing Chinese workers are sitting on overturned wooden vats drinking sweet soymilk. The sun creeps behind a cloud, shrouding the street in gray. She passes a greengrocer's stall piled high with bok choy and shitake mushrooms. Three blocks further on, she looks into the open eye of a giant dead mackerel in the window of the fish market whose devout Buddhist proprietor saves Eikei the freshest, biggest pearly shrimps on Mondays. Next door to the fish market is the basement Dim Sum House where Eikei takes her out for tea and gorges her on sticky sesame dessert buns. Fay hurries on toward the river and climbs the pedestrian ramp of the Camden Bridge.

Except for a lone cyclist in skin-tight gear and a white helmet, she is the only other person on the bridge. Now the sun has disappeared entirely and it looks as if it might rain. She gazes out across the Thames, past the dock where three rickety houseboats are tethered. Tracing the flight of an odd-looking blackbird, she looks down and sees a homeless trio gathered around a fire in a barrel under the bridge. The "bird," she now realizes, is actually a wisp of black newspaper ash blown upward by a wind current. On the turbulent gray river, a garbage scow glides under the bridge with a seagull perched on its head like a living masthead. The river is foul, too pestilent for a pure fish like her. Eikei said he would teach her to swim in filthy water and survive. Now she will prove to him that she can. She will jump into the churning waters of the Thames in the wake of the garbage scow and show him how well she's learned her lesson. A few feet from where she stands looking down at the water there is a construction site. Marked by orange and white striped cones and sawhorses, it opens onto a break in the protective mesh covering the guardrail at the entrance to the pedestrian ramp. She can easily pass through the barrier and climb the guardrail there. Emerging from the wings of her dream theater on cue, she moves toward the orange and white cones providing her stage markings. Preparing herself for a grand jeté, she visualizes herself leaping slow motion into the water in a perfectly curved arc. She's already in position, insteps arched, toes pointed, when she suddenly realizes that she's wearing sneakers. As she bends down to remove them, Eikei appears in front of her in his woolen stocking cap and weskit.

"You okay, Fay-san?"

"I'm fine."

"No. You want to jump off bridge. Don't do it. You do it already. In last life you jump off Uji Bridge and I not there to stop you."

Fay follows Eikei's pointing finger and sees that she is in fact no longer in London but is standing on the western parapet of the Uji Bridge just outside Kyoto.

"Why? Why did I do it?" she asks.

Eikei doesn't answer. Instead, he directs her to join a procession of Shofuji monks in robes and sloped straw hats just then making their way across the bridge.

"Come, I show you."

Fay joins the procession just as Eikei disappears from view. Looking down into the water, she is not at all surprised to find a young Japanese boy in monk's robes reflecting back at her. The boy who is Fay hurries across the bridge and rejoins the Shofuji monks in a narrow alley in Kyoto's Gion Quarter. Without warning, the zendo monk suddenly steps from his place at the head of the line and grabs the boy who is Fay by the collar of his robe and pins him against the wall of a wine shop. "There's no way he can escape from us now, can he, boys?" Another shouts, "That's right! Let's have a go at him!" The zendo monk narrows his eyes. The boy who is Fay feels his assailant's hot, sour breath on his face. "Now's our chance to get what we wanted. Let's have some sake with this boy as our side dish!" cries the zendo monk. He drags the boy who is Fay up to the entrance of the closed wine shop and pounds on the door. A light goes on in the shop and Mrs. Yamato appears, curlers in her hair, cigarette dangling from her mouth. The zendo monk calls for sake, and Mrs. Yamato brings out a bottle and some glasses and sets them down on the counter before ducking into a back room behind the shop curtains. The zendo monk fills a glass full of sake and pries open the mouth of the boy who is Fay, forcing him to drink as he strokes him between the legs. Another monk loosens his sash as the zendo monk pushes him down, pins him against the floor and slips his tongue into his mouth. The boy, who is Fay, gags and weeps. Stretching out beneath him like a vast field, the tatami mat catches his tears.

Over the backs of his attackers, he can see that it is drizzling outside and that there are people walking under huge, gaily-colored parasols. He knows that even if he could scream, not one of those people would come rushing into the wine shop to help him. He knows that being Japanese means keeping to your place—wife, child, boss, monk, samurai, or outcast—you don't step out of your place. Nor do you seek to change it—not if you don't want to be considered a misfit. You simply accept it as your karma, which you perform as silently and unquestioningly as the stars in the sky perform theirs. Even now, as the zendo monk is turning him over onto his stomach and thrusting his huge swollen cock into his tender anus, the boy, who is Fay, knows that what is happening to him is his karma, and that Eikei will not come to his rescue.

There's a sudden thud, and a large black ball rolls across

the tatami mat and comes to a stop beside him. Horrorstruck, the boy, who is Fay, sees that the ball has two wide-open eyes and a nose and a mouth—and that it isn't a ball but the zendo monk's head, which has been lopped off with one swift thrust. Looking up, he sees a samurai in jet-black armor standing over him, blood dripping from the point of his sword. Again, the samurai flashes his terrible blade, and again another head falls. A third monk pleads for his life: "Spare me! I've done nothing at all!" Another heavy blow, and it's his turn to be silenced. The boy, who is Fay, sees the headless torso of the zendo monk lying at his side. Four more blood curdling screams are silenced by blows from the samurai's sword. Convinced that he is next to die, the boy, who is Fay, closes his eyes and starts reciting the Kannon Sutra. Outside, the drizzle has turned to rain, whose steady pounding on the roof accompanies his chanting like a drum. The floor creaks and he feels a light rush of air against his face as the samurai steps over him and turns him onto his back, then kneels at his side.

"Now, my sweet boy . . . why did you run away from your lord?" he chides in a disturbingly familiar voice. "Did I ever harm you? Did I ever once treat you roughly in our love play?" Daring to open his eyes, the boy who is Fay watches the samurai lift his visor to reveal Sam Rubin's face.

Instantly leaping to his feet and pushing Sam aside, he flees from the wine shop into the market. Turning, he sees Sam following close behind him with the bloody sword still in his hand. In the market, the early morning peddlers are unpacking their stalls for business. A tea-seller in headband and tucked trousers is crying, "Tea for sale!" as the boy who is Fay runs past him, almost toppling his wares. The angry peddler steps forward, and is about to berate him, but is knocked aside by Sam, who swats him like a mosquito with the hilt of his sword.

Now the Uji Bridge looms ahead. Breathing fast, pierced

by a stitch in his side, the boy who is Fay tears ahead, his feet sinking into the muddy ooze of the riverbank. He has just reached the western parapet of the bridge when Sam catches up and flings himself at him. For a few seconds, they grapple wildly. The boy who is Fay struggles to pull the heavy sword from Sam's hand while his captor plucks at his robe and tries to drag him across the bridge. The boy who is Fay continues to struggle, but it soon becomes apparent that he is losing the fight and must submit to Sam's superior power or die. He knows that if he wants to go on living, he must surrender himself to Sam's will. Gathering his last bit of strength, the boy who is Fay wrenches free and leaps from the bridge with a bone-shattering cry.

"KAAAAAATZ!"

16
A ZEN MONK IN PARIS

Fay's idea of creating a Shofuji affiliate in New York with Eikei was born when Hiro-san told her that Victorine Carrel, one of Tano Roshi's French students, had approached him in London and received his permission to start looking around Paris for an appropriate place to house a Zen center. Why not a New York affiliate, Fay thought. Tano was due to return to Shofuji in two weeks, and Eikei had already confessed to feeling superfluous— "no monastery need two abbots"— when she proposed her plan to him. "I think about it, Fay-san."

"I'm leaving here before Tano Roshi arrives, so, if you want to come along with me to New York and set up a formal connection with Jessie Kane's group, we have to act fast."

"You not rush me . . . still have duty to Tano and French lady who ask first."

And that was how, instead of flying to New York, Fay and the roshi ended up in Paris.

They left Shofuji early one morning without any fanfare, skulking off like fugitives when only Kosen-san appeared to help them put their bags in the taxi. Handing him the bottle of shaving balm she'd bought him, she wished Kosen-san well and invited him to visit her in New York. Eikei sat in the back seat looking grim as they pulled out of the driveway; he did not stop the driver when Hiro-san sprang out of his office behind the kitchen still in his britches and desperately tried to flag them down. He seemed preoccupied, and Fay didn't want to provoke him, so she too remained silent all the way to the airport. When the Hanakawa clan gathered at the check-in counter to see them off, Eikei instructed her from between clenched teeth on the number of bows she should make as they backed into the jet bridge. As soon as they were seated, he turned his head away from her toward the window and dozed. Fay got up and with help from a flight attendant, changed her seat. Refusing lunch, she turned up the volume on the music channel of her headset.

A second flight attendant stopped at her seat and, kneeling, pointed at Eikei. "Are you traveling with that man? I saw you change your seat. Is there something wrong? Can I help you?" she asked.

"No, everything's fine, thanks. It's . . . just the music. I always cry when I listen to Mozart. It's too beautiful." Fay gave the flight attendant an unconvincing smile. At that moment the plane gained altitude and broke through a cloudbank, and she had the sudden premonition that the worst was not yet behind her.

They arrived to find that Victorine had left Paris for London on a last minute's notice to be at the bedside of her dying ex-husband, and that none of the other five people supposedly involved in the offer to start a Zen center were inclined to help her. It had been a one-woman operation, largely the result of Tano Roshi's pressure, and, as Eikei muttered after reading the hasty letter of apology Victorine had left with her concierge, "another Western pipe dream." The Parisians' loss turned out to be Fay's gain, for in his reluctance to return to Shofuji as second fiddle to the abbot, Eikei agreed to come back with her to New York. To show the roshi how grateful she was, she removed from her bag the three thousand dollars in unspent traveler's cheques she'd been saving and promised him the sightseeing trip of his life. Then thanking the smartly dressed concierge for his help, she raced out of Victorine's fancy Marais apartment building, hailed a taxi, and ordered the driver to the George V hotel. "Now we're on my territory," she told Eikei, who, having rolled down the window, sat grumpily smoking. The driver complained to her in French of the draft coming through the open window and Fay rolled it back up. In a loud voice, Eikei said, "French dirty people never take bath, only apply perfume. It stinks of sweat in here." Fortunately, the driver didn't understand him.

Fay couldn't tell whether the roshi was really bored or so insulted at being unceremoniously ejected from the monastery by Tano and left to the mercy of his unreliable Western Zen students, that he was just pretending not to like Paris. Whatever the reason, nothing she pointed out impressed him: on the *bateau mouche*, as they were passing the Eiffel Tower, he sat smoking and looking in the opposite direction across the Seine. When she told him to turn around or he'd miss it, he said, "So what? We see all this before in Japan. Japan Eiffel Tower is nicer."

"You're just being chauvinistic," Fay said, noting that it was exactly the kind of late summer day, with the leaves on the plane trees just starting to turn gold, that made her nostalgic for her first visit to Paris with Ira as students. In the dump near the University, the only hotel they could afford, the frumpy, bad-tempered girl who'd served them their brioche and coffee breakfasts had worn the same shrunken brown dress smelling of unwashed sex every morning, and a brindled bulldog had sat under the dining room table as they ate, leaving a dried, cigar-shaped turd the color of the girl's dress behind him before ambling out. Fay and Ira had made love every morning and every afternoon in that triangular-shaped hotel on the Rue Jacob, with the faucet dripping in the door-less toilet a few feet from the bed, and the floor-length windows barely hidden by crepe de chine curtains with quarter-sized holes in them. That Paris trip was the first time she'd been moved to tears by a work of art, standing with bowed head in front of a Chinese Kwan-Yin, at the foot of a winding staircase in the Musée Guimet.

Eikei wouldn't hear of going to a museum, he said, when she told him about it. He had seen—and cleaned—enough Buddha statues to last him a lifetime. Besides, he didn't like art; he liked "real life." As for architecture, "Paris not so beautiful," he added in his irritatingly high-pitched voice used to show disdain.

"You don't know what's beautiful," Fay said angrily.

When they got off the tour boat, they were no longer speaking to each other. She was walking a few feet ahead of him in the direction of the hotel, fuming at him for downgrading Paris and her efforts to impress him with everything worthwhile about Western culture, when a Frenchman with beautiful silver hair approached her, extending a pack of Gitanes. Fay smiled and said she didn't smoke. The Frenchman placed the Gitanes in his pocket and walking alongside her asked if she would like to join him for a drink.

"I'm married," she said; technically, at least, she thought.

"To him?" With a derisive laugh, the Frenchman pointed at Eikei shuffling along behind her.

"Of course not. That's my uncle on my mother's side. It

was a marriage made after the war when my aunt was a nurse in Japan. My husband and I sponsored him in the States when my aunt died in Yokohama last year. I'm taking him on a tour of Paris." Having no idea where that came from and why she was rattling on to a perfect stranger, Fay shut herself up.

The Frenchman shook his head and drew his elegantly manicured fingers through his beautiful silver hair. Eikei was as bald as a toad under his absurd pork pie hat. She was tempted to take up the Frenchman's offer, get even with both men—Monsieur Gitanes, for thinking himself so sexy and desirable, and Eikei for his xenophobia. But the Frenchman walked away just then, and Eikei caught up with her.

"I tired sightseeing. I want to go back hotel and take shower."

"That man tried to pick me up."

"Why any man want to pick you up, Fay-san? No man like such strong woman."

Fay couldn't tell whether he was giving her a backhanded Zen compliment or insulting her. Probably both.

Having showered and taken a nap, Eikei knocked on her door and in a much better mood announced that he was hungry for fish. He even seemed impressed by the opulence of the lobby as he stood alongside her looking around at the colorful wall tapestries and Louis XIV furniture, while she conferred with the concierge. After writing down the address of "a superb seafood restaurant not far away, the latest favorite of the diplomatic set, tucked around the corner from the Arc de Triomphe," she happened to glance over the concierge's shoulder into the mirror and was shocked to see herself reflected in the person of a tall, stylish stranger in an expensive white suit and matching Chanel turban carrying a white alligator skin bag on a braided gold chain, her mouth ablaze with red lipstick. Eikei, for some reason known only to himself, had chosen to wear his black monk's robes instead of his "civilian clothes." They were so mismatched that for a moment, she felt like returning to her room, removing her makeup and turban, changing her high heels for flats and her white suit for her blue Zen monk's jacket and pants.

"I am hungry," Eikei said, and Fay knew it was too late to go back, and that on leaving Shofuji behind, their relationship had taken an altogether inevitable unnerving turn.

"We'll take a taxi," she said, after the concierge had telephoned the restaurant and reserved a table.

"To whom shall it be charged, Madame?"

"Me, of course," Fay said impatiently. "Like everything else."

The discreet concierge merely bowed, though, like everyone else on the hotel staff, he must have found the tall American woman and the little bald Japanese monk a bizarre couple for registering in separate rooms, and, in the monk's case, making his own bed and cleaning the bathtub and sink in his bathroom every morning before the maid arrived. As for Fay, who was jumpy and irritable, the concierge and the entire well-trained staff were nothing but deferential; hurrying to satisfy her every whim and caprice no matter the time of day or night: flowers in Japanese vases always accompanied the sushi platters and beer that she ordered sent to Eikei's room; the doormen were always ready to whisk her into waiting taxis, the bellhops always available to carry the booty from her manic shopping sprees along the Rue Saint Honoré to her room for lavish tips—all the while ignoring the fact of her too red cheeks and the sadness in her eyes as she ran ahead of the little Japanese monk with the ever-present cigarette following behind her, trying not to get caught in the revolving door.

What the well-mannered staff at the hotel did not know

was that the harder she tried to impress the irreverent roshi with the splendors of European civilization, the more he scorned them. What could she do with a man who complained that Notre Dame had too many candles and gave him a headache; that the great vaulted domes were too high and gave him a stiff neck, the gargoyles too dirty with pigeon shit and the flea markets along the Seine too filled with thieves and pickpockets to shop in? Now it's my turn to placate him with food, she told herself when a lavish Chinese lunch taken on the Ile Saint-Louis cut off his interminable complaint about the ugliness of "Christian temples." But it didn't stop him from spoiling their walk through the Bois de Boulogne afterward by railing against the couples kissing on the benches under the chestnut trees and extolling their Japanese counterparts who—except for those in the very lowest social classes—never indulged in public displays of affection. Fay tried to divert him, pointing out a child on a red tricycle, a jogger in a white knitted cap, and a man in a tan raincoat reading a Persian newspaper on a bench up ahead. But Eikei ignored her and continued reciting his litany of complaints against Paris, Western behavior, and lewd Western women in particular. Proper Japanese women, he reminded her, did not show their emotions in public, especially when it came to feelings between men and women, not even when married—no, especially when married. He praised the elegant Japanese women mourners at Shofuji funerals for their silent fortitude, and the temple priests' wives for their modesty, and samurai daughters and mothers and grandmothers for their "bravery mind." On and on and on he went, until finally she stopped in her tracks and turned to him saying, "If you hate it here so much, why don't you just go back to Japan?" And he, as always, chastened by the vehemence of her tone and the challenge in her eyes as she looked down into his, and said, "No insult, Fay-san. You take too personally. Come, I treat you to dinner."

They went to the same seafood restaurant three nights in a row and stuffed themselves with creamed fish stews and cognac-laced lobster and emptied two sixty-dollar bottles of amber wine, and the waiters and the maître d' soon recognized them and found them the best table in a corner not too near the kitchen or the toilets, which had offended Eikei's sensibility on the first night, and for which, having changed tables, the maître d' had found an extra twenty dollars in traveler's cheques added to his tip. After dinner on the third night, drunk on food as much as wine, they wove on foot down the Champs Elysées looking into shop windows, and Eikei praised the chef at the seafood restaurant: Paris wasn't so beautiful, he said, but the food was surely the best in the world. To Fay, the crowds along the Champs Elysées appeared vaporous, blue and neon red under the lights—what with the wine throbbing in her head, it was hard to walk straight. It was even harder to concentrate on what Eikei was saying and respond appropriately. Just then she thought she heard him say, "And you too pure, too honest. When you need to cheat, you cheat!" But she couldn't be sure, for it sounded more like, "So sure a love nest can't be beat, too sweet." The next thing he said, however, came out loud and clear:

"We go to sex show, Japanese tourists all go to French sex show, and I want go too. I show you how Zen master discipline work, how control not enough."

They were looking into the window of a fine leather boutique at an expensive set of caramel kidskin suitcases she'd briefly contemplated as a gift for Ira before abandoning the idea as impractical; the fragile bags wouldn't survive his frequent bicoastal flights beyond a couple of months at best. At the sound of Eikei's voice, she looked away from the luggage at his reflection in the window and saw herself towering over him in her high-heeled pumps.

"To the Lido? You mean you want to go to the Lido?" She watched her crimson mouth move in the reflecting glass. Then she burst out laughing. "Yes, yes. Of course I'll take you to the Lido. It's something all Japanese tourists should see."

Then they were in a taxi, speeding through narrow streets to a sex show, with Fay telling the driver in tipsy French about her Japanese uncle's interest in European culture, to which the silent driver responded with a sleazy smile in the rear-view mirror.

"You make fun of me?" Eikei quavered from the dark corner of the taxi. "Fay-san, you my mother. You not make fun of me, you protect me from bad womens."

She could have sworn his upper lip was trembling and that he was on the verge of tears. And this scared her so much she thought her beautiful supper was going to come up all over them both. She was drunk and couldn't be sure she was hearing anything right, couldn't believe the roshi had called her "my mother"—certainly not she, who for thirty-five years had managed not to be anyone's mother, and certainly not Eikei's, because she needed him to be her father, her guide and source of strength, not sitting scrunched in the corner of the cab like a sick pigeon, folding his wings around his head and pleading for her to protect him.

"Your mother is . . . she's always with you." His hat was askew, and she resisted the impulse to reach over and straighten it.

"My mother have same white skin as you, white as clean rice paper. You like my mother . . . egg-shape face. I see you walk like my mother, too; she tall for Japanese womens, not so tall as you, but same straight back and long neck. Strong womens . . . like you . . . she never cry."

Fay felt her bones turn to powder, and her stomach, losing its center of gravity, did a quick flip.

"Lido!" called the driver.

They wandered like dreamers through the mirrored entranceway where a laughing, drink-bearing, ghoulishly lit crowd snake-lined the stairs to the basement theater.

"I avoid many womens in Japan . . . only because my mother always with me. Now, in the West, she send me herself in you . . . Fay-san . . . same white, egg-shape face . . . she say you protect me. I consult with uncle who know such things, see the future, contact dead people. He tell me what mother say. I show you how Zen monk stay pure. I never know lady."

An usher in a tuxedo seated them along with five other waiting couples at a side banquette three rows from a vast circular stage. Sitting on the thick velvet padded banquette with her shoes off under the table and her toes digging into the plush carpet, Fay imagined herself inside a gigantic purple womb. Seeing that Eikei had ordered an enormous bottle of red wine on his own and was holding out a glass for her, she drank some. Then she turned to the stage, where a half dozen extremely tall and beautifully built naked men and women with furs draped around their shoulders and enormous beaver fur Cossack headdresses were pantomiming sex. Feeling she might pass out, Fay put her head down on her arms on the table, almost upsetting the bottle of wine. Eikei sat beside her very still, didn't ask her what was wrong, just sat there watching the naked giants perform their antics with a glassy stare. Fay lifted her head and forced herself to watch. Eikei was now talking to her, but she missed what he was saying. She turned away from the stage and saw him talking, but not to her. The redhead sitting to his right was asking him in

English if he was from Tokyo, curling her lip at him as she spoke over the music, wetting it with her tongue between sips of wine.

"I am country boy from Zen temple. I Zen monk!" Eikei announced, and the redhead giggled at her escort, a wild-eyed man with tufts of gray hair sprouting out of his ears eying the monk.

It's a hooker, thought Fay, as the redhead, giggling again, chucked Eikei's chin with two blood-red mandarin fingernails and said, "I been to Tokyo, you cute Japanese man."

The tufted man bristled, "I paid you already," he said to the redhead in Hungarian-accented English.

"Only for my company at the Lido," said the redhead, "not for the whole evening."

The naked Cossacks left the stage and a man wearing a leopard skin across his chest emerged from the wings leading a stunningly naked blond yoked by a diamond collar to the leash in his hands.

"I never been with lady," Eikei said to the redhead, who had tilted her face close to his.

What would his mother do now? Fay thought. What should I do now? She sat glued to the banquette willing the Hungarian to act. The man reached into his pocket, removed his wallet, and, taking out a fistful of dollars, waved them between the redhead and Eikei, saying, "There, that is payment for the whole night!"

The redhead sprang back like an asp releasing her prey; she belonged to the Hungarian again. Fay breathed silent thanks to the spirit of Eikei's mother.

The roshi seemed to be dozing.

The leopard man and the stunning blond woman at the end of his leash were now lying on his leopard skin simulating intercourse.

Fay stood up and said, "Let's get out of here. I'll pay the waiter."

"We not finish wine," Eikei said, suddenly wide-awake. "No waste, I take bottle with me."

The waiter frowned, looking for a moment as if he were getting ready to retrieve the bottle by force if necessary. Fay mollified him with a fifty-dollar bill, which he pocketed with many thanks as he draped her shawl around her shoulders.

She approached the Avenue George V with no idea of how she'd found it, only a vaguely remembered dream of Eikei weaving alongside her through the Paris streets with the wine bottle in his hand, rambling endlessly, drunkenly, about the school teacher in Japan who wanted to run away with him, leave her husband and children to meet him in the mountains. Then, in front of the waiting doorman at the hotel, he beckoned her to stoop down so he could whisper in her ear. "Okay, I tell you truth, Fay-san. I almost marry once. I almost marry Gretta Lewis, American Zen student in Israel. Almost engaged. I buy her Rolex watch, take her to visit my sister in Japan. Even Ryuho Roshi approve. Gretta a lot like you, independent, strong American lady. But I not love Gretta. Like I not love you. But she love me. She leave Israel because of disappointment in not marrying me. After that, I not wanting zendo members knowing too much about my private business, so I leave Israel, too. But Gretta and me still good friends. She live in Portland, Maine, and we talk on telephone sometimes. You not mad at me?"

Fay stood on the sidewalk in front of the burly doorman, suddenly blinded by the double row of gold buttons and loops of braid on his chest, and wondered if Eikei weren't a fraud after all, and she not the butt of an enormous Japanese joke. Wondered if, in her foolish, idealizing, worshipful head, she hadn't invented him in her image, and not, as she'd always believed, the other way round. So, little innocent "coke-face" Eikei Roshi, mother's precious virgin boy, had been traveling across the globe trailing a string of broken hearts.

"No, I'm not mad," she said, pushing him ahead of her through the revolving door as she handed the three quarter-full wine bottle to the doorman.

In her room she stripped off her clothes and stuffed them into the wastebasket under the Louis XIV desk. Then she ran a steaming tub, emptied an envelope of lavender bath salts into it and got in. When she had finished drying off, still wrapped in the oversized towel, she telephoned Ira in New York. He picked up on the second ring.

"It's me," she said hoarsely into the receiver. "Please come and get me. I'm at the George V in Paris, and I'm afraid I might jump out of the window."

"You're not going to jump out of any window," Ira said, his voice very faint and distant. "I can't come and get you; I'm in the middle of negotiating a publicity tour."

"He's driving me out of my mind."

"It's part of Zen training," Ira said. "You ought to know that. Now go get some sleep; isn't it about four in the morning there?"

"Yeah. Good morning."

"Good night, Fay."

Her body was shaking so hard she thought she might be on the verge of an epileptic seizure and almost called Ira back to tell him so. She lay down on the bed thinking it would somehow make it worse if she cried, maybe choke on her own tears. "You will not cry," she heard herself order so loud that her voice bounced off the wall opposite. She turned on the radio, turned it off again. Then she lost all control and started to wail, crying and screaming like a woman possessed. She leaped up on the bed and pounded the wall dividing Eikei's room from hers; she threw herself on the embroidered carpet near the bed and kicked the wooden frame with her bare feet. She got up again and beat the pillows with her fists, then circled the carpet in front of the window and tore at the drawn yellow brocade draperies. She was on the sixth floor, but six floors up were enough to kill you if you landed on the tar-covered parapet. She had seen it from her window, surrounded by a concrete balustrade, a hidden corner of the courtyard facing the hotel kitchen, with a chimney that could skewer you with its rotating bulb if you happened to land on it.

Despairing, but not yet ready to die, Fay circled the patch of carpet in front of the yellow draperies until the first faint shimmer of dawn stole through. Only then did she drop to the floor and fall asleep where she lay.

She woke up with the sun on her face. After washing and combing her hair, she put on a bathrobe and slippers, went out into the hall and knocked on Eikei's door.

"Come in," he said calmly.

On entering she saw that he was dressed in his brown monk's traveling robes and that his bags were packed and ready. Not a sign of a hangover on him. He sat smoking and drinking a cup of Chinese tea, his face a map of benevolent aplomb.

"Roshi . . ." Her knees buckled and, before she knew it, she was prostrating face to the floor in front of him.

"It okay, Fay-san. You stand up; take some tea. Much wine last night. You strong lady but not strong enough for so much drinking."

When she was on her feet, facing him, she said, "I promise to protect you, like you asked. I'll stand by you no matter what. Even if you—"

Eikei clicked his tongue against his teeth and said, "I protect you, Fay-san. I be your umbrella. So, even if you have nobody, no husband or family to take care of you, I protect you. Like Ryuho Roshi when he come back from Manchuria in very bad condition, nobody to take care of him . . . old Roshi, his teacher, assure him that he will be his umbrella, his protection for life. Nothing else matter."

"Nothing else matters," Fay echoed, convinced the moment she spoke that nothing else did.

17
A BARGAIN

It was raining when their plane finally landed after circling Kennedy airport for two hours. Ira was waiting for them when they came out of Customs, at least ten pounds thinner and almost entirely bald in front. Their diplomatic restraint signaling the latest separate-but-equal terms of their marriage, Fay and Ira hugged without commenting on the changes in their appearance—his weight loss, her cropped hair—both focusing instead on the roshi, whom Ira welcomed with a handshake, adding that he'd prepared the loft for him to stay with them until he got settled.

"I sleep through whole two hours circling," Eikei responded, beaming.

Mindful of the roshi's distaste for Western displays of affection in public, Fay gave her husband a polite bow of thanks but did not kiss him.

No one spoke after that odd little exchange until they were crawling along on the Long Island Expressway, when, apropos of nothing, Eikei said, "New York traffic bad as Tokyo." Then, dropping his chin to his chest, he promptly fell asleep waking only when they'd pulled up in front of their building.

Ira had not only kept up his part of their bargain in opening his home to Fay's Zen master—as she had finally acknowledged his partnership with Sam—but he'd gone out of his way to please her by driving to Fort Lee to stock up on Japanese food. The first thing he did when they arrived at the loft was open the pantry to show her the cellophane-wrapped packages of dried seaweed, udon noodles, and shaved bonito flakes he'd bought. Then claiming he had a meeting uptown, Ira discreetly left them on their own.

Sitting in the loft across the table from Eikei drinking tea, Fay felt herself jolted out of time, as if transported only minutes ago from Shofuji, and even before that, from the tatty zendo kitchen in London, to pick up the thread of their Zen dialogue. Eikei must have felt it too, for immediately after she poured him a second cup of tea, he said, "The teacher is fishing, fishing. He give bait, slowly, slowly, little by little. Then . . . oops, he catches!"

And the fish struggles, Fay thought.

"If my teacher Ryuho Roshi say, 'Jump into water,' I jump. But of course, he never tells me to drown myself. Zen mean so much trust you jump."

His chocolate-brown traveling robes hitched up over his knees, surrounded by her gleaming appliances, the roshi suddenly struck her as out-of-place. Fay wondered if she had done the right thing by bringing him to New York.

"I warn you, Zen is most horrible," he continued, not seeming to notice her discomfort. "It is not from books, not philosophy. I cannot give you the strength, the willpower you need. I cannot change my legs for your legs, my strong stomach for your weak one, because you can only experience every second of your life by yourself."

The hard rain beating on the roof as the roshi talked reminded her of the rainstorm on the day her mother had dropped her off at Sunday school, leaving her to her weekly assignment of placing the Children's Book of New Testament Stories on every little desk in the church basement before class. She'd been so intent on adjusting each book in its proper place that she didn't notice that a half hour had passed, and she was still alone. She had finished her task and was playing chopsticks at the upright piano when she heard a noise in the doorway. Ben was standing there in his galoshes, with a plastic raincoat over his uniform and a transparent plastic shield over his officer's cap, watching her.

"Daddy!"

"It's a flash flood," he drawled. "The river's overflowing. Put on your coat."

"But I don't have boots."

"Don't worry. I'll carry you."

"You can't. I'm too big. You'll drop me."

"Stop the silly talk and put on your coat."

Ben tucked his pants into his galoshes and fastened the little hatchet clips. Hoisting her up on his shoulders, he made his way out into the rain. Each step forward left her wriggling for position. She grew dizzy, feared falling. "Stop moving around." He was breathing hard. "Anyone want to buy my sack of wheat?" he cried into the storm as he ran with her to the car.

Fay had been afraid her father would really sell her for not trusting him to carry her safely through the flood. Now she was gripped by the same fear as the roshi exposed the sham of her vaunted independence, viable only for as long as Ira had demanded it from her secretly needy quivering little girl's heart. She'd exchanged one mask for another and was neither Eikei's boy-monk nor Ira's wife, but her father's fabricated "Number One Son"—an imitation of an imitation.

A coincidental telephone call from Ben, announcing he'd been diagnosed with cancer arrived a day later. Shaken by the call from his hospital bed demanding she fly out to see him for probably the last time— "without letting Mother know"—Fay pleaded with a recalcitrant Eikei to accompany her to San Antonio until he finally gave in. She hadn't seen her father for years, they were hardly on speaking terms, and (absent Ira) only Eikei, her "umbrella," could now protect her from his wrathful disappointment in his "Number One Son."

They entered the hospital room together, Eikei holding a bouquet of flowers. Not giving her father a chance to register his annoyance at seeing her accompanied by a Japanese stranger, Fay immediately introduced Eikei as her Zen teacher, quickly adding that she'd formally become a Buddhist during her stay in Japan and hadn't written home about it so as not to upset her mother any more than she had by marrying a Jew.

Ben turned away from her and said nothing. He lay propped against the pillows sprouting an IV on one side and an assortment of tubes on the other, their ultimate destinations hidden by the bedcovers. Fay braced herself against the bed railing. A second turn—this time toward her—smiling faintly, "Come help me with the urine bottle," her father said hoarsely. Then finally acknowledging Eikei, "Sit down."

"How you feel?" Eikei asked in his mild-mannered Japanese tourist voice.

"How should I feel?"

Fay walked over to the nightstand and fetched the urine bottle, actually a tall pewter pitcher. "Do you want to use it?" she asked.

"No. Stop fooling around with that thing. Go get me a new one. I don't like lying here with stale urine fumes all over the room," he said, sounding exactly like his cranky old meticulous self.

It must have been beyond bearing for him to be dying of bladder cancer, he who had toilet trained her by making her lie in her own wet bed until the sheets grew cold and her mother took pity on her and, while he was shaving, stripped and changed them. *Karmic retribution*, Fay couldn't help herself from thinking.

"Take pitcher from father," Eikei ordered, now sitting in the chair near the window across from the bed still clutching the waterlogged bouquet.

"Unwrap the soggy tissue paper from those flowers and stick them in some water," Ben pointed Eikei toward the sink where an empty opal-colored vase stood on a neighboring shelf.

Fay left the room in search of a nurse and informed the first friendly-looking one she met out in the hall that the Colonel didn't want the urine pitcher left standing in his room.

"Who's that? Ben Watkins?" the nurse asked, breaking into a grin.

"My father," Fay said, reflexively falling into her childhood chest-out-stomach-in military posture.

The nurse chuckled. "He's a character."

"Really?" Fay asked, amazed at the nurse's casual insubordination.

"The girls around here all love him. Doctor Ben's a cutie."

Her father, a "cutie?" The redheaded French hooker in Paris had called Eikei "cute." What, she wondered, did women (including her sex-hating Catholic mother) find so cute about these Napoleonic little bantam cocks? She didn't find either of them cute at all.

She came back into the room carrying a new urine pitcher just as her father was impolitely asking Eikei to leave so he could talk to his daughter alone.

"Of course, understanding perfectly . . ." Eikei murmured, removing himself swiftly and quietly.

Almost before the door closed, Ben sputtered, "Why . . . why did you bring him here? I wanted to see you by yourself. Not even with your mother here. And you bring this . . . this foreigner along. What about your husband, what does he think about it?" Then, looking up at her, his dark eyes suddenly awash in un-spilt tears, he whispered, "What does it all mean?"

Fay leaned over and kissed her father's needle-pricked, blue-veined hand. "It's all a dream," she said. "It means nothing."

"I'm glad you came, Fay," he said, closing his eyes. But I'm getting tired, so tired . . . you can leave me now."

She found Eikei in the hospital cafeteria drinking tea from a Styrofoam cup with the tea bag still in it. "I no like hospitals," he said as she approached the table. "They make nervous. Once, when I was a boy my grandmother make me go with her to hospital clinic. The doctor there want to scare me, so he said, holding long needle in his hand, 'Come here, boy. You are my patient, not your grandmother!' And I try to run away, but my grandmother call me back. And if I didn't listen to grandmother, she beat me hard. Grandmother always beating." He stared down into the Styrofoam cup.

"My father is dying," Fay said.

"Your father really brave soldier."

"He's had a hard life."

"Hard life good. Make brave person. Your father not a greenhouse person like you. He wanted to make your life easy —big mistake. He spoil you."

"Spoil me? Sure, if you mean he failed to turn me into a samurai you could say he spoiled me."

Eikei reached over to the back of the chair for his coat. "I no like hospitals. Make sick."

"Thanks for coming along," Fay said, helping him on with his coat. She noticed that he was wearing his glasses. Before that she'd only seen him wear glasses for reading; now he was wearing them even out on the street. Alarming to think that Eikei was only five years younger than her father, and that there would come a time when he too would die. The stark samurai Zen master in black robes no longer frightened her. Paris had changed all that. Now whenever she looked at him, she saw only the indentation above his eyebrows where he'd perched his glasses as he squinted over the Japanese newspaper, his bald head wrapped in a towel, the hard lines around his mouth deepening every day. Away from the monastery, out of context, even as he bellowed orders at her, he often struck her as pitiable— a dwarf in giant's robes. Had familiarity turned him into just another enlightenment fantasy gone awry?

The cold rain gave way to a spurt of Indian summer, and Ira suggested they take the roshi out to the Hamptons for the weekend. They left in mid-morning, after the heaviest of the commuter traffic. Orange and red leaves blanketed the roadside, and great elliptical pumpkins sat on the porches, Eikei marveling at their size, only interrupting himself to praise "Fay-san and Ira-san" for being such a wonderful, handsome couple, embroidering their strained civility with his unwelcome stream of observations.

They sat at a cramped table in the American Hotel eating duck in wild cherry sauce while the roshi jabbered on about their wonderful marriage. At last sensing that he might be overdoing it, he began praising the food, the wine, and the service until Ira intervened to change the subject.

"Tell me something about Zen enlightenment, Roshi. Is it what you would call a religious experience?" Ira motioned the waiter for more wine.

"No special religious . . . anyone can get enlightened, even Fay-san," Eikei chuckled.

"How long will it take her?"

Fay bristled.

"Very hard to do Zen practice in married life. Fay-san should forget this idea and go back to being good wife."

"No, Roshi, I'm serious." Ira said, exchanging glances with her. "Fay and I have spent many years searching for a spiritual path . . . we've found different ones, but that doesn't matter. We support each other. It's important for her to see this one through on her own, even if it means sacrificing worldly attachments for a time."

"Thanks," Fay said, giving Ira a kick under the table.

"No . . . no . . . woman must take care husband."

"Well, then, what do you say to this? I'll give her as much time off from taking care of me as she needs."

"A lifetime . . ." Fay said, bitter at finding herself bargained over by a husband who dreaded being needed and a Zen master who wasn't sure he wanted to buy.

"Roshi doesn't like talking about Zen stuff when he's eating." She made a face, hoping Ira would let it drop.

"Well, I think maybe if she do zazen all the days and concentrate hard without mix-up cassette tape mind, I think she realize essential nature in three years."

Fay bit down on a cherry and swallowed the pit. What if she didn't do it in three years, would Ira withdraw his support? Would she, like Chu-san, stop sleeping nights and sit up under a blanket, hacking with T.B.? What if her "cassette tape" never got unstuck?

"Okay, Roshi. I'll give her three years," Ira said, and the two men clicked glasses.

Eikei leaned across the table and addressed her directly for the first time that evening. "Fay-san, we take three years to make zendo in New York. If no success, I go back Japan."

Fay had drunk too much wine to know if she was shaking with rage or delight.

18
THE BOWERY ZENDO

Jessie was thrilled to sponsor Eikei Roshi as Shofuji's resident Zen master in New York. But she was too busy running her dance troupe to deal with the details of establishing the monastery's affiliate Zen center. Everyone involved agreed that she'd been more than generous in offering her studio as an interim zendo and helping to fund it. But that left the matter of settling Eikei Roshi, and since it was Fay who'd talked him into leaving Shofuji and coming with her to New York, the task naturally fell to her. Having already designated Fay as her assistant, Jessie gave her a free hand in expanding the Zen training of her dancers and even went so far as to put her in charge of the troupe's spiritual exercises. Assuming a lay version of Hiro-san's monastic role, Fay was both the roshi's personal attendant and "head monk" of a dance company engaged in a unique experiment combining performance and Zen. Though this was not new in the history of Zen (the Japanese arts were suffused with it), it was new for Americans. At first, she was honored to be part of a growing movement to bring Zen to the western art world. But her initial excitement soon disappeared in the daily banalities of administration. She wrote numerous fundraising letters, and despite the increasingly fragile nature of their marriage, even cajoled Ira into donating the monthly rent for the Bowery loft that eventually became the permanent zendo and housed the roshi. Fay was the only one beside Eikei himself to have a key. She appeared every morning at five to ring the opening bell for meditation and was the last to leave at night. On Thursdays, she recorded Eikei's Zen talks, and gradually the center grew. Unobtrusively, at first—until looking up from the tape recorder one Thursday night, she counted thirty people sitting cross-legged on black cushions listening raptly to Eikei's Zen talk.

Still, while he never showed anything but gratitude to Ira—even to the point of unctuousness—it didn't take long for him to level his inevitable complaints against her.

"I not able to concentrate in this small, cramped space. Almost as bad as London zendo," he said, as they stood together appraising the small galley bedroom that had been constructed to his specifications on a platform at one end of the zendo.

Fay looked at the expensive stereo system Ira had bought and installed, and the handmade futon she had ordered from Japan and said, "You'll get used to it."

But Eikei didn't get used to it, and things soon went from bad to worse. The Bowery Zendo's first weekend sesshin in New York was a disaster, and of course he blamed her for scheduling it poorly. Only six women turned up, not even one of the dozen male regulars who meditated with him every morning before going off to work and every evening after rehearsals. At first, she felt it served him right, being surrounded by women. But by the afternoon of the second day, she was sorry she hadn't canceled the whole thing and refunded the women their money. The strain proved too much for him, and he raged at every one of them in turn. Paulina hadn't put the coffee on right. Kate, who studied Tai Chi in addition to Zen had "spoiled" the walking meditation with her "Chinese jerky movements," and Mary dared to complain to him about the "unhealthy" white sugar and caffeinated coffee for breakfast.

"I no like womens," he muttered when Fay brought him tea in his room during afternoon breaks.

On the last day of the dreary sesshin, she took the bag containing the meditation bell and clappers and was placing it along with hers into the trunk of Paulina's car when Eikei came running out into the street after her. "You stupid! You leave that package alone! I tell you never to handle bell and clappers! You not zendo monk! PUT BAG DOWN RIGHT NOW!"

Feeling as if he'd torched her, Fay fought the urge to slap him in front of the women gathered around the car.

"I ring the goddamned bell every morning," she screamed back. "And who do you think paid to bring it here in the first place!"

Kate came over and put her arm around her. "Come on, get into the car. We'll drive you home," she said.

"Yes, I'd like that," Fay said, gingerly standing the bag at his feet.

His eyes bulging, Eikei picked it up and went back inside.

Fay got into the car muttering. "You bow-legged sonofabitch."

Kate, who was toothpick thin and had dark brown bangs let out a whistle. "Well, I've seen it all," she said. "I've been to sesshin with Ryuho Roshi and Tano Roshi, and I've practiced Chinese Zen with Master Wang; they're all 'eccentric'—but Eikei Roshi is the weirdest of them all. How you take it, Fay, I'll never understand. The man is scared out of his wits when it comes to women. I mean he's clearly got a problem. You have to be careful of these Asian men; if you stick around, they eventually grind you down to a fine powder. Women are nothing but slaves and ornaments to them."

"He may not be a seducer, like your run-of-the-mill guru, but he's violent, and that scares me," said Paulina, her eyelids sparkling with the iridescent green shadow that was her trademark.

"Like Catholics," said Fay. "Virgins or whores, that's all we are to them."

Paulina lit a cigarette, and Mary said, "Open the window if you're going to smoke."

"Yeah, they fuck like rabbits too," Paulina said.

Though she was tempted, Fay refrained from telling them about her Paris adventure. She would have liked to join their Zen scandal gossip but was still too deeply rooted in notions of loyalty to her teacher, still harboring her secret hope of becoming his enlightened sergeant one day.

Mary said, "I was brought up Catholic, too. Our parish priest was an alcoholic. He had a red nose, and he tickled the little girls in his Catechism class under their dresses."

The women then launched a discussion about a famous Japanese Zen teacher in California, who had recently confessed to having sex with the teenaged daughters of two of his most committed women students.

"Are there any women roshis?" Kate asked.

"Are there any women popes?" Fay asked, getting a laugh.

Paulina pulled to a stop in front of her building. Fay stepped over Kate's long legs and got out of the car. Kate reached out the window and handed Fay her bag. "Don't worry, you'll toughen up," she said.

"Yeah," Fay said. "Either that or I'll kill him."

Paulina drove off in a cloud of exhaust fumes. Fay waved at the women in the back seat until the car turned the corner, then, picking up her bag, feeling as if she'd been beaten black and blue, she buzzed for Ira to let her in.

December 20, 1984

Ira's book has hit the bestseller lists! I watched him on Oprah the other day, in his brown corduroy jacket and brown tweed slacks, looking heavier than he really is and getting seriously bald. He's grown a mustache, which I'm not sure suits him as well as the baldness, which gives him a certain air of spiritual authority, like Eikei's. I guess it's not for nothing that religions invented tonsure; there's definitely something otherworldly about baldness, as if all that transcendent wisdom can't be contained in a skull covered by a shock of hair. Of course, hair is also connected with women, and sexuality, and, as Tano Roshi believes, women (read "demonic spirits") just get in the way of spirituality . . .

They're calling Ira the latest sensation in "alternative medicine" on the publicity blurbs, and since there's even been some talk about his getting a TV show of his own, he's assumed a new, self-confident, almost glib, speaking style. The women in the audience trusted him right off. You could tell from the way they looked at him when he answered their questions in that reassuring, slightly ironic tone he reserves for women in trouble, which, for Ira, means all women. It made me wonder whether he and Sam aren't being trailed by an army of lost, mostly middle-aged groupies who follow them from seminar to seminar, spending thousands to cure their depression or quit smoking or lose weight by just owning up to their "past life karma" and willing it away. Sure, the money comes rolling in regularly, and he's generous, practically paying for the whole Bowery Zendo enterprise himself, so who am I to complain? But I wonder if there isn't something phony, even unethical, about what he's doing.

Though he tells me it's much less harmful than what the traditional doctors are doing to their patients, and God knows, I have first-hand experience of that. No, Ira's not selling snake oil, not yet. But Sam is another matter . . . Wonder if . . . no, dare I think it . . . if, in addition to their business partnership, they haven't got a thing going. Ira and I sure aren't having much sex lately, what with all his coming and going and TV appearances and a long waiting list of patients scheduled half a year in advance taking up every minute of his time while he's here in New York. Sam has been strangely scarce in all this, leaving Ira to occupy the spotlight. Guess I can't complain about that.

As an early Christmas present, Ira made an appointment for Eikei and me with Ted Zalk, who, he says, is the best Tarot reader in the country. I thought Eikei would laugh in his face when he told him this, but he didn't. And was dead serious about wanting to go, mumbling on about his psychic uncle in Yokohama who he calls every now and then for advice, and who told him to come to America with Fay-san because it was his karma to bring Zen from Japan to a whole new generation of seekers across the ocean—like a latter-day Bodhidharma sailing on a reed to China with the great teaching from India. Eikei, it turns out, is much more superstitious than he at first let on.

So, last Tuesday, after morning zazen, we went to consult with Ted Zalk at the Ansonia Hotel. The lobby was filled with dancers (some of whom I knew), and bookies, and witches, and retired German refugees, all of them smoking. Everything was decorated in purple silk, like in an Oscar Wilde farce, and the players were self-consciously weird. Lest he be recognized (by whom?) Eikei dressed like a Japanese tourist for the occasion: porkpie hat, shirt and tie, blue blazer, and Barney's three-hundred-dollar slacks (courtesy of Ira). Not that there was any danger of anyone recognizing him. The roshi's been looking very wizened lately, more like the night watchman he's been threat-

ening to become if we run out of money to keep the Bowery Zendo going! The truth is I'm beginning to loathe his "civilian" getup; out of his floor-length black robes he's just another Japanese Obasan on the street, helplessly dependent on me for everything. At times like these, I forget that he's as healthy as the proverbial horse, even with all the smoking.

We took the elevator to the fourteenth floor, rang the bell of a purple door, and were asked through the intercom to please wait in the hall for five minutes. Eikei didn't like that, especially since there was no chair or waiting area and no ashtray. He paced the thickly carpeted corridor while I stood in front of the long, shade-less window facing Broadway. I traced the letters on the movie marquee across the street advertising a "Classic Russian Film Festival" on the window with my finger until I heard a door open, and then almost bumped into a woman in a muskrat fur coat with a pair of glasses hanging from a silver string around her neck, who was hurrying toward the elevator. Then Ted Zalk appeared in the doorway to usher us into his tiny studio office, kitchen, bedroom, and meditation room. He is a round man with a red face and a head of unruly brown hair. Good-humored and businesslike at once, he looks and acts more like a financial consultant than a Tarot card reader.

Ted briskly seated us around a bare table and immediately produced from its drawer Eikei's astrological chart cast from the sketchy information I'd related to him through Ira in advance. Eikei removed his hat and sat with it in his hands, beads of sweat forming on his baldpate. Ted asked if he wanted a drink of water or juice, which he refused. My hands were shaking under the table. Eikei only has to be sitting a certain way, with his hip off the side of a chair or his back suddenly stiffening as if he's about to get up, to make me nervous. I only have to anticipate his need of the moment, an impatient gesture indicating his wish to leave, or the onset of a fit of rage, to get the adrenaline pumping.

Without any introduction, Ted plunged right in. "The chart shows that you're particularly influenced by your mother," he said, his eyebrows arching. "Though she's gone, she still strongly lives in your feelings, in your decisions. You are very attached to her."

Eikei sat with his lips compressed in a line and said nothing. Ted again opened the table drawer and took out a packet of Tarot cards. "I have a sense that these will give me a clearer reading of the roshi's situation," he said as he sorted the cards and placed them face down on the table in orderly rows. Eikei pulled his chair closer to the table. The cards were large and glossy, engraved with mythical popes and knights and sword-bearing empresses. Ted asked Eikei to turn over a card. Pointing to the Fool card Eikei had chosen, he sighed. "Ah . . . that's you, roshi." A strand of cowlick came loose and dangled over his forehead. He smoothed his hair into place then turned over two more cards, one on either side of Eikei's emblematic self. "Ah," Ted sighed again, this time pointing to the first upturned card in the top row, an angel. I noticed that he was wearing a silver thumb ring with a jasper stone. "That's you, Fay, his guardian angel, on the right."

"Who is that?" Eikei pointed at the card on the left, a rather pornographic sketch of a nude woman with a lascivious grin.

"That is worldly temptation. Some woman is coming to tempt you, roshi," Ted said smiling and lazily lighting a cigarette. He offered one to Eikei and another to me. I thanked him and refused. Eikei accepted.

"What woman?" Eikei wanted to know.

"That I can't tell you. If she already hasn't appeared, she will, in a short while. And when she does, it will mean Fay will have to exert her efforts on your behalf, because, if you succumb to this worldly temptation, the future of your Zen community is in jeopardy. You can lose it all."

Caught by Ted's certainty, I asked, "Who is she?"

Eikei waved his hand at me and said, "Be quiet. Let him talk."

Ted squinted through the cigarette smoke and said, "There's nothing more to add, really. That's all there is. You, roshi, the Holy Fool, will be tested. And you, Fay, his guardian angel . . . will be the one to suffer either way." Then he nonchalantly launched into a description of some oceanfront property in Canada, which, according to the surrounding cards, someone would soon donate to Eikei for a retreat center. But after that bombshell about the roshi being tested and me suffering, I didn't pay too much attention to what Ted was saying.

Later, over a cup of coffee and a doughnut in a luncheonette on Seventy Second Street, I asked Eikei bluntly if he was secretly harboring a girlfriend.

"Many, many girlfriends," he said with a tinny laugh.

"No kidding, roshi, I mean, is there anyone you can think of, from the zendo or from London?" (Or could Ted have been talking about Gretta Lewis?)

"What you mean? I tell you many, many girlfriends. I most popular, have big girlfriend following."

I ordered a second cup of coffee. Why should a girlfriend spoil things? I thought. Maybe, if he finds someone and gets married, he'll be nicer to me, and to women in general. Right then and there, taking a sip of coffee and burning my tongue, I hatched the plot to find him a wife. Anything would be better than losing him to the lewd woman on the card with the pink belly and the pointed red nipples.

So I called a set designer I knew through Brad, our stage manager, an attractive blond named Kim. Eikei was surprisingly tractable, even admitting that considering the professional and financial investment Jessie and I had made, and with our reputations at stake in the current climate of Zen scandals, it would be better for him to get married and avoid trouble. Surprisingly, rather than order me to stay out of his business, the roshi tasked me with finding just the right kind of wife, insisting that the woman be American, not Japanese, and that she be blond and young enough to bear children. Kim filled the bill, and best of all from his point of view, she had her own car. He refused to call her himself, so I had to arrange the date for him. The funny thing was it seemed like the natural thing to do: a monk calls a girl to fix up a fellow monk who's shy, like one of the guys at Shofuji training to be a temple priest who's looking for a healthy, attractive wife who'll make supper and babies on time. Fact is, ever since Ted's reading, Eikei's been treating me like a guy. He doesn't bother putting on his robes and is still sitting in his pajamas drinking tea when I come into the zendo in the morning, and sometimes even leaves the bathroom door open when he pees!

One morning, he came out of his bedroom carrying one of those self-testing digital blood pressure machines and asked me to note and record his painstaking attempts to take a reading from one minute to the next. He was absolutely mesmerized by the changes. "Feeling strange today," he said, making a routine of taking his blood pressure every morning thereafter. I think he's taking the idea of being "tested" literally. And, as if to prove his invincibility, he's doubled his cigarette intake! That must be what the dating game is all about: he's testing his heroic Zen discipline against the coming onslaught of the she-devil. Here, in a reversal of my lowly novice/guest status at Shofuji, I am the roshi's confidant, not enlightened, but sufficiently neutered to have become a Zen crony . . . his alter ego, his dating self.

Kim said she remembered seeing Eikei at Jessie's company party, a little drunk, but charming. Then she paused and asked how old he was.

"Fifty-three," I said, shaving two years off his age.

"That's a bit old," Kim said. "But okay."

We arranged for me to bring him to her apartment on Waverly Place. After that, Kim said, she would take him to her bungalow in the Catskills, grill a couple of steaks in the fireplace and show him Woodstock, then drive back to the city before nightfall.

Eikei ran around the studio dusting everything in sight the whole time I was on the phone with her. When I'd finished talking, he ran up to me with the dust cloth still in his hands, and, his face glowing, said, "She nice, quiet lady. I remember from party. But I really too drunk to remember good. She not afraid of me?"

"No, she's not afraid of you."

"But I afraid of lady. I never on formal date; Fay-san, you come too."

"Are you kidding? What am I supposed to do, hold both your hands?" Eikei shrank back and gave me a beady-eyed stare. "Do you want me to call her back and cancel the date?" I said.

"No, no," he pleaded.

"Then what do you want me to do?"

"You call back and tell her you come too."

The absolute terror in his voice drove me back to the telephone. "Kim?" I said, trying to sound lighthearted, "Kim, you're not going to believe this, but the roshi wants me to come along on your date."

Kim did not laugh, as I thought she would. Instead, taking a long, audible breath, she said, "Oh, that's just what I'd hoped; only I was ashamed to ask. I want you to come along too. It'll make it easier for me on several counts: first off, I can hardly understand his English."

With a nervous laugh, I said, "Okay, I'll come along as translator."

Eikei stood at the window knotting and unknotting the

Venetian blind cords. As soon as I'd hung up, he ran over and almost fell at my feet. "Thank you, Fay-san. I so grateful you rescue me from womens."

December 28, 1984

The day in the country was a welcome break from the dry stretch of zazen I've been experiencing lately. We sat around the fire grilling steak and potatoes, drinking beer and playing Monopoly, then strolled afterward in the snow-covered vegetable garden where we refilled the bird feeders and talked about nothing in particular. Even Eikei relaxed a little. When Kim dropped us off in front of the zendo that night, he thanked her, bowed several times, and praised her driving. But as I walked with him to the front door, he said he didn't think he wanted to date her again.

"From now on you're on your own. I'm not dating with you anymore."

Eikei gave me a bashful smile. "Thank you, Fay-san. I see it not that bad. But I never touch lady, I never even hold hand. You come upstairs for cup of tea and show me."

"No, let's do it here by the door. I'm tired, and I still have to get the zendo books ready for the accountant before the year is out."

Eikei opened the front door and I followed him into the hallway. "Okay, I'll be the man, you be the girl," I said, taking his elbow and guiding him through the door of a pretend restaurant. "Oh, and above all," I said, "don't make gas." His hard, wiry back grew soft and vulnerable under my touch, and for one sweet moment I felt the raw power of a man over his woman.

Then he ruined everything by getting drunk and phoning Kim at two in the morning to thank her again for her kind hospi-

tality. She called the next day and asked me to meet her at Elephant and Castle to discuss his strange behavior.

She was sitting at a table for two, drinking hot chocolate when I arrived. Her coat and long striped woolen scarf were trailing on the floor behind her chair, and I hung them up along with the down jacket and newsboy cap Eikei had bought me for Christmas. I had barely sat down before Kim snapped at me, "Is your roshi some kind of sex maniac?"

"What . . . are you . . . talking about?" I stammered.

"Mind you, it was two in the morning. He started out thanking me, and blah, blah, blah, but then he got onto this sex jag, and it occurred to me that he's one of these guys who gets off on dirty telephone talk, and that's not my thing." Kim was red in the face. The waitress came by with the menu, and asking for a few more minutes, she waved her away.

"No, you've got him wrong. It's just that he's naïve, really, totally off the wall when it comes to women. They threw him into a monastery at age six and screwed up his sex life . . ."

Kim didn't let me finish, "He kept going on and on about how he's a virgin, kept making nasty remarks about women, and American women in particular, kept deriding my psychoanalysis. I'm not even in psychoanalysis! I tried steering the conversation to Zen, anything to get him off the topic of sex—as I said, it was two in the morning and I was deeply asleep when he called —but sex was on his mind, and I couldn't get him off, so I just hung up on him. I hope it wasn't disrespectful of me, him being your Zen master and all, but I'd had enough."

I assured Kim that she'd done the right thing and promised there'd be no repeat performances. She left and I paid for her hot chocolate, giving the waitress an overly big tip, though I hadn't had anything to eat or drink—and deciding then and there to get out of the dating business for good. Luckily, Eikei and I will be heading for Nova Scotia right after New Years (Ted Zalk was right about the donation of Canadian property; one of Eikei's biggest fans is a Rockefeller cousin who handed him the deed after our end-of-year sesshin—which he promptly put in his pocket and forgot about until two days ago). And that should put the issue of the Tarot card demon lady to rest—at least for the next two weeks. Eikei's reputation is still intact. Kim has agreed to say nothing to anyone about the date or the 2 a.m. phone call, and another Zen scandal has been avoided.

19
NOVA SCOTIA

To drown out the roshi's running criticism of her driving, Fay turned on the radio. She knew he was annoyed at having to travel so far by plane, and then a hundred miles more by car to get to the tip of Nova Scotia Bay, for he'd told her so at least five times since she'd left the airport road and gotten onto the highway. She nodded, thinking, but not saying—as her mother would—that he'd better stop complaining and start counting his blessings. After all, he hadn't spent a dime on his own airfare or on the car rental, she had traded in all her frequent flier miles for an upgrade to Business Class, and, to top it off, he'd been handed the deed to over a hundred acres of valuable seafront property, so the least he could do was *stop bitching and show some gratitude*, she thought. But of course, she said nothing of the sort, because it was no use starting an argument with him, which she'd never win anyway.

Fay turned up the volume and sang along with the Beatles. The road, like the one the Beatles were describing just then, was long and winding, and she was momentarily baffled at Eikei for choosing to provoke her and risk an accident. On the other hand, it could be that he was testing her as usual, to see how she'd react under pressure. Would she fly off the handle and get hysterical like a woman, or should the tire go flat, or the car skid on a patch of ice, would she take control of the situation like a man? Ever since his date with Kim, he'd been goading her about her "female mentality," her emotional and impulsive "lady nature," as if to let her know how she'd failed him.

"You driving too fast around turns," he said.

"What do you think of the countryside around here, isn't it perfect for a retreat center?"

"You cannot drive and sing at same time. Better you pay attention to driving," he said, turning off the radio.

Fay slowed down, "There's got to be a reason for this kind of pressure, right, Eikei? I mean, on such a narrow, unfamiliar road, putting us both in danger—especially since you think I'm such a lousy driver."

He gave her a sheepish smile. "It my technique not to give compliment, because you need to hear sweet words only. You don't like my bitter medicine, but it good for you. Getting nowhere with romantic dream talking, like Ira-san."

Fay switched on the radio again, and pressing her foot hard against the gas pedal, sped toward Mabou Mines.

It's not a good idea to bite the hand that feeds you, she thought, amazed at Eikei's ability to bring out not only his, but her own mother in her as well.

The property the Canadian lawyer showed them was surrounded by spruce trees and led through a snow-covered meadow to a cornucopia-shaped bay of icy green water filled with lobster, herring, and mackerel. *Alive and bountiful as the Buddhist Pure Land Paradise itself,* Fay thought, imagining the place in summer and herself running barefoot through the meadow. The lawyer was accompanied by a surveyor who talked about building codes and property lines, and Eikei nodded, pretending to understand every word while Fay jotted notes on a yellow pad. Shaking Eikei's hand, the lawyer assured him that the paperwork was ready and that all he had to do was come to the office the next day to sign—and the property was his. Then, he and the surveyor got into their blue van and drove away.

Fay and Eikei were having a light supper in the coffee shop of their motel later that evening when, for the first time, she dared to admit to herself that he'd been drinking in his room on the sly, using "the holiday season" as an excuse. He'd overslept three times in the past two weeks, missing morning zazen, and she'd heard him snoring softly on his cushion during evening meditation. Eikei had also started making excuses for the alcoholism among Shofuji monks, even going so far as to whisper in her ear during a Japanese Kabuki performance at Lincoln Center that Ryuho Roshi's talent as a kabuki artist had been inspired by sake. She hadn't taken him seriously until afterward on the subway downtown, when he informed her that the real reason Ryuho was locked up in his mountaintop hut was not because he was crazy, but alcoholic.

Her chest constricting against a rush of images—the circles of little blue men carrying XO Napoleon brandy at Narita airport, the endless wine served at Mr. Yamato's French restaurant, the cook passing a bottle of Johnny Walker to the brutish zendo monk behind the bathhouse—Fay wondered if Eikei weren't alcoholic, too. Certainly, it would explain the mood swings, the insults followed by the baby talk, the obsequiousness toward Ira, and the snide remarks in his absence. Again, like the clever little monkey she'd been with Ben, Fay worked hard not to see, not to speak, not to hear, and not to acknowledge the possibility that her Zen master might be a drunk, even if an enlightened one.

As a child, pretending to be a deaf mute during one of her father's alcoholic rages, she'd sit with her mouth shut and her eyes looking down at his shiny black gum-soled shoes, thinking, if I don't move, he won't hit me, and she was right, because, though he grew angrier when she pretended to be deaf and dumb— "Damn it! You'll answer your father when he talks to you!" and removed his belt (always surprising her when his heavy green military trousers stayed up without it), and she didn't budge. Ben would then toss the belt on the sofa and sobbing, would grab her by the ankles and beg her forgiveness.

The same little red veins she saw in her father's eyes mapped Eikei's, and she smelled the same whiskey on his breath, and detected the same weakness behind his military façade. Now, sitting in this red vinyl booth in Nova Scotia eating whitefish chowder listening to Eikei prattle on about his mother's saintly virtue—how it was because of her that the land had come to him in the first place, and would remain his only if he had nothing to do with impure women, like the walleyed Japanese dancer, Miyako, who, though she could answer koan questions almost as soon as he posed them, was just the sort his mother's spirit was warning him against—Fay at last understood that in drunkenly confusing her with his mother, Eikei feared her more than she feared him. How else to account for his rant against "bad womens," demanding they be barred from attending sesshin in the new retreat center, where only women like his mother, paragons of patience, modesty and forbearance would be welcomed. Even personal details came spilling out: how his father had often come home with a painted geisha on each arm, and his mother had taken her husband from them without so much as a tear or a rebuke. How she would speak only when she had her little boy alone to herself, and never against his father, warning the boy to keep away from women and remain a pure monk for as long as he lived. In college, Eikei said, he had never so much as taken a girl to a movie. On trains, remembering his mother's words, he'd change seats rather than sit next to a pretty woman. When his temple teacher had offered him his beautiful youngest daughter as a wife, Eikei had ridiculed her to make her hate him, causing her father to cancel the match. No woman could ever equal his mother. Most were scum.

The catalog of horrors continued through dessert, but by then Fay had stopped listening. She sat in front of him, mute, as she had with her father, marveling at even the greatest Zen masters' implacable hatred for women in all its guises, and then at the ingenuity of the women who had dealt with it. She thought of the Chinese Ryonen, who had been too beautiful to study Zen; no master would take her on. Waiting until she turned forty-five and was no longer sexually desirable (so she thought). Ryonen left her husband and children and went searching for a Zen master who would teach her. She traveled the length and breadth of China without success. "You're too beautiful," said the abbots of every monastery she tried to enter, "too much trouble around the monks."

Finally, having reached the end of her travels, Ryonen returned home, seized a hot iron, and seared one side of her too beautiful face. "There, that's the end of my looks," she said. The end of her problems too, for Pai Chang, one of China's finest Zen masters, took her on as a disciple and ordained her a nun. Ryonen later became his scar-faced successor, the first female Zen master in his entire illustrious line.

"Much easier dealing with men," Eikei was saying as the waitress appeared with the bill. Though her calves were chunky, and she was barrel hipped, she wore a pink uniform that barely covered her knees. Good for you, Fay thought, paying the bill with her credit card.

In the car, Eikei, who'd grown glum and silent after his tirade, suddenly lashed out at her:

"You are nothing but human toy. When I with you, I talk to you like human toy, become toy. You like talking toys on television shows for children—nothing more than piece of human dust. Like snot."

Fay drove past an Indian reservation, then a town with a surprising number of surly drivers for such an idyllic, white churchy place. Cutting through the traffic, she took the ramp leading to a busy highway. With the light flashing on the incoming lane flashing yellow, she pressed her foot all the way down on the gas pedal and pulled into the stream of passing cars, crossing to the left lane and causing a brown and white station wagon to swerve in order to avoid hitting her broadside, an angry chorus of blasting horns following in her wake. Surely, she'd scared the bejeesus out of Eikei, made him shut up. Surely, she hadn't, for he was still at it. "Your men friends like you only because they are gay and you nothing to them, not a woman. Even Ira-san not want you. To me you nothing more than human toy."

Fay ran through her usual list of infringements and found she hadn't been guilty of even one. She had driven day and night on Canadian roads without getting lost, had dealt with zendo business even more efficiently than Hiro-san, in fact, she had shown neither glee nor disappointment, had scrupulously followed road maps and gotten him to appointments on time with minutes to spare. She had not stopped the car to go to the toilet and had been lectured non-stop about the inferiority of her sex without putting up an argument. Nonetheless, for reasons that were only just becoming clear to her, she was sure that Eikei had chosen this moment to test her ego, to see how she was faring at the outermost limits of her tolerance for humiliation. He'd joked on occasion about her "suicide bravery." In London, fearing that she had gone off and drowned herself in the bathtub, he'd rushed out in the middle of a morning meditation period taking the stairs two at a time and banged on the bathroom door yelling for her to come out or he'd break it down. She had scared him enough then into rewarding her by taking her to Harrods and buying her a beige cashmere cardigan that had cost him a week and a half's worth of pocket money. As they were drinking sake in a Chelsea sushi bar later that afternoon, he'd said, "When you are old and paralyzed, I will buy you golden wheelchair and walk you up and down Hyde Park Road." And she'd replied, "You are old enough to be my father. In all probability, I'll be buying you a golden wheelchair, and walking you up and down Hyde Park Road." And Eikei had roared, "Fay-san, you greatest fighting partner of all!"

Leaving Canada and the Pure Land Paradise behind, as the plane banked through the clouds at five thousand feet, it suddenly occurred to her that she had once again outscored him. Flashing him a wry smile, she said, "Eikei, you greatest fighting partner of all!" But the roshi was fidgeting with his seat belt and didn't hear her over the roar of the engines.

20
FOR THE LOVE OF ZEN

Ira calls Fay from New Mexico and tells her that his lecture tour is going great guns. Fay hears cocktail lounge noises behind him and asks him who he is with, and Ira says he is with Dana Brownell, his publicist. Fay thinks of asking him if he is fucking Dana Brownell, but then remembers that she is the president of the Bowery Zendo board of directors and is supposed to be above such petty wifely carping. So, telling him to send Dana her regards and wishing him well on the next leg of his lecture tour, she hangs up and goes back to the twelve-inch Sony on the kitchen island counter and resumes eating potato chips and feta cheese and drinking diet root beer while watching *My Man Godfrey* on the Turner Movie Classic channel. It is past midnight and Carole Lombard is chasing William Powell to his hobo retreat near the docks of what is supposed to be New York, actually only a few blocks East of where Fay is sitting now. The telephone rings again. Hoping it is Ira calling her back to tell her—as she knows William Powell in the penultimate scene will tell Carole Lombard—that since she has stopped acting like a spoiled brat, he can love her, that she is, after all, his long-held dream of the perfect woman, needing only a shanty and a mattress and a coffee pot to be happy, and not four-hundred thousand dollar lofts and Business Class air tickets for her rummy of a Zen teacher; the kind of woman who would curl up with him as snug as a bug in a rug under the Brooklyn Bridge, if it came to that, and still consider herself the luckiest woman in the world—as Carole is at that very moment saying on soft camera, her eyes glittering like rhinestones on the tiny television screen on the counter. The phone rings seven times before Fay picks it up, for she is thinking about Carole Lombard's dying in an airplane crash, and that sets off a cascade of morbid death fantasies revolving around her Zen teacher Eikei trapped in his Business Class seat belt, red-eyed as he goes down in a fiery crash which he miraculously survives.

On the seventh ring, Fay picks up the telephone. She has not turned on the answering machine in the hope that Ira will call back and say that he has decided to call it quits with his latest foray into the psychic healing business and wants her to leave Eikei and Zen behind and join him in the Algarve, where they'll eat crayfish and write mystery stories together under the combined pseudonym Corman Watkins. Carole and William are kissing; "The End" flashes across their midsections as Fay reaches on top of the refrigerator for the wine rack, takes down and opens a dusty bottle of Beaujolais, and, after pouring herself a glass, picks up the telephone.

It is Walleyed Miyako at the other end, the twenty-four-year-old import from Japan, Eikei's newest favorite Zen student. Fay has tried hard not to bear Miyako a grudge. She's worked for three months since Miyako joined the Zen group on Halloween eve to keep from hating her younger rival for the slinky ease with which she has maneuvered her way ahead of the zendo's senior members and for laughing and exchanging jokes in Japanese in the kitchen with Eikei while Fay stands around feeling superfluous. Most of all, Fay resents Miyako for supplanting her as her teacher's cook and confidante.

Thus, Fay controls the little ripple of pleasure that threatens when she hears Miyako sobbing at the other end of the line. Fay reckons she would be the last person Miyako would be calling in tears on a Saturday night at twenty minutes past twelve, since Miyako (in very un-Japanese fashion) is known for bragging to anyone within earshot that she is seeing Jan Vandenhag, the famous Dutch neon artist who just happens to be in New York enjoying a Whitney retrospective and is in the process of shedding his latest girlfriend, the equally famous, cigar-smoking British feminist writer, Lindsey Polk, in favor of the exotic Miyako.

Fay has had to restrain herself from smashing Miyako's little snub nose further into the fleshy folds of her moon face every morning as she opens the door to the zendo and finds the Japanese woman already perched on her cushion in deep meditation. Lately, Fay has been digging her nails into her palms during interview periods when she hears Miyako and the roshi in his tiny bedroom engaging in what she assumes are brilliant Zen dialogues and laughing so loud that all the other non-Japanese speakers in the room shuffle uncomfortably on their cushions. With great effort she has managed to keep from telling Miyako to please stop bringing her ikebana flower arrangements and setting them on the altar, since two zendo regulars have complained of being allergic to flowers, and she, Fay, is only stuffing them in the trash can in the parking lot behind the zendo afterward. Fay has worked hard not to insult Miyako since the day Eikei informed her that the young woman was some kind of Zen genius, whizzing through koans in a week that even he had struggled with for months. Fay has consequently given Miyako a wide berth. Still stumped by

Eikei's claim that enlightened people came in all shapes and sizes, that, yes, there could be unlikable, drunken, and even immoral ones, Fay has been keeping a sharp eye on Miyako from a distance.

"Fay-san," Miyako says breathily, "I so sorry to disturb you so late. But I have emergency and you the only person I think to talk to."

Fay takes a sip of wine and holds it against her teeth.

"You there, Fay-san?" Miyako asks.

"Mmm," Fay replies in the act of swallowing.

"Can I come over?"

"What about Jan? I thought you said you were going to a party for him tonight." Fay glances at Eikei's sinewy calligraphic circle depicting emptiness hanging on the white brick wall above the sofa across from the counter where she is standing and momentarily entertains a doubt about the authenticity of Miyako's enlightenment. The mind at peace, she thinks, doesn't get this rattled.

"I left the party. I calling you from telephone booth on Canal Street; can see your building from here."

"Sure, come up. I'm not sleeping."

The streets were blanketed in slush, and a wild wind was blowing up from the river; Fay could hear it whining through the elevator shaft out in the hall. Seeing Miyako standing in the doorway underdressed for the weather in only a shabby brown turtle-neck sweater and the tiniest, tightest excuse for a black leather skirt, her Chinese cloth slippers waterlogged, the droplets on her black hair hanging over her face like a beaded curtain, Fay felt sorry for her.

"You're shivering, I'll turn up the heat," she said, leading Miyako into the loft and handing her an oversized orange bath towel from the linen closet in the foyer. "Take it in the bathroom with you; there's a dryer there for your hair, if you want."

"Thank you, Fay-san." Miyako bowed and removed her shoes before stepping inside, and, with atypical humility, continued bowing every step of the way to the bathroom.

With the dryer humming in the background, Fay poured herself another glass of wine and took a seat on the stool at the counter opposite the sofa. Noting that the Saturday Night Horror Special was featuring *The Thing*, she reluctantly switched off the television set. A few minutes later the hair dryer went silent, and Miyako emerged from the bathroom, tiptoeing down the hall on the balls of her bare feet. Fay handed her a pair of socks and a fringed purple afghan and suggested she curl up on the sofa. Then she went to the stove and made a pot of green tea; lacing it with cognac, she passed a cup to Miyako.

"So, what can I do for you?" Fay said, moving the counter stool closer to the sofa and sitting down after placing her wine glass on the Lucite cube coffee table. It was hard not to focus on Miyako's off-center eye, follow its gaze to the window, so Fay concentrated on her perfectly shaped kewpie doll lips instead.

Miyako pulled on the socks. Then placing the purple afghan alongside her on the sofa, she sniffed once and said, "I not so cold anymore. Please, you have patience with me—"

"Did something happen at the party?" Fay leaned forward and asked in a low, comforting voice.

Instead of answering the question directly, Miyako made a recognizably Japanese effort to regain her composure. Looking around the room, she said, "You have beautiful home. I never here before."

Fay nodded and took up her wine glass. She was getting the uneasy feeling that Miyako might be engaged in a bet with Eikei that Fay could easily be manipulated into taking an action she would later regret. Fay pictured him and his star pupil sitting across from each other in the interview room, laughing about the greenhouse gullibility of Westerners. She made an impatient gesture with her glass, and the wine sloshed against it.

Miyako uncrossed her legs and leaned forward. "Fay-san, I tell you the truth about my situation. But you must not interrupt me, must believe every word I say to you. I tell you the whole truth of my situation tonight." Miyako wiped her eyes with the back of her hand and said, "Eikei have visitor. I very upset, I discover her earlier tonight when I come to bring him Japanese newspaper. I see them from window facing parking lot behind, the blinds open and all the lights on. She very tall American lady, very skinny, with brown hair and long braid hanging down her back, and very long skinny legs, like bird legs. I never see her here before. She not zendo member. Coming up the street from parking lot side, it easy to see everything in zendo, and I see lady putting her arms around Eikei's neck, sitting him down on kitchen chair and sitting on top of his lap. They hugging and kissing"—Miyako let out a sob, rattling the teacup against the top of the Lucite cube and startling herself. Both eyes were equally dark now, almost aligned in their misery. Like the two of us, Fay thought, cold sweat running between her breasts. Thinking Fay was about to speak, Miyako held up her hand and said, "No . . . you must let me tell you everything. Say nothing until I finished."

Fay got up and tore a paper towel from the roll on the wall above the sink in the open kitchen. She bunched it up and, tucking it under her sweater, dried her cleavage with it. The paper was harsh against her skin; she had run out of tissues. Very deliberately, she walked over to the shopping list tacked to the refrigerator on a pineapple magnet, taking it down she wrote "Boutique Tissues" on it before tacking it back onto the refrigerator again. Miyako's cup was empty, and the tea had turned cold. Fay opened a cupboard and took out a second wine glass. Without asking Miyako if she wanted any, she poured her the last of the Beaujolais, then opened the refrigerator, took out an open bottle of California Chardonnay and poured some for herself. She brought the two glasses with her back to the Lucite cube, handing Miyako the Beaujolais, then sat down facing her again. If she hadn't moved around while Miyako was talking, she knew she might have blurted words she'd be sorry for afterward—just in case it was another one of those "Zen discipline tests" Eikei had cooked up for her and borrowed Miyako to execute. For now, in the narrow, ungenerous spaces of her envy and mistrust of her Japanese rival, she sensed a far more dangerous presence. She had always pictured Eikei's fiancée manqué as the kind of woman who would have bird legs and a single braid down her back.

Miyako gulped her wine and said, "I get up on top of parked car right under the window to see better, and get full view of them sitting in chair, kissing and hugging. She much bigger than him, long legs hanging over him, making his face disappear in her neck. I jump off car and start running around corner into building, open zendo door with my key, and come right into the room, stand facing them and screaming—"

So, Miyako had a key to the zendo! Fay couldn't help but interrupt her then: "I can understand your shock, your disappointment; I just don't see, though, what makes you feel you have the right to interfere with the roshi's personal life."

Miyako jumped up from the sofa and after putting down her wine glass, came around to where Fay was sitting and knelt down in front of her. With one eye staring directly at her and the other struggling to join it, but gazing off at the window again, Miyako said, "Because I Eikei's lover for all these months, because I teach him how to make love in bed. He virgin, know nothing about where to put penis, know nothing until I teach him! We sleeping in bed together every night, even

I hear you coming into zendo in morning, turning key, sometimes lying without moving in bed, without making a sound, not even able to go to toilet and feeling like bursting, having to pee so much—but Eikei not want you to know, he say you go crazy if you find out."

Holding Miyako's hand, Fay asked, "How many months, exactly?"

"Since I joining zendo and become Eikei's student."

"From the first day?"

"No, not first day, but very soon after, a week, maybe. But Fay-san, you not ask question now. You ask me after. You promised."

Fay removed her hand from Miyako's and sat back on her stool. She would have gotten up and added toothpaste to her shopping list, for, absurdly, the idea had popped into her head that she was almost out of toothpaste. But Miyako remained kneeling in front of her, looking like one of the supplicant women she'd seen praying to the enormous Buddha in Kamakura, so she stayed put. "Okay," she whispered, placing her finger on her lips, "not another word."

"I try to pull her off him. She jump up and slap me in the face, asking him who I am and why I have key. And Eikei then get very red in face and very angry with me, and order me to get out, saying it none of my business who he invite as guest on weekend, saying he not interested in me anymore, I troublemaker, bad woman he would not even look at in Japan, say no nice Japanese man would marry me after I come to America and sleeping with so many Western men. And tall American lady then go into toilet, and I hear her taking shower. Eikei then take me over to Buddha statue on altar and make me swear in front of Buddha never to tell you any of this, saying that woman just very good old friend, that she fly down for weekend from Maine to see him, that she love him, but he not love her. I ask him if we still can be together, if he still want me to sleep in zendo with him, and he say better no more sleeping together. But then I tell him I not getting period and going to doctor for test and test say I pregnant. And Eikei get very red in face then, and very angry, and start yelling that it probably white foreigner's baby, and that I nothing but painted bad woman, probably carrying disease, and that I lying about pregnant . . ." Miyako broke off and buried her face in Fay's lap.

"Can I talk now?" Fay asked.

Miyako's shoulders moved up and down, and Fay said, "Is it true that you're pregnant?" Miyako emitted a muffled wail that left no doubt that she was. Smoothing Miyako's hair, Fay said, "He's partly right, you know, it could be Jan's baby and not his."

Miyako lifted her head, contorting her tear-streaked face and said, "I not sleeping with Jan the whole time I Eikei's lover. I loyal only to Eikei. Making excuses to Jan, saying I sick or I too busy. And Jan very understanding person, not need sex much, having trouble making penis big."

Lifting Miyako to her feet, Fay walked her over to the sofa and sat her down. Then she sat down alongside her and covered herself with the afghan, for it was now she who was shivering. In a very calm voice resembling her mother's, she asked: "Did you leave then?"

Miyako dropped her chin on her chest and shook her head. "No," she said, "I tell him I kill myself if he not want me anymore."

"And did you mean it?"

"Of course. Japanese never joking about suicide. Especially since he shame me, telling me I never can go back to Japan."

"And what did he say then?"

"Eikei light cigarette and say that he not care what I do so long as I not kill myself in zendo and make Buddha statue dirty with my blood."

Fay let out a deep sigh of disgust. "Jesus, Jesus, Jesus!" she heard herself whisper.

"And was that when you left?"

"Yes, I run out of zendo when American lady come out of toilet wearing bathrobe and towel around her head, and she smiling . . ."

"And did you go to the party?"

"No, I walk around in street, in rain, too scared to go home, too scared to kill myself. Don't want to die so young, but don't want baby, either. Then thinking about you and walking from zendo to here and thinking you kind, really loving Eikei, and you husband a doctor who help me get abortion so Eikei not have bad reputation in United States and scandal not spread to Japan."

"What makes you think I love him that much?"

"Fay-san, everyone but you know that you in love with Eikei, only too pure lady. All Zen students here think you sleeping with him, even I thought that, and I very jealous of you at first. But Eikei tell me truth about you, saying you purest person he ever know, and he not want you to go crazy from being disappointed in bad monks. He tell me you have deep karmic relation to him and that you beautiful lady, and he have to make sure you not lose husband and everything because of him. He say he train you very hard and say bad things to you to make you not fall in love with him, like all lady Zen students doing and getting into trouble with teachers, making scandals. He want to protect you."

"Be my umbrella," Fay said.

"What?"

"Nothing."

The two women had folded their legs and were sitting

facing each other, like teacher and student in the interview room. Fay thought of pointing this out to Miyako, but didn't. "I think the best thing for you to do tonight is to sleep here on the sofa. And for me . . . to . . . think over everything you told me. We don't have to act right away, bring on a catastrophe. We have to think first, always, about our practice, about Zen—"

Miyako looked at her and smiled wanly. "You really sincere student, most sincere Zen student, like Eikei say."

Fay's teeth were chattering. She got up and went into the bedroom, fetched her flowered flannel nightgown with the pearl buttons and brought it to Miyako. "You go to sleep now and we'll talk about it tomorrow."

She sat for a while at the counter with her face in her palms, listening to Miyako wash up in the bathroom. Then, before turning off the light in the kitchen, she wrote in block print letters on her shopping list: TOOTHPASTE.

At eight in the morning, with a strong sun warming her back and a cold wind bruising her face, Fay walked East through the slick black and white streets. Miyako had fallen asleep instantly, but Fay had not gone to bed. She had sat in the dark, watching the curve under the afghan on the sofa that marked Miyako's sloping shoulder. Miyako slept without making a sound, and Fay had watched her until the light started filtering through the slatted blinds. Miyako was still deeply asleep when, pulling on her high-top sneakers and tucking twenty dollars into the inside pocket of her down jacket before putting it on, Fay slipped out of the loft.

On Canal Street, the Chinese vegetable vendors were opening for the day, and the parking lot that served as a flea market on Sunday was already filling with salespeople putting up their stalls. A jacketless man in a T-shirt with a handlebar mustache and multiple tattoos was unloading a battered minivan with Alabama plates. As she passed him, Fay saw that the man was carrying a slender gilt-coated Thai Buddha in his arms, and she almost tripped. The mustached man from Alabama called out for her to watch her step, and, taking it as a sign Fay pressed her palms together and bowed.

When she reached the Bowery, she felt her stomach rumble, and the resinous taste of last night's wine mixed with phlegm, forming a clot in her throat. She longed for a cup of coffee but couldn't spare herself the time. Not that she was intent on "catching" Eikei and the tall pigtailed woman in the act (she was half hoping Miyako had made the whole thing up), but because she wanted to talk to him before anyone else did. Now convinced that Miyako was more than a little unstable, Fay wouldn't put it past her to make her story public. Whatever the reason, it was clear that Miyako would not stop until she had brought Fay's world tumbling down.

Fay let herself into the building, bypassing the elevator, climbing the two flights of stairs to the zendo. By the time she reached Eikei's door, she was simultaneously sweating and chilled to the bone. The smell of incense seeped into the hallway. As she would have done three hours earlier on any normal day of the week, Fay noiselessly turned the key in the lock and opened the door. She hung her coat on its usual peg and left her high tops on the rubber runner alongside Eikei's Wellingtons, the only other footgear in the hall. He could be hiding his visitor's shoes in his bedroom closet, she thought, as she walked into the zendo and made the obligatory bow toward the altar. Dressed in his black robes, Eikei was sitting on his cushion, facing the Buddha in meditation. The altar had been given a thorough cleaning; a fresh cup of water and a new dish containing the rice offering were neatly arranged on a beige silk altar cloth she hadn't seen before. Bowing before the cushion nearest her, Fay sat down, crossed her legs, and instantly fell into a deep, dreamless sleep.

She woke to the blissful aroma of brewing coffee and followed it to the elevated kitchen off the entrance hall. Eikei stood with his back to her, talking in Japanese on the telephone. He had removed his robes and was wearing only a sleeveless undershirt and sky-blue monk's work pants with a rope for a belt. He had tied an oversized handkerchief around his head and was smoking. His glasses and the ever-present digital blood pressure machine were side by side on the counter. Moving so as not to disturb him, Fay sidled into the kitchen and poured a mug of coffee. Eikei turned around then, and she offered it to him, but he pointed at her and shook his head, so she took the coffee around to the zendo side of the open kitchen and drank it with her back turned to him.

Eikei yelled "*Mushi mushi*" into the phone twice, and, on hearing him hang up she turned around to face him.

"What happen, Fay-san, you too much drinking last night and falling asleep on Zen cushion?" Eikei laughed, pointing at her with the cigarette nesting between his middle and forefingers.

The mug was shaking in her hands, so she set it down on the counter. "No, it's not a hangover. But I didn't sleep last night . . ."

"What, you have fight on telephone with Ira-san? I tell you many times it better you travel with husband. I take good care of zendo here, no need for you to stay home alone and make husband angry."

"Ira's not angry. He's doing quite well, in fact."

Eikei motioned for her to come around the counter into the kitchen. He placed two chairs so that they were facing each other. "You sit down. You all white in face, no look good." He waited for her to sit, then perched himself on the chair opposite, leaving only about a foot of space between them and forcing her to sit with her legs at prim right angles.

"Miyako came over last night. She . . . Eikei, can you put out the cigarette? The smoke is bothering me."

Eikei turned and tossed the cigarette into the sink.

"Thanks," Fay said.

"You want more coffee?"

She shook her head.

For a minute or two they sat looking at each other. Seeing his swift little brown eyes blinking monkey-like at her made her want to pet him, make it up between them regardless of what he'd done. But then Eikei smiled and was no longer vulnerable, and at that moment she hated him as she had never hated anyone before.

"Miyako says you made her pregnant," she said flatly.

Eikei raised his eyebrows and looked puzzled. "Why she tell you that? You know, Miyako a crazy girl. Not right in here," he said, tapping himself on the temple.

"She also says that you were making love to a strange woman in here last night, that she saw you through the window. A woman with a long braid down her back."

Eikei snorted. "Miyako big liar. I have no womens in here last night." He rose from the chair and turning his back on her went to the sink.

"I don't care what you do with your private life, but fooling around with students is out!" Fay said.

Eikei had turned on the faucet and was scouring the sink with Brillo. "I have guest here; lady friend from Maine, she fly down to New York for weekend to see boyfriend here who work for newspaper. She not making love to me . . . she only have time to stay for one hour before meeting boyfriend for dinner. She want to see zendo and make sure I okay. Japanese girl crazy, I tell you."

"As I said before, what you do on your own time and with anyone who's not a student is your own business . . ."

Eikei turned off the water, threw down the scouring pad and whirled around from the sink. "That's right! My business, not yours! You no come and tell me how to run zendo affairs. I Zen master here, not you!" His face had turned blood red and a vein in his forehead was throbbing.

"What will you do when the crazy girl comes and kills herself in front of the altar?" Fay screamed. She was about to get up from the chair, but Eikei pushed her down again.

"Don't you dare push me!" she cried.

"You too excited, not knowing what you talking about! You going crazy from too much zendo business and not seeing husband, Fay-san. I not wanting you to have nervous breakdown . . ."

Fay could see that he was holding back his own anger now.

"Stop bullshitting me, Eikei," she said. "Are you sleeping with Miyako?"

"She very bad womens, like I told you. She start by making me homesick for Japan, cooking Japanese food very good, then giving me massage. Soon she taking me to bed and making penis big, but I no love her. She very low society girl in Japan; parents own sweet candy factory in Kyushu, very bad manner girl who sleeping around with everybody."

Fay placed her palms against his chest. Under the thin sky-blue cotton of his monk's shirt, she felt his thudding heart and the hardness of his tiny skeleton. "You miserable bastard," she whispered. "You make her pregnant and then tell her you don't care if she kills herself as long as she doesn't get blood on your altar!"

"Fay-san—" Eikei pried her hands from his chest. "You sit down and drink coffee and we talk."

"No!" She flailed her hands in the air and tried to hit him, but he caught them and pressed her down onto the chair.

"You listen to me!" he said hoarsely. "I am your teacher and I order you to listen!"

Fay pulled herself free and jumped to her feet. "Not anymore, you're not! You're nothing to me anymore, you lying piece of shit!" With that, she scooped his glasses and the blood pressure machine from the counter and tossed them at the altar, shattering them against the stone Buddha. Lunging at her, Eikei landed a glancing blow on her cheekbone. Almost as quickly, Fay struck him on the mouth with the back of her hand. Then seeing that she had drawn blood and that he had another blow in store for her, she ran past him to the door, grabbed her shoes and jacket, and quit the zendo. As she took to the stairs, she heard him yell, "What I tell you, Fay-san? From very beginning I say you too pure for enlightenment!"

21
BREAKDOWN

Fay was mortified when Gail Breyer walked into the treatment room and announced that she was the attending psychiatrist assigned to her case. Her first impulse was to head for the Chief of Psychiatry's office and demand a change of therapist. Why couldn't she stick with her admitting doctor, a sympathetic Austrian in a tweed jacket who had talked about Parsifal and didn't think she was nuts for being on a "spiritual quest." It was only after she let him talk her into voluntarily consenting to being admitted and put on suicide watch that she realized he had diagnosed her as dangerous to herself and could possibly have her sealed away for life.

The first week was a nightmare. They took away her clothes, her shoes, her watch, her wedding ring, leaving her with only her underwear and a loose, belt-less smock that snapped at the back, and a pair of flannel slippers. A nurse led her up to the closed ward, clanged the steel door shut behind her, and brought her to her room. After depositing her, she likewise clanged the door shut and locked it behind her. A far cry from the luxurious Lying-In wing of the hospital where she'd had her miscarriage, the room for potential suicides was furnished with only a bed and a small table. No mirrors, no door on the toilet, no shower or bath, and no windows. The door to the room had a barred transom at eye height, through which a patrolling aide might peer at all hours, startling her awake by shining a flashlight in her face at three in the morning to make sure she hadn't found some ingenious way of using the sheets or towel to do the deed.

The initial interview was to be Fay's last encounter as a free person. From the moment the nurse escorted her out of the Admissions Office and up to the ward, she had become a "patient." Fay didn't think of herself as a patient. Yes, she had intended to jump into the East River. No, it wasn't just an "idea" she'd entertained; she had actually gone there. But she hadn't jumped. Wasn't it actually carrying out the deed that counted, and not what psychiatric jargon referred to as "suicidal ideation?" She hadn't heard any voices; she knew who the President was and what day it was and what city she was in. She even got the sympathetic Austrian doctor to call her soon-to-be-ex-husband Ira's office and see that she wasn't delusional claiming to be a famous psychiatrist's wife. What disturbed her most was that, although the admitting psychiatrist, the resident on duty, and the social worker didn't seem to think she was crazy, didn't humor her or talk to her in that condescending singsong voice people use with children or crazy people, once she was lured past the front door by their apparent belief in her normalcy, herded upstairs and deprived of her clothing, Fay was no longer to be trusted.

She was reminded of the wounded feral cat she once rescued and kept secret from her parents for fear they'd say she had rabies and would have her put down: a thickly pregnant tabby with golden globes for eyes, skittish and talkative. Fay lured her for three days with bowls of sugared milk and sardines on a plate. And when the cat finally let her near her after she'd lapped up the last bit of milk, she coaxed her into the garage. The cat eventually grew so dependent on her for food that she had even let Fay handle her kittens when she gave birth. But Fay had been too afraid of her parents finding out, and she had betrayed the cat by bringing her and her kittens to the Humane Society shelter for adoption—or whatever fate might await them. Now it was her turn to be caged.

She slept a lot the first week. And had no dreams. Dr. Susan, the in-house resident assigned to her case, was a plump woman of about thirty-five who favored triple gold chains and blue eyeshadow. She sat on a chair opposite Fay asking questions and writing down everything she said, when, and if, she felt like talking. On the first day, she took down a meticulously detailed history, which, Fay thought, placed undue emphasis on her "hostility" toward Ira. She asked her almost nothing about her childhood. On the third day, when Fay asked what her treatment protocol was going to be, Dr. Susan said she wasn't going to be given any medication because she was being "assessed" by Gail Breyer, her main psychiatrist, along with herself, a panel of psychologists, and a social worker. They wanted to be sure she was no longer suicidal before they commenced on a course of treatment. What was she, then? Fay asked. Depressed? Delusional? Had she suffered a nervous breakdown?

The resident toyed with the outermost of her gold chains. "We don't use that terminology," she said.

Nothing Fay related changed the impassive expression on Dr. Susan's face. But at their third session, she did say that the hospital had contacted Ira and that although he had immediately left his conference in San Diego and was on his way back to New York with the intention of signing her out of the hospital, the staff had unanimously agreed to prevent him from seeing her. Dr. Susan said Ira had threatened to sue the hospital, and that for the moment, it would be better if he and Fay had no telephone contact. Fay felt strangely comforted by that last bit of information.

Within a week she was allowed out of her room to walk around in the locked ward and take her meals in the dayroom, where she could sit in front of the mammoth-sized television set watching soap operas all day long if she wanted to. She did not want to. The other patients, also in smocks and shuffling along in flannel slippers, were as mute as Trappist monks. They too ate in silence and refrained from eye contact. It took her a couple of days to realize that they weren't meditating but were being drugged instead. Only once did someone talk to her: a two-hundred-pound Black woman in a paisley muumuu, who had wandered into the dayroom and insisted that Fay had deliberately changed the channel on her favorite soap opera. She snarled and curled her lip, but before she could get rambunctious, a nurse came between them and humored the muumuu lady out of the day room with a promised slice of marbled chocolate cheesecake.

It was on the Wednesday of the second week that they took Fay off suicide watch and loosened the restrictions on her comings and goings. Dr. Susan told her that the panel was still deliberating on the course of treatment but had agreed to let her talk to Ira on the telephone. That first conversation was awful. Ira broke down and cried as soon as he heard her voice. Fay thought he was crying because she'd wanted to kill herself. But he immediately launched into a tirade. How could she do this to him? How aggressive and hostile of her to sign herself into that particular hospital's psychiatric ward and place herself in the hands of his enemies. She couldn't have done better to ruin his reputation, he said, than if she'd actually jumped!

At their next session, Fay told Dr. Susan that she didn't

want to talk to Ira on the telephone, that she didn't want to talk to anyone on the outside just yet. The resident gave her an approving nod and jotted a note on her chart to that effect.

Gail Breyer spent the first week reminiscing about her psychiatric residency when she and Ira were in training together. Fay was surprised to see how open she was about her feelings (nothing like Ira's strictly impersonal back-of-the-couch approach) telling her she'd loved the department as much as Ira had hated it, and always looked forward to coming back as a full-fledged staff psychiatrist one day. Eased into offering a few revelations of her own, Fay told Gail how much she'd envied her perfect breasts and pouty lips and brilliant reputation. Getting no sign from Gail that she'd taken those remarks as a compliment left Fay feeling a bit testy. So she said she didn't think Gail was as beautiful now, that her breasts were already beginning to sag with age, and she was starting to get thick around the midriff. Gail sat in her brown leather armchair with her long, slim legs crossed and eyed her coolly. "I can't say the same for you, Fay. You don't look a day older than the first time we met. You were . . . in your twenties, right?"

"Twenty-three . . ."

"You've kept your dancer's body, that's for sure," she said.

A week later, Gail started her on what she called "a new treatment regimen"—a combination of Active Imagination and Dream Therapy that she hoped would stimulate Fay's imagination to guide her toward recovery. The treatment, Gail said, was a little like zazen, in that it started with watching the breath and relaxing into it without trying to think about anything special. The difference was that this meditation was "guided," with Gail giving the instructions. At first Fay found her voice intrusive, and she told her so. Fortunately, Gail was flexible, and didn't insist on directing the exercise but left it up to her to raise one finger when she was ready to speak. This being the first session, Fay was more than a little self-conscious, and it took her the better part of the hour to relax into it. Her first images were strictly scenic, no people: an autumn country road with lots of falling leaves and morning ground mist. She strained so hard to fill in the details that she got a headache, and Gail suggested they quit, assuring her it would go better the next time . . .

The treatment room was actually a glassed-in sun porch with a view of Rikers Island. A droopy potted palm stood in one corner flanked by a couple of brown leather armchairs, like the ones Gail and Fay sat facing each other in during their therapy sessions. Unlike Dr. Susan, Gail did not wear a white coat or take notes. She wore tailored suits, lots of navy and mauve, and a variety of beige or black or oxblood-colored mid-heel pumps. She was certainly more toned down than she'd been as a resident, lipstick, and a bit of blush her only makeup. But her nails were professionally manicured and, though her black hair was streaked with gray, it was fashionably cut. No more Dutch boy bangs. Fay asked Gail if she was married, and she told her she was divorced, had a ten-year-old son named Harry, dated, but was not seriously involved with anyone, adding that her ex-husband was a stockbroker.

Gail never once alluded to Fay's "attempted suicide," and therapy sessions with her were more like friendly chats. Nothing traditional. Fay was not asked to lie down on a couch (there was none) or to talk about herself if she wasn't inclined to. Likewise, Gail could answer Fay's questions when and if she felt like it. Fay grew to trust her, and soon started looking forward to their casual encounters. One day, Gail asked if she'd mind having Dr. Susan sit in on occasion, and Fay said, "Why not, the more the merrier—but only if she doesn't take notes."

"That's a good sign," said Gail, looking at her watch and ending the session.

Susan dropped in twice after that. Gail was her training analyst, and Fay was one of the eight patients she saw under Gail's supervision. As resident in charge of the ward, she was kept busy throughout the day and every other night when on duty, reporting back to Gail twice weekly.

Susan's first "drop-in" visit occasioned the first dream Fay could remember since her admittance to the hospital. She still hadn't been put on drugs; Gail said she'd recommended holding off on medication unless she was having trouble sleeping, which was no longer the case since the aide had stopped waking her at three in the morning by beaming a flashlight in her face. Fay did not have to be asked, but spontaneously volunteered to tell Gail the dream. She'd read once that patients matched their dreams to the kind of therapy they were undergoing: Freudian patients dreamt about sex; Adlerian patients dreamt about power, and Jungian patients dreamt about myths. Gail told Fay she thought of herself as an "eclectic" analyst with a preference for Karen Horney. Since Fay had never read any Horney and knew nothing about her, she couldn't say that she'd had a Horneyian dream. Gail laughed when she told her this. "Stop trying to please me," she said. "It's your dream."

An impulse to enact the dream made her get up from her chair and walk around the room a few times before stopping in front of Gail with her arms crossed over her chest.

"I know it's perverse, but I have to tell you that I dreamed Ira was exposed to the incurable strain of TB while treating an old schizophrenic man in the locked ward, who was really his supposedly psychic friend Sam Rubin. And we had to wear masks and rubber gloves around each other and could no longer make love. Ira told me the situation was hopeless, that I'd better not see him anymore. And I don't know what happened after that because the dream ended, and although it was an eerie dream, I woke up feeling better than I have since I got here."

As usual, Gail took no notes, this time only commenting: "Good job, Fay. I think we're finally getting somewhere."

1/12/1985
Patient: Fay Corman
Ward 6 Staff Physician: Susan Redlich, MD

Patient is an attractive childless thirty-six-and-a-half-year-old woman, a former principal in the Jessie Kane Dance Company, who stopped performing three years ago, but remains with the company as a part-time instructor and business manager. Patient states that she and her husband, Ira Corman, a prominent psychiatrist turned self-help guru, are "on the verge of divorcing" because of problems she attributes to her husband's friendship with Sam Rubin, a celebrity psychic. Patient suspects the two may be homosexually involved, though she offered no factual evidence for what she called her "gut feeling." When questioned further, Patient traced her suspicion to an event that occurred early on in her relationship with her husband leading to an assault she suffered on Lexington Avenue. She described the event leading up to, and including, her assault in a matter-of-fact tone that clearly belies her repressed rage against her husband. Inserted here is Patient's handwritten account, which she presented to me at the end of today's session.

Dear Susan,

. . .

Since you keep referring to my 'preoccupation' with Ira's relationship to Sam Rubin, I'm providing some essential background information that might help clarify the situation.

Two weeks before we were married—after all the wedding invitations had been sent and RSVP'd, the hall and caterer and photographer and band hired—Ira announced that, on Sam's advice, he'd decided to take a time out before "sealing the deal." He said Sam thought early marriages were doomed, and who should know better than he, having been married and divorced twice—the first time at nineteen and the second at twenty-five. At first, I treated the whole thing like a joke and went along with the postponement saying I was only marrying Ira for his money anyway. I didn't think Ira would go through with it. But I was wrong. Our wedding was saved only at the last minute when I threatened to walk out on him!

But that was only the beginning. Ira and I had been married for five years when Sam came to live with us after being thrown out of his apartment by his second wife, Charlene. It was supposed to be a "temporary" arrangement until he found his own place. Sam arrived during the Christmas holidays, at the start of what became the worst winter in two decades, so, what started as a "temporary" stay soon threatened to become "permanent." It had already begun snowing heavily the day Sam arrived, and it didn't stop for the next five days in a row. None of us wanted to venture outside, so we'd order Chinese take-out for supper every night from the greasy hole in the wall around the corner, which, amazingly, remained open and continued making deliveries when every supermarket and pizza parlor in the neighborhood had closed down. After supper, I'd clean up the leftovers and throw the garbage into the trash chute in the hall. This went on for a couple of nights until I announced that I was no longer on cleanup and someone else would have to do it. Since neither Ira nor Sam volunteered, the apartment soon became littered with moldy leftover Chinese food in little white cartons, which I refused to deal with. Ira and Sam didn't seem to care about the leftover Chinese food, or about me, because they were too busy playing poker—for hours on end. Once or twice they'd ask, half-heartedly, if I wanted to join them, and I would say I didn't, and they would turn back to their game and ignore me. By the end of the week, I was sick of being ignored. Sick of Chinese take-out. Sick of Sam, whom I'd hated from the first day I laid eyes on him. I would occasionally drop a few hints about this to Ira but nothing directly. Not that he ever asked me; he just assumed I tolerated Sam because he was his best friend since childhood.

Sam has always been, and still is, the most important person in Ira's life. After we were married a few years, I'd almost grown to accept it—but having him live with us was simply more than I could take. To begin with, I was seriously tired of playing along with them for the sake of being "a good sport"—as if I was the kid sister Ira always wished he had—and not his wife. And the fact that the two of them had turned the apartment into a pigsty and didn't seem to care about it didn't help, either. Now, taking out the garbage may seem like a small thing, but it has been known to break up marriages. Or at least represented the last straw in a marriage on the verge of breaking up. I read somewhere that it's what caused Mary McCarthy to divorce Edmund Wilson—his refusal to take out the garbage, that is (FYI: Like Mary, I was once a Catholic).

I asked Ira if he couldn't think of anything better to do than sit around, eat Chinese takeout, and play poker every night and expect me to be his scullery maid. That's how I put it: "scullery maid," hoping the Cinderella allusion might jog his Jungian imagination.

Sam looked up at me and in that snide way of his, said, "See, Ira, she's making a case out of it, as usual."

Ira said nothing, and only gave me his, "What-can-I-do-he's-nasty-short-and-ugly-but-he's- my-psychic-best-friend?" look.

"I'm addressing Ira, not you," I said.

Egged on, I'm sure, by Ira's silence, Sam now turned on me fully. "Quit being such a pain in the ass, Fay."

Suppressing the urge to stick my finger down my throat and spew my undigested General Tso's chicken all over Sam's two-hundred-dollar Nikes, I waited in vain for Ira to intercede on my behalf. But I didn't stick my finger down my throat, and Ira didn't intercede. Ira was too mesmerized by Sam to defend me, and I was too naïve then to realize that moving in with us was a ploy, what the older and wiser me sees as 'Part Two' of Sam's multiple attempts at preventing and failing at breaking up Ira's marriage. In any case, I just stood there, and all Ira did was emit a sycophantic chuckle, the latest in his lineup of reverent responses to Sam's wit. As far as Ira's concerned, everything Sam says is not only uncontestable but also sacrosanct—like a papal pronouncement. Ira's 'magical thinking' (a term I picked up from the American Psychiatric Association's Nosology) has undoubtedly convinced him that, anointed by Sam's psychic power, he'll abandon the medical profession altogether and pursue his life's dream of playing the saxophone with a famous jazz band; that Sam will buy a whitewashed villa somewhere on the Aegean and the three of us will move there together and become a ménage a trois, like in "Jules and Jim"—but only if I quit being a pain in the ass . . .

So, back to that fateful night . . .

Immobilized by frustrated rage, I stood there watching them play poker. Then Sam started tapping his nail against a poker chip, and for some reason that set me off, so I came around from behind to face him and ask him to kindly stop, his tapping was making me nervous.

"See, I told you she was going to be a pain in the ass tonight." Sam sent me a spiteful grin.

At which point, to keep from throwing a carton of Chinese leftovers in his face, I took a mental room inventory, noting the scattered decks of cards, Baby Ruth wrappers, and unwashed coffee-stained mugs crowding Ira's desk. Had the apartment ever been this messy before Sam came to live with us I wondered?

"Come on, honey . . ."

"That's it, Ira, pamper her. Give in . . . go on." Sam pulled an ace of clubs out of his sleeve and executed a perfect magician's pass.

My hands were shaking. I now had to stand there and fight the urge to rip Sam's glasses off and toss them out the window sixteen floors down into the snow.

"Why don't we just watch Sam do card tricks all night?" I said, redirecting my fury at Ira, who was about to make a conciliatory gesture when Sam quickly turned his cards face up and cut him short.

That was when I decided to leave.

I went to the closet, grabbed my coat and got into it. Then I pulled on my boots and stuck my navy wool beanie on my head and stomped out of the apartment. Neither Ira nor Sam made a move to stop me.

Outside, the snow was still falling. I stood looking up at the swirling snowflakes illuminated by the streetlight in front of our building until my eyes blurred over. There were snowdrifts forming on the sidewalk, which the janitor had shoveled clear that afternoon. My feet were getting cold, so I started walking east on Lexington Avenue. I passed a florist, a cocktail lounge, and a Gristedes supermarket—all closed. I was the only person on the street. But then, out of nowhere, a figure appeared, walking toward me. I wasn't sure if the person coming toward me was a man or a homeless woman in an oversized men's jacket. I wanted to avoid whoever it was, so I crossed the street.

As I approached the apartment building on the corner, I spotted a doorman in the lobby sleeping on a chair near the radiator with his head on his chest and a newspaper in his lap. I remember every detail because it was then I saw that the person who'd appeared out of nowhere had crossed over to my side of the street and was walking directly toward me much faster than before. I thought of quickly pushing past the revolving doors into the lobby and waking the doorman, but the sidewalk in front of the building was like a sheet of ice and I was afraid I might slip and break an ankle. (FYI: All dancers are terrified of breaking an ankle. Even if you're young, it can finish your career.) I soon found myself face to face with my pursuer, now visible as a teenager, about sixteen at the most, with porky cheeks and long, soft black hairs growing like mistakes over his upper lip and along his temples. The two of us stood there looking at each other for a few seconds before he pulled me up against him and started rubbing my breasts through my coat with his gloveless hands. I could feel his cock harden against my thigh and I don't know why, but at that very moment I was certain that Ira and Sam were lovers. It hit me, just like that! And it made me so furious that I gave the kid a violent push, and he fell over backwards onto the icy pavement. I didn't stop to see if he'd hit his head or if he was bleeding. I just turned and tracked through the snow . . . back to Ira. Why? I don't know. I've been asking myself that question for twelve years now and still haven't found the answer. Which, I suppose, is why I am here talking to you.

22
FIFTIES MUSIC

The "Patients' Frolic" fell on the Sunday Fay was taken off suicide watch.

Rory, the taciturn elevator man, appeared to be in an unusually good mood as he let her off on the second floor. "Over there, Miss—see that set of doors at the other end of the hall? Just go through there and you'll find it," he pointed down the deserted tile corridor.

Fay was already nervous at the prospect of performing, and Rory's directions were delivered with a sly joviality that might or might not have been intended to mock the dance costume Dr. Susan had provided for the occasion; it was hard to tell. But when the old man picked up his smudged newspaper and slumped down on his three-legged wooden stool—eliciting her pity for having to sit in the loony bin elevator all day—she smiled and mumbled a quick "thank you."

Rory sat with his long, spade-shaped index finger on the Open-Door button and watched her walk down the corridor. "Good luck!" he called after her.

Fay smoothed down her flesh-colored tights and felt the

muscle in her calf tauten. That gesture, and the familiar whiff of resin escaping from her dance slippers as she walked calmed her a little. A final tug on the shoulder straps of her leotard and she was ready to go. Taking a deep breath, she swung open the leather doors.

The air in the rec room was filled with the tropical smell of coconut. On the "stage"—a raised podium at the far end of the room—flanked by two artificial palm trees and swaying their bodies in time to the music—a drummer, vibraphonist, and trumpeter were playing a cha-cha. Cartoon character balloons were strung everywhere: Mickey Mouse, Popeye, Dumbo, and a snarling Captain Hook, complete with eye-patch. Silver and phosphorescent gold and green streamers snaked along the tiled walls and mustard-colored hospital ceilings. The dance floor was empty. The other patients had not come down yet. She was the first one there. Only a very fat nurse's aide she didn't recognize and a handsome Black man in a business suit, wearing sneakers, were drinking coffee in front of an urn that had been set up on a bridge table near the stage. The musicians didn't seem to care that no one was dancing; they played and swayed with their eyes closed. The trumpeter had already loosened his black bow tie and was sweating furiously. The bandleader, who was playing the vibraphone, had a little gray pointed brush mustache that reminded Fay of the civilian who'd managed the PX at the army base where she had grown up. Exuding the "curiously strong" smell of wintergreen Altoids, he'd followed behind her as she'd browsed the cosmetics aisles to make sure she wasn't stealing lipsticks.

"Yoo-hoo, Fay! Over here, dear!"

Fay turned around. "Oh, Gladys, I was wondering where everyone was."

"But, my dear, you didn't think we'd not be here, did you?" Gladys, all pink and platinum blond, her bouffant grazing the crimson-eared Dumbo balloon overhead, stuck a red carnation behind Fay's ear that promptly fell off and had to be "set aside for later," and then slapped a gummed name tag just below her right shoulder. A gold-dipped carnation tucked into the second buttonhole of Gladys's own blouse marked her status as patient ward leader. She was an old-timer, coming and going to and from the hospital as the errant course of her manic-depressive illness dictated. The latest episode had taken place just after New Year's Day when, in the spirit of the season, Gladys forgot to take her lithium and drank six glasses of champagne which sent her on a shopping spree totaling twenty-five hundred dollars' worth of lingerie at Bloomingdale's and charged to her ex-husband's credit card.

"Come and say hello to the rest of the girls," trailing a nimbus of lilac perfume, Gladys pulled Fay along behind her.

Avoiding the dance floor, ten of the "girls" stood bunched in a kitchen alcove where a wiry Puerto Rican in a chef's toque stood over a tray of coconut slivers drizzling rainbow-colored syrup.

"Girls, will you look at this gawjuss creature!" Gladys cried, pushing Fay into their midst.

"Ooooh, aren't you the famous ballerina tonight?" Babs, a long scarecrow of a woman whose cheeks had been rouged in patches plucked at Fay's skirt.

"Careful, Babs," Fay said, "Doctor Susan lent it to me, and I want to get it back to her in good condition."

"Babs, Babs, always grabs," scolded Molly, the purple-haired preschool teacher who suffered from echolalia.

"Oooh . . . isn't she ze sveetest ting!" Dunia, the self-proclaimed Polish "countess," sprang forward and grabbed Fay by the wrist.

Easing herself out of Dunia's dry reptilian grip and away from the girls' medicine-breath, Fay left the kitchen alcove. As she did so, the iron bolt on the ward door was slipped and the first trickle of male patients, their heads bowed so as to avoid eye contact with the women, entered the room. Distracted by the noise, the musicians lost a beat.

"Okay, girls," Gladys commanded as she handed out carnations, "remember, no dancing with anyone more than one dance at a time. And that goes for you too, Thelma." She glared at a carrot-haired woman in a fuchsia pants suit wearing a pair of centaur-shaped drop earrings. An amateur astrologer, who, in group therapy, had attributed her hypersexuality to being a Sagittarius, who vigorously nodded and farted.

Molly fanned the air and said, "Thelma smellma."

Frowning, Gladys said, "And it's 'Goodnight, Ladies' at nine sharp, not a minute later. We're on direct orders from the hospital administrator himself to be cleared out of here and back in our rooms by no later than nine." Aiming a final glare at her charges, Gladys closed the second and third buttons on Thelma's blouse and led the advance toward the men. As she was being pushed forward with the pack, Fay noticed that Dr. Susan had entered the room.

Herded by a hulking aide in green hospital uniform and incongruously pointed tan and white wing-tipped shoes, the men came at them.

"What do I say to them?" Fay whispered into Gladys's ear.

"Nothing . . . first names only. Talk about the weather," Gladys shouted over the music, which had resumed and was louder now, pulsing frantically. The nurse's aide and the man in the business suit (whose sneakers, Fay thought, were more appropriately matched to the hulking aide's hospital greens than the wingtips, and vice versa) left the coffee urn and headed for their posts at opposite sides of the room. Planting herself in front of the podium, the fat nurse's aide motioned for the bandleader to tone it down, and the musicians segued into a subdued version of "April in Paris."

"Who is the man in the suit with the sneakers?" Fay asked.

"A ward clerk or something like that. Quiet now. Pay attention. I think that one is going to ask you to dance." Gladys walked off airily, exploding little rockets of pleasure and hospitality all over the floor as she welcomed everyone in her path to the "frolic."

A hunchback approached Fay with a broad grin, revealing a set of gold, perfectly spaced teeth. Fay felt herself being pushed from behind, and before she could avoid him, she was being carried off in the warm circlet of his tiny bent body.

"Mmmmmmmmmm...mmmmmm...mmm...mm," the hunchback hummed. He was as warm as an oven and smelled of baking bread.

"Hello."

"Mmmmmm...mmmmm...mmm."

"What's your name?"

"Mmmmmm...mmmmm...mmm."

The hunchback, who was a graceful dancer, whirled and dipped Fay across the floor, allowing her only an occasional glimpse of what was going on around them: Gladys dancing with a red-faced man wearing shiny bifocals; Dr. Susan talking to a man in a wheelchair; the band's vibraphone player unknotting his bow tie. The hunchback continued humming in her ear. *No need for talking about the weather with this one; better to keep quiet and let him lead. Palms sweating. I hate that. Maybe we'll dance the whole evening together until they have to pry him loose. Dear God, let the music stop*, she thought as the hunchback droned on, palming her waist and dipping her backward so that her head almost touched the floor. Then the band launched into a waltz and the hunchback spun her around the room.

The music finally stopped in the middle of a misplaced rumba beat, and without warning, the hunchback let her go and whirled away on his own. Fay watched him hold out his arms to Thelma; he was probably still humming. Thelma giggled and clasped the hunchback's long arms around herself as if she were battening the hatches before a storm.

Fay stood at the center of the dance floor with her heart pounding. Several of the men were clustered around the snack tables, waiting to be served coconut slivers and fruit punch by Gladys and her helpers. A toothless man with a dreamy smile on his face danced a dignified pavane alone in a corner. Fay stood watching him until she heard someone ask her to dance. She turned her head and looked into the stunningly handsome face of a man with black hair and green eyes.

"Would you care to dance?" the man asked again when she didn't respond. He had an unlit pipe in his mouth. "They watch us if we just stand around, so I thought I'd rather . . ." he broke off and laughed as if he were a normal man making conversation with a normal woman at a normal cocktail party.

"Of course," she said, giving him her hand.

Fay's partner held her at a distance. They danced together without speaking, their attention fixed on Molly and her partner dancing a mock version of a tango.

"He's an exhibitionist," Fay's partner said with the pipe still in his mouth.

"Who?"

"That one over there. I hate exhibitionists, don't you?"

"Well . . . I . . . I never knew one. What do they do?"

"That." Her partner removed the pipe from his mouth and pointed it at the red-faced man in the shiny bifocals who was now sweeping Molly around like a broom.

The two nurse's aides looked on and grinned, the fat one shaking her head from side to side in mock disapproval. Fay was about to ask her partner why he was smoking an unlit pipe when she remembered that patients weren't permitted matches.

"Oh, he's just having a good time."

"Good time you call that? It's disgusting, carrying on like a caricature of what a nut is supposed to be like, showing off in front of the women . . ." her partner had turned pale, his stunningly handsome face reminding her of an ice sculpture, the cold green unblinking eyes never leaving hers. "I don't want to dance anymore. Let's sit down and talk," he said wearily. "You're the only one here I can talk to."

Fay gave a nervous laugh, then, with Gladys looking on disapprovingly, she followed her partner to a small table draped in pink bunting. "See that fat aide over there," he pointed his pipe to where the jolly nurse's aide and a sandy-haired boy with a face ravaged by acne were now dancing. A few feet away, stood the ward clerk in business suit and sneakers engaged in conversation with the chef. "She watches me constantly. Never gives me a minute's peace. She steals my poetry from my footlocker at night and plagiarizes it. Then she puts it back in the morning because she thinks I'm asleep and don't see her." Fay's handsome partner tapped the empty bowl of his pipe against his palm and pretended to pour invisible shreds of tobacco into a paper cup on the table.

"Listen, would you do me a favor? Would you sneak some of my poems out for me, send them to W.H. Auden? He's familiar with my work. Have you heard of him?" He removed a crumpled envelope from his pants pocket and was about to shove it into her hand when a lanky man with sparse hair and a protruding Adam's apple walked up to the table.

"May I?" The lanky man gave Fay a sweeping bow, and her partner quickly stuffed the envelope back in his pocket. "Can't you see I'm talking to the lady?" he snarled.

"Everybody's supposed to dance." The lanky man spoke with a Southern accent. "What about it, Miss . . . Miss . . . what's your name?"

"Uh . . . Fay."

The handsome poet leaned forward. "How about it, Fay, wouldn't you rather sit here and have an intelligent conversation with me than dance with a slob like him? He never showers."

"Look here, Pike, no use your insultin' anyone here."

W.H. Auden was long dead and Fay was beginning to get really nervous. She stood up and said, "I'm supposed to dance, I think."

Fortunately, the aide in hospital greens was approaching their table. "Fellas, what have we here? Eh? You know there's to be no congregating around the tables! Come on now—we're here to dance, so—LET'S DANCE!" He marched the handsome green-eyed poet over to Babs, who was leaning forlornly against the wall.

"Guess we might as well," said the lanky Southerner. Taking Fay by the hand and thrusting her into the middle of the floor, he launched into a clumsy jig. Luckily, the band switched to a group number just then and the floor filled with patients.

"Yo! Wallyo! You old son-of-a-bitch! Who let you out of the straight jacket?" an olive-skinned man with thick black hair pomaded into an Elvis Presley pompadour called out to Fay's lanky partner.

"Shut up, Gentile, or you'll be sent back up," warned the hulking aide in greens. But he was too late: Gentile's cry had launched the threat of rebellion, illuminating the hollow-eyed dancers and tinting their ashen cheeks red.

"Clap your partner's hand!" the perspiring bandleader shouted in a mock hillbilly drawl, and the loud slap of palm against palm resounded all the way to the ceiling. Even the man in the wheelchair, partnered by Dr. Susan, was brought onto the floor. The young man with the acne rolled his eyes and howled. Slapping himself and making gleeful doggy noises, he waggled one finger and hopped around on one foot, reminding Fay of the Shinto priest she'd seen performing a fox spirit exorcism during a temple tour in Nara. Encouraged by shouts and applause from the men, the boy erupted into such a high-spirited, self-slapping performance that he had to be removed from the dance floor and ushered toward the food tables by an aide who shoved a pill into his mouth. "Yahoo!" the acned young man yelled one last time, but by then he'd lost the interest of his fickle audience. Fay watched him meekly swallow the pill with a cup of fruit punch. When she looked again, he was sitting down and counting time to the music with his fingers on the table.

Fay grew lightheaded; she'd gone too long without eating. Finding a break in the line, she hastened toward the alcove. The wiry chef asked her if she wanted a cup of coffee. "You sure look like you can use it," he said. Thanking him, Fay refused the coffee and walked out of the alcove toward the female patient's toilet.

She was splashing water on her face when she heard what at first sounded like a puppy yelping but which, when she turned off the faucet, turned out to be a woman sobbing inside one of the stalls. "Hello?" she called in the direction of the stall. "Need some help?" The sobs grew louder. Fay approached the stall and knocked. "Can I help you?"

"Who is it?"

"Fay."

"Oh."

Fay heard a nose being blown with great force, after which a weepy and rumpled Thelma emerged from the stall.

"What's wrong? Are you okay?"

"Sure, sure. I'll be alright," Thelma said in a choked voice.

"What happened?"

"Nothing . . . nothing. Oh, I know I shouldn't have taken it to heart, but I can't help it. I've been here for five months already, and it still gets to me." She twisted the bunched-up toilet paper she was using as a handkerchief and dabbed her eyes with it.

"Here, put some water on your face." Fay turned on the taps.

"No . . . no, thanks, it'll ruin my makeup."

"Anything I can do?"

"No, it's just nerves . . . and—" she trailed off and stared down at the tile floor. "Well, one of the fellas, I know he didn't mean it . . . they're not responsible, you know. Well, he sort of insulted me—"

"Physically, do you mean?"

"No! Oh, no. He just—" she shrugged and grinned lamely, "he called me a red-headed tart out of a bottle and said that if I keep shaking it so hard, I'll break it someday."

Without having to ask, Fay knew it was the paranoid poet with the unlit pipe who'd wrecked Thelma's evening. Feeling somehow responsible, she said, "To hell with him, Thelma. Let's go and have a good time just to spite him."

"I'm too thin-skinned, I guess. I shouldn't take them so seriously, these men, should I?"

"Of course not," Fay said, putting her arm around Thelma's plump shoulders and guiding her back to the dance floor. "These men are—well, they're sick, aren't they?"

The dance floor was empty, and the musicians had abandoned the bandstand, leaving behind their instruments amid a tangle of wires. Patients and staff were lined up at the tables for cake a la mode and coffee. An angry looking Gladys approached Fay and Thelma carrying a tray of brownies. Fay took a brownie and excused herself, saying she needed a breather before performing and would they mind if she didn't participate in the raffle drawing. She was walking across the empty dance floor, eating the brownie, when a very dark-skinned Black man beckoned her to join a group of men who hadn't gotten up to dance, yet seemed to be thoroughly enjoying themselves at their self-segregated table. The man, who said to call him "just Horace, if you please," was obviously the leader of this small knot of friends who might, for all she knew, be a group of night duty staffers, not patients.

"This is Brandon," Horace said, pointing to an immaculately groomed Latino man, "and Vinny, Moe, Pinky, and Rip—all of them pass-patients, so you don't need to worry about them acting up." Horace snorted or laughed, she couldn't tell which, and the men nodded at her in turn.

"What's a pass-patient?" she asked, feeling oddly at home.

"Means we come and go, we can smoke, we get little privileges from the nurses" Horace did a little soft shoe shuffle around her.

"Yeah, real privileged characters," said Brandon.

"Yuk yuk," Rip chimed in, holding up his hands for her to see the cruel scars on his wrists.

"You're kidding me, aren't you?"

"It's okay, baby, you don't need to worry. We all had our tranks for today," Moe said, curling his lip.

"Boys, boys, be friendly now. This heah's a nice lady come to dance with us poor souls. Don't go givin' her a hard time." Horace gave her a friendly smile. The others, no longer interested in her, turned back to their refreshments.

"Same goddamn jellybeans . . . Hey, Gladys," Pinky yelled across the floor, "when are we gonna get a steak?"

"Yeah, Gladys, and some champagne–like real people!"

Vinny added in a voice hoarsened by a combination of cigarettes and tranquilizers.

Gladys clucked at them from afar, and two of the men gave her a power salute. "That Gladys sure is something, though," Brandon said absently.

"You've got to give her credit," Horace nodded his approval, and Gladys returned his salute.

"Hey, man—don't eat that, that ain't for eatin . . ." Moe pulled a half-chewed paper doily from Rip's mouth. "No use actin crazy like that. They'll only send you on upstairs to the shock department." Moe spoke with the considered delicacy of an old-world gentleman informing his friend of a spot on his tie. Rip placed the half-chewed doily alongside his plate. The aide in greens approached the table. "Everything copacetic, boys?"

"A-okay, Chief," Horace said, and the aide moved on to another table where someone had started a forbidden game of cards. "He's the best," Horace said. "Never any trouble when Big Stacey's around." The men mumbled their assent. Fay finished the last of her brownie.

"Did you hear the snow-job the Poet's been givin' the new shrink?" said Moe.

"Now him?" Pinky laughed softly, then took a sip of coffee and smacked his lips.

"You mean the Random House-I'm-really-a-famous-author stuff?" Horace yawned and stretched his arms over his head.

"There she goes!"

Gladys climbed the podium and took the microphone from its cradle. "Testing, one-two-three." It was then that Fay saw Gail Breyer enter the room and unobtrusively take a seat near the alcove. She wore a soft gray turtleneck sweater, a blue blazer, smoke-colored slacks, and black suede loafers.

"Roger and out, baby," one of the male patients shouted, and everyone laughed.

"I want you folks to know that in five minutes," Gladys held up five fingers as if to illustrate her point—or maybe it was to cue those patients who weren't listening at all, just sitting and staring into space— "in exactly five minutes there will be a raffle drawing for some wonderful prizes right here in the middle of the floor, and then a professional performance from two superb talents I'm sure you'll enjoy. So, finish up . . . the girls will be clearing the tables . . . and get ready FOR THE FUN!" Greeted by whoops and whistles, Gladys signaled the bandleader, who quickly gathered his musicians to the podium and launched them into The Beer Barrel Polka.

"I guess we ought to start clearing the table," Fay said.

"Yeah, boys. Let's help the lady clean up," Horace ordered.

The men quickly got to work, and Fay was soon faced by two neat piles of paper plates, crumbs all banked into a cup, and plastic spoons gathered for washing. She was about to take as much as she could carry back to the alcove, hoping to thank Gail for coming after hours to watch her perform, when, blocking her path, Horace held out his hand and asked her to dance. Vinny popped a balloon as they left the table. "Lots of luck, Miss, you'll need it dancing with Horace," Moe called out after them.

"He's the Lindy champ of the whole hospital," Pinky shouted.

Horace whirled her past a barefoot man mumbling obscenities. The music slowed and they fell into a pleasant box step. Fay looked down at Horace's white buckskin oxfords.

"Horace, isn't it strange, that man's barefoot and you're wearing shoes with laces? How come?"

Horace either hadn't heard her or pretended not to. The music changed, and they started to rumba. Only two other couples were on the floor: the ward clerk in sneakers, dancing with a much-recovered Thelma, and the heavy aide puffing along with the humming hunchback. Their carnations drooping, three or four "girls" doggedly cleaned the tables, while the men, growing restless, demanded they get on with the raffle drawing. Someone had lowered the floor lights and aimed the spotlight at the podium where the band was playing.

"You want to know why I get to wear shoes with laces?" Horace said suddenly. "It's only for show. You'll get to see in a few minutes."

Fearful now that Horace might be crazier than he let on, Fay nodded and smiled.

"It's the same every time there's a talent show," he said. "I win them all, and for my reward I get to wear an article of clothing from the outside. I've collected quite a snappy wardrobe over the years."

Horace dropped her hand and snapped his fingers. "And since nobody but me around here ever gets to perform, I'm automatically the winner." Taking her hand again and making a bridge of it with his own, he motioned her under it. "But tonight, lovely lady, I hear there's going to be some heavy competition."

"Why are you here, Horace?" Fay asked, her question slipping out unintentionally.

"You know, it's been so damn long I've forgotten," he giggled, covering his mouth.

"What did you do . . . before?"

"I sang tenor with the Tip Tops, but that was before your time."

"I've heard of them. They were a big sensation in the fifties."

The music stopped and the lights flickered. Gladys approached the microphone and called out the winning raffle ticket number, which turned out to belong to the barefoot man mumbling obscenities. The men groaned, but Gentile called out for them to shut up and be fair. The prize, a high-tech stationary bike from Sweden, was duly presented to the winner, who, assisted by the two aides, shuffled up to accept. The contemptuous poet called out that the gift was appropriately bestowed, since the rider could pedal until doomsday without actually going anywhere; several men booed in response, and the drawing was brought to a close.

Gladys took up the microphone again, "Okay, folks, the moment you've been waiting for . . . THE FROLIC TALENT CONTEST!" She paused for a musical flourish from the band then, flashing a huge grin at the audience, pointed around the room calling for volunteers. "Let's see our contestants up front, please! Let's go, people . . . I want to see some good sports around here. Who's going to sing, dance, or tell jokes? Who's brave enough to start us off?"

Horace and Fay had returned to their respective tables at the first drumroll. Now it was so quiet in the room you could hear the thrum of the refrigerator in the alcove; it was as if Gladys had thrown a net over them, even Gentile refrained from issuing a wisecrack. Those patients who had at first appeared hopelessly lost to the world, lounging against the walls on crutches or in wheelchairs, or indulging in forbidden card games at corner tables, even they now sat up and focused their attention on the spotlighted circle in front of the bandstand.

Fay saw Horace pretending to be reluctant, carrying out an annual ritual of waiting to be coaxed and pushed to perform by his tablemates. He sat glued to his chair with his elbows on the table and his eyes closed. Suddenly, from the other side of the room, a deep bass voice (probably belonging to the hulking aide in greens, Fay couldn't tell, because the house lights had been turned down) yelled, "Come on, man . . . let's hear you sing!" Silence. Broken by Gladys, who started clapping rhythmically until everyone joined in, and Horace, propelled from his chair by Vinny and Rip, and followed by the spotlight, made his way to the microphone. He was almost there when the hunchback leapt out of the darkness and blocked his path. Fay sucked in her breath and looked around to see if any of the aides were poised to break up the confrontation that was sure to erupt. Still humming, the hunchback cut into Horace's path and no one was doing a thing to stop him. Fay recognized Thelma's voice as she called out, "Give him the hook!"—Eliciting a barrage of boos and hisses. Clearly, the hunchback was part of the ritual, the villain of the piece, playing his role of spoiler with relish. Only when the catcalls had receded, and with his astute performer's instinct guiding him out of the spotlight, did the hunchback pretend to fall back in defeat. His act now greeted by deafening cheers, he flashed the audience a gold-toothed grin, and bowing, slunk into the shadows. The hunchback having prepared his entrance, Horace now emerged beaming before the microphone. The crowd went wild.

"Quiet! Quiet now! We have our first contestant," Gladys cried above the din; clearly, she too was part of the act. "Horace Fields!" she cried, waving the audience on for further applause, though the room was already shaking with it.

A catatonic at the table next to Fay doubled over in a fit of coughing and was quickly hustled out of the room by the aides.

"Horace, as you all know, is the lead singer for the Tip Tops," Gladys announced, employing the timeless present tense favored by mental patients.

Horace gave his audience a conspiratorial grin and a little bow. "What are you going to sing tonight, Horace?" Gladys asked before stepping back from the microphone.

"Well," Horace paused, taunting his audience. "I think I'll do a little number that won us a Gold Record back in '54, called, 'Shoo, Little Girl.'"

The patients responded with a roar, and Horace turned to the bandleader to ask for the key of G. The catatonic and the two nurse's aides came back into the room and took their seats just as Horace released the first healing strains of his song over every bruised soul in the room. Hitting the chorus in a sweet falsetto that again evoked a roar from the audience, and followed by the spotlight, he removed the microphone from its cradle and walked with it to where Fay was sitting. He motioned her to him, and before she realized what was happening, she had accompanied him to the front of the bandstand and was dancing, charged by Horace's music with the power to fly. Forgetting where she was, effortlessly keying her movements to the sound of his voice, Fay surrendered to its ephemeral sweetness.

It was over quickly. The lights went back on, and the spell was broken. The aides leapt to their posts and patients began milling around the exits; the musicians packed their instruments, and the room emptied. No one bothered to wait around and watch Gladys award Horace and Fay their hand painted "I'm A Winner" T-shirts.

Gladys had gone, and Fay and Horace were still standing at the center of the room, reluctant to leave, when Gail emerged from the alcove to congratulate them. Horace gently let loose the air from a balloon and said, "That was beautiful, girl. Real beautiful." Fay shrugged her shoulders. "You might have given me advance notice, Horace. It wasn't at all what I'd prepared."

Gail placed her hand on Fay's shoulder and said, "That's what made it so spontaneous. You were great, both of you."

Fay took a closer look at Horace; he was actually older than he appeared. As he turned to thank Gail, she glimpsed a clump of nappy gray hairs on the back of his neck that had escaped processing, which, for some unfathomable reason, made her want to cry.

23
ALA MOANA

Diane, the woman Fay had met in Israel who'd invited her to Honolulu to sit with her Zen group, was on a textile-buying trip in Bali and could not pick her up at the airport. Diane's substitute was a sour-faced woman with straw-colored frizzy hair named Linda. Standing off to one side of the arrivals lounge and holding up a cardboard sign reading "Honolulu Zen Center," Linda didn't so much as crack a smile when Fay came up and introduced herself. Unprepared for the heat, and rubber-kneed with exhaustion after the twelve-hour flight from New York, she had a hard time navigating her way through the crowd of tourists around the baggage carousel, and when Linda didn't offer any help, she wearily retrieved and rolled her bags out of the lounge herself. The strong scent of perfume followed her as she left the airport.

"What's that incredible fragrance?" Fay said.

"Plumeria," Linda said, "from the leis they bring the tour groups."

The zendo car—an ancient yellow two-door Toyota, its passenger door rusted permanently shut, and the one on the driver's side missing a handle and held partly closed by a rope—could only be entered if the passenger got in first and climbed over the stick shift. When Fay had accomplished this feat after first hauling her bags into the back seat, Linda, who still hadn't offered her any help, smiled for the first time, and said, "You won't need half of what you've got back there."

The car's air conditioner wasn't working. Fay struggled to open the window, which got stuck a quarter of the way down. "Yeah, well, I'm coming from New York, where it's still cold, so I've got my heavy clothes with me."

"Uh-huh." Linda didn't appear interested in pursuing further conversation and drove the rest of the way in silence.

In addition to being stuck, the window was caked with dust, casting a brown patina over the passing scenery. From the little Fay could make out, they were on a nondescript freeway bordered by pink and ochre sandstone apartment buildings that reminded her of Los Angeles. The only difference was that here the air was free of smog and the light was magical, like none she'd ever seen before.

Leaving the freeway, Linda pulled the reluctant yellow heap first uphill and then downhill, into a lush residential neighborhood in a deep green valley surrounded by Day-Glo green mountains. She stopped on a paved incline and parked the car in a narrow lane bordered by mango and avocado trees that all but hid a big weathered white clapboard house with a lava stone chimney. Suggesting Fay leave her bags in the back seat after they got out of the car, Linda led her down four steep steps onto a stone path dividing a vegetable patch from a miniature Japanese rock garden where a baby Buddha sat facing a tiny goldfish pond. After depositing their shoes in a wooden cupboard filled with an assortment of sneakers, zoris, and two mud-caked pairs of Wellingtons, they entered a shabby, forlorn-looking kitchen, which, except for the birds chirping in the trees outside the louvered windows was monastically silent. From the foyer leading to what Fay presumed was the zendo, came the fragrant whiff of sandalwood incense.

"Are they meditating?" she whispered.

"No need to whisper," Linda said. "Everyone's at the beach." She pointed at the refrigerator. "Want some apple juice?"

Fay shook her head. "The beach?"

"This is a lay Zen Center in Hawai'i, not a monastery in Japan, like the kind you're used to," Linda replied—somewhat snidely, Fay thought. "When we're not in sesshin, and there's no visiting roshi in residence, we sit only twice a day, at six in the morning and seven in the evening. We eat breakfast together in silence after chanting meal sutras, do two hours of *samu*—you'll most likely be assigned to tending the compost heap out back—and then we're off on our own till five, when we eat supper together out on the porch."

Linda opened the refrigerator, poured herself a glass of apple juice and was about to drink it when, hearing someone moving around in the next room, she put the glass down and motioned for Fay to follow her into the zendo. "Oh, lucky for you, Gen's here. He'll be able to help you upstairs with your luggage."

Originally a combined living/dining room, the zendo was a long narrow affair carpeted in what had once been ivory shag, but, like the Zen Center's Toyota, was now a faded yellow relic. Midway into the room a screen door led out onto a large hardwood-floor porch. A long oak table stood in the middle of the porch surrounded by two long benches on either side. A massive bronze monastery bell and clapper set in a wooden frame occupied the far corner to the left of the dining table, and above that hung a thick wooden board and mallet used for striking calls to meditation and meals. In the zendo, opposite the screen door opening to the porch, Linda pointed out the staircase leading to the residents' sleeping quarters: "two bedrooms for men to the right, one large bedroom to the left for women, and a bathroom between them." At the far end of the zendo, set against a lava rock fireplace, stood a huge mahogany altar, where a peeling red and gold statue of Bodhidharma, surrounded by an incense pot and bowls containing rice and water offerings, sat scowling down on the rows of black meditation cushions lined up against the walls.

A very tall man in black monk's robes had just gotten up from the cushion closest to the altar and was heading for the porch when Linda blocked his path to the door.

"Gotcha!"

The man, who looked to be in his early thirties, had a strong, square face and was wearing wire rimmed glasses, instantly reminding Fay of Hiro-san. Yet, unlike Hiro-san, this "monk"—despite the black robes—was not bald but sported a mane of shoulder-length brown hair, a thick brown beard, and a gold earring in his left ear.

"Gen, this is Fay Corman. She just arrived from New York and has hundreds of bags and with my bad back I can't help her lift them, so will you help her bring them upstairs? Please, pretty please?" Fay was so transfixed by Linda, chirping, and batting her eyelashes as she transformed herself from sour-faced spinster to seductive flirt, that she didn't notice that the tall man had removed his glasses and was talking to her.

"Gen is my monk's name, but as I'm no longer a monk, I'd rather you call me Harald, Harald Schoerner," he said, in pleasantly accented English.

"Oh, I'm sorry."

"You look very familiar, have you ever sat with Ryuho Roshi in Europe?"

"No, I'm afraid I wasn't lucky enough to sit with him before he retired."

Seeing she'd lost Gen-Harald's attention, Linda interrupted, "Well, you two seem to be hitting it off just fine. I'm going down to the Food Co-op. We're running low on brown rice. Bye." Forgetting that Fay's bags were still in the car, Linda dashed through the screen door to the porch, slipped into a pair of zoris, and drove off before she could stop her.

Harald laughed. "Linda's absent-minded, but she's okay." Then putting on his glasses and ushering Fay out the porch door into the garden toward a cottage behind the house, he said, "Never mind the bags for now. Let's go to the library. There's a sofa where we can sit down and talk. I have a feeling we have a lot to talk about."

Fay leans against a coconut palm tree in Ala Moana Beach Park watching Harald swim. The tree's thinning fronds are etched in yellow because it hasn't rained in two weeks. If you were seeking shade, you wouldn't sit under this particular palm tree, but Fay and Harald favor it because it's the site of their first kiss.

It happened after a particularly grinding seven-day leaderless sesshin. Fay was in a funk, and Harald was trying to get her out of it by taking her to the beach to read "Zen shit," as he called it. Fay found it funny hearing Harald curse in English; he had a way of drawing out the American "i," so that "shit" came out sounding more like "sheit." She once said his accent sounded German, and Harald hadn't liked it at all. He was Dutch, and very touchy about being mistaken for German. They were having coffee at the Café Manoa when Fay said she didn't care whether he was Dutch or German or Swiss or whatever, and they got into their first fight. Harald simply unfolded all six-foot-four of himself and walked away, leaving her staring into the face of the crazy flute player in the jester outfit sitting at the opposite table telling jokes to his imaginary friends and giggling to himself. It wasn't until later that day, when Harald told her that his aunt had been a member of the Dutch Resistance who'd been executed by the Nazis, that she realized why he was so sensitive about being taken for German.

Harald had just finished reading the last lines of Zen master Ikkyu's love poem to his blind mistress, Lady Shin, when he leaned over and kissed her.

"Why did you do that?" Fay asked, although she'd never enjoyed a kiss so much and wished it had lasted longer.

The periwinkle blue sky was spinning overhead, and a naked Hawaiian toddler with a pail in one hand and a shovel in the other was standing near their blanket and staring at them.

"I don't even know myself," Harald whispered. "It was a spontaneous urge."

"But does this mean you love me, that we're not Zen friends anymore . . . that we're adulterers?" Fay asked, her voice cracking.

"Yes," he said, "I love you, and you love me. We're bound to each other by karma, you said so yourself when we first met. But I wouldn't call us adulterers."

"But we're both married. Wouldn't you say we're being unfaithful to our spouses, which makes us adulterers? You're always trying to get me to 'think things through before acting,' telling me you're a rationalist. That kiss wasn't rational. You yourself said you acted on a 'spontaneous urge.' And it's only because of a 'spontaneous urge' that we met in the first place. It would never have happened if I hadn't 'spontaneously' followed Eikei Roshi to Israel, and then 'spontaneously' flown to Honolulu simply because I'd once met a woman in

Jerusalem for less than half an hour who invited me to sit zazen with her group."

Recalling Harald's unwavering patience when she'd poured out her story to him in the zendo library at their first meeting, Fay knew better than to keep harping on her break with Eikei. And if she wanted to be truly honest about it, it wasn't karma that had prompted her question on the day of "Ikkyu's Kiss"—as they referred to it ever after—but her overwhelming guilt about cheating on Ira, who that very same morning had called her from California to say he would be coming to visit her in Hawai'i in two weeks, and that, instead of being pleased at the opportunity to reconcile with a husband from whom she'd been separated for almost a year, she was sitting in Ala Moana Beach Park, swooning over a man with a wife in Amsterdam.

Fay was wrong: their affair did not begin with that kiss but in a car that broke down in a rainforest behind the valley housing the Honolulu Zen Center. Bent on bypassing the Byzantine regulations governing zendo car use, and its five-page waiting list, Fay had leased an old orange Tercel from Rent-a-Wreck that had the perverse habit of breaking down in out-of-the-way places, like the lush green rainforest of erotically charged birdcalls and phallic miniature banana trees now surrounding them. They had planned to hike around the Arboretum gardens, because the big winter sesshin was coming up, and Harald, who was slated to lead it, wanted to get Fay's opinion of the radical new approach to sesshin he'd been planning. The idea of "getting out into nature" to discuss it was hers.

Harald was driving. He'd mentioned to her that he'd been a racing car driver back in Europe. And Fay, who hadn't paid much attention to the details, casually let drop that she hated car racing because the fans were just sitting there in the stands waiting to see someone crash. She called it "a macho blood sport, like bullfighting." Harald tried to convince her otherwise, and Fay resisted him, getting huffy and shrill as they debated the issue. Harald said he felt as if he were grinding a huge mill-wheel by hand whenever they argued, and Fay said that meant he wanted to grind her down to a fine powder, adding that she would fight him to the death because she'd had enough of that kind of treatment from Eikei and her father and pretty much all the men in her life. That set off their first big fight (there had been a few smaller skirmishes before that, like the one at the Café Manoa), which ended abruptly when, staring each other down, they simultaneously burst out laughing. Reflecting on it afterward, both realized that they had fought the hardest before actually becoming lovers. Not wanting to cheat on their spouses, they had agreed there would be no further physical contact after that first and only kiss under the palm tree at Ala Moana Beach Park. The truth was, they couldn't stand not touching, so they fought instead. Which was often, given that they were zendo residents who ate, slept, and meditated together every day of the two-month spring training period, and did not leave for a year after the center erupted and they were virtually kicked out and had to move into their own apartment. How could it be otherwise? The Honolulu Zen Center was one of Ryuho Roshi's American affiliates and the Shofuji curse was bound to follow her before all the "bad karma" with Eikei was exhausted.

There they were, driving along, when all of a sudden, the clutch emitted a hideous screech and the Tercel stopped dead. They had been too busy arguing to notice that Harald had made a wrong turn on a muddy dead-end road. Fay suggested shifting the car into reverse, so Harald got out and pushed from the front while she worked the clutch. For the next fifteen minutes, he pushed and Fay shifted, but the car would not budge. Fay next suggested they leave the car, walk back to the Arboretum and call the Rent-a-Wreck people to tow them out and exchange the old wreck for a new one.

Harald got back into the car and sat down in the passenger seat next to her. "I know you believe in prescient dreams and stuff like that, but I usually don't. But there are times when I'll have one of those dreams. Like last night."

"Really?"

Harald looked straight ahead at the windshield. "I dreamed we were sitting here, in this car, in exactly this place, with exactly this problem."

"No surprise, since we've had two breakdowns already."

"Right. But in the dream, we were making love.

"Did you like it?"

"Yes, very much."

Fay didn't know if it was because he'd said it so matter-of-factly, or because she'd been fantasizing what it would be like to feel his body pressed against hers, but that is exactly what happened when Harald leaned toward her, and the front seat lurched forward landing her in his arms.

24
PARTINGS

The trouble at the Honolulu Zen Center had started after Ryuho Roshi had retreated to his mountain hut at Shofuji and stopped coming to lead sesshin at the monastery's Western affiliates. By the time Fay arrived, the center was in the middle of a full-blown identity crisis. Though he'd been ordained by Ryuho Roshi and sent from Amsterdam to lead the zendo in Honolulu, Harald had decided that he no longer wanted to be a monk. At a membership meeting, he'd announced that he didn't want to be called by his monk's name — "Gen"—and recommended that, having been set adrift by Ryuho Roshi's retirement, the center break off ties with Japan and create a Western democratic style of Zen practice instead.

Harald's announcement had split the membership in two. The conservative, pro-clerical faction he called "the baldies," stood firmly against him. Pedro Brown, the politically sophisticated, half-British son of a Brazilian diplomat was their leader. He'd responded to Harald's suggestion by publicly denouncing him as "a power-hungry manipulator." His followers, the "baldies," were not monks but people of means, loyal to Ryuho

Roshi who continued to patronize the monastery even after he'd retired. There were ten of them, all active zendo members and permanent residents of Hawai'i. Harald's second most powerful enemy was Marilyn Omeru, a rich Japanese American divorcée famous for wearing string bikinis at zendo beach outings. She'd been unsuccessfully trying to seduce Harald from the day he landed in Hawai'i, eight months before Fay appeared to leaven the mix.

The pro-Harald faction consisted of an unreliable set of oddballs who came and went as the spirit moved them: a California woman and karate black belt who wore a Japanese hakama in the zendo and sold Cuisinart's at the Shirokiya Department Store for a living; a purple-haired University of Hawai'i music student and self-described "street performer" who played the guitar in front of the Royal Hawaiian Shopping Center in Waikiki on weekends, and survived on tips from tourists; a peripatetic Israeli who slept in a tent in the zendo garden when in Hawai'i; a brown-eyed civil rights lawyer with a Zapata mustache; his radical feminist girlfriend just returned from Nicaragua; along with other assorted transients. It did not take long for Fay to realize that, as the old Zen saying went, she had "leapt into fire to escape from drowning."

She and Harald embarked on the first leg of their Zen experiment during his last sesshin as leader by leaving the zendo after the bell had ended the last period of zazen. Harald had arranged for them to take their meals and sleep in the Manoa Valley apartment of a professor friend of his on sabbatical who had left them the key. Fay was nervous about not sleeping in the zendo during sesshin, and, as she had been at Shofuji, she was reflexively anxious about missing the four a.m. wake-up bell and being late for the first period of zazen. Still, she'd had enough of communal living and was grateful for the privacy. Sleeping head to foot on the zendo floor with five deep ecologists who saved water by not flushing the toilet after themselves had quickly sent her packing.

She was putting away groceries in the professor's apartment when she opened the refrigerator door and encountered an army of cockroaches scurrying around the empty shelves. Opening the kitchen cupboards, she was again met by roaches. Looking into the oven . . . roaches. Big black ones. Bigger than any she'd ever seen in New York—and with wings! Fay went into the bedroom to tell Harald; finding him sprawled out on the bed, fast asleep, she decided to tackle the kitchen on her own. It was well past midnight when she dropped onto the bed alongside him and immediately entered a dream in which Harald and Hiro-san, dressed in monks' robes and sloping straw hats, were walking together in an autumn forest during *takehatsu*—alms-begging season. She watched them shuffle through heaped red, yellow, and orange leaves toward the barnyard of a farm bordering the forest, where she stood shaking a flock of migrating geese out of a carpet. As they approached, she heard Harald complaining to Hiro-san about his life at the monastery, and Hiro-san responding, "I'm glad we left. I never want to see the place again."

". . . Sitting like a lump of cow shit, parading the fire in your belly, crushing your balls but never daring to move an inch for fear the stick might come crashing down on your head . . ." Harald took off his robe and spread it on the ground. "Come on. Let's stretch out here under this tree and take a nap. We have a long way ahead of us."

The two monks were about to lie down when Eikei's voice suddenly thundered through the trees. "Sleeping outside zendo, leaving cushion during sesshin—that greenhouse person Zen!"

Jumping up and looking around the unfamiliar room, Fay was startled to find that she was no longer in Japan but in

Hawai'i, and that the man sleeping next to her wasn't Ira but Harald. Taking her diary and a pen out of her bag, she went into the bathroom, closed the door behind her, and turned on the light. Softly putting down the lid, she sat down on the toilet and entered the dream in her diary, so she'd remember it the next time she wrote to Gail.

April 10, 1985
Honolulu

Despite breaking with Eikei and destroying my chances for practicing Zen in Japan, I'm not sorry I left Shofuji. Yet, a secret part of me still seems to want the roshi's approval. I wanted to shake Harald awake and tell him the dream. I wanted him to assure me that we weren't going to become a pair of outcasts. But we were in the middle of a sesshin, and we had to get up at four, so I didn't have the heart to do it. I just sat there watching him sleep, envying his self-confidence.

I thought of the three magical days we spent at Turtle Bay after the last sesshin, and Harald's promise to go there again after this one. How worried he'd been about the cost, and grumpy he was during the entire drive to the North Shore. Having separated from his wife and quit his job as a civil engineer to come to Honolulu, he was living on his savings and was on a restricted budget. Who could blame him? As if that weren't enough, my spending appalled him. His mood lightened after we'd checked in at the hotel and made love among the bubbles in the Jacuzzi. He didn't even protest when I ordered up an expensive fruit and cheese platter and a bottle of champagne. We sat on the lanai overlooking the ocean wearing nothing but our guest bathrobes, feeding each other grapes and drinking champagne. After a few glasses, the "other Harald" came out, the one who hates asceticism as much as he hates bourgeois self-indulgence, the wild Dutchman whose lusty appetite for food and drink and sex reminds me of Frans Hals and borders on the hedonic, the one who loves Ikkyu and his erotic poetry.

"Here's an Ikkyu story you'll like," he said. "When told about the venerable Chinese Zen master who had driven stakes into his knees to keep from stirring during meditation, Ikkyu replied that he would rather drive his 'stake' into his lady love."

"Is Ikkyu your hero?" I asked, smearing a thick slab of melted brie on a cracker and putting it into his mouth.

"Mmm . . . along with Rinzai, Bankei, Danton, and Immanuel Kant, yes."

"How typical of you to combine the wildest kind of antinomianism with the most Protestant form of duty."

"It's where our morality meets, wouldn't you say? You, the lapsed Catholic Zen Buddhist, and me, the pagan stoic."

"I'm not Catholic anymore, and I'm not even a real Buddhist. I never took the Precepts, and I don't wear a rakusu—Eikei wouldn't let me."

"Do you really want a rakusu? I'll give you mine."

"No. I'll stick with your pagan style of Zen. It's hard getting used to, but I have to say that, for the first time since I started sitting, I don't feel I have to be punished."

Seeing we were on the verge of entering one of those long, psychological discussions that make him antsy, Harald jumped up from his chair and enacted a Zen koan. It was a game we'd play whenever the conversation got too heavy.

"Ma-yu came to see Lin-chi. He spread his bowing mat in front of him, gave a bow and asked, 'Which is the true face of the twelve-faced Kuan-yin? Getting down from his High Seat, the master seized the mat with one hand and with the other grabbed hold of Ma-yu. 'Where has the twelve-faced Kuan-yin gone?' he shouted. Ma-yu jerked himself free and tried to sit on the High

Seat. The master picked up his stick and made as if to hit him. Ma-yu seized the stick and holding it between them, both of them entered the master's room."

Jumping up, I jabbed and feinted at Harald, as he taunted me with, "Where has the twelve-faced Kuan-yin gone? Show me, Fay, show me!"

We leapt around the lanai having our pretend boxing match until we ran out of steam. Then Harald picked me up and carried me back into the room. After gently placing me down on the bed, he began nibbling at my toes. "Here she is," I heard him say in a muffled voice as his tongue made its way north.

It was three in the afternoon on a humid day in May when Dr. Ira Corman burst into the Honolulu Zen Center kitchen and, quickly introducing himself to Pat Darling (a recently arrived resident from Western Australia who was in the middle of preparing a smoothie), asked for his wife, Fay. Startled as much by Ira's abrupt entry into the Zen Center kitchen as by his expensive designer sportswear, Pat had at first taken him for a tourist who'd lost his way and come looking for directions back to Waikiki. She was having a hard time imagining Fay as the wife of the balding man with the distinctly New York accent and, turning off the blender, she stood there thinking of what to say next. Though recently involved with a married man back in Perth, Pat did not approve of Fay's affair with Harald; for she, like several other women at the Zen Center, had quietly fancied him, too. Yet the fact that the balding man in the expensive sportswear who'd just burst into the kitchen demanding to see his wife could actually be Fay's lawfully wedded husband had proved so unsettling that Pat's first instinct was to head him off.

"I'm making a mango-peach smoothie. Want some?" she asked.

Ira's manner was both officious and urgent. "No thanks. I'd really like to see Fay. Do you know where I can find her?"

Now confronted with the undeniable physical reality of a husband, Pat's protective instinct toward Fay proved short-lived.

"She's at the beach, at Ala Moana. It's not far from here. You just take University Avenue—the street you took to get up here—back down to Kapiolani Boulevard, where you'll make a right turn; stay on Kapiolani until you get to Atkinson Drive, where you take a left. Atkinson Drive will take you straight on to Ala Moana Beach Park. There's a huge shopping mall right across the street, and a marina at the park entrance. The beach she goes to is bordered by a reef and shaped like a bathtub encased in a half-moon of rocks. You can't miss it."

Ira thanked her and backed out the kitchen door. It was only after he'd brushed past the shoe rack and found himself facing the Buddha in the garden that he realized he'd committed a breach of zendo etiquette by entering the house with his shoes on. He got into the jaunty white rented convertible and pressed the button rolling the top down. Fay always liked riding in convertibles with the top down and the radio blaring. He'd surprise her, casually approach her on the beach and ask if she'd like to take a ride. First, he'd have to remove his shoes and socks and roll up his slacks; he didn't want to get sand in the cuffs. He reached for a map in the glove compartment and located "Ala Moana." The beach was small, a cove, actually, and shaped like a bathtub, as Pat had described. He'd find Fay easily.

. . .

Fay had turned to look back at Mount Tantalus, where a rainbow had just pierced the dark gray cloud cover, so she didn't see Ira at first. When she finally did see him, she quickly turned away to face the ocean. So, he'd come to get her. Had she not known him better, she might have attributed a more benevolent reason for Ira's showing up unannounced than a warning from his "psychic" friend Sam to reclaim her in person, if he wanted to save his marriage. After all, Ira was a famous self-help medical doctor on the verge of getting his own cable TV show and a divorce would be bad for business. Why else would he do it? Spontaneous acts of loving-kindness were not part of Ira's repertoire. It would be entirely out of character for him to fly to Hawai'i on impulse and whisk her back into his arms unless Sam had put the idea into his head.

Harald had reached the reef and climbed onto the rocks. He was waving his arms, beckoning her to swim out and join him. Harald was forever coaxing her to swim out to the reef with him, but she'd always made an excuse not to because of her fear of drowning. She'd been phobic about swimming in deep water ever since she was fourteen and had to be dragged half dead from the neighborhood pool where her friend Barb, a champion swimmer, was teaching her to dive. Until that day at Ala Moana, with Ira approaching her from behind and Harald waving to her from the reef, Fay would probably have just continued sitting there, paralyzed with fear. But today was different. Something compelled her to get up, and before she knew it, she was walking briskly toward the water. As if it were the most natural thing to do. As if she'd done so hundreds of times before. As if this weren't the very first time. As if her heart weren't pounding and her hands weren't curled into fists and white at the knuckles. As if Ira weren't there to reclaim her.

. . .

Reaching the curved shoreline, she entered the water. When it was waist-high, she closed her eyes and dove straight into the first oncoming wave. Suddenly realizing she'd reached the point where the sandbank dropped off and she could no longer stand, she thought of returning to the safety of the shore. But didn't. Dog paddling to stay afloat, she calculated whether drowning could be worse than returning to Ira, who was now standing on the beach ready to reel her back into their sham marriage. As he had no matter how many times she'd fled from him—to Jerusalem, Japan, Paris, the hospital psychiatric ward in New York where he'd trained . . . and now Hawai'i—Ira would always be there to lure her back to him, and Sam, and their dysfunctional ménage-a-trois.

Nor did she look out toward the reef where Harald was beckoning her to join him. Plenty of time for that . . . Instead, she did something she hadn't done since her fourteen-year-old self had bravely climbed the stairs of the high diving board ready to meet the water lapping in the pool beneath her.

Unclasping her fists, she flipped over on her back and floated. The water was warm. It cupped her body like a hand. Sticking her feet out in front of her, she wiggled her toes. Then looking up and seeing that the sky had broken open to reveal a double rainbow, Fay disappeared into it.

AUTHOR BIO

Perle Besserman is the recipient of the Theodore Hoepfner Fiction Award and past writer-in-residence at the *Mishkenot Sha'ananim* Art Colony in Jerusalem. She was praised by **Isaac Bashevis Singer** for the "clarity and feeling for mystic lore" of her writing and by *Publisher's Weekly* for its "wisdom [that] points to a universal practice of the heart." Her autobiographical novel, ***PILGRIMAGE***, was published by Houghton Mifflin, and her Pushcart Prize-nominated short fiction has appeared in ***The Southern Humanities Review, The Nebraska Review, Briarcliff Review, Transatlantic Review, 13th Moon, Bamboo Ridge, Lilith, Hurricane Alice, Crab Creek Review, Solstice, Other Voices, Agni, Southerly***, ***North American Review***, ***Page Seventeen***, ***Midstream***, and in many national and international literary journals, both print and online. Her most recent books of fiction include a linked story collection ***Yeshiva Girl*** (Homebound Publications) and two novels, ***Kabuki Boy*** (Aqueous Books) and ***Widow Zion*** (Pinyon Publishing). Her latest novel is ***The Kabbalah Master*** (Monkfish).

Besserman's creative non-fiction includes ***Oriental Mystics and Magicians, The Way of Witches***, ***Monsters: Their Histories, Homes, and Habits*** (Doubleday); ***The Private Labyrinth of Malcolm***

Lowry: Under the Volcano and the Cabbala (Holt); ***Kabbalah: The Way of the Jewish Mystic*** (Doubleday/Random House/Barnes and Noble); ***The Way of the Jewish Mystics*** (Shambhala/Random House); ***Crazy Clouds: Zen Radicals, Rebels and Reformers*** (with Manfred Steger, Shambhala/Random House); ***Owning It: Zen and the Art of Facing Life*** (Kodansha); ***The Shambhala Guide to Kabbalah and Jewish Mysticism*** (Shambhala/Random House); ***Teachings of the Jewish Mystics*** (Shambhala/Random House); ***Grassroots Zen*** (with Manfred Steger, Tuttle), ***Grassroots Zen: Community and Practice in the 21st-Century*** (with Manfred Steger, Monkfish) ***A New Kabbalah for Women*** (Palgrave Macmillan), and ***A New Zen for Women*** (Palgrave Macmillan). Her books have been translated into German, Spanish, Japanese, Czech, Italian, Hebrew, Portuguese, Russian, Dutch, Hungarian, and Thai.

She has written for publications as varied as ***Mademoiselle, Mānoa*** (Honolulu), ***The Boston Globe***, ***The Village Voice***, ***A Different Drummer***, ***Canadian Literature***, and ***East West***. ***Kabbalah: The Way of the Jewish Mystic*** has been recorded as a "book on tape" (***Sounds True Audio Editions***) and in a new Shambhala Pocket Edition.

Based in Hawai'i, the author travels frequently throughout the U.S., Europe, Australia, Asia, and the Middle East, and has appeared on national and international radio and television and in two documentary films in connection with her work. Perle and her husband Manfred Steger are the co-founding teachers of the Princeton Area Zen Group.

Visit Perle on the Web at: www.perlebesserman.net.

SYNOPSIS

Fay's Men traces the adventures and misadventures of Fay Watkins, a Texas-born dancer and spiritual seeker, on the poignantly funny, circuitous path to self-realization. Prompted by her naïve, almost quixotic idealism, Fay's quest inspires hasty decisions in love and a disillusioning spiritual encounter that nearly knocks her off course. Undaunted, she boldly pursues her goal, journeying from home to an initiatory stint as a revolutionary in Mexico, then to New York, where she leaps into marriage with a wacky psychiatrist, then to an Israeli Zen center and a Japanese monastery, followed by a hilariously disastrous trip to Paris with her Zen master, and an unintended admission as a patient in the psychiatric ward of her husband's hospital—an experience that finally propels her to self-discovery on a palm-fringed beach in Hawaii.

ACKNOWLEDGMENTS

Because so many people have encouraged, fortified, and contributed to the creation of *Fay's Men* throughout the years, I cannot manage to thank them all individually, so I'm dividing my acknowledgments into groups to facilitate the process. In doing so, I know I'll inadvertently leave some out, and I apologize to all those unnamed here who nonetheless remain vitally important to the making of my novel.

Fay's Women:

Thanks are due to all the women spiritual seekers encountered in my travels around the world. A deep bow goes to the late Jennie Martinez Peterson, my dearest friend and sister Zen rebel who, especially, inspired Fay's creation. My longtime Zen women friends, Hetty Baiz, Ursula Baatz, Brigid Lowry, and Kathy Shiels continue to provide models of endurance and commitment to the practice. K.A., a beautiful dancer from Texas, taught me a whole lot about strength and kindness in the face of rejection and adversity, particularly in her relationships with men. In addition to their warmth, encouragement, and appreciation of my work, my brilliant New York friends, Ellen Gibbs and Renate Latimer continue to keep me on my toes about literature, music, art, and culture in an age increasingly devoid of beauty.

Hanan Nassar, Nancie Carraway, Maya Soetoro, and Clare Hanusz model my idea of brave women warriors dedicated to saving the world. I can always count on my friends Diane Reitsperger, Yumi Fujii, Keiko Neubauer, and Etsuko Douglass to provide comfort, healing, and delicious meals in good times and bad. A special nod goes to Gloria Brasuel, an enthusiastic reader of my work, who fortified me with excellent wine and homemade pastries.

My niece, Shatay Trigère, is all I could have wished for in a daughter. And she's got "golden hands", business savvy, and a big, loving heart that I continue to rely on for everything I can't do myself.

My Australian women's cohort, Chris Hudson, Jan Seely, Farzaneh Ghaffari, Nina Killham, and Supriya Singh are paragons of loyalty and tough love, not to mention great readers. Special thanks to Mariella Barbara, who never fails to graciously record and offer incisive commentary on my writing.

Fay's Men:

I'm grateful to teachers Bill and David Boyle, and the members of the Princeton Area Zen Group for embracing "Philia"— friendship— and powerful women's leadership as the basis for a contemporary Western Zen sangha.

Brilliant poet and fiction writer, Paul Nelson, has provided remarkable insights into my work and all things literary for many years. My wish is that our dialogues continue for decades to come.

Fortnightly virtual conversations about Zen and creativity with Paul Boston, dear dharma brother and superb visual artist, never fail to evoke joy and delight. Sharing experiences as spiritual seekers and creative artists is one of the most precious rewards of our friendship.

Combining political savvy and intellectual heft, Governor Neil Abercrombie also knows his way around the art of fiction. I'm honored by his generous private and public support of my work.

Tommaso Durante, a true Renaissance man whose art, scholarship, and magnificent meals have galvanized my efforts to keep writing in the face of overwhelming professional and social change.

Always to be counted on for offering a fresh reading of my work, Emmet Blanchette, my intellectually curious and artistically talented grandnephew, keeps me focused on the future.

Fay's Producers:

A big Mahalo to the Running Wild Team—Lisa Kastner, Rudolfo Serna, and Evangeline Estropia, for carefully, gently, and respectfully shepherding this wayward, technically challenged author in bringing Fay's story into the world.

No amount of gratitude can express my love and appreciation for my husband, Manfred Steger, light of my life.

Running Wild Press publishes stories that cross genres with great stories and writing. RIZE publishes great genre stories written by people of color and by authors who identify with other marginalized groups. Our team consists of:

Lisa Diane Kastner, Founder and Executive Editor
Mona Bethke, Acquisitions Editor, RIZE
Benjamin White, Acquisition Editor, Running Wild
Peter A. Wright, Acquisition Editor, Running Wild
Resa Alboher, Editor
Rebecca Dimyan, Editor
Andrew DiPrinzio, Editor
Abigail Efird, Editor
Henry L. Herz, Editor
Laura Huie, Editor
Cecilia Kennedy, Editor
Barbara Lockwood, Editor
Kelly Powers, Reader
Cody Sisco, Editor
Chih Wang, Editor
Pulp Art Studios, Cover Design
Standout Books, Interior Design
Polgarus Studios, Interior Design

Learn more about us and our stories at www.runningwild-press.com

Loved these stories and want more? Follow us at www.runningwildpress.com, www.facebook.com/running-wildpress, on Twitter @lisadkastner @RunWildBooks

RUNNING
Wild
PRESS